EDGE of HONOR

Also by Gilbert Morris
Jacob's Way
Jordan's Star

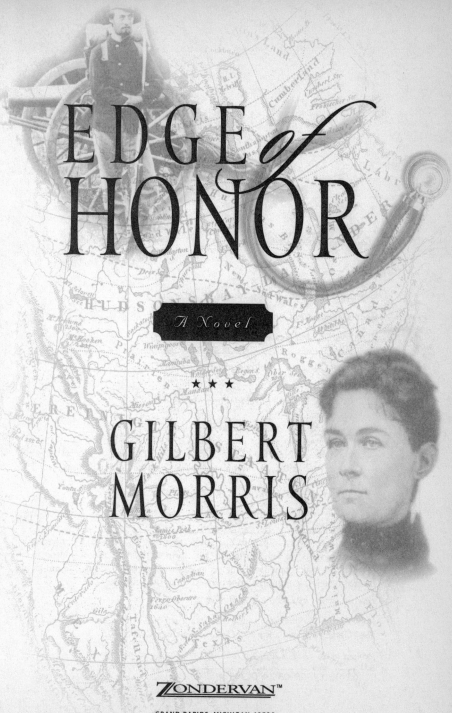

EDGE *of* HONOR

A Novel

★ ★ ★

GILBERT MORRIS

ZONDERVAN™

GRAND RAPIDS, MICHIGAN 49530

ZONDERVAN™

Edge of Honor
Copyright © 2000 by Gilbert Morris

Requests for information should be addressed to:

Zondervan, *Grand Rapids, Michigan 49530*

Library of Congress Cataloging-in-Publication Data

Morris, Gilbert.
    Edge of honor: a novel / Gilbert Morris.
    p.   cm.
    ISBN: 0-310-24302-5 (Softcover)
      1. United States—History—Civil War 1861-1865—Fiction.
2. Physicians—New York (State)—New York—Fiction. 3. Physicians—
Arkansas—Fiction. 4. New York (N.Y.)—Fiction. I. 5. Arkansas—
Fiction. I. Title.
PS3563.O8742 E34 2000
813'.54—dc21 99-089972

                                        CIP

Interior design by Laura Klynstra Blost

Published in association with the literary agency of Alive Communications, Inc.,
7680 Goddard Street, Suite 200, Colorado Springs, CO 80920.

Printed in the United States of America

  02 03 04 05 06 /❖ DC/ 5 4 3 2

To Johnnie
Thanks for fifty years of joy
I couldn't have made it without you!

PART
One

CHAPTER One

"Well, Quent Larribee will never win a prize for beauty, will he, Charlie?"

The speaker was a sharp-faced young man, one of twenty medical students who lined the balcony of the operating room. They were peering down on five doctors circled around a middle-aged woman with a pale, perspiring face. She lay rigidly on the operating table, her eyes quick with fear. "Quent always reminds me of old Abe Lincoln—when he was a younger man, of course."

"No, Rob. Quent's not quite as ugly as Abe." The pudgy student who sat beside the first speaker shrugged. The two students spoke in lowered tones, hoping to catch some of the conversation from the doctors gathered below. "Anyway, he doesn't have to look like one of Charles Dana's spiffy young men. He's got it made, Larribee has. Soon as he's fully qualified he'll start right at the top. I wish *I* had it so good!"

The sharp-faced Rob chewed on a petulant lower lip, studying the lanky figure of Larribee. Envy glowed in his eyes as he said, "I wouldn't mind being as homely as Quent if I could pull off what he's done. He'll have it made the rest of his life, Charlie."

"You're right about that. I'd marry old Doc Chambers's daughter myself if I could get his practice to go along with it. She's a good-looking woman, and Chambers is ready to step down."

The tallest doctor in the operating room below was also the youngest. At the age of twenty-eight, Quentin Larribee seemed overly tall and gangly among the other physicians, towering over them. He was wearing, as were the others, a dark suit, white shirt, and tie. His sleeves were rolled up to the elbow, revealing stringy but strong-looking forearms; his fingers were long and almost delicate. His hair was crisp brown, with a stubborn curl that insisted on falling over his forehead, and his sideburns were long, though not bushy as was the custom of the day. He had straight eyebrows under which warm, deep-set brown eyes studied the woman carefully. He did indeed look like a young Abe Lincoln, as his observer had mentioned. His features were homely enough: hollow cheeks, prominent cheekbones, and a pronounced lower lip. His nose was large, and twin creases led from it down beside his extremely wide mouth.

Quentin, seeming somewhat hesitant, glanced at Doctor Franklin Sutter. "Doctor, I would be glad to have you do the surgery today."

"Why, not at all, Larribee. This calls for younger hands than mine. I understand she's had oestrus cessation for over two months."

"Yes, sir. That is correct. The patient has one fairly sizable tumor on her uterus and possibly two on the left ovary."

Quentin turned suddenly and looked into the face of the frightened woman, chiding himself for speaking so unfeelingly about her condition while standing beside her; she was frightened enough as it was. Moving quickly to his right, he picked up a brown bottle and poured a small amount of clear liquid into a glass. "This morning, gentlemen," he said, looking up now and speaking to the gallery, "we're going to use a technique that I've found most helpful. This is absinthe. I've found it to be excellent in calming patients. A very fine preoperative, much more effective than laudanum. The dose is smaller, and I add some anise to calm the stomach."

"And why do you do that, sir?" The question came from another of the doctors gathered around the patient, Leslie Simmons, a short, stocky man with black hair and sharp black eyes. Simmons was already well aware of the reasons for the use of the drug, but he let no opportunity pass to call attention to himself.

Across the table Doctor Sutter studied Simmons, not surprised by his challenging manner toward Quentin Larribee. Sutter was well aware of the private drama developing between the two younger men. Then Sutter's eyes flicked to Oscar Chambers. *Chambers is a rotten doctor*, he thought sourly, *but he's got a good bedside manner and he knows how to use other men to do his work for him. That's his real talent.* Sutter himself was one of those men. For years he had done the difficult tasks that Doctor Oscar Chambers was unable to accomplish. But the arrangement had suited Sutter, for he liked the operating room best and was happy to leave the handholding and bedside manners up to Chambers.

Quentin Larribee regarded Simmons. "The anise," he said evenly, "calms the stomach so that there's less danger of the patient vomiting while under anesthesia." Moving to the head of the table, he murmured, "Mrs. Johnson, just lift your head and sip this."

The woman lifted her head obediently and drank the mixture. She made a face, then spoke in a thin whisper audible to all. "Doctor, am I going to die?"

"Certainly not, Mrs. Johnson. You're going to get very sleepy, and then Doctor Simmons here is going to give you an anesthetic. You'll go off to sleep, and when you wake up you will be fine." Quentin used the title "Doctor" even though neither he nor Simmons had yet been certified, feeling that it gave the patient confidence.

Like most patients who came under the knife in the year 1865, Matilda Johnson, age forty, was afraid of the men who surrounded her. Her eyes searched their faces for some assurance but found none. This tall young man, however, had warmth in his expression as he took her hand, his large fingers wrapping it completely. "You'll be just fine, Mrs. Johnson. Just lie quietly now and wait for the drugs to take effect."

Up in the gallery, the two young medical students were whispering as they watched. "Watch what he does now," Rob said, digging his elbow into his friend's side. "He'll go over and wash his hands."

"Wash his hands! What for?"

"He believes in everybody being as clean as possible. Some of the other doctors don't like it. Look at Simmons there. Ho, he looks like he's bit into a wormy apple!"

"I thought those two were good friends."

"They were until both of them started courting Oscar's daughter, Irene. Les can't believe a homely gent like Quent beat him out. He's like a bear with a sore tail!"

The late afternoon sunlight threw down lambent bars through the skylight as Larribee, accompanied by a reluctant Les Simmons, moved to a side table. Simmons dipped his hands gingerly into a basin provided by a nurse, muttering, "Blasted foolishness! That's what this is, Larribee!"

Accustomed to resistance from Les Simmons, Quentin Larribee did not reply. He cleaned his hands and forearms, then dried them on a towel that a nurse handed him. "Thank you, Agnes," he murmured. Turning back, he stood beside the patient whose eyes were already drooping from the powerful drug. He was aware, as he waited, of the pressure that always came with an operation. It was not only that the medical students upstairs were watching, nor that the doctors gathered with him were there to judge any false move he made. This was enough to disturb some men, but Quentin had learned to ignore it. He had, in fact, learned to block out everything but the needs of patients. During his brief medical career, he had seen many callous doctors who treated patients as sides of beef, never showing any interest or compassion. He prayed every day that he would never become one of them, and even now he prayed silently that God would give him sure hands and wisdom to do what was best for Mrs. Johnson.

Taking a deep breath, Quentin nodded. "All right, Doctor Simmons, you may administer the anesthetic." He watched as Simmons picked up a small bottle, put several drops of a yellow-green substance on a cloth, and then laid it across Mrs. Johnson's face. From that moment, Quentin Larribee became almost another man. His face grew stern and his voice clipped as he gave orders. Picking up a scalpel, he waited with one hand on the patient's pulse, then finally made the incision.

"Will you look at him go!" Rob whispered, nudging Charlie with an elbow. "How fast his hands are! He's got the best hands for a surgeon I ever saw."

Charlie nodded. "You're right about that. His hands are big, aren't they? I don't see how he manages to get inside like he does."

"He's born for it, I think. Some men are like that. You can either do surgery or you can't. If you can't, you'd better look for another line of work."

The room was quiet, broken only by the voice of Larribee as he performed the operation. By habit, he spoke directly to the students in the balcony, describing exactly what he was doing. Finally he straightened and stood absolutely rigid for a moment. His voice contained a note of satisfaction as he turned to the stubby physician standing beside him. "Doctor Chambers, I think we may congratulate ourselves on a successful surgery."

"A pleasure to work with you, my boy! A pleasure!" Oscar Chambers beamed.

The other doctors in that small group traded glances, each of them thinking, *It must have been a pleasure for Chambers, all right—he never touched the patient.*

Simmons made himself say heartily, "Fine job, Larribee."

"Thank you, Les."

Doctor Sutter put out his hand. "Fine job, Doctor."

"Why, that's good to hear from you, Doctor Sutter."

Sutter turned to leave but was stopped by Oscar Chambers, his eyes gleaming. "What did you think of that, Sutter?"

"I think he's got the surest touch of any young surgeon I've ever seen." He hesitated, then his eyes grew hard. "You will, of course, know how to take advantage of that."

Chambers was speechless for a moment, but then he cleared his throat before saying in a half-defensive tone, "Why, I want to give the young man every opportunity. He'll be my son-in-law, of course, so it'll all be in the family. Well, I've got to hurry." Wheeling, Chambers half ran to catch his future son-in-law. "You'd better get a move on, Quentin. If you're late to that ball tonight, Irene will skin you alive. She gave me strict orders to remind you to be at the house on time."

"Yes, sir. I will be." Larribee shook his head ruefully. "But I wish I could like dancing as much as I like surgery. I cut a poor figure, I'm afraid. Two left feet."

"Why, you do the surgery, I'll do the dancing, my boy," Chambers smiled. He laughed aloud, pleased with himself, reached up again and slapped Quentin on the back, then scurried away.

★ ★ ★

A keening wind rattled the windows, and Hannah Larribee felt a cold breath as the January gust forced its way through the cracks around the facing. A look of annoyance crossed her face, and she drew the faded, green woolen shawl around her shoulders. This did not suffice, and she glanced at the fireplace, finding with some surprise that the fire had guttered down to a single tiny yellow tongue. Shivering, she placed a faded ribbon carefully in the Bible she was reading. Putting the thick volume on the mahogany side table beside her chair, she rose, reaching for the worn crutch balanced against the Pembroke table. Slipping it under her arm, she moved across the room. She had used a crutch since she was ten, when she had lost most of the use of her right leg. Like all of her other dresses, the dark brown dress she wore was long, sweeping the floor, so that her crippled leg was not visible, and she had learned to use her crutch so effectively that she could cover ground almost as fast as a woman without her handicap. Moving to the fireplace, she picked up the bellows and blew the coals until they glowed like cherry and a yellow blaze sprang up. She blinked her eyes against the acrid fumes of coal. Picking up the brassbound, mahogany coal bucket, she scattered several chunks over the coals, then set the bucket down and straightened up.

A black-and-white marble mantel clock ticked solemnly with a stately cadence, its pendulum swinging from side to side. She stared at the hands, then murmured, "Quentin's late."

Only a few seconds later she heard the sound of whistling, and her eyes softened. "He's always whistling no matter what happens." She stood waiting a moment longer, a well-shaped woman of twenty-seven with direct, gray-green eyes set in an oval face. Her hair, when it was let down, reached below her belt, but she kept it braided and woven in a hair corona that framed her head. She never complained about her handicap. Still, there was something in her face that should not be there: a dissatisfaction over what she felt she had missed, a slight chronic look of discontent that she tried to mask but could not. She had seen her youthful companions grow up, marry, and now with children about their feet. She kept house for her brother, and long ago had buried all her youthful romantic dreams behind a rather stern exterior.

Now the door opened and she moved forward, saying, "You're late—and close that door. It's cold in here."

"Why have you let the fire go down?" Quentin jammed his soft, felt hat on a hook beside the door, then hung his gray woolen overcoat carelessly beside it. He cared little for clothes, and the suit he wore was too large, hanging loosely on his lanky frame. He gave the impression of a man who had grabbed up clothes to escape a burning building.

Going to the fireplace, he picked up the bucket of coals and dumped the remainder on the fire. He turned and grinned at his sister, saying lightly, "Now, that'll put some heat in here." He set the bucket down, then realized he hadn't removed his gloves, so he stripped them off and tossed them down beside the fireplace.

"Pick those up and put them in your pocket, Quentin!" Hannah Larribee spoke sharply, as was her custom. She moved away toward the kitchen, saying, "I'll fix you something to eat before you leave. I'll be bound you haven't had a bite all day."

"Oh, I grabbed a little at noon. Don't bother." He watched her, knowing that she paid him no heed. Her halting gait suddenly brought a pang to him and he wondered, as he had many times in the past, if she hadn't had that accident and been made a cripple, what would she have been like? He had no answer, despite his great love for this still-faced woman whose life might have been so different. "I'm going to get dressed," he called. "I'll eat just a bite."

He moved out of the living room and down the hall, turning into his bedroom. The apartment they had rented on Thirty-second Street was close to the hospital—which was almost its only virtue. It was stuffed with furniture the two of them had brought from their old homestead, for Hannah had insisted on saving as much as possible. Stripping off his clothes, Quentin whistled "Lorena," adding a few trills to what he considered a rather sad song. He knew that the troops, both Confederate and Federals, were singing the song, but he liked it for its tune rather than for any political reasons. Yanking open both doors of a George Third mahogany clothespress, he pulled out a white shirt and tossed it on the old bed, which dated back to his grandfather or, perhaps, even farther than that. It was made with walnut spindles and glowed with a rich sheen under the decrescent afternoon light that slanted in through the high window beside it. He put on fresh underwear, then stared doubtfully at the evening suit he had not worn for several years. Hannah had cleaned and pressed it, but as he put it on he was apprehensive. It was a square-cut, dress-coat evening suit with narrow skirts. The sleeves were close fitting, with turned-back cuffs, and under it he wore a single-breasted waistcoat with a V-shaped front. The trousers were narrow with a braid running down either side. He noticed with concern that they were too short for him—which shouldn't surprise him, since they had been too short when he had worn them before. He eyed the high, closed collar and struggled with a well-worn black cambric tie until finally he gave up in disgust. Leaving the room, he entered the combination kitchen and dining room where Hannah was setting food on the table.

"Hannah, help me tie this blasted thing, will you?"

Hannah set a steaming plate of beef down on the table, then came to stand before him. Balancing herself on her left foot and expertly keeping the crutch trapped under the pit of her right arm, she reached up and swiftly tied the narrow tie. "It's strange to me that a doctor who can tie a fine knot in a little cord with one hand can't tie his own necktie." She jerked at the ends of the tie and started to move away, but Quentin suddenly reached out and caught her by the arm. He grinned down at her, and said, "I have to leave something for you to do around here." He was used to her abrasive manner, having long understood that beneath it lay a heart that was quite different. It was a measure of their closeness that she sometimes allowed him to see this more tender side of her, since she showed it to no one else.

Hannah scowled at him and pulled back. "Stop pawing me!" she said sharply. "Let me see!" She looked at the suit, and said, "That's too small for you. Look at those sleeves. Are you going to a fancy ball in that ratty thing?"

"Reckon I'll have to." Quentin shrugged. He tried to pull the sleeves down but, seeing it was hopeless, gave an embarrassed laugh. "Irene will probably refuse to go with a tramp like me."

No answer came, and Quentin saw that his sister's lips were drawn into a thin line. He was well aware that she did not like Irene Chambers and was highly unhappy with the engagement.

Quentin had done all he could to encourage friendship between the two, but they were like oil and water. "Any mail?" he asked as he sat down. He bowed his head and said a quick blessing, then looked up for her answer.

"A letter from Lucille." This was the youngest Larribee, the last to marry.

"How is she?"

"Fine. The baby will come next month. She's hoping it's a boy."

"Nothing from Ann or Elizabeth?"

"No, but there's a letter from Frank. He's doing well. I don't see how he gets along with that father-in-law of his, but he does somehow."

Quentin suddenly leaned back. He had been poised to take a bite of beef, but now he let the heel of his hand rest on the table, the beef morsel forgotten for the moment. His gaunt face was tranquil, and his deep brown eyes thoughtful. Finally he looked up, a quizzical light in his warm brown eyes. "We had a time raising that bunch, didn't we, Hannah?"

Hannah did not answer, but the two of them were thinking of the hard, lean years. Their father had died when Quentin was only sixteen and he had had to take over as breadwinner. When their mother had died three years after this, Hannah had, in effect, become the mother of the younger girls and the younger brother. She and Quentin had been more like a married couple than brother and sister as far as housekeeping and struggling to make ends meet were concerned. They had determined that they would keep the family together, and although it had been hard and the winters had been lean at times, they had managed to eke out a living on the farm, although it had cost them both. Quentin had longed to be a doctor since he'd been thirteen years old, but his education had been delayed until his sisters were all married and his younger brother had married into a wealthy family. Only then had he thrown himself into medical studies, taking it in huge gulps, and he had quickly caught the eye of Doctor Oscar

Chambers, who had at once started working him long and hard for a small wage.

"You did a fine job on us, Hannah," Quentin said quietly, his fine eyes warm as they studied her face. "I don't know what any of us would have done if it hadn't been for you."

Hannah was startled and for one moment, almost, it seemed that she would break down. Her face softened and she could not speak for the fullness in her throat. Then she straightened up and said rather roughly, "Never mind all that. It's time for you to go, if you must."

Quentin finished his meal quickly, then rose and took his dishes over to the cabinet by the sink. Hannah was standing by the stove heating water to wash them, and he laid his hand on her shoulder. "I'll be late coming back." When she did not answer, he said, "Maybe tomorrow we can get out of here. Go around and watch the skaters."

"You'll be busy at the hospital. You always are."

"I'll take tomorrow afternoon off. We'll watch the skaters, maybe go by Barnum's Museum, and then we'll eat out at Luigi's." He put his arms around her, squeezed her, and lifted her up off the floor.

"Put me down, you crazy fool!" When he did put her down, she turned and reached up and gave his tie one more twist. "Go on with you now!"

"I'd better. Doctor Chambers said Irene would skin me if I was late." He leaned over, kissed her cheek, and left—whistling "Dixie" as the door slammed.

For a moment Hannah stood there. She felt no affection for anyone but her family. Her three sisters and Frank, her younger brother, had lives of their own now in distant places, and they had never been affectionate with her. She had been forced to be so strict with them that she knew they feared her, and this was something she regretted. But with Quentin it was different, and her eyes softened as she crossed her arms, thinking, *It'll be over soon.*

He'll marry her, and I'll be here in this little place alone. The thought frightened her, but it was true enough. Irene Chambers was not a woman who would share her husband. That had been clear from the beginning. On the few occasions Quentin had taken her to the Chambers's mansion, she had been treated politely enough, but there was a wall between her and the family that she knew would never be broken down. She moved across the room and sat down on the horsehide chair, holding her crutch and staring at it as if she had never seen it before. Long thoughts ran through her mind and a sadness came to her. Her eyes suddenly blurred, and she let the crutch drop to the floor with a clatter and closed her eyes, fighting against the tears that gathered there. But she was not a crying woman, Hannah Larribee, and with a distinct effort she picked up her Bible and began to read.

★   ★   ★

"Betty, watch what you're doing! You're pulling my hair out by the roots!"

The maid, a shapely young blonde woman of only seventeen, bit her lip, saying nervously, "I'm sorry, Miss Irene. Truly I am. I'll be more careful."

"See that you do!" Irene Chambers sat impatiently, back straight, and studied herself in the mirror over her vanity. She was conscious, as always, of her appearance, especially her clothes. Now she studied her face and reached up to smooth back one arched eyebrow. Her hair was dark brown with a slight touch of red. She wore it pulled back and parted in the middle, which she thought gave her an artistic look. She rather fancied herself as being artistic and had some talent with the piano and painting. Her brown eyes were bright but rather too small, she thought, and she now drew a careful line with a small charcoal pencil to make them appear larger. Her face was too narrow, but she had found ways, by the use of cosmetics, to make it appear broader. Her features were really rather aristocratic, of which she was proud. She glanced up and said impatiently, "That's enough, Betty! You're just making it worse."

"Yes, ma'am. I'm sorry."

Irene stood and crossed the room to examine her dress in the full-length mirror. She had shopped for days before finding this particular dress, for the ball was one she had looked forward to all year long. She knew that the Astors and the Vanderbilts would be there, and she was determined to be perfectly dressed. The gown was a yellow, off-the-shoulder affair ornamented with deep lace and a velvet fichu. She plucked at the short puffed sleeves wondering if the velvet ribbons and bows were a bit much, but it was too late to think about that. She moved back and forth, keeping an eye on the mirror, making sure that the train skirt decorated with lace and velvet ruching trailed properly. The cost of the dress would have made middle-class families flinch, but Irene had felt that she must have it. Besides, her father seldom asked anymore how much her clothes cost.

"Betty, go down and tell George to be sure to have the carriage ready." She glanced at the clock on the mantel and shook her head. "We're going to have to hurry when Doctor Larribee gets here."

"Yes, ma'am. I'll go right now."

As soon as Betty scurried from the room, Irene paced back and forth, looking up only when her mother came in. "Mother, is he here yet?"

"Not yet, but he will be, I'm sure." Louise Chambers was overweight, and her face was flushed from the exertion of climbing the stairs. No more than five feet two, she could not seem to control her appetite, and now the cherry pink dress that she wore made her look even larger. "I wish he'd hurry! Your father's ready to go."

"I'll have to take Quentin to task," Irene said. She took a deep breath and forced herself to be calm. She prided herself on calmness and had long ago learned to control her explosive temper. Now when she grew angry she actually spoke more slowly in her effort to maintain control. Forcing herself to calmly take a seat, she began to buff her fingernails. "He'll be here on time, I'm sure, Mother."

"I'll be glad when you're married," Louise said, eyeing her daughter rather carefully.

Surprise washed across Irene's face, but when she met her mother's eyes, suddenly she was able to read her thoughts. The two of them were much alike. Now Irene thought, *She still hasn't given up on my marrying someone from the aristocracy. Well, she might as well, because that's not going to happen.*

Indeed, few young ladies had been so groomed for the pursuit of an aristocratic, wealthy, and socially prominent husband as had Irene Chambers. It was what her mother had first desired, and from the time Irene could walk she had been tutored in the principle that her whole life must be focused on marrying someone in Mrs. Astor's Four Hundred. The husband she found must be socially acceptable, wealthy, and respectable in every way.

But the years had passed, and now at the age of twenty-eight, time's winged chariot had suddenly caught up with Irene. It had been just the previous year that she had taken stock of herself and faced the reality that she was not going to marry an Astor or a Vanderbilt. A hard realistic streak in Irene had surfaced and she had made her decision. She remembered it as she sat buffing her nails, for it had been in this very room, seated in this very chair, after weeks of depression and frustration over her unmarried status, that she had suddenly announced—within her own mind, of course—*I'll marry Quentin.*

As if she had read her daughter's thoughts, Louise Chambers said, "Quentin isn't exactly what we had planned for you—for a husband, I mean."

"No, but he will be."

"Will be? What do you mean, Irene?"

"I mean he is the most brilliant young surgeon in New York, which means in the United States. And when he takes over Father's practice, it will grow even more than it has already."

"Well, I suppose that's true," Louise said slowly. She was a great reader of romances, and now sadness tinged her voice. "He doesn't look like much. He's not at all handsome."

"He'll look better as he grows older. He'll have dignity. All he needs is someone to help him with his clothes, and I can attend to that."

Irene had made a separate peace with herself and was now satisfied. True, Quentin Larribee was not handsome and his manners were not fine, but she knew him to be honorable, honest, and a tremendously talented doctor bound to rise in his profession. Even better, he was easy to mold. She had persuaded him to court her, leading him to think it was his own doing, just as she had led him only a month later to propose. She had accepted gracefully. Now she looked at her mother and said, "We'll be happy, Quentin and I."

"Have you never regretted breaking your engagement to Les?"

"No. Les is handsome enough, but he's only a mediocre doctor. Turn the practice over to him and it would be gone in five years." Quietly Betty opened the door, and said, "Doctor Larribee is here, Miss Irene."

"Good. Help me with my coat, Betty."

Slipping into a thick ermine coat with matching muff and hat, Irene stopped long enough to look down at her mother and smile. "Don't worry. He'll be a good son-in-law to you."

She found Quentin waiting for her downstairs. Her heart sank, for his suit did not fit, and she knew he would be sadly out of place at the ball. Still, she knew how to handle him. "Hello, darling," she said, lifting her face to be kissed on the cheek. "You're a little late. We'd better hurry."

"I'm sorry. The operation took longer than I thought. I'll tell you about it on the way, though. It was very interesting."

The two left at once, and he asked, "Aren't your parents coming?"

"They'll be along later. I wanted us to get there early."

The carriage was waiting in the fresh-fallen snow, and as Quentin helped Irene inside the landau, he said, "Hello, George. How are you?"

"Fine, sir."

"Catch those rats in the barn yet?"

"Yes, sir. I'm working on it."

"George, drive quickly. We're going to be late," Irene said sharply. As soon as Quentin was inside, she said, "You ought not to be so familiar with the help."

"With George?"

"Yes, with George! You've got to learn to be firm with hired servants."

"Well, I've never had any, so I guess you'll have to teach me, Irene."

"Of course I will." Irene leaned over, and slipping her hand out of the muff, held his. It gave her a feeling of security. She held his hand up for a moment and saw how small hers looked. "You have the most beautiful hands," she said. Then she laughed and reached up her other hand to his lean jaw. "If only the rest of you were as beautiful as your hands!"

"Too late to pray for that, I'm afraid. But anyway, if some parts of me have to be right, I guess the hands and the eyes are most important."

The carriage rolled along, Irene listening absently as he described the operation. The daughter of a surgeon, she was not squeamish at the details, but her mind was not on his description. Finally she said, "You didn't mention my dress."

"Oh, it's beautiful! I meant to tell you, but we left in such a hurry. But then your dresses are always beautiful." Clumsily he tried to turn his gaffe into a compliment. "And you are beautiful too, my dear."

I don't suppose I'll ever make a courtier out of him, Irene thought. *But I can smooth over his roughness a bit.* "We'll see about getting you a new suit."

"You don't like this one? I was afraid you wouldn't."

"You've got to keep your appearance up. After all, being a doctor is more than cutting someone open."

Surprised, Quentin looked at her and then grinned. "Well, that's a big part of it."

"I know, dear, but you'll be treating some of the most important men and women in the world, and they'll expect you to have polish."

Ruefully Quentin shook his head. "I'm afraid I didn't get any of that. I was behind the door when the Lord passed it out, I guess."

"Don't worry," she said. "We'll work it out, you and I. And you know what?"

"What?"

"We can start looking at houses. I thought maybe next month."

"Houses!" Quentin gave her a blank look. "Look at houses?"

"Certainly! We're going to have to live somewhere." She softened her tone and laughed. "You didn't plan to live in a cave, I trust."

"Why, I thought we'd live in an apartment, at least for a while."

"Don't be silly! We can't do that," Irene said firmly. "I think a brownstone would be nice. There are some over on Third Avenue. I made an appointment for us to look at one of them."

"But I don't have the money for a thing like that."

"As soon as you finish your training you will, and Father can help in the meantime."

Quentin swallowed hard and shook his head. "Well, you know best, I suppose."

"Oh, just about some things!" She put her hand on his knee and squeezed his leg rather suggestively. "You know about operating, and I suppose I've had more time to think about houses and things like that. Anyway, I want you to be very attentive to the Vanderbilts tonight."

"You mean Cornelius Vanderbilt?"

"Yes. The Commodore. He'll be there. One of these days he's going to be your patient."

"I doubt that. The Vanderbilts are pretty well set with Doctor Jacobs. They've been with him for years."

"Jacobs is getting old. They're going to need a new doctor, a young man like you."

Quentin said no more, and for a moment Irene felt that she had gone too far. Studying his gaunt face, she saw the soberness there and took his hand again. "Put your hand inside the muff where it's warm." She held it there. Sensing that he was discouraged, she said, "Don't worry about the house. It will come." She waited for him to lean and kiss her, and when he did not she turned to him. Pressing herself against him, she put her free hand on his neck. He turned to meet her and she held him firmly. He wrapped his arms around her and held her roughly, and although she enjoyed it, she thought it better not to allow too much freedom. Putting her hand on his chest, she pulled back with a short laugh. "Now, Quentin, that's for after marriage."

Quentin tried to calm himself, concentrating on breathing slowly and deeply, the warmth of Irene's hand in his a powerful reminder of the longing he'd just felt. He had been dazzled by the attentions of Irene Chambers from the first, not quite believing his good fortune. He knew that many young doctors would be happy to marry this woman just to inherit her father's practice, but there was more to her than that—and much of it, despite his admiration for her, made him uneasy. For one thing, she was far above him in social awareness, and he felt awkward and out of place. For another, she knew how to stir him physically, and sometimes he was sure she was purposely tormenting him.

The carriage rolled on, its two passengers facing the evening with quite different attitudes. Quentin Larribee dreaded it, as he did most social events. His bride-to-be, on the other hand, looked forward to it with exultation. An evening with the Vanderbilts, the Astors, and the cream of New York society . . . there was no other way she'd rather spend an evening. And by her side, a young fiancé—not handsome, but soon to be rich and very famous indeed! Life was good, and Irene Chambers was happy.

CHAPTER Two

"Like I always say, you must make the best breakfast in the United States, Hannah." Quentin sliced another thick slice from the large ham, placed a piece in his mouth, and chewed with contentment. He savored the pleasant aroma of fried eggs, fresh bread, and chicory coffee. "I don't see why I'm not as fat as a pig."

"You're like Father was. No matter how much he ate he never gained an ounce." Hannah remarked. She took a sip of the thick, black coffee that both of them drank without sugar and regarded him thoughtfully. "How was the ball last night?"

"Oh, not bad—as such things go." Quentin forced a grin, adding, "You know how I hate those formal things, but it's part of the profession."

"I can't see that going to a ball makes you a better doctor."

"You're right, but Irene says I have to learn how to move in the proper circles." Quentin pulled his shoulders together, then slumped back in his chair. "I suppose she's right. I was as out of place last night as a man could be. I just don't fit in with the Vanderbilts." The thought was unpleasant to him, so he changed the subject. Looking around the dining room with a fond light in his eyes, he said, "I'm glad you talked me into saving all the furniture we could. It makes this place feel more like home, even if it is only rented."

The room was filled with furniture that both of them had seen all of their lives—a Federal carved mahogany sideboard, a country Queen Anne maple table with the same style of chairs painted black, and a large cherrywood corner cupboard decorated with fine china plates and crystal goblets. Quentin finished off his coffee, and Hannah got up at once to refill it. Sitting down again, she said quietly, "I miss the old place, Quentin." Then, as if she had said something amiss, she added quickly, "I'm not complaining. This is a nice place, and we had no choice—we had to leave the farm and come here for you to finish your studies."

"You never complain." Quentin reached over, squeezed Hannah's wrist, then sliced open a biscuit and spread one half with butter, the other with blackberry jam. Putting the biscuit back together, he took a generous bite and chewed with thorough enjoyment. "The war will be over soon," he remarked.

"Do you really think so?"

"Sure. It'll have to be. Grant's got Lee penned up in Richmond. There's no way he can fight his way out of that. It's just a matter of time."

"It's been a terrible war. So many young men have died."

Quentin had lifted the second half of the biscuit to his lips but suddenly lowered his hand and examined Hannah carefully. She was looking down into her coffee cup, swirling the thick ebony liquid. "Are you thinking of Richard Grierson?"

Startled, Hannah looked up—then back down at her cup again, and was quiet for a few moments before she spoke. "I've never gotten over his loss. I know you haven't either."

"He was the best friend I ever had."

Richard Grierson had been killed at Antietam. He had been the only man that had ever shown any interest in Hannah as a woman.

Quentin knew without being told that Hannah had loved Richard, and Richard had confided in him that he loved her also. "After the war," Richard had told Quentin confidently, "I'm going to marry Hannah."

But that had not happened, and after they received the news of Richard's death at Cold Harbor, Hannah, always quiet, became even more so.

Quentin regretted mentioning Grierson. Quickly he popped the remains of the biscuit into his mouth, chewed on it, then washed it down with the remainder of his coffee. Getting up, he crossed the room and pulled his worn black overcoat from a peg. He shrugged himself into it, jammed his hat firmly on his head, then leaned over and kissed Hannah's cheek. "Don't forget, now, I'm coming home early. We're going to Barnum's Museum."

"Why, that man's just a charlatan!"

"But he's entertaining. You'll have to admit that."

As he left the house, Quentin muttered, "Why did I have to mention Richard Grierson? I ought to have better sense." He trudged on through the light snow that had fallen the previous night, resolving to make it up to Hannah by taking her out to a fine restaurant after they had visited the museum.

At the hospital, he threw himself into the work as usual, and time went quickly for him. He moved among the patients, many of them wounded men from the war, with a calm manner and reassuring words. He knew most of them by name, for he had a good memory and had long ago decided that his patients would not be faceless bodies. He had seen enough callousness on the part of physicians, and it always sickened him. Many times he had asked himself, *Why did they become doctors if they care nothing about people?* Many physicians seemed to be very mediocre doctors who cared little for those they ministered to. Their indifference and callous behavior had made him determined to be different.

Just before noon he was in a small ward occupied by eight men, all wounded veterans. Each of them brightened as he came by—except for Lonnie Prather, a small young man of no more than eighteen, who looked up at him fearfully. Lonnie had received a severe wound to his right side that had done serious damage to his digestive system. Sitting beside the young man, Quentin removed the bandage. The wound, he saw, was not healing well. Some men healed as easily as animals, and others did not—just why, no one knew. When Quentin had skillfully applied a clean bandage, Lonnie swallowed hard and whispered, "Am . . . am I going to die, Doc?"

"Why, you mustn't talk like that, Lonnie," Quentin said quickly. He smiled and leaned toward Lonnie, placing his hand over the bandage. It was something he often did: touching a wound and breathing a quick prayer. There was no medical reason for it, of course, but Quentin felt that it made a difference. Perhaps it was just the human touch, something that drew him a little closer to his patients.

His use of touch in healing had its roots in his childhood. His aunt, a gaunt woman who had lived close to the Larribee family, had been widowed early. While still a small boy, Quentin had found out a strange thing. Often when he was bruised or had a stomachache, his Aunt Minnie had laid her hand on the hurt and somehow made the pain go away. He asked her once how she did it, and she had said, "Oh, child, I don't know. It just happens."

Aunt Minnie's gift, or whatever it was, had strongly impressed Quentin. He had never mentioned it to a living a soul—certainly not to his colleagues!

Now, as he kept his hand pressed firmly against the terrible wound, Quentin said, "I'm going to pray for you, Lonnie. You've got a future ahead of you. Are you a Christian man?"

"Yes, sir. I am."

"Good. So am I." Quentin bowed his head, and said, "Lord, I ask you to help Lonnie get well. You have made us, and it's your mighty power that keeps us alive. Now, I ask that you undertake a healing in his body in the name of Jesus." He kept his hand on the bandage for a moment, and when he looked up he saw that the fear had left Lonnie's eyes.

"That's good, Doc! That prayer and just putting your hands on me like that. I guess it's crazy, but my side seems sort of warm and it doesn't hurt as much."

"That's good, Lonnie. We doctors do all we can, but we are only the servants of the Lord. He's the one who does the healing. Now, I'll be back to see you tomorrow. Eat all you can. You need to take good care of yourself."

Quentin rose and turned—then stopped abruptly, for Les Simmons was standing right behind him. "What in the world was *that* all about, Quent?" he demanded.

A quick flush rose to Quentin's cheeks. "What do you mean?" he said. "I was just changing the bandage."

"You were putting your hands on that patient—and praying for him. You don't think you're some kind of faith healer, do you?"

"No. I just think these poor fellows need all the encouragement they can get."

Les Simmons stared at Quentin, then shook his head. "You're an odd fellow. I still can't understand how you beat me out with Irene."

"To be truthful, Les, I don't understand it either." Quentin had, in fact, often wondered why Irene preferred him to Simmons, who was far more polished in his manners and certainly handsome enough. There was little egotism in Quentin Larribee, and he had once asked Irene why she had chosen him instead of Simmons. She had merely laughed at him, saying, "You're the man for me. Les is handsome and charming, but in the long run you'll beat him out."

A scrawny orderly stuck his head inside the door. "Doctor Larribee, there's a major who wants to see you. He's in the office. I told him I'd send you down."

"Thanks, Bob."

Leaving the ward, Quentin made his way to the lobby. As soon as he saw the Union officer, he smiled, putting his hand out. "Well, Major Billings. Good to see you again."

Major Todd Billings returned Quentin's smile. A small but upright man, he had red hair and a lean face. His grip was hard, and he observed Quentin with level gray eyes. "It's good to see you again, Quentin."

"How's that wound?"

"Never bothers me a bit. You did a fine job." Major Billings had been one of those brought back from the carnage at Fredricksburg. The hospitals were so jammed that many men had died simply from lack of care. Quentin had been overwhelmed with the sheer numbers of wounded and dying men, but had taken a special interest in Billings, at that time a captain. He had fought for Billings's life with all of his energy and skill, and the officer had never forgotten it. The two men had become close friends, meeting from time to time to share a meal.

"Come along. I'm about through here. We can have lunch."

"All right," Billings said. "Where shall we go?"

"How about Delmonico's? You still like Italian cooking?"

"That sounds good to me."

An hour later the two men were finishing a meal of lasagna, accompanied by smoking, fragrant garlic bread. Billings had said little during the meal, listening as Quentin told of his experiences with patients.

Finally Billings sat up straighter and said abruptly, "I've got some bad news for you, Quentin."

Quentin blinked with surprise. "For me! What is it, Todd?"

"This war's about over. Nothing's going to stop Grant now. The South can't hold out another six months—if that long."

"That's what I understand, but what's the bad news?"

Billings gnawed on his lower lip for a moment then shook his head, disgust sweeping across his face. "We've got a new brigadier who's taken over at the Department of Conscription down at the War Department. He was a coward on the battlefield—ran away the first time a shot was fired—but he's got political influence, so he had to be put somewhere. I guess," he said thoughtfully, "they thought he could do less damage at the Department of Conscription than anywhere else."

An alarm went off suddenly in Quentin's mind. "Conscription— is that still going on?"

"Oh, there's still a law on the books."

Both North and South, long ago, had seen that volunteers could not be obtained in sufficient numbers and had passed laws conscripting men into the army. The South had reached the bottom of the barrel, drafting men in their sixties and boys less than sixteen. The North had an enormous amount of manpower available, and with the end of the war in sight, Quentin would have thought there was little need for additional conscriptions.

"This General Hastings has to prove something to somebody," Billings said. "He's a pompous fool, but he is a general."

"Am I going to be conscripted? Is that it?"

"That's it, Quent. A friend of mine in the department knew that you and I were friends, so he brought the list to me. Your name's on it for immediate conscription."

Quentin sat quietly, leaning back in his chair. The pleasant sounds of laughter and rattling dishes filled the room. He did not reply for a moment, then he said slowly, "This catches me a little off guard, Todd. I never anticipated anything like this."

"Quent, I tried to do something about it, but I'm only a major. The place is literally crawling with colonels and generals. I didn't get anywhere at all." Billings rapped his knuckles on the red-and-white checkered tablecloth. "If you've got any important friends in government who owe you a favor, now's the time to call it in. This general is brass bound. He excuses nobody."

"I don't have any friends like that, Todd."

Major Todd Billings sighed heavily. He tapped the water glass with his fingernails impatiently, then shrugged. "Well, it'll just be a short chunk out of your life. There's not going to be any action to speak of. Hopefully Lee will see that it's hopeless and surrender." He summoned a grin, and said, "I think the worse that can happen is you might have to spend a few weeks in a camp learning to soldier. Try to think of it as a sort of vacation."

Quent grinned suddenly. He had absorbed the news, and now it did not seem quite as bad. After all, the war would be over soon. "Thanks for coming to tell me, Todd. The only thing that bothers me is having to leave my sister alone."

"Well, if you do have to go, I'll keep an eye out for Hannah. I'm stuck in Washington. Now, I've got to get back . . ."

The two left the restaurant and parted. A light snow was beginning to powder down in small, grainy flakes. The icy fragments bit at Quentin's face and lips, giving them a tingling sensation. He looked up at the slate gray sky, then moved on, his mind occupied with the news that Billings had brought. He was not a man given to excessive worry, so now he contented himself by thinking, *Well, the war will be over soon. If it takes a few months, I can stand that, I suppose.*

He tried to put the news out of his mind and quickened his pace. *I won't mention this to Hannah until after our trip to Barnum's Museum. I don't want to spoil her good time. She has few enough of them.*

★　★　★

Quentin glanced down and saw the pleasure in Hannah's eyes. The two were walking along Broadway toward Ann Street, where Barnum's American Museum was located. Pleased that he was able to bring some pleasure into her life, he asked, "Are you cold?"

"No. I like the cold."

Heavy snow slowed their steps, and the icy wind nipped at their faces. Men clutched at their derbies and women kept their hands inside their muffs. The sun was filtered by ragged clouds and the falling flakes gathered atop the gaslights in pristine mounds. The tops of the buildings were softly rounded, their sharp edges contoured by the snow, and the fetlocks of the horses were clogged with slush and dirty snow.

"It's so quiet!" Hannah exclaimed. "I think that's why I like the snow. It muffles everything."

Usually Broadway in New York City was a noisy scene—the steel shoes of the horses ringing on the stone, steel-clad wagon wheels rumbling, the cries of street merchants rich and boisterous. But now even the voice of the church bell was muffled, and the traffic of horses, wagons, and buggies seemed almost silent in the world of white that had wrapped New York in a blanket of soft snow.

"I'd like to go for a sleigh ride, Quentin."

Turning his head, Quentin blinked as the snow bit at his eyes. In the open sleigh passing by, a man and a woman were laughing as they faced each other. Both wore fur caps. Suddenly the man leaned and kissed the woman, who laughed and shoved him away.

The hissing of the runners and the jingling of bells became fainter as Quentin and Hannah watched the sleigh move down the street. Quentin said, "I miss sleigh rides. Remember how I used to put runners under the small wagon?"

"I remember. And you'd hitch up Hector and Blaze and off we'd go." Hannah laughed suddenly, her eyes shining as she turned to him. She made an attractive picture, the snow clinging to her lashes. "It's a wonder we weren't all killed, the way you drove that team."

"Good days."

"Yes, I miss them."

Quentin saw that the memory had brought a sadness to Hannah, and he said quickly, "Well, there's Barnum's. Looks like a mob going in—as usual." He motioned toward the five-story building draped with banners of all sorts, including the Stars and Stripes. The gaslights were on, even though it was early afternoon, and Quentin protected Hannah from the jostling of the crowd.

Barnum's Museum was, without a doubt, New York's most popular tourist attraction. P. T. Barnum had been, for at least two decades, the premier showman of the United States, and had attracted both his admirers and his detractors. After purchasing the large, five-story building that had previously housed Scutter's American Museum, he had decided that people liked to be fooled.

As he put it, "People like to be humbugged, don't you know, and I'm just the man to do it!"

During the early days, Barnum had certainly placed a few fraudulent attractions in his museum. His first exhibit was the "Feejee Mermaid"—the thin body of a fish topped with what seemed to be a human head. It was, of course, not a mermaid or anything else except a device that popped into the great Barnum's mind. Shortly after this was exposed, apparently doing Barnum no harm, he advertised, "The great model of Niagara Falls with real water." Many newlyweds who could not take a trip to the real falls flocked to Barnum's Museum—where they were surprised to find that Barnum's Niagara was a miniature model only eighteen inches high, but Barnum defended himself by saying, "They only paid twenty-five cents, and they've got the rest of the museum to fall back on."

Indeed, one could have a good time at Barnum's Museum all day long for only a quarter. It became customary for people to bring their lunches and spend the whole day. On one occasion so many Irish families packed into the museum it was filled by noon, and the sale of tickets had to be stopped. The line outside got longer and longer, and those waiting began to be restless. Some effort was made to persuade those inside to leave, but as one man put it, "I'm not going outside at all. Not at all, sir. Nor the children either. We've brought our dinners and we're going to stay all day!"

Barnum had solved the problem in a way that became typical of his methods and made him almost into a legend. He had been exposed to Latin at some point in his life, and he happened to know that the word *egress* was Latin for exit. Quickly Barnum made several signs that blazoned in bold letters, "THIS WAY TO THE EGRESS!" These signs were placed over the exit doors and person after person passed through the doors to see an egress, which they imagined to be some sort of fabulous monster. One Irishman read the sign aloud, "The Aigress! Sure, that's an animal we've never seen," and boldly plunged through the door with his family—only to find himself standing outside on the street.

Hannah and Quentin roamed the museum for two hours. They laughed at the puppet shows and studied the miniature models of Paris, Jerusalem, and Dublin. They were fascinated by the anaconda, the orangutan, the alligator. As they moved through the waxworks which was devoted to the evils of drink, Quentin commented, "Barnum is a teetotaler, I can see." They were treated to exhibitions of glassblowing, singing, dancing, and an art gallery featuring paintings of famous Americans.

"I don't wonder that the crowds come here," Quentin said. "There's not much else going on in the city. No zoo, no aquarium, no museum of natural history." He was suddenly conscious that they had been on their feet for hours. Though she never complained, he was always afraid that, due to her handicap, Hannah would tire quickly.

"We came on a good day," he said.

Hannah glanced up at him. "Why's that?"

"Because Tom Thumb and his bride are here."

"Oh, I'd love to see them."

"They're making a special appearance. If we go down now, we can get a good look at them."

The two hurried to join the crowd that was already gathering to see Barnum's triumph. Barnum's brother had found a remarkably small child in Bridgeport, a perfectly formed, bright-eyed little fellow with light hair and ruddy cheeks. Barnum, on seeing the boy, at once had signed him to a contract and the rest became history. The boy became General Tom Thumb, and all America wanted to see him, including the president of the United States. Lincoln attended the wedding of Tom Thumb, and Queen Victoria welcomed him to Buckingham Palace.

The crowd swelled, jostling them, but Quentin managed to secure a tall stool for Hannah to sit on. They were delighted with Tom Thumb, who was, indeed, a quick-witted man. He was evidently well-informed about politics, for he made pertinent remarks about political figures and finally, when someone asked him what he would do to end the war if he were in charge, General Tom Thumb said, "I would put my friend Barnum in charge of the whole thing. It would be over in a week."

After leaving the museum, Quentin took Hannah to Luigi's, for she loved Italian food almost as much as he did. They had a fine meal, and Quentin noticed with satisfaction that Hannah's eyes were bright with laughter. Unusual, indeed, for her!

When the meal was over, they sat talking quietly. "You remember Captain Billings?" Quentin asked.

"Of course I do."

"He came to see me today. He's a major now."

"Is his wound healed?"

"Completely. He's doing fine. He came on another matter." Quentin drew a design on the tablecloth, wondering how best to put it, then realized there was only one way. Lifting his eyes to meet Hannah's, who was watching him curiously, he said, "I'm going to be conscripted." Alarm leapt into her eyes, and he added hurriedly, "It won't amount to much. The war's almost over, Todd says, and everybody else I know says the same thing. I'll probably wind up in a training camp for a few weeks. Lee can't hold out."

Hannah did not speak for a moment, and Quentin knew that she was examining this startling news from every angle. Finally she asked, "What will this do to your training at the hospital?"

"It has to be put off, but I can finish it as soon as I get out. I'm sure Doctor Chambers will understand."

"And you won't be fighting?"

"Certainly not. They've got plenty of troops surrounding Lee already. I just hate to leave you alone."

Hannah straightened up and her eyes flashed. "Don't worry about me! I can take care of myself!"

"I never doubted that. You always took care of me and the others, so I reckon you can take care of yourself." He smiled and patted her hand. "As a matter of fact, it'll be easier. You won't have to cook and wash my clothes."

Hannah studied him skeptically, then repeated, "Don't you worry about me, Quent. I know you do, but you mustn't. Go do this thing, and then come back. You'll finish your training, you'll marry Irene, and you'll have all you ever wanted."

★ ★ ★

The following evening, Quentin made his way to the Chambers's mansion for dinner. As always, when Quentin approached the Chambers's home he was uneasy. Indeed, on his first visit he had been almost paralyzed by shyness. He had been a poor boy and had become a poor man, and the ornate structure that housed the doctor and his family had intimidated him.

The mansion was done in the style of the Second Empire. It rose three stories, capped with a concave, mansard roof with slates in a contrasting pattern; atop this, a deck with a decorative iron crest was centered between the two tall chimneys. The four windows across the second floor had white louvered shutters and were trimmed with fancily carved cornices. On the first floor, the massive doorway was flanked with full-length windows on both sides. Quentin paused now before the front door, wondering suddenly why he should be so depressed about such a fine home. *I hope*, he thought, *Irene doesn't want us to have a home this fancy. It's too big for a young married couple.*

He rang the bell and was met at once by Lois, a thin, intense young woman. "Hello, Lois. How's that ankle of yours doing?"

"Oh, very well, Doctor!" Lois said. "Those hot compresses you ordered seemed to take the pain away at once."

"Is the family home?"

"Yes. They're all in the large parlor. Come along, sir, they'll be happy to see you."

Walking down the wide hallway, Quentin felt a stir of something very like apprehension. He was confident when he was operating and in most other circumstances, but this ornate house and the opulence of the Chambers's lifestyle he had never gotten used to. Now as he turned into the large parlor, he thought, *Why does a parlor have to be this fancy?* It was the biggest parlor Quentin had ever seen, about sixteen by sixteen with fawn brown painted walls; the carved molding was painted gold. Pictures with heavily gilded frames decorated the walls. The floor was covered with wall-to-wall deep brown carpet. The furniture was all massive, made of mahogany and cherry, each piece intricately carved, overstuffed, and covered in bright fabrics—reds, greens, and golds.

"Well, my boy, it's good to see you!" Oscar Chambers had stood and now he strode forward to shake Quentin's hand firmly. "Come and take a seat over here by the fire."

Quentin greeted his host, then crossed the room to shake hands with his future mother-in-law. "Is that the thickest coat you have, Quentin? You need to get something warmer."

"I suppose I do." He was accustomed to Mrs. Chambers's comments on his wardrobe. It had annoyed him at first, but he had learned to shrug it off.

Irene put her hands out, and he took them, asking, "What have you been doing all day?"

"Oh, just a little shopping." A stray thought came into Quentin's mind: *Why does she dress up to stay at home like this? It seems she'd have a more casual dress she could put on to relax.* Then in one of those strange tricks of the mind, he saw the scene that he himself was a part of. He saw the four of them as if they were actors on a stage. It should have been a pleasing figure, for the room was beautiful and three of the actors, at least, were extremely well dressed and appeared to be contented. But in his imagination he also saw his own face—and on it was a look of dissatisfaction.

"Well," he said, turning to face them, "I have a bit of news that hopefully you won't be too glad to hear."

"Hopefully! Of course we won't be glad to hear any news introduced like that!" Irene said. "What is it?"

Quentin shrugged his shoulders. "I'm going to be conscripted."

"Impossible!" Irene exclaimed. "You're joking!"

Quentin quickly explained, adding, "It won't amount to much. I might be gone three months. Probably not that long. Lee can't hold out much longer."

Irene at once took her father's arm. "You must know somebody in the War Department, Father."

"Well, I can't think of anyone . . ." Chambers muttered, thinking not so much of Quentin's dilemma as of how he would find someone to replace him in surgery. He blinked and pursed his lips together firmly. "I'll see what I can do." Then a thought came to him and he brightened. "Why, Quentin, it's simple enough! All you have to do is hire a substitute."

Many men, on both sides of this war, had hired other men to serve in their place. But as the war had progressed, the practice had become more unpopular. Still, it was possible, and at once Irene and her parents formed a united front, insisting that it was exactly what Quentin should do.

"I don't feel free to do that," Quentin said firmly.

"But, Quentin, it will interrupt everything if you go into the army! You can't finish your training! Why, we can't get married."

"I'm sorry, Irene, but this is a part of life I must face."

It was not a pleasant evening, and when Quentin left he felt depressed—not at having to serve in the army; he could bear that as others had. Rather, it was the displeasure of the entire Chambers family that bore down on him. He felt pressured by their reaction, and it irritated him. *Why can't they see,* he thought, *that this is something a man has to do?*

★   ★   ★

For a week Quentin went about his duties, saying nothing about his problem to anyone in the hospital. But such things cannot be kept hidden, and several of his colleagues found out—perhaps as a result of Doctor Chambers's attempts to get Quentin excluded—and expressed sympathy and concern.

Les Simmons said carefully, "You'd better watch out for yourself, Quent."

"Oh, I doubt that there'll be any fighting involved, for me at least."

"I didn't mean that. I mean if you stay gone too long, you may find things changed around here when you get back."

Quentin knew exactly what Simmons meant. He smiled crookedly. "Well, you'll have an open field with Irene. Maybe you can gain back the ground you lost."

Near the end of the week, Hannah was at home—alone, as usual—when there came a knock at the door. Picking up her crutch, she moved swiftly to open it and found Irene Chambers standing there.

"Why, Miss Chambers!" Hannah said with surprise. Then added, "Come in. It's cold."

Irene stepped inside and removed her coat and hat. "I can only stay a minute, Miss Larribee," she said quickly. "But I did want to talk to you."

"Come in by the fire." She led the way, moving very swiftly across the floor and motioning toward one of the Louis XVI chairs. "That chair is very comfortable."

Irene did not waste time. "I've come to talk to you about Quentin, of course. About his going into the army."

"Yes?"

"I think, perhaps, we've done all we can to prevent it. Father tried to use his influence, but it hasn't worked. What we think you should do is talk to Quentin about hiring a substitute."

"He would never do that," Hannah said quietly. "He's against the practice. Always has been."

"But you must consider yourself, Hannah." It was the first time Hannah had heard Irene call her by her first name. Now Irene leaned forward, saying with intensity, "It's very simple. If you tell him that you can't get along without him, which indeed I find quite believable, he would hire a substitute. You have great influence with him, Hannah."

"I wouldn't care to do that."

Impatience swept across Irene Chambers's face. "It's true enough. You're a cripple. You do need your brother."

"I don't need anyone except God, Miss Chambers. And I might give you one bit of advice. If you're going to marry my brother, there's something you need to know." Hannah's voice was slow and deliberate. "Quentin is very amiable. He's easily swayed, for he always likes to please people, but I'll tell you this." Here Hannah's voice took on a steely edge. "When Quentin does set his foot down, it's hard enough to shake the world. He won't be changed in this matter, Miss Chambers, no matter how hard you try."

Later, when Quentin came home, Hannah told him about Irene's visit.

"She wanted me to use my influence to get you to hire a substitute."

"You told her I wouldn't, didn't you?"

"In no uncertain terms!"

"I'm glad you did." Quentin had been thinking hard, and he said quietly, "I've decided to enlist, Hannah."

"I thought you might. It's the only thing to do. But you mustn't worry about me. I'll take care of myself."

★   ★   ★

"Irene, I wish you could see things my way."

Quentin had packed his bag and was on his way to take his place with the Seventh New York Infantry. After being informed of Quentin's decision, Dr. Chambers had said, "I've been working on something, Quentin. I suspected you were going to do this, so I've been speaking with a former colleague of mine, a Doctor Keith Alexander. He's an army surgeon now, with the New York Seventh, and he's agreed to find a place for you with his unit. You'll be assigned to him at one of the big army hospitals right here in New York. Why, it's even possible you can continue your training."

This had pleased everyone, including Irene and her mother. Quentin had agreed, and now that it was time to go, he said, "Irene, I wish this hadn't happened, but it has, and we just have to make the best of it."

It was Irene, although Quentin himself was not aware of it, who had been behind her father's attempts to find a place for Quentin. Now she felt victorious—she had once again succeeded in turning adversity to her advantage.

"Quentin, darling, it won't be bad at all. You'll be right here in New York. We'll see each other often, and this awful war will be over soon and we can go right on with our plans."

Irene stepped into Quentin's arms, pulled his head down, and kissed him thoroughly. She had planned this embrace well, as she had planned everything else, and now she moved her lips away and whispered in his ear, "I want you, Quentin—what we have now is not enough. I want you to be my husband. Come back quickly, Quentin!"

CHAPTER
Three

Quentin's induction into the Union Army was more painless than he had anticipated. True, he had to sleep on a hard mattress in a barrack with six other men, but aside from this loss of privacy, his days were not a great deal different from what they had been while serving his internship at Mercy Hospital. He had been issued an ill-fitting uniform with some parts too small and others too large, but other than this his military training was practically nonexistent. He was assigned to serve as an aide to Doctor Alexander, and he found the duties not at all rigorous. The hours were long, for the hospital was packed with wounded men, but he was accustomed to hard work.

He had long been aware of the difficulties of transporting sick and wounded men from the battlefield to a hospital. Immediately after the Battle of the Wilderness, when the wounded men had flowed back in a steady stream, he had helped all the other doctors in the city tend to them. The plight of wounded soldiers, he had found, generally was no better than that of someone imprisoned in the dungeon of a medieval castle. He had seen rough surgery where field surgeons had lopped off arms and legs carelessly in a manner that was unthinkable to Quentin.

Washington itself had been transformed into one gigantic hospital, while New York received thousands of wounded who had survived rough treatment and terrible suffering. The Empire Hospital, where Quentin had put in the first two weeks of his military service, was an ancient building that had served as a hospital for civilians at one time; now it was crumbling with age, and the sanitary facilities were abysmal. The orderlies worked constantly under the supervision of medical officers, and the hospital was a beehive of activity. Quent looked at the hundreds of wounded men who lay here and tried to grasp the truth that these were only a small percentage of those in other facilities throughout the North. And when he considered that the South had at least as many wounded, he found himself bitter and deeply grieved about the great struggle that had destroyed so many fine young men.

He had seen Irene only once since his induction, a quick unsatisfactory visit to the Chambers's home. Dr. Chambers had been irritable, saying, "I'll be glad when this nonsense is over. That fellow I hired to take your place is a butterfingered moron! I wouldn't trust him to operate on a squirrel."

Irene had been most considerate. When he had left early to get back to the hospital, she had held him closely and whispered, "It won't be long, dear. Then we'll be together again."

"Maybe longer than you think."

"No, I don't think so. Everyone says the South can't last much longer." Irene put herself against him and looked up, whispering with excitement, "I have good news."

"What's that?"

"I found the most darling house. It's just exactly what we need. Can you get off tomorrow so that we can go look at it together?"

"No, I'm afraid I can't."

"Oh, what a shame! Well, as soon as you can get a day off you'll see it. You're going to love it, Quentin!"

For the next three days Quentin had felt uncertain and somewhat depressed about Irene's determination to buy a house. He moved along the line of wounded men, forcing all thoughts of Irene and the future out of his head, concentrating totally on his patients in the strong belief that each one of them deserved his complete attention. As he moved down the line, he was suddenly interrupted by Jim Peters, one of Doctor Alexander's orderlies. "Hey, Quentin. When you get through here, let's go get something to eat. Maybe that cook will come up with something that tastes better than a dead horse."

Jim was a wiry, undersized young man of twenty-six, with a shock of thick brown hair and a pair of merry gray eyes. He had sharp features and would have been nice-looking except that his teeth were bad. They also gave him a great deal of discomfort, and now he leaned forward and said, "My teeth are killing me, Quentin. I'm going to have to have some more laudanum."

"You're taking too much of that, Jim."

"Aw, I know when to quit. Anyhow, I just need a little to get me through the day. Hey," he said, "how about you and me go out and do the town tonight? I found a place where there's lots of good-looking women. What do you say?"

"I guess you'd better count me out, Jim." Quentin smiled at his friend and shook his head. "You never give up, do you? Don't you understand I'm an engaged man?"

"Ah, that don't mean nothing." Peters shrugged carelessly. He grinned, exposing his bad teeth. "I've been engaged half a dozen times. Managed to get away every time, though. Anyhow, you need to have some fun. You don't do nothing but work."

"That's what I'm here for, Jim. Let me get to the end of this row, then we'll go see what they've got to eat."

The room in which Quentin moved from bed to bed was very large, with high windows letting in sunlight. As in all hospitals, the smell was rank from unwashed bodies and waste that was not always removed quickly enough by the orderlies. Every bed was occupied, although some patients were able to move around. A few of them had gathered at a table and were playing a game of checkers. Their voices rose in an argument as Quentin left one patient and stepped to the next. Looking down, he said, "How is it with you, soldier?"

"Not so good, Doc."

Quentin searched his mind for the man's name. He had a fine memory for names, and now said cheerfully, "Well, Daniel, let me take a look at this." He pulled the sheet down and saw that the bandage on the soldier's side had bled so that the sheets were stained. "Let me get a fresh bandage on this and then we'll get your bed changed."

"All right, Doc."

Carefully Quentin pulled away the sodden bandages, letting no reaction show in his face. The bullet had struck young Daniel Smith in the back, plowed through some of his intestines, and exited in the lower right part of his side. It was impossible to tell how much damage had been done, but Quentin was well aware of the statistics concerning stomach wounds. Very few survived. As he cleansed the wound, both front and back, he saw that there was drainage and made up his mind to keep the wound as clean as possible. It was about all that could be done for such a wound. He fastened a clean bandage on the front and back, called for an orderly, saw to it that the sheets were changed, then assisted the man back into bed.

He saw the young man's lips tighten in pain, and said, "Easy there, Daniel." As he adjusted the pillow under Daniel's head, Quentin noticed that he had a fever. With a cold compress, he bathed the sick man's face. This was usually the duty of the orderlies, but for some reason Quentin felt a particular interest in this young man. It happened that way sometimes. He tried to show concern for all his patients, but occasionally he would encounter one that drew a deeper sympathy from him.

"You've got a family, Daniel?" he asked, and listened as the young man whispered about his parents and brothers and sisters.

"Got a sweetheart?" As he asked this question, Quentin put his right hand under Daniel's side on the wound of his back. His left hand he put over the bandage in the front.

Abruptly the soldier broke off and stared up at him with surprise. "What are you doing that for, Doctor?"

"Just to give you a little comfort."

"That feels—" The soldier's speech broke off and he closed his eyes. Relief eased across his face, and he whispered almost inaudibly, "That feels better."

Quentin Larribee looked down at the face of the young soldier, aware that, for some reason he could not explain, this young man had stirred something within him. He prayed for all his patients, but from time to time, the impulse to pray for some patients was stronger than for others. Now as he sat feeling the heat of the wounded man's body, he began to pray silently. He said nothing aloud, and was unaware that young Daniel Smith was watching him carefully, his lips parted and his eyes hooded. The sounds of the hospital seemed suddenly muted. Without warning, something came into Quentin's mind. It was nothing that could have been heard by the young man under his hands—simply a thought. But it was so clear that it was startling:

If you will believe me, I will give this man life.

Startled by the intensity of the thought, Quentin sat perfectly still. Although he was a man of prayer, this was the clearest, strongest impulse that had ever come to him while praying, and he could not tell if it was from God or simply a thought manufactured by his own mind. For an instant he hesitated, then he prayed, *Well, Lord, I want this man to live, so I'm asking you to heal him. He's beyond the help of any medical care, but not beyond your power. So I'm asking you in the name of Jesus to give him life.*

Quentin was not sure how long he kept his hands on Daniel Smith, for after his prayer he simply sat there, unaware of the passage of time.

"Thanks, Doc." The eyes of Daniel Smith were opened wide now, and he took a deep breath carefully, as if he were afraid he would damage something within.

"You just take care of yourself and rest, Daniel. I'll see you tomorrow."

The next day he followed Doctor Alexander as he made his rounds. When they came to Daniel Smith's cot, Quentin watched carefully as Alexander examined the wound. The young man's fever was down.

When they had moved to the next ward, Alexander said, "Well, that's a puzzle."

"What's that, Doctor?"

"Private Smith back there. I've been keeping a close watch on him. You probably have too."

"Yes, sir, I have."

"Well, then you know he's been going down every day." Alexander shook his head. "I thought he'd be dead by now, but somehow he seems to have made it."

"How do you account for that, Doctor?"

"Can't. We do the best we can, but with a wound like he has it's just mostly in the hands of God."

Quentin looked up sharply at Doctor Alexander, who caught his glance. "What's the matter?"

"Nothing. I just hope we can see him make it."

"You have a special interest in him?"

For a moment Quentin was tempted to tell Doctor Alexander about the prayer but decided that it was best not to. He said quietly, "I have a feeling for some patients. Some more than others. Does that ever happen to you, Doctor Alexander?"

"Sometimes it does. Can't explain it, but it just happens that way."

The experience troubled Quentin. He watched day by day as the young man grew better and stronger, the wound healing rapidly. One evening, when Doctor Alexander had given him permission to visit his sister and he had taken the day off, Quentin spoke of it to Hannah. He had spent the day attending to several things that Hannah needed done, glad to be able to help. After they finished dinner and sat down in the parlor, she talked more than usual, by which Quentin knew that she had been lonely. He listened, trying to encourage her all he could. Finally Hannah looked up from her knitting and said, "Have you had any interesting patients, Quentin?"

"Well, they're all pitiful. I don't know if you'd call them interesting." He hesitated for a moment, his thoughts wandering to Daniel Smith. He leaned back in his chair and stared into the fire silently for so long that Hannah finally said, "What are you thinking about?"

"One of the wounded men who came in about a week ago. Everybody thought he would die. He took a bullet in the back, came out the front. Those wounds usually are fatal."

Hannah put her knitting down. His lean face seemed almost skull-like in the flickering reflection of the fire. When he said no more, she asked quietly, "What is it, Quentin? What happened?" Then she listened carefully as he related how he had put his hands on the man and prayed with the assurance that, if he did, the man would be healed. Hannah's face was still as she asked, "And is he doing well?"

"He's going to live, Doctor Alexander says, and I agree. But if—" He broke off for a moment, ran his hands through his hair, and then looked at her with confusion in his dark eyes. "I don't know what to make of it, Hannah."

"I don't see what's so difficult about it. You always pray for your patients."

"I know, but this is—well, it's different. This man was dying, and when I put my hands on him, something happened. And I don't know what that 'something' was. There's no medical explanation for it. He should be dead."

"Nothing is too difficult for God. You remember the Scripture?"

"Which Scripture?"

"Genesis 18:14," Hannah said promptly. She had an almost encyclopedic knowledge of the Bible, and it always amused Quentin that she could find a Scripture for any circumstance. He listened as she said, "You remember that God told Abraham he would have a son, and Sarah overheard it. She was an old woman in her nineties and Abraham was an old man, but you remember in the fourteenth verse the Lord said unto Abraham, 'Is any thing too hard for the LORD?'" For a moment she paused, and then said, "And then in Jeremiah 32, after Jeremiah prayed, in verse twenty-seven God said, 'Behold, I am the LORD, the God of all flesh: is there any thing too hard for me?'"

"I've always admired the way you can use the Bible. You know it better than anyone I know. Any more?"

Hannah thought hard for a moment, then she smiled and turned her gaze on Quentin. "Do you remember when the angel appeared to Mary and told her that she would bear a son, even though she was a virgin? And she asked how this could be. I've always liked verse thirty-seven of Luke 1. I've used it many times. 'For with God nothing shall be impossible.'"

Quentin looked fondly at his sister. "You're a comfort, Hannah," he said quietly. "I don't know why I should be troubled. God's always spoken to you—more than to me, I think. But you know—I believe it *was* the Lord. As soon as I touched him, I felt something happen."

The two sat in that meditative silence that comes when two people have learned to live together. They felt no need for speech, but after a time Quentin shifted, got up, and added more coal to the fire. After poking it and watching the sparks rise up like myriads of tiny stars, he came back, sat down in his chair, and sighed deeply. "I think a lot about Aunt Minnie."

"I'm surprised you can remember her. She died when you were only six."

"Oh, I remember her all right. She always brought us cookies when she came to visit. I never told you about this, but there was something odd about Aunt Minnie," Quentin said quietly.

"Odd? What do you mean odd? She was a fine woman."

"Yes, and she was always good to me, I remember. But I recall several times I'd go out and bang myself up. I was always getting cuts, or scrapes, or bumps." He paused then and passed his hand over his hair. "I remember I came in once. I had taken a pretty bad fall and hurt my ankle. I was crying, or trying not to, and Aunt Minnie sat me down on the couch. She began to rub my ankle and you know, the hurt just went away." Quentin chewed his lower lip thoughtfully, looking more than ever like a young Abraham Lincoln in the light of the fire. "I've never forgotten it. Twice more while she was there, I hurt myself somehow. I went to her and she rubbed it and the pain would go away. And once she healed my stomachache." He looked at his sister. "What do you think about that, Hannah?"

"I don't know, Quentin. With God all things are possible. Maybe he just used Aunt Minnie to heal your hurts."

"Once or twice before, I've had the impulse to just lay hands on patients and pray for them. Of course, I wasn't thinking that they would be healed by my touch or anything—I just thought of it as praying. But when I put my hands on Daniel Smith, there was something about it that was different."

"Could you have the gift of healing, Quentin?"

"Oh no, nothing like that! Except maybe there's comfort in some hands. Aunt Minnie had it. Maybe I've got a little bit of it."

"How does that line up with your medical science?"

"It doesn't." Quentin grinned suddenly. "Don't worry. I'm not going to give up doctoring and start laying hands on people. I've read about too many so-called faith healers who turned out to be not altogether honest."

Once again the silence ran on, and finally Hannah said, "Do as God tells you. If he speaks to your heart and tells you to pray, then you must pray." Her eyes were soft as she looked at Quentin. "God has given you great skill, Quentin. And he's given you a heart softer and gentler than most men. I want you to promise me that whatever God tells you to do, you'll do it—matter how foolish it is."

Surprised, Quentin said, "Guess I can promise that, Hannah. You just keep praying for me."

★ ★ ★

The next morning when Quentin went back on duty, Jim Peters ran up to him, eyes wide with apprehension. "Well, I knew it was too blamed good to last."

"What are you talking about, Jim?"

"I've been bragging about how we were safe here and not likely to get shot. Well, that's all over."

Quentin stared at the short young man. "What's happened?"

"Doctor Alexander popped in here earlier this morning and he told me he'd been transferred to the lines around Richmond. Gave me a list of supplies to pull together, and he wants you to help." Pulling out a thin sheaf of papers from his tunic, Peters handed the list to Quentin. "He wants to see you. You'll be going with him and so will I, worst luck!"

To conceal the shock that ran through him, Quentin stared at the list of medical supplies. He was worrying about leaving Hannah alone—then with a guilty start he realized he was not thinking of Irene. *But she's got her folks to take care of her,* he thought. Then he looked up and demanded, "When do we leave?"

"Tomorrow. Can you beat that?" Peters was despondent. He suddenly slammed a fist into his palm. "If they'd just wait another two or three months, this war would be over and we'd never get shot at!"

"We'll be all right," Quentin said. "We won't be on the battle lines. We'll be back in a field hospital somewhere."

But Jim Peters would not be consoled. "Just got that little blonde filly in a notion to be nice to me. Now there's a line of fellows right behind me. Tom Sterling is already laughing, saying how he'll comfort Lily while I'm gone. Blast it! Why did this have to happen?"

Taking a deep breath, Quentin shook his head. "I don't know why these things happen, but I know one thing. We're going to have to scramble to get all the equipment and supplies together. Come along."

After Doctor Alexander had confirmed Jim's news, Quentin and Jim were busy all day assembling supplies. The last thing Quentin did after they'd finished was go by Daniel Smith's bed. Smith was sitting up, and he smiled at once. "Hey, Doc! Good to see you!"

"I came to say good-bye, Daniel."

"You're leaving the hospital?"

"Yes. Doc Alexander's been transferred to Virginia. Jim Peters and I will be going with him." Smiling, he reached down and took the hand of the young man. "You're going to be fine, Daniel. Drop me a line when you get back home."

"I'll do that, Doc." Smith struggled with words, and finally said simply, "You know, somehow I think you saved my life."

"No. It wasn't me."

"You remember that time you prayed for me and you put your hand under me and the other hand right here? Something happened then, Doc. From that minute on I started gettin' better."

"You'd better give the glory to God, then. I did pray for you, Daniel, but I'm sure your family has been praying too. You go home, get well, and God bless you."

"I'll do it, Doc, and I ain't never going to forget you!"

★   ★   ★

There was no question, really, in anyone's mind that the end of the bloody struggle was at hand. The politicians began to turn their attention to a peace settlement, and on March 4, 1865, Abraham Lincoln was inaugurated president for four more years. He faced a split over Reconstruction policy and growing dismay in the South: Now that slavery was dead, what would happen to the Negroes?

At his inauguration, Abraham Lincoln spoke words that he hoped would bring healing. "With malice toward none; with charity to all; with firmness in the right; as God gives us to see the right, let us strive on to finish the work we are in; to bind up the nation's wounded; to care for him who shall have borne the battle, and for his widow, and his orphan—to do all which may achieve and cherish a just and lasting peace among ourselves, and with all nations."

Quentin read these words in a New York newspaper and felt hope stirring. He looked over at Jim Peters, who was cleaning the mud off his boots. "I like what Lincoln says. We need to show we're a people of charity."

"Well, I don't care what he says as long as the Rebs over there give up soon. I'm freezin' to death!"

The tent, indeed, was cold, as was all of Virginia. The spring had not yet come, and the small woodstove sputtered and spat as the green wood was slowly transformed into a great deal of smoke and little heat. The two men sat huddled by it and as Jim raked at the mud with his knife, he complained, "I wish every one of them Rebs would just throw their muskets down and go on home. The war's lost. I don't see why they hang on."

"I don't either, Jim," Quentin said wearily. He was seated in a fragile camp chair, and now held his hands out, almost touching the sides of the stove. Dark had come early, and it was time for him to make one more round of the hospital, which consisted of a series of large tents and two old mansions that had been riddled by shell fire. It wasn't much, but it was the best that could be had. The cots were packed now with men—not only wounded, but also those sick with the diseases that had plagued the Union Army, and the Confederate as well, throughout the war.

The fire sputtered and spat with what seemed like malice. Finally Jim threw his boots down and lay down on his cot, pulling both of his blankets up over him. He shivered and said, "When this war is over, I'm gettin' out and I hope I never see a musket again, or an army tent!"

"I'll agree with you there," Quentin murmured.

"You know what I'm going to do when the war's over? I'm going to get rich."

"A noble ambition. How do you plan to do that?"

"Oh, I've got a plan, don't doubt it," Peters declared. He pulled the blankets up to his chin, still shaking with the cold. "I ain't told nobody about it. I'm afraid somebody will steal my idea."

"Well, if it doesn't involve medicine, I don't guess I'll be a candidate for stealing it."

"That's true, Quent. Well, here it is. You know I've been on a riverboat all my life. Just a deckhand. Never had nothin'. My folks didn't have nothin' either. Grew up in a shack in St. Louis by the river. It was a mighty rough life. I never told you how rough."

Outside, a wind was keening around the tents and the flaps rattled suddenly with a staccato sound. The thin cry of a bugle sounded, plaintive and mournful, carried in by the night wind. Jim Peters listened to it, then rolled over and propped his head up on his fists. His eyes shone in the yellow lamplight. "Just before the war," he said, "I got on as a cook on the *Memphis Belle*. Now *there* was a boat for you, Quent! I mean it was downright fancy! Of course my quarters wasn't too fancy." He laughed shortly, then he sat up and wrapped the blankets around him with his legs crossed under him. "Well, it was while I was cookin' I got to thinkin'. You know they eat mighty fancy food on them steamboats. You ever been on one, Quent?"

"Never have."

"Oh, well, they're floatin' palaces! I'd go in sometimes to the dining room to help out." Jim's eyes grew dreamy. "White tablecloths, silver gleaming under chandeliers big as this tent, orchestra playing over at one end with the prettiest music you ever heard. There was wine in crystal goblets flowing like a river. Oh, it was something to see!"

"Like to get on one some day. Sounds like a good way to travel."

"Well, some say a riverboat's the best way on this earth to go anywhere. Of course, there's lots of gamblin', but I never had the money to get into any of the big games. Anyways, while I was cookin' I noticed there was quite a struggle to stock up on fancy food. We could always buy potatoes, and beef and pigs were plentiful enough. We'd stop at little river towns and just go out and buy 'em from farmers or at a market. But I got to thinkin' about that, Quent, and I decided that there's somethin' better."

"What's the scheme, Jim?"

"Well, those rich folks on those boats, they like fancy foods. So I decided I'm gonna go to raisin' foods like pigeons and quail."

"That's pretty fancy."

"Oh, yeah!" Jim said quickly. "Sometimes we'd find a hunter who'd go out and shoot us some quail, but there wasn't never enough. And pigeons—they like them, too. And even rabbits. You see, my plan is," he said eagerly, "to raise 'em in cages. That way you don't have to go huntin' for 'em and they'll be fatter and juicier. Don't you see?"

Quentin sat for a time listening as Jim Peters built castles in the air. Finally he rose and said, "Well, time for me to go make rounds."

"You just wait." Jim Peters nodded as he tossed another stick of green oak into the small stove and poked the ashes until he got a blaze going. "You just wait, Quent. One of these days you're going to say, 'I knowed Jim Peters when he didn't have nothin'—but look at him now!'"

"I hope it works out for you, Jim." Quent grinned.

As he walked through the tents toward the hospital, Quentin thought about the days he'd spent here outside of Richmond. He thought mostly about the Confederates trapped inside the steel ring of Union forces. The Confederate prisoners taken had been little more than skeletons, their eyes large in sunken sockets. One of them had been shot, and Quentin had dressed the wound after Doctor Alexander had removed the musket ball from his leg. He had found that the young soldier, seventeen years old, had little hope of any sort of good ending to the war. His name was Ossie

Mayfair, and he was from Mississippi. When his leg was bandaged, he said in a thick, Southern accent, "Thanks a heap. Purely do 'preciate it."

"What will you do when the war's over, Ossie?"

"Go back to raisin' taters, I reckon, and cotton. It's all I know."

"Why do you fellows keep fighting? You can't win. You know that."

"I knowed that when I joined up last May. Don't know why. Just seemed the thing to do. My pa got killed in the Wilderness. Look like he left a gap, so I come to fill it up."

"You fightin' for slavery?"

"Slavery? I ain't fightin' for that!" Ossie snorted with disgust. "We ain't never had a slave. Never want one neither."

"What for then?"

But Ossie Mayfair could not express what was in his mind, and Quentin was convinced that most of the men behind the lines could not have answered this question either.

"I don't think Jeff Davis could answer it," he murmured as he moved along toward the hospital. He entered and gave his best attention to the wounded, wondering what kind of insanity would make men endure things like this. He had no notion whatsoever of the glory and grandeur of war, nor had he ever. Even before the few days he had spent on the front lines here, he had been convinced that there was a perverse streak running through the minds of men, and that it grew even stronger during such times as these.

CHAPTER *Four*

𝒯he face of General Robert E. Lee was drawn, and fatigue clouded his eyes. He stood with shoulders slumped, looking out over the fortifications that kept the Federal forces from entering Richmond. General John B. Gordon stood to Lee's left, preserving space between them. Neither General Gordon nor any of Lee's other aides could fathom his thoughts. It was that way with General Lee. His men loved him and would lay down their lives for him, but none of them ever clapped him on the shoulder. Lee had become a symbol of the South, and already myths had begun to surround him, elevating him to a level beyond the reach or understanding of common soldiers.

The rattle of musketry broke the night silence, sounding like the breaking of hundreds of dry sticks. This was followed by a cadence of booming cannons far off to the right. Lee turned his head slightly and was still. Gordon did not move, and the two men remained in that position for some time.

"Come and walk with me, General Gordon."

"Yes, sir."

Lee turned and made his way along the lines of men. They were thin lines now, for every Confederate who fell left a gap that could not be filled. The circle of defense around Richmond had shrunk until the city itself was practically all that was left for the Union Army to take.

Lee walked silently, and the ragged Confederates followed him with their eyes. They were almost starving now, but still were not ready to give up—not as long as Robert E. Lee was with them!

Finally Lee stopped on a parapet and turned to face Gordon. "It's been a long day, General."

"Yes it has, General Lee."

Lee studied the lean face of Gordon, and said quietly, "We cannot remain in Richmond. That much is clear, is it not?"

"That would be untenable, General Lee." He waited for Lee to speak. When he did not, Gordon said, "Do you have a plan for our retreat?"

"Depending upon how alert the Yankees are, I have in mind something that might be done. We must get away from Richmond and join with General Johnson."

"That will be difficult," Gordon said. He looked out over the lines again, his eyes narrowed. He was a fighting general, one of the best Robert E. Lee had ever trained, but now he was impatient, knowing that it was all over except for the finale. Turning back, he waited, unwilling to break the silence.

"If the siege line could be broken, General Gordon, I think Grant would shorten his lines."

"What is your command, General Lee?"

"You will make an attack on Fort Stedman. If the line can be broken there, it's possible that we can get this army away."

Gordon's eyes gleamed as always when battle was imminent. "Yes, sir!" he said. "What forces should I take?"

"Whatever you can gather. When can you be ready?"

Gordon considered briefly. "Today is Thursday the twenty-third—I think by Saturday. That will give me all day tomorrow to collect whatever forces are available."

"Then God go with you, General Gordon, and may he keep you safe in his hand."

"And you too, General Lee." Gordon stared at the gray-haired man, wanting to say more. He wanted to offer comfort, for this was the man who had borne the Army of Northern Virginia and the fate of the Confederacy on his shoulders throughout the hard, arduous struggle. Phrases came to his mind, but finally, concluding that talk was now superfluous, he bowed slightly. "Good evening, General. I will send you word at what hour the attack will be made."

Lee spoke quietly, "Thank you, General," then turned and gazed through the darkness that lay outside the lines. Somewhere, he knew, General Ulysses S. Grant was there, perhaps directly ahead of him. Lee had beaten all the Federal generals—Burnside, Pope, McClellan—but he could not beat General Grant, for Grant was a butcher. Grant had worn down the Army of Northern Virginia by attrition, losing five Union soldiers in order to kill one Confederate. For every Union soldier that fell, there was another back in Indiana or Ohio or New York to take his place. But for every fallen Confederate, there was nothing but a vacancy that could not be filled—and no one knew this better than Robert E. Lee.

From overhead came the cry of a hunting owl. Lee looked up but could not see it. The stars were faint, although one glittered brightly. Lee fastened his eyes upon it and for a time did not move. In the east a faint opalescent glow marked the beginning of dawn, but it brought no pleasure to Lee. He had known for a long time that the war was lost, and now the end was upon the South. A pain took him in the chest—something, he knew, that would kill him eventually. But he gave that no thought as he simply turned and walked back along the lines, saying a word of encouragement to the scarecrow soldiers who greeted him with such enthusiasm that it pained him.

★ ★ ★

"Larribee, pull together what supplies you can. We've been ordered to another hospital."

Looking up with surprise from the man whose arm he was bandaging, Quentin responded quickly, "Yes, sir! What sort of supplies?"

"All that you can liberate," Doctor Alexander said gruffly. He slapped his hands together, then impatiently shook his head. "Just as we get settled in here they move us. Well, that's the army for you."

Quentin suddenly grinned and straightened up. "Yes, sir. If they'd let the doctors run it, it'd be a smoother operation."

Alexander grinned slowly. "You're a saucy fellow, Larribee, blast your eyes! Well, do what you can."

"Yes, sir. Will Peters be going with us?"

"Yes. If you can find him."

As it happened, Quentin was unable to find Peters. He suspected that the undersized young assistant had slipped away to enjoy what was left of his level of society in Richmond. There were sutlers and camp followers everywhere, and by the time Alexander had commandeered a wagon and the two of them had seen to the loading of the supplies, Peters had not surfaced.

"The rascal! He's probably hiding over there watching us somewhere," Alexander muttered. "Can you drive a team?"

"Yes, sir. I grew up on a farm."

"Well, let's get going."

The wagon creaked and the team's harness jingled almost pleasantly. The winter had mitigated, to some extent, and now, although the air was cold, the sun was out. Larribee glanced up, noting a flotilla of Canada geese flying high in a perfect V.

By the time the two had ridden for several hours down the rough, muddy roads, both men came out of their heavy coats. They talked about medicine, which was all that really interested either man, and Alexander, at one point, gave Quentin a sharp glance. "You'll be going back to work under Doctor Chambers when the war is over, I suppose?"

"Yes, sir. That's my plan."

"Going to marry his daughter? Did I hear that?"

A slight silence followed Doctor Alexander's question, and then seeing the other man's rather careful look Quentin said hastily, "Yes, sir. We'll be married as soon as I get back."

"A wonderful institution, marriage," Alexander said, then added dryly, "but who wants to live in an institution?"

Quentin laughed. The doctor had a sly wit that surfaced from time to time. "It'll be a good situation for me. Doctor Chambers has a thriving practice."

"Yes, so I've heard. Do you like the big city?"

"Not as well as I like small towns, but still, that's where one builds a big practice, I suppose. I've had most of my training there."

The wagon rattled and jounced along. From time to time they passed lines of mud-splattered soldiers, weariness pulling their shoulders down. A troop of cavalry dashed by once, galloping with sabers clinging to their sides. The hooves of the horses threw mud all over a squad of soldiers, who screamed curses and oaths after them.

Thick chunks of mud splattered Quentin and Alexander. Quentin scraped his face, saying, "I could have done without that."

"The cavalry is always dramatic. They never go anywhere at a walk—always at a mad charge."

When they arrived at Fort Stedman, they found themselves very busy indeed. There had been no doctor to take care of this segment of the Union Army, and many of the men were down with fevers. They worked steadily, seeing man after man until they were both exhausted.

"What time is it?" Alexander whispered hoarsely.

"I don't know, sir," Quentin said. His eyes were blurry with fatigue and he straightened up with an effort. "It must be after ten."

"Been a long day. Well . . ." Alexander shrugged. "I think this is the last group over here. Let's see what's there and then we can get some rest."

Inside a large tent, which served as a shelter for ten men, they found every cot full; several of the men were so ill they were only semiconscious. Doctor Alexander examined each man with Quentin beside him, and finally they came to one man who watched them with frightened eyes. His head was bandaged, and one of his fellow soldiers said, "That's Quigby. Got shot in the head three days ago. He loses his mind, it seems like, sometimes. I hope it didn't hit his brain."

The man called Quigby did not speak as the two doctors bent over him. He was very weak, obviously, and a film covered his light blue eyes. His lips moved slightly, and as Alexander removed the bandage the two men studied the wound, then Alexander murmured, "Impossible to do much."

"I suppose so," Quentin said. It was indeed a terrible wound. It had crushed the skull, but there was no telling how much damage was done inside the bone. "I'll bandage it up, sir."

"Very well."

Quentin quickly cleaned the wound and bandaged it. As soon as he was finished he started to leave, indeed had risen and half turned—when an impulse came to him. *Pray for him.*

Feeling somewhat foolish, Quentin turned back and sat down beside the man, aware that the soldiers on either side of the wounded man were watching. Reaching out, he put his hand on the bandage that he had just applied. He bowed his head and prayed a quick prayer. He felt nothing, and there was no change in the patient's eyes or in his attitude. Still feeling somewhat foolish, he rose—nearly running into Doctor Alexander, who had come to stand beside him.

"What were you doing there?"

"Oh, nothing!"

When they were outside the tent, Alexander remarked as they strolled along, "I've seen you do that before, put your hands on the men after they were bandaged. I take it you're praying for them?"

"Well—yes, sir, I am."

"Well, it can do no harm," Alexander remarked. Together they headed for the tent where bunks had been provided by a sergeant. Both men pulled off their boots and tunics and lay down, pulling the blankets up.

Quentin was sleepy, but he heard Alexander ask, "Do you think it does any good? Prayer, I mean."

"Yes, sir. I think it does."

"I could never figure prayer out. Sometimes it seems to work and sometimes it doesn't. Is God that undependable?"

Quentin stirred restlessly. He was tired to the bone, but he knew that Alexander was a sincere and earnest man, though not particularly religious so far as he could discover. "I think we pray a lot of prayers that are out of the will of God. When I was a boy, only eight or nine, I prayed for a pistol. I would probably have blown my brains out with it if God had granted that prayer."

"But among all these wounded men, it's God's will to heal some and not to heal others?"

Hesitating for a moment, Quentin said, "I don't know, sir. I only know that from time to time I feel a special compassion for a man—like that soldier with the head wound. I just felt like I should pray for him."

"And the laying on of hands. Is that a religious thing?"

"Well, I don't know how to put it, sir. Sometimes I think it gives patients confidence. Do you think it's wrong?"

"Not much you do with these poor fellows would be wrong, I think. Some of them haven't felt a kindly hand in a long time— some maybe never. Good night, Quentin."

"Good night, Doctor."

★　★　★

The next day Quentin rose early and found breakfast, which amounted to very little except biscuits and bacon. Doctor Alexander wandered off somewhere, and Quentin visited the patients he had seen the night before. When he entered the tent of the man with the head wound, Quentin went to him at once and saw that he was sleeping peacefully.

"I think he's gettin' better," the soldier next to him said.

"That's good. I hope all of you will get well."

Leaving the tent, Quentin walked along the lines. From time to time a shot rang out and once a burly sergeant said, "Better keep your head down. Them Rebs got some good sharpshooters over there—a few anyhow."

"Thanks, Sergeant."

Quentin spent the day in an almost leisurely fashion. Doctor Alexander did not return, and by three o'clock Quentin was preparing to visit the patients again. He was gathering supplies out of the wagon when a sudden sound caught his attention—musket fire. He spun toward it, listening intently. The sound increased in intensity, and a sour taste came to his mouth—which he recognized with surprise as fear. He had never been tried in battle; he was not a soldier. One had to be trained for that. Suddenly a group of Union soldiers ran toward him, shouting, as the sound of a bugle erupted.

"What's happening?" Quentin asked a private running past. "What's going on?"

"It's an attack! The Rebs are coming!" the private gasped, his eyes wide and staring. "They're comin' this way! You better get back if you don't want to get shot."

Quentin's first thought was the wounded men. If the makeshift hospital was about to be overrun, perhaps his place was with them. He left the wagon at a dead run, but a sergeant with a group of soldiers behind him charged across Quentin's path. "Hey!" the sergeant yelled. "Come on! Grab a musket!"

"But I don't even know how to shoot one! I'm a doctor's assistant!"

"I don't give a blast what you are!" the sergeant roared. "The Rebs are breakin' through, and we need every man we can get to stop 'em! Hey, Clyde, show this fellow how to load a musket."

A young man with a pale face and unsteady hands came forward. "Here," he said, "do you know how to load a musket?"

"I've shot a few, but maybe you'd better show me again."

"Well, we ain't got much time, but look. Here's what you do. You take this ball . . ."

After hurried instruction, Quentin found himself running along with an escorted group including cooks and wood haulers. A major charged by, his face red with exertion. He waved his hand in the air and said, "All of you men! Get in the line over there! We've got to stop 'em—we've got to stop 'em!"

Suddenly Quentin heard the hoarse whistling sound of an incoming cannon shell, quickly growing louder. The more experienced soldiers threw themselves down, but Quentin simply stood there.

A sudden explosion shook the earth, and the concussion of the shell struck him like a fist. Dirt flew into his face, and he fell backwards, dropping the musket. Clawing at his eyes, he rolled over, groping blindly for the musket. His hand found it and he crawled to his feet.

"Come on. Let's go!" A hand grasped Quentin's arm and he felt himself pulled along.

"Wait a minute! I can't see!"

"You're all right. Just a little dirt. Come on!"

Ten minutes later Quentin found himself amidst a bunch of screaming, shouting men. He could see only faintly, and he held his musket awkwardly. From every side came the rattling of musket fire, and he heard the whistling of bullets around his head. Frantically the command came: "Spread out! Spread out! We got to cover this whole gap!"

For Quentin the world seemed to have turned upside down. The explosion had not only half-blinded him, but also confused him terribly. Now he sensed that the men on his right and his left had moved away, and he found himself alone in what seemed to be a field with deep gullies. He scrambled down one, stopped at the bottom to pull out his handkerchief, and tried once more to rub the dirt from his stinging eyes. *If I could only find a stream—something to wash out my eyes!* But the musket fire was getting heavier, and fear swept over him. *To get killed here, at the end of the war—what a tremendous waste!* He stumbled on, trying to see, but his foot dropped into a hole and he fell full-length. The fall knocked the breath out of him and he lay there for a while. The rattle of musket fire seemed to fall off. He heard the crash of Union cannon fire coming from the right flank, and then from the left. A troop galloped past, the officer cursing and waving his sword. Quentin scrambled to his feet, confused and frightened, but stumbled forward almost blindly. Afterwards, he could not remember how long he lurched through the woods. Branches struck him across the face—once across an open eye, which made his vision even worse.

Unable to see anything but shadows, he knew he would be useless in the front line. But which way back to his own lines? He chose a direction and forced his way through the undergrowth, listening carefully to the sound of gunfire, which seemed to be tapering off.

The ground dropped away from him and he fell headlong into a small gully, rolling wildly down the steep side. The ground at the bottom knocked the breath out of him, but struggling to his feet, he scrambled up the other side. As he hauled himself over the lip, he heard a bugle blowing, thin and clear, somewhere to his right. Turning toward the sound, he saw a sudden movement—a soldier emerging from a thicket not twenty feet away. Shock ran through Quentin, freezing him in place, and he peered at the man through dirt-filled eyes. He could see only one detail—the soldier was wearing a gray uniform, not the blue of a Union soldier!

Time stopped, and Quentin heard his own raspy breathing and the silver snarling of the distant bugle. His legs trembled, and his hands grasped the musket so hard that his fingers ached.

For one terrible instant Quentin almost threw his musket down and fled. But when he dimly saw that the Confederate was moving toward him, some primal instinct was triggered. Fear robbed Quentin of all thought, and his musket seemed to level itself, as if it had a life of its own. He watched the long barrel lift, and then he heard the sound of a shot. For a split second he thought that the enemy soldier had fired—then his musket kicked violently, its muzzle lifting to the gray sky overhead. The acrid smell of burning powder stung Quentin's nostrils, and he saw the soldier throw his hands skyward, then fall over backward.

Quentin had no memory of pulling the trigger, but as the gray-clad soldier thrashed wildly, crying out, Quentin felt the musket slip to the ground as if it had grown too heavy for him to hold. Even as it struck the ground, a rough voice sounded almost in his ear and his arm was seized with an iron hand.

"What did you shoot for? He was trying to surrender, you blasted fool!"

Quentin shut his eyes and dug his knuckles into them. When he opened them, he saw the red face of a sergeant. He was glaring at Quentin, his face twisted with rage and battle fury.

Quentin could not speak for a moment. He had never before shot at anyone. His boyhood fistfights were faint memories now, and like all other men he had wondered if he would have whatever it takes to pull a trigger and send another human being into eternity. Now the sergeant was cursing, and Quentin said, "I–I couldn't see!"

"He was waving a white handkerchief! Are you blind?" The sergeant suddenly struck Quentin in the chest with the flat of his hand. He turned to spit a stream of amber juice on the ground, then shook his head in disgust. "Well, he's done for. Come on, we've got to plug up this line!" He whirled and ran awkwardly toward the woods ahead, but Quentin made no move to follow.

The sound of firing grew more fierce, but Quentin paid no heed. His stomach suddenly heaved, and he began to tremble violently. For a moment he could not seem to move, his legs were so weak. Then he knew he had to do *something*. He stumbled forward until he came to the limp body of the man he had shot. Kneeling down, he squinted and saw a bearded face, the eyes wide and staring. Wiping his eyes, Quentin saw that bright crimson arterial blood was forming a pool in the hollow of the man's throat. The shot had taken the Confederate high in the chest, and blood bubbled up through the hole as air escaped from the lung.

Anguish and grief suddenly gripped Quentin. There was nothing he could do to help this man, and life was leaking out of him with every breath. Leaning forward, Quentin cried, "I'm sorry! I'm sorry!"

And then the eyes of the dying soldier focused on Quentin. They were filled with hatred. "You shot me!" he gasped. "I was . . . trying to surrender."

Quentin's throat grew thick and he felt sick—so sick that he wanted to vomit. The man he'd shot had been faceless at the time, just a vague shape in a Confederate uniform, but now that his vision had cleared somewhat, he saw every detail of the dying man's face. He was a good-looking man, though his face had been thinned by hunger. His eyes were dark blue and his hair a tawny yellow. It was a strong face, tough and hard, contorted now with pain and hatred. He cursed Quentin and, doubling up his fist, tried to strike him. But his life was pouring out in a steady stream, staining his shirt, and his blow had no force.

The sounds of battle had faded away now. Quentin would discover later that the attack on Fort Stedman had failed. Now, he was conscious only of the man whose life was running out to stain the Virginia earth. Quentin felt as if a giant hand were squeezing his chest, and he tried to think of something to say—but no words came, and he simply knelt there, looking down at the ruin of the man glaring up at him.

Quentin had heard many stories from soldiers about dying men. Most of them stressed how men turned to God in their last few moments. Some called out for their mothers or their sweethearts. None of them had spoken of a man going into eternity with his mouth filled with cursing.

Suddenly the Confederate gave a desperate lunge, his arms flinging outward and his body arching like a bow. Quentin tried to speak, but nothing came. He finally cried, "Can I take a message to anyone—your family—?"

"I'd like—to send you—to hell!"

The words were forced from stiffening lips and the hate-filled eyes were fixed on Quentin. A fountain of scarlet blood suddenly gushed from the mouth of the dying man. He cried out in a gurgling scream and tried to rise, clawing at his chest feebly—and then the lean body relaxed and a terrible stillness came to his features. His eyes did not close, and not even death softened the rage that burned in them.

"Please—forgive me!"

Quentin knelt in the middle of a battlefield holding a dead man in his arms, and he knew that as long as he lived he would never forget that face.

How long Quentin sat there he didn't know. It was as if the earth had stopped. Finally a voice close to him said, "Is he dead?"

Looking up, Quentin saw through blurred eyes a youthful lieutenant, his face smeared with powder, bending over to peer at the Confederate.

"Yes, sir. He's dead."

"We'll have to bury him then. They're making a common grave right over there."

Quentin clung to the body of the man as if it were a treasure. "No," he gasped. "No, I won't do that! I killed him!"

"He was the enemy," the officer said with surprise. "What outfit are you with?"

"I'm Doctor Alexander's assistant."

"What were you doing fighting in the line?" When he saw that Quentin could not answer, he said impatiently, "Well, he'll have to be buried. Just leave him—you'd better get back to your post. We've got plenty of wounded."

"No!" Quentin said. He looked up. Shock had rendered his face stiff and immobile. His hands and feet felt numb. Vaguely, he knew that he could not refuse an order from an officer, but he shook his head stubbornly. "I'm going to bury him by himself."

The lieutenant's face showed exhaustion. He cursed, saying, "All right. Dig your own hole then!"

Quentin waited until the lieutenant left. Then he rose and made his way back to the camp. He hitched up the team and, without saying a word to anyone, drove back. Pulling up beside the body, he looked around and spotted a pair of privates headed back toward camp. "Can you give me a hand here?"

The privates, surprised, came over asking, "What do you need?"

"Help me get him up into the wagon."

Quentin helped the two pick up the limp form. As they placed it in the wagon, he murmured his thanks and then got back up onto the seat. He spoke to the horses and they moved out at a fast trot.

Quentin had no idea where he was going, but he knew what he was going to do. He drove away from the site of Fort Stedman down a road that led vaguely toward the east. When he had ridden for twenty minutes or so, he saw a small farmhouse off to one side. It was a humble place, a frame house with white paint. Smoke curled out of the chimney. Driving up to the front door, he got down stiffly, his mind working very slowly.

"Can I help you, soldier?"

Quentin turned to see a man and a woman who had stepped outside. They were an older couple, in their middle fifties, both dressed in the usual garb of country people.

"I need to make a coffin and . . . and bury this man somewhere."

The couple exchanged glances, and the woman said, "Is he your kin?"

"No, but I've got to see him buried right. It's very . . . important to me."

"My name's Hawkins. This is my wife, Ethel." The farmer was a short, stocky man with strong-looking, bulky arms and toilworn hands. He came closer to Quentin and stared up into his face. Something that he saw there made him say quietly, "Friend of yours then?"

"I have to bury him—properly," Quentin managed to say.

"Well, I reckon we can work out something," Hawkins said. "I made many a coffin in my day. Carpentered a little when I was a younger man. Why don't you take him out to the barn? We'll see what we can do."

As Quentin drove the team to the barn, Hawkins turned to his wife. "That fellow looks like he's been shot himself! He's wearing a blue uniform and that's a Confederate's body. I don't understand it."

"Neither do I, but you help him, Cyrus, all you can."

★   ★   ★

The coffin had been made, and Cyrus Hawkins had told his hired hand to dig a grave on the back side of his farm. It was by a small stream with large oak trees all around. Cyrus and his wife had come along with the hired hand for the burial.

The burial was simple. The hired hand and Cyrus lowered the coffin into the grave. That done, they stood respectfully while Ethel Hawkins said, "Do you want to say some words over him, soldier?"

"I'd be obliged if one of you would."

Again Hawkins and his wife exchanged glances and seemed to come to an agreement. They all bowed their heads and Hawkins began to quote the Twenty-third Psalm. He quoted it completely and finally said, "Lord, you know this man. He's got one friend that loves him anyhow, so we ask you to have mercy on him. In the name of Jesus."

Ethel Hawkins said, "You come away. You can bring a stone back sometime and put it over him."

Numbly Quentin nodded, then moved away with the woman. She led him inside the house and insisted that he drink a cup of coffee while her husband and the hired hand filled in the grave. She said little to him. After a while, she saw that tears were running down his face. "Some say a man ain't supposed to cry," she murmured, "but I don't see as how it hurts any. I think it does good."

Quentin looked up, only half hearing her. She left the room then and he was alone. Reaching into his inner pocket with a trembling hand, he pulled out the leather wallet that he had removed from the dead man's pocket. He opened it with hands that trembled so violently he could hardly manage. A picture was inside, an old tintype. It was a woman, her eyes seeming to look right at him, surrounded by three children—and the man he had killed was beside her.

As Quentin stared at the picture, he fingered the letter that was with it, knowing that in all probability it was from this woman whose eyes seemed to fix upon him with accusation.

"I can't read it—I just can't!"

He pushed the letter back into the wallet, stuffed it into his coat, and then went outside where the woman was standing. "I've got to go," he said hoarsely. "I'll come back tomorrow and see to some kind of a marker."

"That'll be all right. What did you say your name was?"

"Quentin Larribee."

Ethel Hawkins stared at the man with compassionate eyes. "I can see you're plumb hurt bad, Mr. Larribee. He's put in a nice place, though. You can come back anytime you want and visit him."

Quentin wheeled and turned away. He made his way to the wagon and had to make two attempts to get up, so violently did his legs tremble. Sitting down on the seat, he picked up the lines and slapped the backs of the horses. When they started up, he turned once on the seat and looked back. He could not see the grave, but he knew that he would never forget it. Not as long as he lived.

CHAPTER
Five

And so finally it ended—the most terrible war America had ever known. On April 9, 1865, Robert E. Lee surrendered the Army of Northern Virginia to General Ulysses S. Grant at Appomattox. It had been almost five years to the day—April 12, 1860—when the first shot of the war had been fired at Fort Sumter, and now it was all over.

Or was it? On April 14, John Wilkes Booth assassinated President Abraham Lincoln. It was not only the North that grieved the loss of this man but many in the South as well, for some understood that Lincoln had planned a gentle and generous reunion of the North and the South. That plan ended with the death of Lincoln. On Saturday the sixteenth, President Johnson was sworn into office. On April 19, the funeral of Abraham Lincoln was held in Washington, D.C., and on the twenty-fifth his body left the capital to be buried in Springfield. Only five days after that, the twenty-sixth of the month, John Wilkes Booth was shot to death as he attempted to evade capture. On that same day

General Joseph Johnson surrendered the last Confederate force to the Union Army.

Even then, the war was not over for many. Those who had empty places at their table—sons, brothers, husbands, fathers, cousins buried in far-off fields—it was not over for them. Those who came home maimed, missing limbs, blinded—it was not over for them, either. And for the wounded South, which would undergo the hardships of reconstruction, the war and its effects were not over.

And the war was not over for Private Quentin Larribee. He was unable to purge himself of the memory that had become a nightmare. Night after night he would awaken, sometimes with a wild cry, dreaming that he was pulling the trigger of the musket and seeing the man in gray go down, shot to death by his hand. He moved mechanically, almost like a robot, going through his duties.

Early in June Doctor Alexander spoke to Major Horace Simpkins, commanding officer of the regiment. After explaining at some length what had happened to Quentin, he said, "The boy is shattered emotionally. He needs to get away from here."

Simpkins had seen a great deal of death, but he was basically a kindly man. He came from Illinois and at one time had entertained thoughts of being a minister. He still had a Christian charity about him. "Well, of course, Doctor. If you feel that's best. You can do without him, I assume?"

"Yes." Doctor Alexander nodded, feeling greatly relieved. "I appreciate your help in this matter. When do you think we could release him?"

"Send him right away, Alexander. From what you tell me, he's not really a soldier. Killing another human being is hard enough for someone who's trained for it. As you've described Larribee to be, it must be traumatic. Use my name with the orderly. Have him make out the proper papers and have Larribee taken to the train."

"Thank you, Major."

★　★　★

At that exact moment, the subject of their conversation was sitting on his cot staring at the wall. He had been there for some time, unable to comprehend what Jim Peters, who sat across from him, was saying. Quentin had always been careful to listen when people spoke, but since the dreadful day he had shot the Confederate soldier, he had found himself drifting, unable to concentrate on the conversations that went on around him.

Peters was cleaning his fingernails with a huge Bowie knife he had found on the battlefield. But when he looked up and saw that Quentin was paying no attention to what he was saying, he barked, "Hey, what's the matter with you, Quent?"

"What . . . what did you say, Jim?"

Peters threw the knife down into the dirt floor of the tent, burying it halfway up to the hilt, and shook his head almost angrily. "I might as well be talking to this tent pole as you! I was telling you what I was going to do when I get back on the Mississippi."

"Sorry, Jim. I guess my mind wandered a little bit."

Peters removed the knife and carefully wiped it on his boot. He admired the sheen of it, tested the blade with his thumb, then nodded as if satisfied. He stuck it in the sheath fastened to his belt, then leaned forward to study the face of his companion. "You still worried about that Reb you shot?" When he received no answer but saw the swift reaction in Quentin's eyes, he shook his head and said roughly, "Forget about that. It's a war and people get killed in a war. It wasn't your fault."

"I don't see it that way—"

At that moment Doctor Alexander walked through the entrance of the tent, and both men stood up at once in the presence of the officer. "Peters, I've got to talk to Larribee. Go do something useful for a change."

"Yes, sir, Doctor. I certainly will." Peters scurried out but did not go far. He began throwing his knife at a large cedar tree, grunting with satisfaction when the huge blade sank into the soft wood.

"Quentin, I want you to get your things together. You're going home."

Quentin stared at the tall surgeon and for a moment could not understand what he was hearing. "Home? You mean the regiment's pulling out?"

"No. I mean *you're* going home. You're not doing yourself any good around here. It's been a hard time for you."

"Well, it doesn't seem right, Doctor, my going home and everyone else staying."

"We'll all be going home soon enough," Alexander said. He pulled his hat off, removed a handkerchief from his pocket, and wiped his forehead. June was hot, and even though the tent was in the shade, it was still stuffy. He replaced the handkerchief, and then said, "I want you to go as soon as possible."

"Well, sir, there's something I need to do."

"Something to do with that Confederate you shot?"

Quentin dropped his eyes and did not answer for a time. Finally he murmured, "Yes, sir."

Alexander had grown fond of Quentin Larribee. Now he stepped forward and put his hand on Quentin's shoulder, saying quietly, "Look, it's been a terrible thing for you, but you've got to put it behind you."

"That's what Jim says. But it's not easy to do."

"Why, blast it, man—you're too sensitive!"

Quentin tried to smile and failed. "I thought it was good for a doctor to be sensitive."

"It is, ordinarily, but—look, he was a casualty of war. It wasn't personal."

Quentin Larribee lifted his eyes. An enormous sobriety had drawn lines in his face. Fatigue was part of it, but the grief in his eyes spoke of something much deeper. "Yes, it was personal, Doctor."

Alexander stared at the tall, lanky man before him, and finally said quietly, "Look, Quentin, some day you'll make a mistake on the operating table and your patient will die. That may have happened already. If it hasn't, it will sooner or later. What are you going to do then?"

"That's different."

"Not a great deal. You'll be trying to help that patient, just as you were trying to help your country when you came here to serve. You've told me what happened, Quentin—you had debris in your eyes; you couldn't see that the man was trying to surrender. You made a mistake, but it was the kind of mistake that happens in the confusion of war. Now it's time to go on, and the best thing is for you to get away from here."

"Yes, sir."

"Finish up your business. Tomorrow morning I'll have Peters take you to the train."

"Yes, sir, and—and thank you, Doctor. I know this is your doing."

"You're too good a doctor to waste. I've known men before who made a mistake and couldn't walk away from it. Some of them took to drink, some of them just walked away from their profession, their families. Don't let that happen to you, Quentin. God's put something in you. Don't waste it."

"I'll do my best, Doctor Alexander."

Doctor Alexander left the tent and Quentin stood staring after him. Jim came in almost at once. "What did he say, Quent?"

"He said he's sending me home."

"Me too? Am I going with you?"

"I don't think so. He said you were to take me to the train tomorrow."

"That's rotten! I'm going to see if I can talk him into letting me go with you."

Peters left the tent at once and Quentin Larribee called out, "I'll be ready to go at noon, Jim."

★   ★   ★

The sun was warm on the back of Quentin's neck as he stood beside the mound of raw, red dirt. He wondered why a brand-new grave was always so much more tragic than an old one. "Some day," he murmured, "when his wife comes here with her children, the grave will be sunken and there will be grass on it. They won't have to see it looking like this."

The branches on the huge oak tree that shaded the grave moved slightly in the breeze; flickering shades of light danced on the ground at Quentin's feet. He bowed his head and closed his eyes, but found that he could not pray. It was almost as if God had erected a huge, steel barrier, and Quentin's words, broken and fragmented, dissipated. Finally he simply stood, head bowed, unable to say a word. Then he looked up at the stone that Cyrus Hawkins had arranged to have carved and set. It simply said, "William Breckenridge." Below the name were the simple words, "A soldier," and the date, "March 25, 1865."

Quentin knelt beside the fresh, new stone, its edges sharp and clear, and ran his fingers through the V-shaped gaps the engraver had made. *Some day,* he thought, *this stone will be soft and round and the letters will wear away. It will have lichen on it and green moss.* He thought, as he knelt, of how time changes things inexorably, and he remembered a line from a poem one of his professors had made him memorize. The poet was Andrew Marvell; Quentin had never liked it. It was called "To His Coy Mistress," and it was a plea from a lover to his mistress, urging her to give herself up to his lust. As much as Quentin had disliked the poem, a few words had become fixed in his memory, and they came to him now:

> But at my back I always hear
> Time's winged chariot hurrying near.

Those lines seemed poignant and sad and tragic. "I guess time's winged chariot's at my back, too. Coming nearer every day."

He knelt for a while with his hand resting lightly on the stone, then took a deep breath and stood. He put his hand into his pocket and felt Breckenridge's letter. He had not been able to read it yet, but he knew someday he would have to. Now he took one final look at the mound, thinking of the agony on the face of the man he had killed.

Wheeling suddenly, unable to bear the thought, he moved away from the grave. When he approached the house he saw the Hawkinses waiting for him. He shook hands with both of them. "Thank you for all you've done," he said. "You've been kind."

Cyrus Hawkins said quietly, "I was born on this farm. Expect to die here. My boys will take it over afterward. Any of his people that want to come, it will be all right."

"I thank you."

Quentin wheeled and moved away quickly. He got into the wagon, drove it back to camp, but as he left he did not hear the remark of Cyrus Hawkins to his wife. "He's a right nice fellow— for a Yankee."

Arriving back at camp, he found Jim Peters waiting for him. "Got your stuff, Quentin. Here, I'll load it up for you." When he had tossed the black bag of medical instruments and the single valise of clothing into the back, Jim jumped in and took the reins, forcing Quent to move over. "I'll drive," he said cheerfully.

Several times during the four-hour trip to the station, Jim tried to engage Quentin in conversation, but received only monosyllabic replies. Finally, when they arrived, Peters said, "I'll get your stuff, Quent."

"Thanks, Jim."

Quentin handed his pass, written out by Major Simpkins, to the agent, who winked at him and handed him a ticket. "Going home, are you, son?"

"Yes, sir. Going home."

"Want to get something to eat while we're waiting?" Jim Peters asked.

"No, but if you're hungry, I'll drink a cup of coffee, if there is any."

The two men found a small café and Peters ate a huge meal, but Quentin could only drink a little black coffee. He knew that he needed to eat, but he couldn't manage it. Finally the train gave a blast, and he said quickly, "I guess I've got to be going, Jim."

The two walked to the train, which was quickly filling with soldiers, most of them on their way home. Turning, Quentin put out his hand and shook with Jim. "I hope I see you again. If you're in New York, look me up at Central Hospital."

"I'll write you a letter and tell you where I'll be. I'll wind up in Memphis someday. I'll be on a boat, that's pretty sure, for a while anyway." Peters was usually a happy young man but something saddened him now. He wanted to do something to shake Quentin out of the depression he had fallen into, but he had no skill for this. Now he simply struck him sharply on the shoulder with his fist, saying, "Take care of yourself, hear?"

"You too, Jim."

Getting on board the train, Quentin found most of the seats already taken. He found one at the back of the car, and through the window he saw Jim climbing aboard the wagon and turning the team around. Then the whistle uttered a piercing blast that shattered the silence, and a few moments later the car lurched, throwing every passenger in it back against the seats. It eased out of the station, and soon the *clickety-clack* settled into a regular, rapid pace.

For two hours Quentin watched the scenery flow by, wondering what life would be like when he got back to New York City. Once he saw a bluebird perched on a telegraph line. He'd always loved this small, beautifully colored bird, seeing it as a harbinger of spring and good things, but none of those feelings came now. Finally he grew sleepy. He had missed a great deal of rest, and the rhythm of the wheels on the rails lulled him to sleep.

The air was full of smoke and he could not see. He could feel grit in his eyes, and all around him he heard the rattle of far-off musket fire, and the booming of cannons. As he scrambled down into a ravine, he fell and opened a cut in the palm of his right hand, but he barely noticed it. He scrambled up on the lip of the gully, and there right before him was dimly outlined a man who was not wearing blue. The enemy! He threw up his weapon and fired and saw the form driven back by the force of the fifty-caliber minié ball, a slug powerful enough to knock down a horse. And then he heard, "You fool! Why'd you shoot him? He was trying to surrender. . . ."

"No! No!—" Quentin suddenly threw his arms out and his left arm hit something. He turned to see a woman staring at him angrily.

"What are you doing? What's wrong with you?" she demanded.

"I'm . . . sorry. I had a dream."

"Well, keep your hands to yourself!"

"I'm sorry," Quentin muttered again. He got up at once and made his way down the aisle. He felt the eyes of everyone on him and quickly stumbled to the door. He moved outside and stood on the platform, taking deep breaths of air. His hands were shaking. He leaned backward against the steel wall of the railroad car and cried out, "Oh, God, am I never going to be able to get away from it?"

★　★　★

The train reached New York just as the afternoon was ending. Quentin, carrying his valise in one hand and his medical bag in the other, moved along the streets. He considered catching a cab, but his money was limited. He stopped at the trolley station and shoved two nickels across the counter to a tall man with sweeping mustaches who nodded pleasantly enough and gave him a small piece of cardboard. Quentin moved outside, and even as he did the wooden bus drawn by two weary-looking horses pulled up beside the curb. Stepping through the door, Quentin glanced at the driver who sat on an outside seat at the front. The driver made no attempt to collect the ticket, so Quentin shrugged and stepped inside. He glanced down the length of the bus, noting that the two benches which ran from front to back contained only five passengers. He took his seat, plopped his bags down, and soon he heard the driver say, "Hup!" and the bus moved forward slowly. The steel-shod hooves of the horses rang against the cobblestones, but Quentin paid little attention. He looked outside and saw that he was at Fifty-eighth Street, and the houses all seemed to be made of white marble. It was a familiar scene, for he had taken this tram often before.

Suddenly he heard the sound of a bell ringing and his eyes brightened with interest when he saw a wagon painted light blue with the words "Central Hospital" on it in gold leaf lettering. He knew the driver, an Irishman named Daniel Sullivan, and had indeed ridden with the man on several occasions.

It was strange to be back, and he noted listlessly that a new business had gone in, Miss Clara Longstreet's School for Young Ladies, identified by a sign propped in the window in front of a large brownstone. Two young women wearing long, gaily colored dresses were entering, chattering happily to each other.

The tram clattered on, but Quentin paid little heed as the streets slipped by until he got to Forty-sixth Street. He suddenly realized that he must get off and stood. He waited until the tram stopped, then, moving to the front, he handed his ticket to the driver, who took it with a grunt that could have been interpreted as thanks.

Stepping down to the pavement, he caught a glimpse of what looked to be the base of an enormous pyramid—the Croton Reservoir, which supplied the water for most of New York City. He walked slowly to his own street, then turned and trudged until he turned into the entrance to his building. The steps seemed to be half a mile high, for he was weary—he had eaten and slept little since Breckenridge's death. He entered the apartment house, climbed to the second floor, and then stood looking at his own door. Putting the cases down, he knocked, for he had lost his key.

The door opened—and Hannah stood before him, stock-still for a moment, then her face lit up wonderfully. She threw her arms around him, which she had not done for many years. He could tell that her body was shuddering with suppressed weeping. "It's all right. I'm back," he said quietly. When she stepped back, he saw that the tears were gathered in her eyes. She turned quickly, saying, "Well, don't stand out there forever! Come on inside." Her familiar gruff manner amused Quentin. Picking up his cases, he walked inside and shut the door as she turned to say, "Are you all right?"

"Yes. Fine. How are you, Hannah?"

"Me? Well, I'm the same as I always was. You go clean up and I'll have something ready for you to eat."

"I'm not very hungry."

"Don't be foolish! You've got to eat. You've lost weight." She reached up suddenly and touched the hollows in his cheeks. "I can tell it here." There was concern in her eyes and she shook her head almost angrily. "You go clean up. Lie down and take a nap and I'll call you when it's ready."

In his room, Quentin unpacked his bag and washed his face. Familiar things seemed somehow strange. The blue delft pitcher and matching basin had been his grandmother's—he had seen them all of his life. But now, somehow, he was looking at things through a filter, and he stood there with the water he had splashed onto his face dripping from his chin, studying the intricate designs of the beautifully wrought china. He took a towel from the rack at the end of the walnut washstand, dried his face, then neatly hung the cloth up and turned to study the room. He had hoped to feel some sort of ebullience to be back home again, much as a bird would be happy to get back to a nest, a place of safety after a terrible storm.

But there was no joy in him, only a heaviness that bowed his shoulders. He knew that although he had slept on this bed for years, tonight it would be torture for him, as every night for the past few weeks had been. He stared out the window at the street which had grown dark. The gaslights were on, and he studied the long shadows of the people. The streets were familiar, or had been, but now there was a strangeness about it all and he could not understand it. Everything had changed, and he was frightened. He had thought of himself as being fairly strong, maybe infrangible—but now he knew that he was broken in some way that he could not repair by strength of character.

He sat down on the bed, not moving for a long time. He had acquired the habit of just staring at what was in front of him and trying to make his mind as blank as a wall. He succeeded—but after some time, he realized that his name was being called. Looking up with a start, he saw Hannah standing before him, framed in the doorway.

"Didn't you hear me call?"

"Oh, I guess I was thinking." Getting to his feet, he followed her out to take his seat at the dining table.

"I fixed a roast yesterday. It's still nice and juicy and the vegetables are good. I fixed those early peas and the squash that you always liked so much."

As soon as Hannah sat down, he said awkwardly, "Why don't you ask the blessing, Hannah?"

Surprised, Hannah stared at him, then bowed her head and asked a brief blessing. "Now, fill your plate up," she said.

Knowing that he would eat almost nothing, Quentin took small portions and succeeded in making Hannah do most of the talking. He asked her about their neighbors, then about their family, and she spoke of the letters she had received from them.

"Why, you haven't eaten a thing!" Hannah exclaimed. "What's wrong with you? Are you sick?"

"I guess my stomach's a little upset. I'll be all right now that I'm home."

"Well, you go on in the sitting room and I'll bring you some tea. That'll be good for your stomach, and I have a pound cake, too. Maybe you can eat a little of that."

"All right, Hannah."

Ten minutes later the two were seated in the small, comfortable room lined with books, mostly medical tomes, but also some of the childhood books that both of them had loved. The glass fronts of the bookcases caught the reflection of a gaslight overhead and threw beams across the room.

"What was it like, Quentin? Tell me about it."

Knowing that he would have to say something, Quentin talked for some time of the more mundane things that had happened, of his patients, and of Jim Peters and the men in his unit.

His voice grew lower and he spoke more slowly, then finally he broke off completely and fell into a silence.

As Hannah watched him she was troubled. She sat silently for a long time, then crossed to the sofa to sit beside him. It was a horse-hair sofa that had been built by their father when he was a young man, but it was still sturdy and they both treasured it. Putting her hand on his shoulder, she asked quietly, "What is it, Quentin?"

For a long time Hannah did not think he meant to answer, but then he swallowed and drew a deep breath. He expelled it, then began, in a low monotone, to tell her of how he had been given a musket and taken to the battle line at Fort Stedman. He spoke haltingly of how the shell had driven dirt into his eyes so that he was half blind. His speech became more and more broken as he continued.

Hannah listened as he described how he had crawled up out of the gully. His hands trembled as he said, "And . . . and then I saw someone in front of me. He wasn't wearing a blue uniform. I thought he was a Confederate, so I just threw up my musket and pulled the trigger, and—" Hannah saw that he could no longer speak. His chest was heaving and his face working as he stared blindly past her at the wall. She waited. Finally he turned to her and said with a sob in his voice, "And—I killed him, Hannah. He was trying to surrender and I killed him!"

Hannah Larribee had practically raised her brothers and sisters. Quentin was the oldest, but she could remember when he was a child and had injured himself and come to her and she had put her arms around him. She had not done so for many years, but now she saw the hurt and the grief and agony in him and she reached out and pulled him forward. He fell against her, his face pressed against her shoulder, and she put her arms around him. His body was shaking as she patted him on the back. "It's all right, Quentin," she said. "It's all right."

And then Quentin began to shed the tears he had withheld. He wept like a small boy who had lost everything. Hannah saw that he was stricken beyond all that he could bear. She held him tightly and stroked his hair. "It's all right, Quentin. It will pass. God will take it away from you."

The two sat for a long time, Quentin limp in her arms. *Oh, God, be with him,* she prayed, *for he needs you now as he never has before!*

CHAPTER
Six

"I'm very concerned about Quentin, Brother Pettigrew."

The Reverend Horace Pettigrew, pastor of Calvary Baptist Church, leaned forward in his chair and placed his hands on his desk. Interlocking his fingers, he studied the face of Hannah Larribee, who sat across from him nervously twisting a handkerchief. He had a special affection for both of the Larribees, having been impressed from the beginning of his ministry at Calvary Baptist with the sincere devotion of both of them. He had come to depend upon seeing their faces out in the congregation, for it was his habit to pick out several of his hearers who listened with intelligence. Always there were those who simply listened, seeming to endure the sermon; others slept, and many appeared to have their eyes glazed over. But both Quentin Larribee and his sister, Hannah, were among that small group who listened with an intensity that would have pleased any minister. Now as he studied the face of Hannah, he asked, "I haven't spoken with him since he came home. How long has that been now?"

"Over three months."

"He's been to church every Sunday, but I haven't noticed anything unusual. Of course," the pastor added, shrugging his burly shoulders, "I haven't had a chance to spend any time with him personally. What seems to be his problem?"

"He . . . he's just not himself, Pastor."

"Not himself in what way?"

"Well—Quentin's always been outgoing and pleasant, usually with a smile on his face, and he's . . . always enjoyed everything so much. But ever since he came back from the army, he's been different." Hannah twisted the handkerchief in her hands and lifted her eyes to the heavy gold frame containing a picture of Dwight L. Moody, the pastor's hero. Pettigrew quoted him often in his sermons. "He seems to be in some sort of deep depression, and he doesn't listen to what I say. That's very unusual for Quentin."

"What do you mean he doesn't listen?"

"Why, I'll be talking to him and ask him a question, and when he won't answer, I realize that he's gone off somewhere in his mind. When I call to him, he'll snap out of it and pretend that nothing happened."

"You think it has something to do with the war? He was all right when he left, wasn't he?"

"Yes. Quite all right. He was doing well with his work and, of course, he's engaged to be married to Miss Chambers."

Pettigrew suddenly unlocked his fingers and leaned back. He jingled the heavy gold watch chain that lay across his stomach, a habit he was trying to break, and then abruptly jerked his hand away. "You must have some idea. He must have said something. It has to do with the army, I suppose."

For a moment Hannah hesitated, uncertain whether to tell the pastor about what Quentin had told her on his first night home. But she had grown almost desperate now. Quentin was getting no better—in fact, he was getting worse. Making a quick decision, she said, "He told about something that happened. He was terribly broken up about it."

Then she repeated, as closely as she could, the words that Quentin had used to describe the incident. She ended by saying, "Quentin has never been one to cry, even when he was a small boy. But he did this time, almost like he was a baby." She looked down at her handkerchief, twisted into a thin rope, and shook her head. "Quentin is sensitive—more than any man I've ever known."

"Yes. I've noticed that about him. He blames himself for things—like losing patients."

She hesitated for a moment, then lifted her eyes to meet those of the pastor. "He blames himself for my handicap." She had never spoken of this to a living human being, but now she was so apprehensive about Quentin that she felt she must. "We were in a buggy and I was driving. I was really too young to be driving a buggy and I wasn't good at it. Quentin had some stones in his pocket that he had been throwing at squirrels, I suppose. He pulled one out and hit the horse, and the horse bolted. The wagon turned over and injured my leg." Biting her lip, she shook her head sorrowfully. "Quentin's never forgiven himself for that. He feels responsible."

A silence surrounded the two. The light from the tall window to Hannah's right shed pale bars of sunlight on the carpet, illuminating the massive bookcases that flanked the walls, holding hundreds of leather-bound books. The carpet was a pale salmon color. All around, those walls not covered with books were thick with pictures of the pastor's wife and children. For a long time Hannah said nothing. Then she looked up and said, "He's eaten up with remorse, Pastor."

"What does he say about all this?"

"He won't talk about it. I try to bring up the subject, but it's as if he's so ashamed of it he can't bear to have anyone mention it."

Pettigrew shook his head. "That's bad. Very bad. He needs to talk about it. Do you suppose he would talk with me?"

"I've been hoping that he would, but when I suggested it he put me off—I suppose he wasn't ready yet."

They talked for some time, but the pastor had no solution. Finally he rose and came around to stand beside her. He knelt down and bowed his head. "We'll just pray about the matter, Hannah. God's able. I know you're aware of that."

As the pastor prayed, Hannah tried to bolster her faith. But she knew well that faith came from God himself. One could not work it up. Still, she had learned over the hard, lean years when she and Quentin had struggled to raise their brothers and sisters that one must pray even when faith was less than a grain of mustard seed. The pastor's voice was low but his tone was intense, and she knew that this man of God was sincerely concerned about her brother. She joined him silently, asking God to restore and heal Quentin.

Finally Hannah rose and, slipping her crutch under her arm, said, "Thank you, Pastor. I'll try to get Quentin to come and talk with you. It's always good for us to talk our problems out."

"Yes, it is. I'll be here anytime, and I pray that God will do a work in him."

"He's so completely changed, Father. I simply can't understand it." Irene had sought her father out in his study.

Putting the book down, Oscar Chambers listened as Irene spoke with more intensity than he had seen in her in a long time. Her face was tense, and he noticed that she had been rather careless with her dress. Anytime this daughter of his was careless with her appearance, she was in trouble.

"I don't know what's wrong with him," Irene said. "It's hard to even carry on a conversation. He just drifts off. I tried to talk to him about the house over on Fifteenth Street, but he won't even go look at it. And as for marriage plans, all he says is he's got some things to work out."

Oscar Chambers chewed his lower lip and nodded slowly. "I know what you mean, Irene. He's not the same at the hospital either. He's always been so—well, on top of everything, you might

say. He's always known everything that happened. Now he [...]
forgetful. And I'm not the only one who has noticed it. [...]
Miles came to me the other day and asked what was wro[...]
him. He was rather upset, actually. Quentin had done a p[...]
of assisting him in a delicate operation. That's not like Que[...]

"No, but we've got to find out what's wrong with him."

"Have you talked to him about it?"

"I haven't asked him directly, but I'm going to. I wa[...]
announce our wedding day."

"Well, he'll want to finish his training before that, and I c[...]
say that I blame him."

"That's fine, Father, as long as we can be definite and come [...]
with it. I don't understand why he's so reluctant to talk about i[...]
Her eyes narrowed. "I'll talk to him after supper tonight. You a[...]
Mother go off and leave us alone."

Dr. Chambers nodded. "He's got to snap out of it, whatever it is."

All day, Irene thought about Quentin. In fact, she thought
about little else. That night after supper, her father and mother left
early exactly as she had instructed him. As soon as they were out
of the room, she turned to Quentin and said, "Darling, I've tried
to talk to you about this before but you've put me off." She smiled
at him and reached out and put her hand on his cheek. He had
been attentive enough during dinner, and now as he turned to look
at her, she said sweetly, "I thought as soon as you came back we'd
announce our engagement."

"Irene, we can't get married until I'm fully qualified."

"Oh, I know that, darling. But I would like for us to be engaged
and to set a date. It would make me feel so wonderful just to know
that much. Won't you help me with this?" She pulled him forward
and kissed him, but his slow response felt almost like reluctance.

"I'd rather not, Irene. So many things can happen."

"What could happen?" Irene said. She wanted to force him to
give her a date, but she had learned that once Quentin Larribee
made up his mind there was little one could do with him—in

major things, that is, for in small things he was easy for her to manipulate. Now she studied him and, with an effort, kept the irritation out of her voice. "I can't understand why you're so reluctant. You love me, don't you?"

"Of course I do, but—I guess I just learned to be careful, Irene. Things have been different for me. I've had a different kind of life."

"What does that have to do with it?"

"Well, it means that you've never had many disappointments. But I've had quite a few—and I just learned not to plan so far ahead." Summoning an effort, Quentin smiled. "I'll be through with my training in a few months, then there'll be nothing to stand in the way."

Irene tried as hard as she could to persuade him to change his mind, but he remained adamant—not angry, but unmovable.

★   ★   ★

When Quentin left the house it was still early, and the streets were lit with gaslights that illuminated the passersby. When he came to Broadway, he then turned and continued his stroll, not wanting to go home. He heard a clock strike, its chimes echoing in the quiet air—Trinity Church. He counted the eight strokes of the bell. Soon he stood before the church, which rose high against the night sky, blotting out the stars behind it. A man standing in front of the building nodded to him and said pleasantly, "Good evening, sir."

On impulse Quentin stopped and said, "Good evening. Beautiful night."

"Yes, sir. It is." The speaker was an undersized man wearing a pair of black trousers and a checkered shirt. He had a soft cap on his head and his quick eyes took Quentin in. "Pretty warm for this time of the year."

"Yes. It is very warm." Quentin looked up at the tower and said, "That's one of the highest points in New York. I wonder what it looks like from up there."

"Why, you've got the best view in the city. Would you like to have a look?"

Quentin stared at the man. "Would it be all right?"

"Well, we don't ordinarily let people in at night. Lots of sight-seers come in the daytime, though. My name's Giles. I'm the custodian."

Oddly excited, Quentin said, "I'd like to see, if you don't mind."

"Why, no trouble at all." The man turned, and Quentin followed him inside. He came to a stone staircase and motioned, saying, "I've got a little rheumatism in my legs and it's quite a climb. But you go right ahead, sir. Here's a lantern to help you up and down the stairs."

Quentin took the lantern and then moved up what seemed to be an endlessly winding stone staircase. He passed by the rooms housing the bells that sounded so clearly and wondered what they would sound like if you were in the same room. *Probably deafening,* he thought.

Finally he reached the top and stepped to a stone windowsill. He stared out over the city, amazed at how many lights he could see. He would have thought that most of the city would be dark at this time of the night, but then he remembered that there were large residential areas; the lights that he saw must be from homes. He looked down at the street below where, by the gaslight, he could see Giles, the caretaker, lounging on the stone steps. He had never been particularly fond of high places, and for a moment, dizziness took him.

He sat for a long time, noting that the moon was only a fine sliver but the stars were very bright in the sky. The three hundred or so feet he had climbed away from earth seemed to bring him much closer to the stars, and they seemed to twinkle—perhaps because there were no other lights above him to take away from their glory.

It was very quiet. He could hear nothing except the faint whistling of the breeze as it moved across the tower that rose like a needle pointing toward the sky. The air was very clear, and peace washed over him with a warmth that surprised him.

For some time he sat. Finally, he thought, *I can't go on living like this. I've got to talk to somebody.* He had been thinking of this for some time and now made up his mind. *I'll go talk to Brother Pettigrew tomorrow.*

He descended the staircase and thanked Giles, then made his way home. Hannah greeted him and asked how his evening had been. For a time they sat and talked, but then he said, "I think I'll go to bed early. I have a long day tomorrow." He went to his room at once, but did not undress. He sat in the chair beside the window, looking out at the street, not really seeing it. He thought of the release of spirit he had felt while on top of Trinity Church, and a longing for peace that would last came to him.

When he went to bed, he tossed and turned. Finally, miserable and exhausted, he got out of bed and turned up the gas lamp on the wall beside his bed. He stood for a moment, dreading what he was about to do, but knowing that the time had come when he could no longer avoid it. Opening the drawer beside him, he took out the letter he had taken from the dead soldier and sat down. For a long time he sat holding it in his hands, wondering if it would make things worse; then, impulsively, he opened the envelope and pulled out a single page. It was a very short letter, he saw, covering only one page. The handwriting was firm and well-shaped, easily readable. His hands were unsteady as he read:

> *Dear Will:*
>
> *I take this opportunity to send this letter by the hand of Fred Hendricks who will be returning to the army tomorrow. His wound has not healed completely but he must go back he says.*
>
> *The children are both well. Johnny and Prudence had the measles, but Stuart was spared. They all miss you very much, especially Johnny. I shouldn't say that, for Prudence asks every day when you will be back.*

Do not worry about us. Food is plentiful, and God is good to us. Soon the war will be over, and you will be here.

The mortgage on the house will be due soon, and I have worried about it. So many have lost their farms, and I could not bear to lose this one.

Try to be careful, for the children need you.

> *I remain your obedient wife,*
> EDEN BRECKENRIDGE

Quentin read the letter several times. It had a formality that seemed odd in a letter from a wife to her husband. *But then,* he thought, *I have a hard time expressing affection myself.* He looked for a long time at the picture of the family, focusing on the face of Eden Breckenridge. The picture was of poor quality, but he thought he saw signs of strength in her face. She looked like the kind of woman who could shoot a man down if she had to—and then get on with living.

He slowly put the letter and the photograph back in his desk, then went to bed. Even when his eyes were shut, he could remember every word of the letter. But he could not put his finger on what was so odd about it. Finally he dropped off to sleep, but it was a fitful sort of night for him, filled with vague dreams that would not leave his mind.

For three days after reading Eden Breckenridge's letter, Quentin was even quieter than he had been previously. He went about his work mechanically, and after leaving the hospital would walk the streets of New York for hours before going home. It was as if something were locked inside of him, struggling to get out, but he could not imagine what it was. Hannah, he knew, was concerned about him, as were those he worked with at the hospital, but he could not find his way out.

On Wednesday, he started to walk again as soon as he left the hospital, but weariness and despair combined to force him to a decision. He went at once to the church and found the pastor very glad to see him.

"Well, come in, Quentin. I haven't had a chance to talk to you since you got back. Here, take a seat. Let me fix us some coffee, or perhaps tea."

Quentin didn't really want anything, but when he saw that the pastor was determined to do something to put him at ease, he agreed. At first, the pastor made small talk about the church and the members, while Quentin gave short answers.

Fifteen minutes later, Quentin said abruptly, "Pastor, I've got a problem."

"What is it, Quentin? Something I can help with?"

"I don't know if anyone can help with it. I don't think so."

"Don't say that. There's always a way. You're a man of faith and God is able. Tell me about it."

And Quentin did, while the pastor sat quietly listening, noting the strain in Quentin's eyes. Quentin had always been a lean, hollow-cheeked young man, but now it was obvious that he was even thinner, and did not look healthy. He wrung his hands, something the pastor had never seen him do before. Suddenly Quentin stood and began to pace the floor as the story came out of him in bits, in broken speech. When he had choked out the last bitter words, he said, "I killed him—and he was trying to surrender. I can't get it out of my mind, Pastor."

"Sit down, Quentin. Let's talk about this." When Quentin was seated Pettigrew said, "War's always a tragedy. If we had a list of all the things like this that happened in this war, it would be a long one. Think about that Confederate who fired the shot that killed Stonewall Jackson, the most beloved general except for Lee in the whole Confederacy. Think what it must have felt like to the man who fired the shot. That happened more than once. Union men died from wounds inflicted by other Union soldiers . . ."

Quentin sat listening for what seemed like a long time. He admired Horace Pettigrew, but doubted that even a man of his compassion knew what terrible things had happened in the war.

When the pastor's voice stopped, Quentin pulled out the letter and handed it to him. "Read that, Pastor." He watched the pastor's face as his eyes scanned the letter. "That's what's driving me crazy. It's bad enough that I killed a father, but now what are the widow and the orphans going to do?"

"I think this is something you're going to have to pray much about. Do you feel any inclination to help them?"

"I've thought about it and prayed about it until I've almost lost my mind. I've got to do *something* to help them!"

"Well, you have the woman's name."

"I don't know her address, though. All she puts is the name Helena. That's a little town in Arkansas just south of Memphis."

"I'm sure a letter would reach her if you'd care to send money."

"Yes, I suppose I will."

"I think you ought to write first before you send money, just to make sure it doesn't get lost."

"But what am I going to say in the letter?" Despair washed across Quentin's face as his chin sank down on his chest. "'I killed your husband. Here's some money.'"

Quick compassion swept through Pettigrew. "You don't have to say that."

"How else would I account for sending her money?"

Pettigrew thought for a moment, then shrugged. "I can't think of any way right now, but between the two of us, and with Hannah's help, we can come up with something. Perhaps you can send it anonymously. You just have to be sure that she gets it."

Quentin heaved a sigh, then nodded. "I suppose it'll have to be that way." He got to his feet and tried to smile, but failed. "Thanks for listening to me. I suppose you listen to stories like mine all day long."

Coming around his desk, Pettigrew shook his head. "Not like this one. I've never heard of anything quite like this, Quentin. Let's pray that God will give us wisdom."

They prayed, and Quentin left. He had taken off from the hospital early, so the afternoon sun was still relatively high in the sky. Not wanting to go home, he began to walk. As was his custom, he found himself moving toward Central Park. With his mind full of what the pastor had said, he struggled violently to find a way out of the guilt that lay so heavily upon him.

At the corner of Seventy-fourth Street and Central Park West, he noticed something he'd never noticed before: an open space adjacent to the park itself. Here people were actually farming—right in the middle of New York City! Women were out weeding their gardens, and as he moved closer he saw two enormous goats with curving horns. One of them made a run at him, but stopped abruptly, changed directions, and galloped away. Continuing his stroll, he saw children playing and dogs barking amid garden patches tended by city dwellers who grew their vegetables here.

The miniature farms brought back memories of his younger days, and he sat down on a slight knoll and watched the activities. *One day*, he thought, *there'll be nothing here but big buildings, some maybe as big as twenty stories. New York's growing that way. No one then would believe that they're actually farming right here by Central Park.*

As dusk came, Quentin remained where he was. He could hear the voices of boys playing baseball in an open spot, and remembered when he had done much the same back on the farm. Time and again he tried to pray; finally despair welled up in him. "Lord, what can I do? How can I help this woman and those poor children? I'm responsible for them. Help me, Lord! Give me wisdom!"

And immediately, God answered his prayer.

Quentin knew vaguely that the Catholics celebrated the Feast of Epiphany, and he had heard that it was to celebrate the annunciation of the birth of the coming Christ child to Mary. He suddenly remembered Pastor Pettigrew saying, "An epiphany is a sudden revelation. It doesn't come from study, it doesn't come from education, it comes directly from God, just as the angel spoke to Mary and told her that she would bear the child who would be the

Savior. Mary did not arrive at that knowledge through her own faculties. God sent her that word, and from time to time, God still speaks and tells us things that we can't learn in other ways."

Quentin Larribee suddenly knew, without any doubt whatsoever, what he must do. The revelation came so simply—yet so clearly that it made him catch his breath. It was as if he had been sitting in darkness and someone had turned a light on. "Why, of course," he whispered, "that's what I must do!" Relief washed through him, and all the weeks of doubt and fear and despair seemed to fade. "That's what I have to do. Why didn't I see it before?"

And then he realized that this idea was from God, the answer to his prayer. He had not arrived at it by any logical procession of thought. He stood, looked up, and said quietly, "Thank you, Lord, for your guidance, and I'll do my best to be obedient to what you're telling me."

★   ★   ★

"But you can send money!" Irene said, her voice rather shrill. She had been glad, at first, when Quentin had finally decided to talk to her of what had been bothering him, and now the two of them were sequestered in the parlor. Quentin had paced the floor as he related how he had killed a Confederate soldier. She had listened sympathetically, trying to understand why this had affected him so powerfully. But after she had read the letter he gave her, and he had told her what he intended to do, she felt more shock than sympathy.

Quentin shook his head. He had thought all this out and now he said, "No. I've got to help them financially, of course, but I can't just put money in an envelope. I can't just send it off and wash my hands of the whole affair. I've got to go to Helena."

"But that doesn't make any sense, Quentin."

"It may not to anybody else, but let me tell you how God spoke to me just this afternoon." Quickly he related his experience near

Central Park. But as he spoke, he saw Irene's brow knit and he saw the disagreement in her eyes. "I know," he said, "this is a disappointment to you. But it shouldn't take too long."

Irene tried once again. "It's money she needs, obviously, and if you don't have enough, I have some. We can take care of this woman and her children, you and I together."

Quentin suddenly smiled. It was the first real smile she had seen on his face since he came home. "I'm glad you feel that way, Irene. I have enough money, but I've got to go see for myself that this man's family is all right. You'll understand. It won't take long."

Irene was a good tactician. She knew when the battle was lost—and how to plan for the next campaign. Coming to him, she put her arms around his neck. "Well, it's as you say then, Quentin, but do hurry."

"It shouldn't take over a week at most. I just have to go down and find some way to help. She has a note at the bank. Maybe I could pay that anonymously."

"Come back as soon as you can!" Irene kissed him and felt his arms tighten around her.

She held him for a long time. Pressing herself against him, she whispered, "Hurry back. Don't stay away from me too long, dear."

★ ★ ★

Hurrying home, Quentin entered the apartment and found Hannah cooking supper. "Hannah, let me tell you what's happened. Come here."

Hannah saw at once that something was different with Quentin. "What is it?" she asked. She stood listening while Quentin told her everything.

Finally, he said, "Do you think it's right, Hannah?"

"Do you really believe that God has told you to do it?"

"I'm as certain of it as I am of anything in life."

"Then you must do what God put into your heart."

The two talked for a long time. Quentin was hardly able to eat, he was so caught up with the idea.

Afterwards, however, as he helped her with the dishes, he turned to her, his face clouded over. "I—I don't see how I can face her and those children."

Hannah asked quietly, "Will you tell her what you've done?"

"I don't think so. She might not take help from her husband's murderer."

Instantly Hannah grasped Quentin's arm and turned him around. "You are *not* a murderer, Quentin! You were a soldier!" Her voice softened, and then she said, "I'm glad you're going. I feel God has been leading you toward this for some time, although I don't understand it all. But you've got to do it, or you'll never be the man God wants you to be."

"It's always good to talk to you, Hannah. You always give good advice." He hugged her, then stepped back. "We can't change what's done, can we?"

"No," Hannah said. "But sometimes God can bring something good out of it—and I think that's what he's going to do for Eden Breckenridge and her children!"

PART
Two

CHAPTER *Seven*

ine particles of spray caused Quentin to turn his head slightly, and he lifted a hand, waving vigorously as the *Memphis Belle*'s massive wheels churned the muddy Mississippi water into a froth. He called out, "Take care of yourself, Jim!" although he knew his voice would not be heard over the rumbling of the engines and the sound of the huge blades striking the water. He saw Jim Peters wave back from the dock, a broad grin on his face, and murmured, "I'm glad you made it, Jim. You deserve it."

The steamboat shook under Quentin's feet as it nosed out into the Mississippi, and he stayed at the rail until the docks faded from view and farms began to appear along the banks. He watched as a man rode along the levee, head down, legs dangling beside the lanky gray mule that plodded slowly along, outlined against the sky. September had been cool, and Quentin pulled his coat about him, shivering slightly.

He walked around the deck, speaking to no one, his mind running over the visit he had had with Jim Peters. It had been a good time, something he had needed. His leave-taking from New York had been difficult. He had known that Irene had disapproved strongly of every part of his plan, but there was nothing he could do about that. He had found Jim Peters without difficulty, for the wiry ex-soldier had sent Quentin two letters describing the ten acres he had bought just outside of Memphis where he was launching his new venture. Hiring a buggy, Quentin had found the farm without much trouble. Peters had been very glad to see him indeed, and had shown him his operation with great pride. Quentin smiled as he remembered how Peters had shown him the cages for pigeons and quail and the hutches for rabbits.

"I sell everything I can fatten up, Quent. I'm making money hand over fist. I'm gonna double this operation. Just wait. You'd better come down and join up with me. Sure beats bein' in the army."

The *Memphis Belle* suddenly lurched to one side as the boat hit the middle of the channel, causing Quentin to grab at the rail. As he did, an unpleasant sensation arose in him. He had eaten little breakfast, although Jim had urged him on, and now he felt slightly nauseated. Automatically he checked his symptoms and was disturbed to notice that his temperature seemed to be higher than usual. "Coming down with a cold," he muttered, then continued his tour of the floating palace.

The distance from Memphis to Helena, as the crow flies, was not great, but the Mississippi made a serpentine path across the Delta, winding, cutting back in on itself, and Quentin had no idea how many actual miles the boat would travel. He had boarded at St. Louis, and since he had never been on a riverboat before, at first it was interesting just to stay on deck and watch the land roll by. Most of the trees were dead, so it seemed to be a dead land that he rolled through.

When he had tired of that, he had visited the gambling salon, which was filled with people anxious to lose their money. Every kind of gambling was available—blackjack, poker, roulette wheels—and the huge chandeliers threw their glittering lights over the participants. The carpet was thick, the white-jacketed waiters brought drinks and food constantly, and if Quentin had been a gambling man, he might have enjoyed it. Tiring of the noise and the smoke, he left the casino and moved down the deck toward his cabin.

A tall, gaunt man wearing a black suit and a tall stovepipe hat was standing at the rail smoking a cheroot. He turned and said, "Good evening." When Quentin returned his greeting, he looked up and said, "Rain tomorrow."

This comment seemed to be some sort of invitation, so Quentin turned to the rail and the two spoke of the weather briefly, then the man said, "I'm Charles Taliferro from New Orleans." He pronounced his city as "N'allins." Quentin asked if he was on business, and he nodded. "Been to St. Louis for the past few months."

Taliferro didn't state his business, but turned a pair of sharp black eyes on Quentin. "You're from the North, sir?"

"Yes. New York." He hesitated, then said, "I've never been in the South before—except for one brief visit to Virginia." He did not think it wise to mention the nature of that visit, but added, "I'm a physician—or soon will be."

"Don't suppose you're thinking of moving down heah to practice?"

"No, not really. I have an obligation to take care of in Helena."

Taliferro studied Quentin with a quizzical look in his eyes. "Just as well you've got no plans to stay."

"Why is that, Mr. Taliferro?"

"Yankees aren't too popular in the South right now."

"But then that's been true ever since the war—or even before."

"You have me there, sir—but now it's worse."

Quentin stared down at the muddy brown water that rushed by with sibilant whispers. The banks swept by as the vessel wound its way around a sharp bend, and the whistle suddenly broke the silence of the evening, uttering a banshee scream shrill enough to startle the dead. "You mean Reconstruction, I take it."

"That's it. For many of us, it's worse than the war."

Reconstruction—the attempt to bring the South back into its proper place in the Union—had been a nightmare since the end of the war. If Lincoln had lived, the people of the South would have been treated more gently, for it had been his intention to deal with the defeated people with compassion. But John Wilkes Booth had prevented that with his mindless violence. To many in the North, the murder of Lincoln proved that the South was unrepentant, and many of the North's powerful leaders determined to apply merciless pressure.

Andrew Johnson was not the man to handle such a crisis as this. A Southerner and a former slaveholder, he was an intemperate and tactless man, filled with resentments and insecurities, and plagued with a serious drinking problem. Actually, his plan for Reconstruction was sound, resembling Lincoln's proposal. He preferred to act as if the Confederate states had never left the Union, and he offered amnesty to all who would take an oath of allegiance, although high-ranking Confederate leaders would have to apply to the president for a pardon.

Under Johnson's proposal, each of the Southern states would have a provisional governor appointed by the president. Each state would have to revoke the ordinance of secession, abolish slavery, and ratify the Thirteenth Amendment. Then each Southern state would elect a new state government and send representatives to Congress.

"It was a tragedy when Lincoln was killed," Quentin remarked. "But if President Johnson's plan had been followed, things would have gone much smoother."

"You're right, sir, but the radicals in Congress put a stop to that." Taliferro's face grew hard and he threw his cheroot into the river. "The South was just beginning to recover when Congress passed its own plan—and every Southerner hates what's being done to it."

"I can understand that," Quentin agreed. He had been opposed to the congressional plan to crush the South, to humiliate her.

Congress had first declared that the Lincoln-Johnson governments had no legal standing, and then had imposed on the South a military government of five districts. Each district would have a military commander supported by troops, and was to institute a registration of voters.

"There's already talk of violence against the scalawags and the carpetbaggers, sir," Taliferro said. "And any man from the North who shows up in the South is suspect. I'd advise you to be alert, Dr. Larribee."

"But I have no politics. I'm coming to Arkansas on a personal matter."

"When people are being crushed, they aren't likely to examine your motives too closely." A bitter smile touched the thin lips of Taliferro. "An Arkansas farmer who's being forced off his land by a hostile military government can't shoot a congressman in Washington—but he can take a shot at a visiting Yankee who comes under his sights."

Quentin was disturbed by Taliferro's words, but there was nothing he could do. "I've got to make my visit," he said finally. "The Lord will just have to take care of me."

These words interested the Southerner. He studied Quentin thoughtfully, as he might have studied a new species of animal, then pulled another cheroot from his pocket and lit it with a match. The blue smoke rose and was carried away by the breeze as he quietly remarked, "I think it will take God to put this country back together." He nodded as he turned. "I wish you good fortune, Doctor."

Quentin went back to his cabin and read a book on the diseases of the heart for a while, but to his annoyance grew somewhat dizzy. He lay down on the cot fully dressed and sank into a fitful sleep.

He was awakened sometime later by a banging on the door. "Helena!" a porter shouted. "All who want Helena get off!"

Coming off the bunk quickly, Quentin swayed slightly, dizzy, and grabbed for the bulkhead. The room seemed to go in circles.

For a moment he stood there, nauseated and sick. "What a time to come down with this," he muttered. Quickly he changed clothes, putting on a pair of worn, faded blue trousers, a checkered shirt much the worse for wear, and a pair of worn brogans. It was the outfit he worked in at home anytime there was outside labor to be performed. He donned a worn gray overcoat and pulled on a black slouch hat he had picked up to complete his outfit. Putting his other clothes and few belongings into a carpetbag, he left the cabin. From the deck, he watched as the *Memphis* pulled in and the gangplank was lowered. Four other passengers got off, three men and a woman, and he followed. The gangplank swayed up and down as the water rose and fell, and Quentin was glad to put his feet on shore again. A chill struck him, causing him to pull his coat tighter around him. It was almost noon, but he was not hungry.

Helena looked much like the other river towns the *Memphis* had passed. It was a rather squalid place, especially after New York. The main part of town ran parallel with the river, sheltered from it by a tall levee that hid the river itself. The main street was identified by a single homemade sign that said, "Cherry Street." He strolled along the wooden sidewalks, noting the wide cobblestone street, and wondered how he would find the Breckenridge place without calling attention to himself.

For ten minutes he walked, simply studying the town, which showed the effects of hard times. Like all Southern towns, Helena had been ground down by the war until nothing was new and everything was shabby. Quentin had read about the plight of the South, but it had not struck home to him until now, as he walked along the streets of Helena, for even the horses seemed exhausted and scarcely able to move. Everyone he passed was dressed pitifully. The women's dresses were faded and worn and patched. Many of the men wore belt buckles with "CSA" on them.

Tired and shaky, Quentin found a bench and sat down, continuing to absorb the town. Union soldiers were common. Their blue uniforms put a splash of color on the drabness of the town. Quentin realized that he was surprised to see the troops there, even though he was aware that most towns in the South were garrisoned by Federal troops to carry out Reconstruction.

Quentin sat for a long while, feeling worse all the time. "Got to do something," he said finally. Getting to his feet, he saw the Palace Hotel and crossed the street. A team of rangy mules pulling a wagon loaded with grain was approaching, and Quentin tried to get out of the way, but he moved so slowly that the driver cursed and told him in no uncertain terms to move faster.

Quentin stepped inside the lobby, a small room with a hall leading down the center and a pair of rickety-looking steps leading to a second floor.

"Howdy. Need a place?" The speaker was a bald man with one arm missing. He had sharp, black eyes and studied Quentin slyly.

"No. I don't need a room, but I'm looking for some information."

"What do you need?"

"I'm looking for the Breckenridge place."

"Don't know 'em," the clerk said and then turned and began reading the newspaper.

Quentin was taken aback. Then he suddenly realized that his accent was a dead giveaway. The further south he had come, the more he had been aware of the difference in speech patterns. Southerners generally spoke at a much slower pace, and they slurred their words, especially the endings. It was so different from the sharp, clipped speech Quentin was accustomed to. *Every time I open my mouth, it's just like wearing a sign "Here's a Yankee,"* he thought. He walked outside and stood on the sidewalk, hesitating for a moment. A wagon was pulled up in front of a general store, and several men sat in worn, straight-backed chairs on the sidewalk, studying the people who passed. Quentin approached them and said, "Good day. I wonder if any of you gentlemen could direct me to the Breckenridge farm."

All of the loafers looked at him. All were bearded, and suspicion clouded their eyes. No one answered. Finally one of them, a tall, lanky man with a dark complexion, spat down at Quentin's feet. "Don't know 'em," he muttered.

Quentin hesitated, but he knew that he would get no more information from them. He turned away, but had not gone far when he heard a voice say, "Mistuh?"

Turning, he saw a very large, strongly built black man, the one he had noticed loading the wagon, standing a few steps behind him.

Quentin studied the man, then asked, "Yes?"

"You're looking for the Breckenridge farm?"

A slight hope penetrated his nausea and weakness. "Yes, I am."

"Well, I'se going out dat way if you wants a ride. Be glad to accommodate you."

"Well, that's very kind of you," Quentin said quickly.

He followed the man, who gestured toward the wagon bed, saying, "You kin put yo' bag there, suh."

Quentin put the bag into the wagon, which was loaded with a sack of some sort of grain and two boxes. He pulled himself up onto the seat. Looking back, he saw the eyes of the men lined along the porch studying him. *They don't like it that I'm riding with a Negro,* he thought.

The black man spoke to the rawboned mules, and they lurched into a walk. Then he turned and said, "My name is Trumbo. Trumbo Jones."

"I'm Quentin Larribee. I sure appreciate your help."

"Ain't no trouble a'tall, Mistuh Larribee."

"Is the Breckenridge place far?"

"Eight miles. I stays a mile past their place."

Quentin felt uncomfortable sitting beside the large black man. He had never known a Southern black and wanted to ask Jones if he had been a slave, but decided that that would not be the way to start a conversation.

Trumbo Jones sat idly on the seat, his powerful muscles relaxed, the reins looking like threads in his large, hamlike hands. He had on a battered straw hat that shaded his face and a pair of ragged overalls covered with a short wool jacket. The large boots that came up to his knees were spattered with mud.

Finally Quentin remarked, "Things have changed a lot since the war, I suppose. Have you lived here a long time?"

"Born on Mistuh Greer's place. Not Mistuh Riley—his daddy, Jacob Greer. They lives just a few miles past the Breckenridge's."

Shifting on the seat nervously, Quentin said, "You probably notice by the way I talk that I'm not from the South."

A broad grin touched the black man's lips. "I did notice that."

"I don't know much about the South. Were you a slave?" he asked directly.

"Yes, I was. Like I said, I belonged to Mistuh Jacob Greer."

"I suppose it feels good to be free."

Trumbo Jones did not answer for a moment. His hands, however, tightened on the lines, and when he did speak there was a deceptive softness in his voice. "No man likes to be a slave, Mistuh Larribee."

The plodding of the hooves of the mules had a rhythm that lulled Quentin almost to sleep. In fact, he probably would have slept if he hadn't felt so terrible, and once Trumbo looked over and said, "You don't look too good, suh."

"Guess I picked up a cold or something. Have you known the Breckenridge family long?"

"Nigh onto seventeen years. Dey bought the place from the old Mistuh Thomas. He moved off to Louisiana to be with his youn-guns, I guess. They's mighty fine folks. I'm 'specially fond of Miss Eden. She's a mighty kind lady."

"They have three children now, I understand."

"Well, suh, you know that Mistuh William, he got kilt in the war. Fought all the way through and almost made it. He got kilt at the very last."

"Yes, I heard about that."

"I reckon you knowed the family a long time?"

"No. Not really." Quentin was not thinking clearly. He had developed a splitting headache, and it was beyond him, at the moment, to make up a story. He said almost desperately, "What kind of a man was Mr. Breckenridge?"

"Oh, he wuz all right, I reckon."

There was something in his tone that caught Quentin's flagging attention. He looked quickly and saw that the black man's lips were tightly pulled together. *Something's wrong here,* Quentin thought. *He didn't like William Breckenridge.* But he didn't feel capable of inquiring into it. In fact, he was feeling worse by the moment. He kept himself upright in the seat with an effort. He noticed that the black man had taken off his coat and seemed comfortable, while he himself shivered from time to time. *I'll have to dose myself up the first chance I get.* He had brought a small bag full of medical supplies, not knowing when he might encounter an emergency. He strongly suspected that he was coming down with something that might be more serious than a cold.

"There's the place, Mistuh Larribee," Trumbo said, his voice breaking into Quentin's thoughts. "Mighty good farm, but it's done gone downhill since Mistuh Will went off to fight."

Quentin got out of the wagon slowly. Sharp pains shot through his head as he reached up to pluck his bag out of the wagon. Looking up, he said, "You've been a great help to me, Mr. Jones."

The black man suddenly grinned. "Dat sho' is a good way to make yourself unpopular. Calling a black man 'mistuh.' We ain't dat fer along yet. Jist Trumbo will do."

Reaching into his pants pocket, Quentin pulled out a wallet and extracted a Federal bank note from it. He handed it up, saying, "All right, Trumbo. I'm grateful to you."

The black man hesitated, then reached out and took the note. "You don't have to gimme nothin', Mistuh Larribee."

"Yes, I guess I do." Quentin smiled. "You don't mind taking money from a Yankee?"

"Come in mighty handy." Trumbo folded the note carefully, stuck it in his shirt pocket, and then looked over toward the house. His voice was soft as a summer breeze when he said, "Miss Breckenridge, she don't need no mo' trouble. She's had plenty of dat."

"I'm sorry to hear it."

"You needs to get back to town, I stays one mile down there. Be glad to take you anytime."

Quentin had not thought of getting back to town, and now his mind was so confused all he could do was nod and say, "Thanks again." He turned and started for the house which was set at least two hundred yards off the road. As he moved toward it, he noticed that everything was falling down. The fences were leaning at a dangerous angle and in two places were completely down. A windmill was obviously out of operation, two of the blades broken off and the other two turning crazily as a slight breeze moved across the upper air. The house itself was of frame construction; it had been painted once, but now most of the white color was gone, exposing the aging wood underneath. The yard itself was cluttered in the way a poorly run farm is, or one with bad help. A plow lay with its handles sticking up like skinny arms toward the sky, one of them fastened on with heavy bands of wire. Two reddish cows and two lanky mules occupied a pasture grown rank with weeds, and as he approached, a sound of furious barking brought him up short. A large dark red hound had appeared, approaching him with his head down and a growl deep in his throat. Two other dogs, one a blue tick, the other a small hound, danced around him yapping, but it was the large red dog that Quentin concentrated on. It was enormous, and there was something menacing about the way that he did not bark but approached slowly and steadily, without hesitation.

"Ben, you stop that!"

A young boy Quentin recognized instantly from the picture had come out of the house and across the yard. He had bright red hair and dark blue eyes. His skin was fair, and freckles dotted his face.

He wore a pair of faded overalls and was barefooted despite the cold weather. "What do you want?" he said.

Licking his lips and eyeing the dog cautiously, Quentin said, "I'd like to see Mrs. Breckenridge."

"Whatcha want with her?"

Quentin had to steady himself; the attack of dizziness that had been troubling him all day was getting worse. He could not think quickly enough to come up with an answer—and then, lifting his eyes away from the hound, he saw a woman step out the door, off the porch, and toward him quickly. He recognized her immediately, but she was much more attractive than in the picture. He took off his hat as she approached and said, "My name is Quentin Larribee, ma'am. I'm looking for Mrs. Breckenridge."

"I'm Mrs. Breckenridge. What can I do for you?"

The dog named Ben was still growling deep in his throat. Mrs. Breckenridge bent and slapped him on the shoulder. "Be quiet, Ben," she said quietly. Straightening up, she turned her head to one side and studied Quentin. She did not speak for a moment, then said, "Do you have business with me?"

"Yes, ma'am. I do."

Eden Breckenridge studied the man's face and so did the boy. They both had caught his Yankee accent, and the boy's thin face was filled with suspicion. The woman said, "Well, you'd better come inside."

Quentin hesitated and looked at the boy. "You have other children, Mrs. Breckenridge?"

"Yes, I do. Why do you ask?"

"I don't think I'd better come in your house. I'm coming down with something, and I wouldn't want to pass it on."

The dark blue eyes of the woman softened at this and some of the stiffness went out of her back. "Come into the kitchen. John, you stay away from this man—and take care of your brother and sister while I talk with him."

"Yes, ma'am."

"Come around this way, Mr. Larribee."

Following the woman around the house, Quentin was almost desperate. If he ever needed a clear mind it was now, and yet he was dizzy and his head felt worse than ever. He knew he could not restrain the shivers that came to him, and he knew that soon that would change to a raging fever. On the porch, the woman opened the door and stepped inside; he followed.

"Sit over there. Are you thirsty?"

"Yes, ma'am, I am."

Using a gourd, she dipped a cup of water from a bucket. She watched him carefully as he drank, and when he handed the glass back, she said, "What is it you've got, do you think?"

"I thought it was just a cold, but it's worse than that. But I shouldn't be around your children—or you either, for that matter."

Eden Breckenridge put the glass down and turned to face him. She was wearing a simple, light blue dress that outlined her strong form. Despite having three children, she still had a trim waist and a full figure. "What did you want to see me about?" she asked.

"I was working in Virginia, and I stayed the night with a family there, Mrs. Breckenridge. They were real nice people. Their name was Hawkins," Quentin said following, as well he could, the story he had made up. "I was there for a few days and got to know them pretty well."

"Where was this in Virginia?"

"It was out in the country, outside of Richmond a few miles. When Mr. Hawkins found out I was going down the Mississippi River he asked me if I'd do him a favor." Shifting on his chair, suddenly heat seemed to rise up in Quentin's body. He knew it was the fever, and soon he would be drenched with sweat. His voice sounded hollow to his own ears, but he continued, "He told me that a Confederate soldier was killed in the fighting there, and he had buried him on his farm. His name was William Breckenridge."

"That was my husband." Shock was evident on her face, and she stared intently at Quentin. "What else did he say? And why did he bury him?"

"I couldn't say. I think that must have happened a lot with good-hearted people there. Anyway, he didn't talk much about it, but I assume that your husband died there and these folks had a heart to bury him. In any case, he gave me these things and said if I was coming your way, it would be a help, maybe, if I dropped them off."

Leaning over, Quentin pulled from his bundle the small bag containing Will Breckenridge's personal effects that he had saved. The effort made him dizzy, and he swayed in the chair suddenly.

"You're not well at all," Mrs. Breckenridge said.

"No. I'm feeling poorly. But anyway I agreed, and here they are."

Eden Breckenridge took the small bag and opened it. She looked at the wallet, the pictures, the letters, and the watch. "I'm beholden to you, sir."

"I was glad to do it."

"This watch belonged to his father. He always said he was going to give it to Johnny. Now he'll get it." She held the watch in her hands and a beam of pale yellow sunlight fell through the windows and highlighted her face. As sick as he was, Quentin saw the quiet beauty and the fine bone structure of the smooth line of the jaw.

"Well, I guess I'll get back to town. Maybe I could get a room there." Quentin stood up, but suddenly he was totally nauseated. He stumbled hurriedly out the door and vomited violently. Then he wiped his face with a shaky hand. He turned to find the woman standing beside him.

"You're not able to get anywhere, Mr. Larribee," she said. "There's a room fixed up out in the barn. A hired hand used to stay there when we had one. No one's in it now. Here, take your bag, and I'll show it to you."

Quentin was in no mood to argue. His face was burning, and he knew that he was much sicker than he had thought, and likely to get worse. He followed her on rubbery legs to the barn and was glad to see that the room was built off the side, a lean-to affair with nothing much in it but a single bed, a table, and a chair. There was a window, however, that let in light, and he said huskily, "Thank you very much. I hope I won't be much trouble to you."

"You've got a fever coming up. I'll have to bring you some more blankets. I'll see if we have anything for it. Now you go to bed."

Quentin was too sick to argue. He pulled off his boots and his clothes and pulled the single blanket over him. He began sweating at once, the nausea came and went, and his teeth chattered although he was sweating profusely. He was aware, vaguely, when the woman came back and lifted his head and commanded him to drink. He swallowed a bitter-tasting concoction without argument, lay down, and through feverish eyes saw her putting more blankets over him. Then he closed his eyes and began to struggle with the raging fever that enveloped him.

CHAPTER *Eight*

Grandpa, why don't you just chop this dern old tree down! It ain't good for nothin'! I mean, it ain't like you could get apples off of it, or pears, or somethin' good to eat!"

Thomas York leaned against the crooked trunk of the stunted tree. The bark was dark and roughly squared, and for a time he gazed silently and fondly down at the ten-year-old boy whose bright red hair caught the sun. There were traces of fine gold in it, and the blue eyes were dark like his mother's. "Well, I'll tell you now, John. A man don't want to go around killin' trees any more than he wants to go around killin' anything else."

"Why, it's just a dern old tree!"

"No, it ain't," Thomas said. He was a tall man, very thin, with silver hair and light blue eyes. He moved to change position, dragging his right leg. A stroke three years earlier had deadened his right arm, leaving it of little use to him, and he used a cane to make walking easier. At the age of sixty-three, prematurely aged by hard work on an Arkansas farm, he still retained some of his youthful good looks. His features were patrician, handsome in a Grecian fashion. Now he reached out his left hand, touched the bark of the tree, and said quietly, "This is a sourwood tree, Johnny. Some folks call them a sorrel tree. My daddy always called them lily-of-the-valley tree. My daddy always loved sourwood trees."

"What's to love about an ugly twisted old tree like that?" Johnny suddenly grinned and a mischievous light leaped into his eyes. "Why, if they had trees in hell, I'd bet it would look just like this one."

Despite himself, Thomas York had to smile. "Better not let your ma hear you talkin' about hell like that. She'd skin you alive." He had found a wicked sense of humor in the boy and recognized it as a gift from his own blood. He himself had kept that sense of the ridiculous, and although he tried to restrain it, it would jump out from time to time. He glanced up at the tree and said, "This here sourwood tree does feed you, Johnny."

"I ain't eatin' no sourwood trees!"

"Sure you do. That honey you had on your biscuit this mornin'. Where do you think it came from?"

"Come from bees, of course."

"That's right. And the bees came to this tree when it was blossoming, and you seen it. Don't you remember? Bees go crazy when they get around sourwood. They stay at the flowers even in the rain and all through the day. You remember. We could stand under it and you could hear the hum of the bees in the blossoms."

Johnny Breckenridge was very quick. "Why, I remember that," he said, then he laughed. "But I didn't think about eatin' honey. It's hard to think that far ahead."

"Well, you got to learn, Johnny. Life's pretty tough. A fellow don't think ahead, he's gonna get himself in big trouble."

Johnny thought about what his grandfather had said. Although his young face was unmarked as yet, there was a painful expression in his eyes. He was a sensitive young man, physically tough, sturdy like his father. Still, there was a touchiness about him that covered a sensitive spirit.

"What's wrong with that fellow that's out in the barn, Grandpa?"

"Some kind of fever."

"He looks terrible. Is he gonna die?"

"I hope not, boy," Thomas murmured. "Your ma sent for Granny Spears."

"The herb woman? She's comin' here?"

"Yes, she is. Now, you've loafed long enough, boy. Get on with your chores."

"All right, Grandpa." Johnny Breckenridge looked up at the sourwood tree and shook his head. "Sure is an ugly thing to put out such good tastin' stuff as that honey we had this morning."

"Some of the homeliest things you'll see in this life produce some of the nicest things, Johnny."

Puzzled, Johnny stared at his grandfather. He was accustomed to the rather strange sayings that issued from the old man's lips. He treasured them up and pondered them when he was alone. "And I reckon some of the pretty things"—Johnny grinned suddenly—"come out with some awful things. Like a snake now. Some of 'em are mighty pretty, but they can kill a feller."

"That's right, Johnny. As the sayin' goes, 'All that glitters is not gold.' So you'd better watch out."

As Johnny walked away, the old man remained under the sourwood tree, thinking about how much the boy resembled his dead father physically—and how little he was like him in other ways. "He's like me and Eden," Thomas murmured. And there was a sense of something like joy in him as he realized it. His son-in-law had been a rough man in many ways, and Thomas had always felt that Eden had married the wrong man. He had said nothing to his daughter about it, but he had known that Eden and Will Breckenridge had had some difficult times. He glanced up once more into the sourwood tree, thinking of when he was a boy. He had gathered the long, narrow, glossy leaves and chewed them. They had a tart, sour taste and made a good thirst quencher. He had chewed many a leaf of this very tree as he had plowed the fields that lay along the Mississippi River.

Finally he turned and made his way slowly to the house. He found Eden hanging clothes on the line and asked, "Granny Spears not here yet?"

"Not yet." Eden Breckenridge was wearing a thin cotton dress; the September wind whipped it around her, molding it to her body. She pushed her fine blonde hair back from her forehead. Impatiently, she gave it a twist and tried to pin it. "It's windy today." Then her brow furrowed. "I hope Granny can help that man. He's about as sick as a person can be."

"I hope it's nothin' catchin', Eden. Scarlet fever or somethin' like that."

"I don't know. I hope not," she said briefly.

She looked up and saw a mule plodding down the road. "There's Granny," she said.

"That mule must be older than dirt," Thomas said. "Granny's had him as long as I can remember."

"How old do you reckon she is, anyway?"

"She ain't no spring chicken." Thomas smiled. "Eighty somethin', I reckon."

Granny Spears looked every day of her eighty-something years. She wore a snuff-brown dress that came down to her ankles, but it was hiked up as she straddled the mule. Her legs were clad with black stockings, and she wore a man's rough brogans. With the agility of one much younger, she slid off the mule and stood before the two. Her face was lined, but her eyes were sharp and black still, as was her hair except for a few streaks of white. She had Indian blood, everyone knew. Cherokee, she claimed. Now she said, "Well, where is he?"

"I'll take you, Granny," Eden said. "He's out in that room in the barn."

The two women made their way to the barn, and Eden opened the door. Granny stepped inside and went at once to the cot where the sick man lay. She leaned over and stared at his face. With one hand she touched his forehead. "He been throwin' up any?" she asked.

"Yes. He can't keep anything down."

Granny's remedies were widely sought after by the Delta people in the area around Helena, especially those who could not afford a doctor. "Give me a chair, Eden," she said abruptly.

Eden at once pulled up a cane-bottomed chair, and Granny sat down and began to strip the clothes from the lanky man. "He's burnin' up. Go get some cool springwater. And lots of towels and cloths. We've got to get this fever down or he'll die."

"All right, Granny." Eden hesitated, turning as she arrived at the door. "What do you think it is?"

"I think he's sick with fever. What difference it make what name you put to it?" she demanded, her black eyes snapping. "Now get that water, girl! And don't dawdle!"

Eden hurried to the house and stepped inside calling out, "Prudence! Where are you?"

"Right here, Mama." Prudence looked almost comically like her mother. She had the same blonde hair, the same features. Only the shape of her dark blue eyes had she inherited from her father. She said, "Is he gonna die?"

"No, he's not going to die," Eden said. "Go out to the spring and get a bucket full of cool water and take it out to the barn. I've got to get some cloths. And take care of Stuart."

"I will, Mama." Prudence snatched up the one-year-old who had the same red hair and blue eyes as his older brother. "Come on, Stuart. We're going to get water."

As Eden gathered cloths, a spirit of fatigue and discouragement came to her. "As if we didn't have enough trouble. Now we've got a sick man that we know nothing about to take care of." Her lips tightened and she shook her head, trying to drive the thoughts out. She knew that the war had hardened her, as it had almost every woman she knew. The men had gone off and died or come back broken and maimed, and the women had been wounded just as critically. Their wounds did not show, but the wolf-lean years of making it through, finding food, keeping children from starving, making do with threadbare, oft-mended clothes, and always the threat of death, always the shadow of what hung over the South—it had done something to all of them. The war had, indeed, inflicted a wound—not as obvious as an amputated leg or a missing arm, but Eden knew that she was not the same woman she had been before the war started.

Gathering up all the cloths she could find, she hurried out the door. When she entered the barn room again, she saw that Granny had stripped the man's clothing off except for a pair of drawers. "Well, where's the water?" Granny snapped.

"Prudence is bringing it." Eden moved closer to the bed and looked down at the face of the man, studying it without speaking.

"Right homely fellow, ain't he now?" Granny said.

"Yes, he is. He's lean too. You can count his ribs."

"Just one of them naturally lean fellows, I reckon. Does look kind of like a skinned rabbit though, don't he?" Granny put her hand on the man's chest and was silent for a moment. "Heart's beatin' good, but he's burnin' like a furnace."

At that moment Prudence came in, a bucket of water in her hand. "Here, Mama," she said.

"What did you do with Stuart?"

"He's right outside."

"You go watch him."

Prudence looked at the almost naked man and said, "He's skinny, ain't he, Mama?"

"You get out of here, Prudence. Take care of your brother."

Granny Spears cackled suddenly as Prudence left. "First time she ever saw a fellow without no more clothes on than this. Well, it won't hurt her none, I reckon. Now, come on. Let's get this fever down, girl, or we'll be plantin' this fellow sure as the world."

★ ★ ★

The virulent fever that had prostrated Quentin rose and fell with no pattern or regularity. Sometimes he would burn for what seemed like half a day, with the women struggling to bring the fever down. He would cry out sometimes in his sleep, often for Hannah.

"You reckon Hannah's his wife?" Granny asked Eden once.

"I don't know. He sure calls for her a lot."

For Quentin, life had become nothing but a red darkness. The fever that burned him seemed to start in his bones, and when he did approach consciousness he felt that he was in flames. Other times the chills would come, and he would shake so violently that the bed itself seemed to tremble. At those times he was vaguely aware that there were voices, and that the touch of rough wool blankets brought a welcoming warmth.

He had no sense of the passage of time. The pyramids might have been built while he was sick, or it could have been an hour.

He opened his eyes and saw a lamp burning. The amber glow caught his eye, and he blinked trying to understand what it was. He was conscious of nothing except that the red burning pain had gone away. Then he heard a raucous voice say, "Well, you decided to live, did you?"

Quentin blinked with surprise. The voice seemed very close to him. Turning his head slightly, he saw the wrinkled face of an elderly woman. Her hair was black with streaks of white. Quentin tried to speak, but his lips were dry as dust. "Water," he managed to gasp.

Granny Spears took the glass off the table beside the bunk and with surprising strength lifted the sick man to a sitting position. "Here," she said, holding the glass and watching as he gulped it down thirstily.

"That's enough. You'll make yourself sick. You can have some more in a little bit. Maybe a spoonful at a time."

Quentin tried to make sense of what was happening. Memories began to filter back. "I've been sick."

"I should smile you've been sick," Granny said sternly.

"What's wrong with me?"

"You had a fever. It like to have kilt you."

Quentin thought about that for a moment. Weariness was creeping up on him again, and he whispered, "How long have I been here?"

"Three days. Now you hush. We've got to get some food into you."

Granny saw the eyes flutter, then close, but she was satisfied. Getting up stiffly, she left the room and walked toward the house. Eden came out with Stuart on her hip and asked, "How is he?"

"He's awake. I think the devil missed out on him this time. Fix up some of that stew for him. I'm going to lay me down and take a nap."

"All right, Granny. Go in the side room. You deserve a rest."

"Folks deserve lots of things they don't get," Granny grumbled. However, she felt a familiar sense of satisfaction that came when she was able to help someone. She was uneducated, illiterate, and life had worn her down, but she knew that she served God in ministering to the poor people of the Delta who had no other hope but her. Wearily she made her way to the room, lay down, and went to sleep immediately.

Eden quickly called for Prudence to take care of Stuart and then went to the kitchen. A stew was simmering on the stove, and she filled a gray pottery bowl full of it. Sticking a spoon in it, she hurried to the cabin. The man was asleep, but his breathing was regular. She set the bowl down and shook him slightly by the shoulder. "Mister," she said. "Wake up."

The gaunt man started as if in fear, and when his eyes opened she saw, indeed, confusion. "It's all right," she whispered. "You've got to eat something to get your strength back. You haven't eaten a bite in three days." She watched his eyes until the confusion disappeared and comprehension returned, then said, "Here. Let me help you sit up."

Eden pulled him into a sitting position, then sat down on the cane-bottomed chair and filled the spoon with the stew. She held it to his lips, and he opened them and swallowed it. Carefully she spoon-fed him. When the stew was gone, she asked, "How do you feel?"

"I feel like . . . I feel weak as a kitten."

"You were pretty sick. For a time we thought you'd die."

Hoarsely, Quentin said, "Sorry to be so much trouble, Mrs. Breckenridge."

"Don't be foolish. You didn't decide to get sick." She spoke brusquely, but then a smile turned up the corners of her lips. "It's a good thing Granny was here."

"She's the woman I saw before?"

"She's the herb woman. We can't afford a doctor so we have to depend on Granny for most of our aches and pains."

The man seemed to be growing more alert as Eden watched. "Could I have some more of that stew?" he asked.

"I'll go get it. You sit right there. Here's some water. Just take a few sips."

Eden left the room, and Quentin reached up and ran his fingers through his hair. *Well, this is a pretty come-off,* he thought. *I come down to help the woman and turn out to be nothing but a burden.* He lifted his arms and studied them. Weak as a kitten. That's what he was. But whatever it was had gone now. He'd been afraid it was scarlet fever or cholera.

Impressions of Eden washed through Quentin's mind as he sat passively waiting. He had been surprised by her strength when she had helped him to sit up, but beneath the strength he sensed softness and gentleness. There was a smell of jasmine about her, and she seemed to have the darkest blue eyes he had ever seen.

When Eden came back with another bowl of steaming stew, Quentin said, "I think I can feed myself, Mrs. Breckenridge."

"All right." Eden handed him the bowl and sat down to watch. He ate hungrily, and when he had almost finished he handed the bowl back. "That was mighty good."

"Squirrel stew. Johnny shot three of them yesterday."

"He must be a good shot."

"Yes, he is. Not many ten-year-olds have an eye like my Johnny. His father was like that. Could hit anything."

At the mention of Will Breckenridge, the dead husband put in his grave by the very hands that had taken this bowl of stew, Quentin grew silent. Gradually, he felt himself strengthened by a renewed sense of determination. *I'm going to help this woman and these children if it kills me!* he thought sternly.

★　★　★

Quentin was sitting on the bed shaving himself carefully. The boy, Johnny, had brought him hot water from the house, and Quentin had fished a mirror out of the kit he had brought. Now the boy stood watching him quietly with a rather suspicious expression. Quentin carefully drew the razor down his lean cheeks, wiped the foam on a towel, then smiled slightly. "Won't be long and you'll have to be doing this, Johnny. It's a real pest. I remember the first time I shaved. I cut myself half a dozen times. Thought I'd have to have a beard for the rest of my life."

Johnny did not answer. He stood beside the door as if he were prepared to flee. Quentin had been able to coax almost no conversation out of Johnny, and all he knew about the boy was what he'd been able to observe: he was physically sturdy, but at the same time highly sensitive. Now as he drew the razor down his other cheek, Quentin said, "Where did you get the squirrels your mother made the stew out of?"

"Down by the river. There's a bunch of big pecan trees down there. Squirrels is thicker than you'd believe."

"You must be a good shot. I'm not," he said wryly. "I couldn't hit a squirrel in a hundred years. Doubt if I could hit an elephant."

"No elephants around here."

"Well, I didn't figure there were." Quentin smiled. He studied the face of the boy with a quick glance and tried to remember the face of the man that he had killed. The memory was fleeting, and he had not seen Will Breckenridge's face clearly. He did have the impression that the dark blue eyes came from his father, but then Eden Breckenridge had the same tint in her eyes. He finished shaving, aware of the boy's intense scrutiny, and as he put his shaving kit away he pulled on a shirt and stood up. For a moment he swayed, and the room seemed to go around. He closed his eyes for a moment, bracing himself against the wall. When his balance returned, he opened his eyes and saw Johnny staring at him. "Guess I've forgotten how to walk."

"Ma says for you to come up to the house and eat."

"All right," Quentin said. He walked to the door, light-headed and aware of his weakness. Outside stood a huge blue tick hound with a philosophical face. "Hello, boy, what's your name?" Quentin said.

"That's Blue. And that's Banjo." A smaller hound, motley white, had come up sniffing at Quentin's legs.

Stooping, Quentin patted Banjo's white head. But when he tried to do the same to Blue, the big hound moved his head quickly aside.

"Blue don't take to folks. Just to me," Johnny said.

"Well, I'll have to be friends with Banjo then, I guess."

The sun was shining but the wind was sharp as the two crossed from the barn to the house. Climbing the steps was more difficult than Quentin had expected, and he held onto the banister as he ascended. The boy stood back, and Quentin entered the kitchen. The smell of cooking was rich in the air; across the kitchen, Eden, in an apron, held a pan full of meat.

"You sit down over there, Mr. Larribee," Eden said. "This is my pa, Thomas York."

"I'm glad to meet you, sir," Larribee said. The older man was standing with his back to the wall and extended his left hand. Quentin's experienced eye at once saw that there was some sort of paralysis in his right arm and that his right leg was weak.

"Glad to meet you, Mr. Larribee. You're doing a might better, I take it?"

As the two men sat down at the table, Quentin said, "I'm sorry to be such a bother. I didn't do it on purpose, of course."

Thomas studied the face of the younger man and said, "You're lucky to get out alive with a fever like that, so Eden tells me. Granny said she's seen fellers just die with fevers that went that high."

"I was pretty sick, but I'm feeling better now."

The little girl shyly lifted her eyes as she put a plate full of meat in front of Quentin. "My name is Prudence," she said.

"I'm Quentin."

"This is my brother, Stuart." She laid her hand on the red hair of the baby who stared owlishly at Quentin.

"I'm glad to meet you, Prudence. And you, too, Stuart."

Eden had put a pan of fresh bread on the table, its aroma reaching Quentin's nose and stirring the hunger in him. When Eden sat down, she glanced at him momentarily and then at her father. "All right, Pa," she said quietly.

Thomas York bowed his head. Quentin saw that the others all did the same, and then bowed his own head. He listened as Thomas asked a simple blessing, which concluded, "And bless our guest. And thank you for your mercies and healing him. Amen." He turned to Quentin with a smile. "Well, I hope you like venison, because that's what we got."

"I don't get much of it in the city, but when I was a boy we had quite a bit."

"Where did you grow up, if I might ask?"

"I grew up on a farm up in the North, but we moved to a small town."

Quentin was aware that the boy was watching him, and finally the question popped out. "You're a Yankee?"

"I guess I am," Quentin said.

"Was you in the war?"

Quentin had prepared his answer. "I worked in a hospital for a few weeks. I helped take care of wounded soldiers." It was not the exact truth, but it was the best he could do. Aware that the two adults were watching him carefully, he said, "I guess Yankees aren't very welcome in this part of the world."

"The war is over," Thomas York said quietly. "Best to put it all behind us."

Eden did not speak, but a stubbornness came to Johnny Breckenridge's dark blue eyes. He said nothing but Quentin thought, *The war's not over for him. It killed his father. And there are thousands like him all over the South.*

The food was good, including the fresh bread that Quentin layered with rich, yellow butter. He sat quietly listening as the others talked of everyday things on the farm. Soon he heard the sound of a wagon, then footsteps, then a knock on the door, and Eden said, "I guess that's Riley." She went to the door, and Quentin heard her say, "We're having dinner, Riley. Could you take a meal with us?"

A man's voice rumbled. "No, Eden. I got to get to town. I just thought I'd stop and see if you needed anything."

"Come on in and you can meet Mr. Larribee."

The man who entered, Quentin saw, was very large—over six feet tall and strongly built. He had tow-colored hair and pale green eyes that met Larribee's at once.

"This is Mr. Larribee. This is Mr. Greer. Riley Greer, our neighbor down the road."

"Glad to know you, Larribee. Hear you been ailin'."

Quentin, still feeling woozy, decided not to risk standing. "Yes. I was just on my way through when I got laid low. It was very fortunate that Mrs. Breckenridge and Granny Spears were on hand to take care of me."

Riley Greer studied him intently. "Not from these parts, I take it?"

"No. From the North. I was just passing through on my way to the coast."

"On business, are you?"

Quentin hesitated. "More or less," he said noncommittally.

Something, discontent or anger, gleamed from Riley's pale green eyes. He studied Quentin carefully, then shrugged. "Glad you didn't die," he said almost grudgingly. "Anything you want from town, Eden?"

"You might bring some sugar. We're down to using honey for sweetening."

"I'll bring you a bit."

Riley's eyes came again to rest on Quentin with a vague antagonism, then looked back at Eden—with, Quentin noticed, a mixture of possession and desire. *He wants this woman,* he thought. *And I would bet that he's a man who usually gets what he wants.*

As soon as Greer left, Johnny said, "He fought in the war. He was with the Army of the Tennessee."

"Is that right?"

"Yep. He was captured; he was a prisoner of war. Nearly died. They nearly starved him to death." Johnny's eyes were accusing, as if Quentin himself were responsible for the atrocities of the war.

Quickly, Eden changed the subject.

After the meal was over, Quentin and York went out on the porch where they sat side by side in a pair of worn, wooden rockers.

"I made these rockers myself back before I had my stroke. Not much good for anything anymore."

"When was your stroke, Mr. York?"

"Three years ago. Came on me one night. The next day I couldn't move much of anything. Never did get the full use of this arm and this leg."

"Well," Quentin said thoughtfully, "you lived through it. That's something to thank God for."

"You a man of God, Mr. Larribee?"

Quentin hesitated. "I'm a believer. Yes."

Thomas did not answer, and after a time he got up and hobbled away saying, "I've got to go feed the chickens."

A few minutes later, Johnny came out of the house. The shotgun in his hands looked too large for him. "Goin' huntin'," he announced.

"Rabbits or squirrels?"

"Anything that we can eat," Johnny said. He stood looking at Quentin, then said, "Mr. Greer, he don't like you."

Startled, Quentin said, "Why not?"

"He wants to marry with my mama, and he don't like no men around here."

With that announcement, Johnny's lips suddenly tightened and his eyes became hooded. Without another word he turned and marched away, his back stiff, the gun held under his arm pointed at the ground. The dogs, Blue and Banjo, followed him, yelping and anxious for the hunt.

Eden came outside almost at once. She stood watching Johnny go off and said nothing.

Hoping she wouldn't notice his gaze, Quentin watched her as she stood there. The lines of her body were clean and pleasing, and he sensed that there was a woman's soft depth in her—but that time and trouble had covered it. A curtain of reserve was about her, but he could already sense that deep within her was a bright, strong spirit. *She's self-sufficient,* he thought. *And she's on guard. I guess she has reason, with the war, and losing her husband.* He wondered how she felt about Riley Greer. The sudden thought came to him: *If she marries a man who's well off, that would take a burden off me. She'd be cared for.* But Quentin was uneasy about Riley Greer. In the few minutes they'd been together, Quentin had glimpsed a roughness and a scarcely covered brutality in the man that disturbed him.

"I hate to be a burden," Quentin spoke up suddenly. "I'll be moving on."

"Better not. Stay for a time until you get your strength back."

She turned toward him, looking at him directly and intently, without pretext or apology, and Quentin realized that there was a complexity in Eden Breckenridge that was surprising in a woman of her station. She had a direct way of evaluating things that was uncommon among women of his acquaintance. Finally she turned away without another word and left him alone with his thoughts. "I've got to find a way to help," he muttered to himself.

★ ★ ★

Four buzzards were circling in the east, and Quentin stopped chopping wood long enough to study them. He admired the birds—ugly and ungainly seen up close, but there were no flyers like them. It was only ten o'clock in the morning, the third day since he had gotten on his feet. Every day he had thought that he should leave, but he had stayed, frustrated that he had not yet found a way to accomplish what he had come for. Now sweat dripped down his face onto his neck, cooling him. Nearby, Banjo, the whitish hound, studied him thoughtfully, his red tongue lolling out like a piece of red flannel. Picking up the splitting maul, Quentin balanced it, then brought it down, and the white oak split as clean as a piece of rock. There was a pleasure in splitting the wood, and the exercise would help him recover. He rubbed his hands and felt the blisters beginning, but he did not care.

He heard a sound and looked up to see a wagon approaching. As it came closer he saw the large form of Trumbo Jones, the ex-slave who had brought him to the Breckenridge place. He waited until the wagon stopped and said, "Hello, Trumbo."

"Howdy."

There was something unnatural in the way the man spoke and held himself that caught Quentin's attention. "What's the matter, Trumbo?" he asked at once.

"Somethin' wrong with my shoulder."

Quentin stepped to the other side of the wagon, saying, "Get down."

Trumbo climbed down awkwardly, saying, "I can't move very good. Never had nothin' hurt me like this."

Quentin was aware that Eden had come out of the house followed by Prudence and Johnny.

"What's wrong, Trumbo?" Eden said quickly. "Are you sick?"

"I hurts my shoulder, Mrs. Breckenridge."

"Is it broken?"

"I don't know, ma'am. It hurts plum fierce."

Quentin hesitated for only an instant, then said, "Mind if I see how it is, Trumbo?"

Trumbo's dark brown eyes fastened on the smaller man. "You know about hurt shoulders?"

"Well, maybe a little bit."

Quentin's hands began to touch the flesh, and it was as if he sensed where the pain lay. "Is it right there?"

"Yes, sir. It's right there."

"Not broken. It's just dislocated, but I know that hurts bad enough."

"Dislocated? What dat mean, Mistuh Quentin?"

Quentin hesitated, needing an answer that used no medical terms. "It just means the bones have kind of popped out of place. I think I can help you, but it might hurt a little at first."

"Anything to stop this achin'. I'd appreciate it, Mistuh Quentin."

"Come over here and sit down." The large stump that Quentin had been using to split the wood served as a seat for the suffering black man. He sat down carefully and Quentin moved in front of him. "Put your right hand right here on the other shoulder and hold it right there."

"Like this?"

"Yes. Just like that. Now, put your other arm right here. All right? Now, this is going to hurt some, but I want you to be relaxed." He smiled as he saw the worry in the black man's face. "I know it's hard to relax when you know you're going to be hurt. The natural thing is to tense up. But you're big and strong and I'm not. I'll be pulling against your muscles and if you resist, I can't do it. Just be absolutely as relaxed as you can. Think of yourself, Trumbo, as a piece of liver. No bones, no nothing. Think you can do that?"

Trumbo studied the lean face of Larribee. "I do my best, Mistuh Quentin."

Quentin moved around and put his arms into position. He got ready and knew that the action had to be swift and powerful. "Now you just relax and I'll count to three, and then I'll try to pop this back into place. One," he said. "Two," he intoned, and then suddenly he threw all of his strength into the action of pulling with his arm and shoving with his hand.

Trumbo grunted with pain and surprise. Caught off guard, he had not had time to resist. Then his eyes went wide with astonishment. He lifted his left arm, and he said, "It's fixed! How'd you do that?"

"Well, I had a friend who was a pretty good man with bones. Kind of a male Granny Spears. I saw him do this a few times," Quentin said.

Eden was staring at the two men. "Is it really all right, Trumbo?"

Trumbo lifted his huge arm rather carefully. He moved them forward, lifted them again, and shook his head. "Dat's a miracle, Mistuh Quentin!"

"No, it's not a miracle," Quentin laughed. "It's just pushing a bone or two back into place. But I'll have to tell you, with a thing like this it can happen again."

"Well, as long as I got you here to pop it back in, I guess I'll be all right."

"But I won't be here. You'll have to go to the doctor."

"Doctor! I ain't got no money for doctors," Trumbo said.

Johnny said nothing but his eyes were watchful, staring at Quentin with an expression Quentin could not read. "Maybe you got some of that lemonade for me and Trumbo, Mrs. Breckenridge," Quentin said.

"Yes. Come on the porch. Pru, you get some lemonade, will you?"

"Yes, Mama."

The two men, five minutes later, were sitting on the porch holding glasses of lemonade. Johnny had gone to do his chores, and Stuart was crawling around and pulling himself up on Trumbo's knee. Eden had gone back inside, leaving the two men alone.

"This sure is a fine little fellow. He look somethin' like his daddy."

Quentin stirred uneasily but said nothing. He watched as the baby sat on Trumbo's lap pulling at the buttons on his vest. Trumbo said, "You met Mistuh Greer, I reckon."

"Yes. He came by yesterday."

"He don't like you bein' here."

"Well, I guess I won't be here very long. I take it he wants to marry Mrs. Breckenridge?"

"You seed that already? Well, it's true enough. He's a right mean man. I hates to talk bad about any man, but everybody knows it. He's hard on his chilluns."

"How many children does he have?"

"He's got three. One girl and two boys. All of 'em about thirteen up to fifteen, maybe. He ain't a good daddy to 'em. He's a widower, you know. His wife, she died. Real unhappy woman she was."

Quentin mulled over what Trumbo had said. "This family is having a hard time, isn't it, Trumbo?"

"Every family I know is havin' a hard time, Mistuh Quentin." Trumbo hesitated, then shook his head sadly. "Miss Breckenridge, she's going to lose dis place. The money, hit's due, and she ain't got no money to pay it at the bank. That bank done took over half the places I know here on the Delta. It shore is sad."

Trumbo's words troubled Quentin, and though the two men continued talking for some time about a variety of things, he couldn't get the thought of Eden Breckenridge's financial problems off his mind. Finally Trumbo got up, saying, "Thank you for helpin' my shoulder. It's jist like a miracle to me." He looked around the place and said, "I wish you could help Miss Breckenridge as easy as you helped my shoulder. But I reckon dat's a different sort of thing, ain't it, Mistuh Quentin?"

"I guess it is, Trumbo."

An unhappiness and dissatisfaction swept over Quentin as he watched Trumbo drive his wagon back up the road. He stepped inside the door and said, "Mrs. Breckenridge, I'm going to walk down by the river for a while."

"All right," she said, looking up at him intently in that disturbing way she had, as if nothing about him was hidden from her. "That was wonderful how you helped Trumbo's shoulder. I never saw anything like it."

"Just a little trick. I'll be back—but I may stay a while by the river."

Quentin made his way across the fields. When he got to the river, which was lined with trees, he walked for a time along the banks. The Mississippi fascinated him. It was a big, brown god, some said. He had heard some call it simply "The Old Man." All morning long he walked, sometimes pausing, his mind grasping at straws. Noon came, and he had found no answers. He sat down on a big tree that had been overturned and watched the roiling waters of the Mississippi. Overhead the sky was blue and hard enough, it seemed, to strike a match on. For a long time he sat silently, then he gave an impulsive, dissatisfied gesture with his hands. "Lord," he said, "help me! I've come to help this woman, and I don't see any way. You know all things and you know my heart. All I want to do is to help put right what I have ruined."

He didn't know how long he sat there on that log. Eventually a paddle wheeler came by, one of the floating palaces that plied the Mississippi. He watched the wheels churn the water into a froth. The decks seemed to be filled with finely dressed people. He watched it until it disappeared—and suddenly a thought came to him. He froze—then jumped to his feet, his eyes alive. "Why, Lord, you must have put this in my mind! I could never have thought of this on my own! I thank you, Lord, and I ask you to help me with what I've got to do."

★　★　★

As soon as he came into the kitchen, Eden saw that there was an excitement in Quentin Larribee she had not seen before. The two smaller children were napping and Johnny was out with the dogs somewhere. "Mrs. Breckenridge," he said somewhat breathlessly, "may I talk with you? Something's come to my mind that I'd like for you to hear."

Cautiously, Eden Breckenridge stared at him. Since she had become a widow, many men had tried to court her. She had grown wary of them. *I'm alone here now,* she thought, *and I don't know this man.*

"Let's go sit on the porch," she said. She moved outside and took a seat in one of the rockers. He sat in the other, apparently nervous, and she said, "Are you feeling worse?"

"No. I feel fine, but there's something I want to talk to you about." He hesitated then said, "I'm broke, Mrs. Breckenridge. I came this way thinking I might find work down here."

"I can't give you work," Eden said quickly. "There's no money. As a matter of fact—"

Quentin heard her break off and knew she had been about to say, *I may even lose this place.* He said quickly, "No, that's not what I'm trying to say. I've got an idea that might work for both of us. It's something that I've thought about for some time. I have a friend named Jim Peters. He started a new venture right here on the Mississippi. It has to do with riverboats . . ."

Eden listened carefully as Quentin explained the proposition. When he was finished, she said, "So you think there would be money to be made by raising rabbits and quail and things like that?"

"It's working for Jim, and it could work here."

"But it would take money to go into it."

"Not much," he said quickly. "Just a little wire. We can use saplings for the posts to make pens for the quail and maybe even pheasants. Rabbit hutches would be easy to build. I think my friend would help us get started with some stock. You wouldn't believe how quickly rabbits multiply."

Quentin was speaking rapidly, enthusiastically—but seeing the hope beginning to glow in her eyes, he drew back, calmed himself, and said, "It's just an idea, and it might not work, but I've got time, and it wouldn't cost much to try it. What I would like to do is to go into Helena and talk to some people there. I think we can get a contract to supply some of the boats. Jim's had no trouble selling all he can grow."

Eden Breckenridge sat quietly, looking back at Quentin, and he had the impression that she was thinking over not only his idea, but also himself—asking herself whether he was the kind of man she could trust to hold up his end of a bargain. Eventually she seemed to come to some kind of decision. "I'll talk to my father, but I think he will say yes, provided you find any interest among the riverboat captains. We have no money to put into it," she warned again.

"I think we can get around that, Mrs. Breckenridge. I'll go into Helena today, if your father agrees."

A few minutes later, they were sitting in the kitchen while Eden explained the proposition to Thomas York. As he listened carefully, hope came to his eyes as it had come to the eyes of his daughter. "It sounds like it might work. There's not going to be any money in cotton around here—not for a long time. But this is something new. I'd say try it, Eden. And, Quentin, if you'd help us this way, I'd say you're an angel from heaven."

Quentin shook his head. A wry smile touched his lips. "I've been called a lot of things, but not that. I'll go into town right away."

"Take the wagon," Thomas said.

An hour later, as Quentin drove out of the yard, Eden said, "Daddy, you think anything will come of it?"

"I've got hopes, daughter. I think he's a good man, and I've been praying that God would send us something to do."

"I'd hate to lose this place," Eden said. She watched the wagon disappear and thought how odd it was that a stranger could bring such hope to her heart. She only said, "I hope it works, Daddy."

Thomas York looked at his daughter with fondness. He put his arm around her and said, "It'll be all right. God hasn't forgotten us, Eden."

CHAPTER
Nine

*A*s Quentin pulled up the team, the shrill cry of whistles
from steamboats split the afternoon air. "Sounds like a banshee,"
he muttered. "Or what I reckon a banshee would sound like."
Leaping down from the wagon, he tied up the team and then
stood irresolutely for a moment. The town of Helena was dominated by the coming and going of the paddle wheelers that plied
the Mississippi, hauling freight and passengers up and down its
muddy waters. He lifted his eyes and there, a mile across the roiling waters, lay Mississippi. Since there was no bridge, all that
moved across the river had to be ferried on the stern-wheelers.

He caught sight of an enormous steamboat called the *Bright
Era* and walked determinedly up the gangplank. He had no idea
how to market the product that he had in mind; Jim had said little of that. *Might as well talk to one of the captains,* Quentin
thought. *He could put me right.*

The crew had evidently finished their unloading, for they were
lolling on the deck. Four of them were playing a card game,

slapping the cards down forcefully on the deck. They were rough-looking men, and one of them shot a curious glance at Quentin.

"Howdy," he said. "Lookin' for somebody?"

"I'd like to speak to the captain."

"He's up in the wheelhouse. Better be careful. He'll throw you off there if you interrupt him."

Another hand, a burly man with bright hazel eyes and a full beard, laughed. "He ain't up there. He's down at Mamie's Place."

Knowing looks ran around the crew, and the bearded one laughed again. "You know Mamie's Place?"

"Don't know it."

"Got the best-lookin' girls on the Mississippi. Ask for Pearl. She'll show you a good time."

Quentin hesitated for a moment but determination came to him. "What's the captain's name? And can you tell me how to get there?"

"Sure can," a skinny deckhand grinned. "When we're in Helena, you can always find Captain Tucker down at Mamie's. Go on down Cherry Street to the end, then turn left. 'Bout a quarter of a mile, you'll see a big white house with colors out in front. Used to belong to a senator, but Mamie took it over during the war. Never mind about Pearl. She ain't got nothin'. Ask for Julie."

"Thanks a lot," Quentin nodded. He went back down the gangplank and climbed up into the seat of the wagon. "Get up!" he said, and turned the team in a short circle. The main street, Cherry Street, ran parallel to the river, and the wheels of the wagon rumbled over the brick pavement. He noted again, as he drove the team down the length of the street, how dilapidated everything seemed to be. The war had ruined the town—including many of the men that he saw, some on crutches, some with only one arm. It was as if a giant scythe had gone through the South, harvesting the finest and strongest of the youth so that now all that was left was the very young, the very old, or the maimed.

He reached the end of Cherry Street and turned the team. The brick pavement stopped and the street turned to mud. Houses lined the street on both sides, some of them very fine antebellum structures, all looking the worse for wear. Mamie's Place was just where the deckhand had said it would be—a fine example of Southern architecture, two stories with a high, steep-pitched roof, and four dormers flanked across the tile roof. Six white pillars rose from the porch to the roofline in front. Unlike most of the other houses on the street, a fresh coat of paint made this one pristine white. A black man approached as Quentin stopped the team. "I'll tie the team up, suh."

"Thanks," Quentin murmured. "I'm looking for Captain Tucker."

The black man's expression, which had been sour, softened into a small grin. "You come to the right place. The captain, he stays here most of the time when he's tied up in Helena. Don't know where you'll find him right now, but Miss Mamie, she'll know. Just go right on in."

Quentin climbed the steps and paused on the high porch. The ornately carved oak door, highly polished, had panes of glass in it. He knocked with a heavy brass knocker and waited for what seemed like a long time. Finally the door opened and he was met by a large woman, mannish in appearance. She was massive in every respect, and her hard, greenish eyes studied Quentin clinically. An artificial smile came to her lips, and she said, "Don't believe I know you."

"My name's Quentin Larribee."

"Well, come on in, Quentin." She stepped back, and Quentin awkwardly entered the foyer, immediately struck by the very high ceilings, white with gold paint around the edges, by walls painted dark blue with gold flocked paper around the dark mahogany windows and door frames, and by highly polished white marble floors. It was ornate and overdone, like the woman's costume, which was a brilliant emerald green. "Come on into the parlor. I'll have some of the girls come in and you can choose."

"Well, no, ma'am. Really, I'm here to see Captain Tucker."

"Caleb, he's playing poker. You got business with him?"

"Yes, ma'am."

The woman turned her head to one side, and her thin, hard lips pursed for a moment. "You've got good manners. Brought up right, sonny," she said. "Come along." Her weight caused the boards to creak as she made her way down the polished pine corridor. At the last door on the right, she turned and said, "Go on in. I expect they're still sober enough to talk a little bit." She hesitated, then winked. "After you get through with your business, come and see me. I'll see you're taken care of."

Quentin had never been in a brothel in his life. He flushed and said, "Don't reckon I can do that, Miss Mamie. I'll have to be on my way."

Mamie suddenly laughed—a girlish laugh that did not go with her massive form or the adamant features of her face. "Well, if you change your mind, let me know."

Quentin nodded, then turned quickly and opened the door. Inside, five men sat around a poker table. The air was hazy and blue with cigar smoke, and the odor of alcohol was raw in Quentin's nostrils. The poker players looked up and one of them, a tall thin man with a pencil-line black mustache and cold gray eyes, snapped, "This is a private game!"

Quentin said quickly, "I didn't come to play poker. I'm looking for Captain Tucker."

A small dapper man with a russet VanDyke beard and carefully trimmed hair looked up quickly. He was wearing a white suit, spotless and well cut, and a large diamond glittered on the forefinger of his left hand. "I'm Tucker," he said. "What can I do for you, son?"

Quentin hesitated. "I . . . well, I have a proposition for you, Captain, if I could meet with you after you are through playing."

Laughter went around the table, and a large man wearing a white shirt and a black string tie said, "That won't be for a while. He's losing and he never quits until he's lost it all."

Captain Tucker glowered at the man. "You just wait, Bill. We'll see who walks away the winner." He leaned back, picked up a glass, and drained it of the amber fluid. "What kind of business, son? Something to do with steamboats, I imagine."

"Well, sir, it's about supplying your boat with food. I'm going into the business of raising delicacies for the table. Quail, pheasants, domesticated rabbits, things like that. Much better than the wild game that you can buy."

While Quentin explained his idea, Captain Tucker filled his glass from a bottle, then held it in his hand for a moment, savoring the odor as if it were fine perfume. When Quentin finished, he nodded. "Sounds all right to me. What's your name?"

"Quentin Larribee."

"Tell you what, Larribee. These fellas are laboring under the mistaken idea that they're captains. Impostors, every one of them."

"Good poker players, though," the tall, thin man smiled. He turned to Larribee and said, "I'm Captain Black of the *Sunset Queen*. I'd be interested in your proposition, Larribee. Have anything now? I'll be pulling out tomorrow."

"No, Captain Black. I just started. It'll be at least a month before I have product."

Black looked away and said with irritation, "Well, come back when you got something to sell!"

Captain Tucker sipped his drink, then put it down. He had a kindly face. "I'll tell you what, Larribee," he said. "You go down and talk to Otis Sanderson. Got the biggest store in town. Get him to handle the stuff for you. All the captains go to Sanderson. Once word gets around that there's quail and dove and what all available, I think you'll get business. He'll charge you a commission—Otis has to have his pound of flesh. But he's a square one. He'll treat you right. I think you got a good idea there, boy. Everybody gets tired of the same old meals. I do myself. Go see Otis Sanderson."

"Thank you, Captain. I hope we'll do a lot of business together."

Turning quickly, Quentin stepped into the hall and started for the door, elated by the interest the captains had shown. Suddenly his path was blocked by a short young woman, full-figured, wearing an extremely low-cut dress. She took his arm and said, "Come with me, sweetheart. You won't be sorry. My, you're a tall one, aren't you?"

Quentin didn't want to be rude, but neither did he want to encourage the young woman. "Sorry," he murmured. "I . . . I . . ." Unable to think of a single thing to say, he disengaged himself and fled out the front door.

Shaken by his awkward encounter with the prostitute, he drove faster than usual back toward the center of Helena and had no trouble finding Sanderson's store. It was the largest building on the main street, with "Sanderson's General Merchandise" printed in foot-high black letters. He tied up the team, went inside, and asked a clerk, "Is Mr. Sanderson here?"

"Sure. Back in his office. Right back behind the harnesses."

Quentin passed pottery, canned goods, dress goods, and practically everything else that could be imagined until he came to a small office almost filled by a huge desk. The man who sat behind it looked very much like a small version of General Ulysses S. Grant. There was an alert look in his small gray eyes, but most of his face was concealed by an auburn beard. "Do for you?" he asked curtly.

"Mr. Sanderson?"

"That's me."

"Can I have a minute of your time? I have a proposition that I'd like to talk with you about. I'm Quentin Larribee."

"Sit down."

Sanderson listened carefully without saying a word as Quentin outlined his proposition.

"I'd have to have ten percent," he said when Quentin was finished.

"Commission? That sounds a little high."

"Nope. It ain't high. I'll raise the price twenty percent so you're actually getting my services for nothing." He watched Quentin's reaction, then said, "You're not used to doing business, are you, Larribee?"

"Not really. My first venture in the business world. I'll be working with Mrs. Eden Breckenridge and her father."

"That so? You're the fellow from the North that got sick on 'em."

Larribee was accustomed by this time to the intensely effective system of communication that existed in the South. Apparently, everyone he met knew about his coming to town, and now he nodded with resignation. "Yes, sir. I have a friend who started a game-raising business up around Memphis. He's doing real well at it, so I talked to the Breckenridges, and we decided to give it a try."

Sanderson studied Quentin quietly, then said, "I hope it works. Mrs. Breckenridge is a fine woman, and I've known Tom York all my life, I guess. I'll do the best I can for you. How long do you think it will be before you have some stock to sell?"

"Well, I'm new at this, Mr. Sanderson. But you know how rabbits are."

"Just call me Otis, Quentin. Bring the critters in as soon as you get anything. These pleasure boats got plenty of money to spend and the folks on 'em like delicacies. How about quail eggs?"

"Not at first—we'll need all we can get. But that's an idea, Otis. Of course, the first thing we'll have to do is build a lot of hutches, and I'll need wire for fencing in quail and pheasant runs."

"Got plenty of wire and lots of lumber. Tell you what," Sanderson said, clawing at his beard. "I bought a piece of property that had an old house on it. Got to tear it down. Want to build another business there. How'd you like to tear it down for the lumber that's in it?"

"That'd be fine, Otis."

"Good. Ought to be enough lumber to build you a shed or two."

"I need to send a wire to Jim Peters, the friend I mentioned in Memphis."

"Write it out. Telegraph office is right across the way. You tell me how much wire you need, and I'll have it ready by the time you get back."

"Well, I don't have much money, you understand."

"We'll start an account." Sanderson grinned, his lips barely visible behind the thick beard and mustache. "Don't usually take to Yankees, but anybody that'll help the Breckenridges is all right in my book."

"I'll be back after I send the wire."

Quentin crossed the street and soon found the telegraph office. He wrote out a long wire to Jim asking him to ship immediately breeding stock of everything he had. He thought for a moment and said, "Send instructions on how to do this, Jim. I'm a babe in the woods."

The telegraph operator, a youngish man with a round cherubic face and a pair of merry bright eyes, said, "You the fellow stayin' with the Breckenridges, I guess."

"That's right. Quentin Larribee."

The young man read the telegram and said, "That'll cost you two dollars."

Quentin fished in his pocket and came out with the Federal notes. The young man took them and said, "Anything else for you?"

"I'd like to get a letter off. Is the post office close?"

"Right down the street beside the blacksmith's shop. What's this breeding stock? You gonna start raisin' cattle?"

"Nope," Quentin grinned. "Rabbits and quail."

"Why, you don't need to do that. You can shoot all you want."

Quentin grinned. At the post office, he bought a sheet of paper and an envelope from the postmaster and stood at the desk. He wanted to write to Irene, but he found it far more difficult than he had thought. He finally decided to make it as simple as possible:

> *Dear Irene,*
>
> *I arrived in Helena but got sick almost at once and am just now beginning to recover my strength.*

I have contacted the Breckenridges and they are in poor condition indeed. They are going to lose their farm if something isn't done. I have found a way to help them, but it will require my being here for a little longer than we had anticipated. I will write you later this week explaining what I feel I must do. In the meantime, I'll try to help the family all I can.

I miss you a great deal and wish that I were back in New York. I know this is hard for you, but it's something I must do. Please try to understand.

He hesitated about the closing and finally put: "With all my love, Quentin."

Then he added a postscript: "Just write me in care of General Delivery here in Helena. Give my regards to your parents and to our friends."

Folding the single sheet of paper, he stuffed it in the envelope, sealed it, and handed it to the postmaster, an elderly man with inquisitive, brown eyes. "Going all the way to New York," the man observed.

"That's my hope."

"This is you, Quentin Larribee, I take it?"

"Yes, sir." Quentin had become slightly amused at the townspeople's interest in him. "I'm the fellow who's staying with the Breckenridges."

"Oh, yeah! I heard about that. You got sick."

"Yes. We're going into business together raising delicacies, domesticated rabbits and so on, for the riverboat trade. You might pass that along in case somebody hadn't heard about it."

The postmaster dropped his eyes, then looked up and grinned sheepishly. "We don't have much to do here. No entertainment, you know, so I guess strangers have to put up with a little idle curiosity." He put his hand out and said, "Glad to meet you, Larribee. My name's Abe Fritch. Come in any time."

"Thank you, Mr. Fritch."

Leaving the post office, Quentin thought how strange it was, this matter of being known to almost everyone. He had forgotten what a small town was like. *Not much privacy here, but there are worse things,* he thought. *Could drop dead in some places in New York, and people would never even know it. Here every time you sneeze, word gets around.*

He returned to Sanderson's store, loaded the wagon with wire and staples, and said, "I'll be here early in the morning to start dismantling that house, Otis."

"I got some hired help here that's doin' nothin' but loafin' anyway. I'll let him give you a hand with the heavy stuff."

"Thanks a lot. I'll tell Mrs. Breckenridge and Tom how much help you've been."

Climbing into the wagon he waved a hand at the storekeeper and then spoke to the team. He moved over the bricks, the wagon wheels rumbling, and once again he heard the shrill scream of a steamboat. "Keep screaming," he said. "Keep coming to this town and come hungry, because we're depending on your riverboats to pull us out of trouble."

★   ★   ★

"Mama, can I get the brains, please?"

"I think it'd be too hard for you to crack these squirrel skulls." Eden smiled. "I'll tell you what. Let me crack 'em, and you can take the brains out with a spoon. Okay?"

"All right, Mama." Prudence loved to cook and she loved to sing, and she usually combined those two things. Now, wearing a white apron over her gray dress, she said, "You want me to sing you a song, Mama?"

"Why, I think that'd be mighty fine, Prudence." She picked up a squirrel skull that had been simmering in boiling water, cracked it, and laid it on a plate in front of Prudence. Prudence carefully separated it with a fork and knife, scooped the grayish contents out, and put them on a white saucer. As she did, she began to sing:

"There was a little chigger
And he wasn't any bigger
Than the wee small head of a pin.
But the bump that he raises
Well, it itches like blazes
And that's where the rub comes in."

Eden joined in with the chorus: "Comes in, comes in, and that's where the rub comes in."

The two collected the squirrel brains and the sweet-tasting cheek meat from the head. Prudence put a spoonful on a cracker and munched it contentedly. "Nothing better than squirrel brains, is there, Mama?"

"They're right good, but you stop eatin' 'em. You'll spoil your supper. Sing me another song."

Immediately Pru broke out singing.

"You're as lovely as a rose
As sweet as any blossom.
If you want to get your finger bit
Poke it at a possum."

"Wherever did you learn that?"

"I learned that one from Matilda. She knows lots of songs like that. Another verse is:

"Love it is a teasing thing,
Acts just like a lizard.
Crawls up and down your old backbone
And nibbles at your gizzard."

Eden looked up and laughed out loud. "Well, I never heard a thing like that before."

"Oh, she knows lots of 'em like that! I'll teach it to you, Mama."

Eden had a beautiful, strong contralto voice, and soon the kitchen was filled with the sound of two voices.

When the squirrels' brains were all extracted, Eden began making the crackling cornbread. She was gratified to see that Pru, as always, was right underfoot. "You're going to be a fine cook, Prudence. You'll make the best crackling cornbread in Arkansas, I'll bet."

The pieces of skin and meat remaining after lard had been rendered were called crackling. Eden measured a cup of diced crackling, a cup and a half of cornmeal, a cup of flour, half a tablespoon of soda, a quarter tablespoon of salt, and a cup of sour milk. She mixed it all together, explaining carefully what she was doing. Pru's face grew very serious, and finally Eden said, "We're going to add some buttermilk, some eggs, and some shortening."

"Can I put 'em on the pan, Mama?"

"Yes. If you'll be careful and not burn yourself."

Prudence, using a large spoon, made patties in the huge blackened skillet, and the room was soon full of the delicious smell of fresh crackling cornbread.

Eden continued preparing the rest of the meal: fried squirrel, grits, and greasy greens. When she was nearly finished, she realized that Pru had said nothing for some time. Turning, she saw a troubled look in Pru's clear blue eyes. "What's the matter, honey?"

Looking up, Prudence did not answer for a moment. Then she swallowed and said, "Mama, are we going to have to leave here?"

Eden put her arm around her daughter. "Why do you ask that, honey?"

"Johnny heard somebody say we were going to lose this place. Where would we go to, Mama?"

Eden Breckenridge stood quietly for a moment holding the girl within the crook of her arm. She studied the face of this daughter of hers, so expressive, and marveled again about how many things one small head could hold. Finally she said, "I hope not, sweetheart. A lot of our friends and neighbors have lost their places, but we're praying that God will let us stay here."

"You think Mr. Quentin can help us by raising quail and rabbits?"

The question stirred Eden for a moment, and she suddenly realized how much hope she had put into the tall, lanky man who had come seemingly out of nowhere. She had had little hope, or none, of hanging onto the place aside from marrying Riley Greer, but now that Pru had asked, she understood how much their future depended on Larribee and his scheme.

"I think it'll work."

"I like him, Mama. But Johnny don't."

"He doesn't like Quentin? Why not?"

"Because he doesn't like any man that you might marry."

"Why, what a foolish thing to say! I've got no idea of marrying Quentin Larribee! We're just going to do some business together."

Prudence did not speak for a moment, and when she did there was an anxiety in her eyes that Eden did not like. "Are you going to marry Mr. Greer?"

Eden had known for some time that both Johnny and Prudence did not like Riley Greer. "Don't worry about that, honey. I think—"

She was interrupted when her father came through the door saying, "Quentin's back."

Relieved that she did not have to answer the question put by Prudence, she said, "Come on. Let's see what he's found out."

As she stepped out onto the front porch, she saw Quentin climbing out of the wagon. She studied his face. He was smiling, and her heart rose. "Come inside. I know you're thirsty."

Quentin stopped in front of her as Johnny came around the corner, holding Stuart, the whole family now waiting to hear what Quentin would say.

"I'll take the lemonade," he said. "But it's good news."

"They want to buy the game, Quentin?" Eden asked quickly, breathlessly.

Quentin nodded. "I think we can sell all we can grow. All we have to do now is learn to raise the pesky varmints."

They peppered Quentin with questions as he drank his lemonade—without ice, of course, but still good to a thirsty man. They insisted on hearing everything, and he did his best to tell them. He concluded with, "Captain Tucker thinks it'll work, and so does Mr. Sanderson."

"He's been a good friend," Thomas said. "A lot of families around here wouldn't have made it without Otis. He gives away more stuff than he's sold out of that store."

Johnny had said little, but finally he said with a rather sullen look, "It won't never work."

"What are you talking about, son?" Thomas said with surprise. "Of course it'll work."

Johnny gave an odd look at Quentin and shook his head. "It ain't gonna work," he said firmly.

Eden broke the embarrassed silence that followed by saying, "Come on. I've got a good supper fixed. Do you like squirrel brains, Quentin?"

A shiver went over Quentin. "Brains?"

"Yes. Squirrel brains," Eden said. She laughed. "You've never eaten squirrel brains?"

"No. Never have."

"Well, it'll be a first. Come along. You go wash up."

The supper was a success. Quentin enjoyed the fried squirrel and grits, and especially the greasy greens. He had never had them before and he found them to be delicious—but he firmly refused to experiment with the squirrel brains.

After the meal was over, Thomas took Quentin into the parlor where they sat while Eden and the children cleaned up. As they were talking about raising rabbits, Quentin's eyes fell on the picture of Will Breckenridge. It puzzled him that the children had said so little about their father, that Eden had not spoken at all of her husband. Trying not to sound curious, he said, "You've had a lot of grief since your son-in-law was killed."

"He was a good man in many ways," Thomas said slowly. "He worked hard. Of course he drank hard, too."

"I guess the children must miss him a lot, and I'm sure Eden is grieved."

For some reason, Thomas York did not answer. His eyes were fixed on the picture of his dead son-in-law. Long thoughts seemed to be running through his mind, and Quentin was puzzled. Finally Thomas said, "He was a hard man to know, Quentin. I was always grieved that he didn't spend much time with his children. They never really got to know him—not even Johnny."

Quentin silently studied the face of Will Breckenridge. It was a stern face, without the light of humor that he saw in Eden and Prudence. He listened while Thomas spoke briefly of the man who had been his son-in-law, but the one thing he did not speak about was the one thing Quentin wanted to hear. What sort of husband had he been? Quentin didn't know women, but it had surprised him that Eden never mentioned her husband. He could not ask, but as he listened to Thomas, he got the impression that Will and Eden had not had a good marriage.

Later, after the children were in bed, Quentin sat out on the porch, his back against one of the columns that held up the roof. Thomas and Eden sat in the two rockers, rocking rhythmically in the night air.

"Kind of warm tonight," Quentin observed casually. "Temperature's seventy-one degrees."

"How do you know that?" Thomas asked with surprise.

"Why, by the crickets."

"The crickets! You can tell the temperature by the crickets?"

"Sure. You count the number of chirps during a quarter of a minute, and then you add forty."

"I never heard of such a thing," Thomas said with surprise.

"Probably doesn't work. I had an aunt taught me that."

"What a funny thing, to tell the temperature by the crickets," Eden said.

"Not too funny," Thomas said. "You can tell whether there's going to be a hard winter by how thick the caterpillars' fur is or how thick the hull is on an acorn."

Their talk went on softly. Once a huge shadowy form sailed overhead. Quentin looked up, startled. "What was that?"

"Big hunting owl," Thomas said. "Big enough to take a rabbit."

"We'll have to be sure ours don't get loose. When we get some, that is."

For Quentin it was a fine evening. The air grew cooler, but he was not sleepy. Thomas finally rose and hobbled off to bed, stopping to say, "I appreciate what you're doing for the family, Quentin."

Quentin mumbled a reply, and after Thomas had gone, he said, "I like your father very much."

"He likes you, too."

The two sat listening to the sounds of the night. Overhead, the stars were spangled like tiny dots of fire across the ebony sky. Eden stood and stepped away from the house to get a better view of the astral display. Quentin came down to stand beside her. As she looked up, he studied her face by the silvery moonlight. She was a tall woman and shapely, and as he watched her he noted again that she had a curtain of reserve. But then she looked at him, and she saw that her face was a mirror that changed as her feelings changed. The bones of her face made strong and pleasant contours. And suddenly a small dimple appeared at the left of her mouth, and light danced in her eyes. "I wish I knew the names of the stars," she murmured.

Quentin looked up and then pointed. "I know a few. That's Venus over there." He moved his arm and said, "And that's Polaris, the North Star. Everybody knows that one."

"I don't. What's its name again?"

"Polaris. Sailors use it to steer by. Other stars seem to change positions, but Polaris is always the same."

She turned her face back up toward the stars, and he studied her again, the moonlight coating her face with silver. There was a fire in this woman that made her lovely. She had a woman's soft depth and a woman's spirit, and buried beneath her reserve was a great vitality and imagination. She turned toward him again, and he caught the smell of jasmine. She seemed to be struggling to say something, and finally she put out her hand. Confused, Quentin took it. It was a strong hand, hardened with work, but with the soft suppleness of a woman.

"I—wanted to thank you for all you've done, Quentin."

Like her hand, her voice was soft and gentle, yet containing an underlying power. He was unable to answer for a moment. Her fragrance came to him powerfully, and he noted again the shape of her eyes. She was a strong woman who could charm a man or chill him to the bone. She was smiling at him now, not teasingly, but with a smile that came from deep within.

Quentin admitted to himself that he was attracted to this woman. He was not and never had been a womanizer, and yet in the few brief days he had been here, he had watched Eden. He had seen her steadiness and her strength, and now he saw her beauty, inside and out. An impulse came to put his arms around her, but he knew that that would be fatal and wrong.

He cleared his throat finally and said, "I haven't done anything really, Eden."

"Yes, you have." Her hand closed more tightly on his, and then she pulled away and turned away from him—but not before he had seen silver in her eyes, the beginning of tears. "You've given me hope," she whispered. "Not many people can do that."

At that moment, Quentin had the feeling that if he moved toward her, if he but touched her, she would turn to him and come into his arms. She was a lonely woman, one who wanted comfort as much as he wanted to comfort her, to tell her that all would be well.

But he did not. He murmured, "I hope it goes well for us, Eden." Then he turned and went at once to his room in the barn. He undressed and went to bed. But as he lay in the darkness listening to the night sounds just outside his window, he was disturbed by what he felt for this woman. He tried to concentrate on Irene and on his life in New York, but all he could think of was the sound of her voice as she had said, "You've given me hope." Finally he turned over and willed himself not to think of Eden Breckenridge.

CHAPTER Ten

*A*n unusual sense of satisfaction filled Quentin as he surveyed the line of rabbit hutches, each filled with a thumping fat female. He walked along poking his finger into the wire netting, speaking to the does, calling their names. Pru had named them all, going to the Bible for most and making up others out of her own rich imagination. He stopped by one, a snow-white doe who nibbled at his finger. "Hello, Rachel," he grinned. "I hope you're feeling well this morning." He paused—then looked up to see Johnny standing by the quail run. "Hey, Johnny," he said. "How about quail for breakfast?"

Johnny smiled briefly. That was rare, for he had still not warmed toward Quentin. As a matter of fact, during the tearing down of the house in Helena and the building of the hutches and the runs, the boy had often expressed his contemptuous amazement at Quentin's ineptness with tools. Trumbo Jones had helped with tearing the house down and hauling the lumber, and his knowledge of rabbit hutches had been of invaluable help. Quentin had overheard Johnny saying to the big black man one day, "He don't know nothin'! He can't even drive a nail!"

"Well, he's a city boy, I guess, Johnny," Trumbo had said gently. "You have to make exceptions. City folks ain't had the advantages of us folks raised in the country. Give him time. He'll come around."

Indeed, Quentin had never been any good with tools—except for a scalpel and a needle. With these, for some reason, he was expert, but now as Johnny ambled over Quentin looked down at his hands and saw that the blisters there were only partially healed. He had cut his fingers time and again and wondered whether the damage to his hands would have any effect on his skills in the operating room.

"I wish we could finish up them boxes for the pigeons," Johnny said. "But Ma says we got to go to church."

"I guess we'd better do what your ma says," Quentin remarked quietly. He studied the boy's face, noting again the strange combination of shyness and stubbornness. Quentin had thought himself to be rather good with young people, since he had helped raise his younger brother and sisters, but he had gotten nowhere with Johnny. The boy resented him, and Quentin knew the reason: *He's afraid his mother will marry again, and that scares him.* Quentin wondered again what kind of relationship had existed between Johnny and his father.

"I guess I'll fix them boxes when we get home from church, if that old preacher don't preach all day."

Quentin grinned. "Long sermons are pretty hard to take, aren't they?" He looked at the shed that housed the pigeons and the feed, sturdily built, and felt a sense of pride. It was mostly Trumbo's doing, but Quentin had at least driven some of the nails and sawed some of the boards. He had forgotten what it meant to take pride in such simple things. But since he had been at the farm, life had slowed down, and he found himself liking it. Back at the hospital he had risen early each day and worked long hours, with little time for relaxation. Now the days passed, it seemed, as slowly as a river flowing, and although he worked hard, he had found a peace in his spirit that had been lacking. This had come as a surprise to him, for he had thought his life was complete. But now as he gazed at the quail scurrying around pecking at each other and at the feed on the ground, he was aware that something in him loved this quiet life.

"All this couldn't have happened without you, Johnny," Quentin said. "I'm not much of a carpenter. You're a lot better than I am."

Johnny's face turned shy for a moment at Quentin's simple admission, and he kicked at the dirt with the toe of his half boot. "Well," he said finally, "I reckon I've had more practice than you have."

"You sure have. You're a fine carpenter. Trumbo says so." He saw the pleasure flicker across the boy's face and added, "I hope you know more about breeding than I do. I don't know much."

Johnny poked his fingers into Romeo's cage, the big black-and-white buck. "I reckon you breed rabbits just like you do cows." He stroked the silky fur and shrugged. "It's just quicker, I guess."

"You ready to get started?" The two looked up to see Eden approaching. She was wearing an ankle-length, light blue cotton skirt with darker blue flowers scattered over it. The matching blouse had a high collar buttoned up the front and long sleeves that buttoned at the wrist. She wasn't smiling exactly, but the thought of a smile was hinting at the corners of her mouth, and her head tilted to one side slightly. She had a way of laughing that was very attractive, and now she lifted her chin and her lips curved in beautiful lines.

She looked at the rabbits and said, "I can't believe it's all happening."

"Well, I hope it happens. I don't know anything about breeding rabbits. I reckon Johnny does."

Pru came up carrying Stuart, who was almost too big for her. She wore a faded pink dress; Stuart wore short pants and a blue shirt. He was yelling loudly in protest. "Be quiet, Stuart!" Pru said, putting him down. She looked at Quentin and said, "Rabbits are different from people. People have one daddy and one mama and lots of babies. Rabbits have one daddy who has lots of wives and they have lots of babies."

"Is that so? Well, I like to have things simplified, Pru. My, don't you look nice this morning!" He went over and picked her up, giving her a hug. He had learned that she warmed to any kind of affection, and now she smiled at him. He studied her and put her down, but he put his hand on her cheek, holding it there for a minute.

Eden had not missed this, and she said, "What's the matter, Quentin?"

"She looks like she might have a little fever."

Quickly Eden came over and held her hand on Pru's forehead. "Do you feel warm, honey?"

"A little bit, I guess."

"Maybe you'd better stay home."

"Oh, I'm all right, Mama! *Please* can I go with you?" Pru said. And she begged so hard that Eden reluctantly agreed.

"You children get in the wagon now. Johnny, your grandpa said you could drive this morning."

"Come on!" Johnny yelled and sprinted toward the wagon.

Eden turned toward Quentin. "You really think she's got a fever? I could hardly tell."

"A little bit maybe." Quentin was apprehensive about his reputation with sick people. Word had gotten around since he had first popped Trumbo's shoulder into place and then treated his small son. Several others had dropped by, asking if he had any idea about different kinds of ailments. For the most part he had managed to turn them away, for none of them seemed serious. He had determined to hide his background as much as possible, though he understood there was no real reason for this. But he had planned everything carefully, and it seemed best to keep his medical background out of the picture. Now he said quickly, "You might have Granny take a look at her if she's at church."

"Granny will be jealous if you keep on stealing her thunder," Eden laughed. She had a teasing look in her eyes that quickened Quentin's pulse, and as she watched him there was a strange expression on her wide, shapely mouth. "Well, time to go to church. You'll have to make your own peace with Granny."

Thomas was waiting in the backseat of the wagon, and Quentin handed Stuart up, then climbed in and took the boy in his lap. Stuart was fascinated with Quentin's watch and held it to his ear, a simple entertainment that held his attention for some time.

The air was getting cold; October had arrived, and now the trees were a flaming riot of yellow and red and gold. Thomas said, "I always like this time of the year. Seems like them bright colors always rest your eyes a little bit. You ever see anything prettier?"

"Never have. Beautiful country."

Pru climbed back and sat between the two men. Without appearing to, Quentin gauged her temperature again, and took her pulse simply by holding her hand and putting his finger on her wrist. *A little fast. And there's a little fever. I hope it's nothing serious,* he thought.

This was the third time Quentin had come to church with the Breckenridges, and as he got down and joined the family walking toward the white frame building with the small belfry, he felt a yearning to belong. The looks he got, for the most part, were either curious or, occasionally, antagonistic. Those who were still fighting the war in their hearts and minds would not be changed for a long time, maybe never. As he passed by, he heard one girl no more than five whisper, "Is that a damn Yankee, Mama?"

He saw that Eden had heard too and gave him a swift look. He heard the mother say, "Hush, Janie, don't say things like that."

As they entered and took their seats, Eden said, "I'm sorry about what Janie said."

"It's all right. I'd probably feel the same way if I were from this part of the world."

His answer did not make Eden happy, but the service began and she, as usual, put herself into it.

The song leader was Otis Sanderson, who had a powerful baritone voice. He had greeted Quentin cordially, even warmly, the first time Quentin had accompanied the family to church and each time since. He was one of the few men who had not been physically scarred by the war, although he had lost a brother at Cold Harbor and a nephew at Gettysburg. "Can't live in the past," he had said to Quentin. "It was a terrible war but it's over, and we've got to move on."

The song service was loud, and Quentin, who had been accustomed to organs and ornate buildings and pews made of polished oak, had found it somewhat difficult at first. The ceiling was fifteen feet high, which gave a sense of spaciousness to the interior. The pews were made of rough, four-inch pine boards nailed together; the backs were hard and uncomfortable. The pulpit sat on a platform, along with two chairs occupied by the song leader and the preacher. The pastor was the Reverend Nelson Jordan, a lean man of twenty-nine with black hair and dark brown eyes. He was lean as a rake, one of those men who never gained a pound, and his wife, Elizabeth, always sat in the front row. She was a small blonde woman of twenty-five and kept strict watch over their four small children, a pair of twin boys and two older girls. Reverend Jordan had served as a lieutenant under Stonewall Jackson. He had survived the worst fighting of the war, but now he never mentioned it, at least not from the pulpit.

As the song service went on, Quentin found himself, as always, conscious that he was the object of many gazes. He sat beside Thomas on the very end and tried to show no self-consciousness. He could catch a glimpse of Eden's profile and thought again how she loved to sing. She had a beautiful voice, clear and true. She seemed to become another woman in a worship service. Her attention was wholly on singing, and there was an air of worship about her that Quentin had rarely seen. He could not explain it exactly, but he knew that this woman was somehow in the presence of God in a way that few ever achieve.

After the song service the minister preached an excellent sermon on sanctification—deep, profound, yet expressed in simple terms. Jordan had a way of teaching unlike anything Quentin had ever heard. He found himself, after each sermon, thinking all week of things the preacher had drawn forth from Scripture, and now he leaned forward listening intently. The sermon was about holiness, about purity, about goodness in the human spirit. The text was "Be ye holy as I am holy."

As he filed out after the service, he shook hands with the preacher. "I've always had trouble with that particular text, Brother Jordan," he said. "I never feel holy."

Nelson Jordan smiled. "I don't feel holy either, but God says we are holy and that's the end of it."

"Even when we do wrong?"

"Well, we don't have time for a theological contest here. Why don't you come by the church some afternoon and we'll talk about it."

"I'd like that very much."

As they left, Eden said, "He's the best preacher we've ever had in this church. We're going to have a revival one day."

"A revival?"

"Yes," she said quietly. "The Spirit of God is going to move. If you're here, Quentin, you'll see it. God's going to do great and marvelous things. Some of us have been praying for years, and God is not going to let our prayers just fall to the ground."

They were almost to the wagon when Quentin felt a tug at his sleeve. He turned to see a rather frightened girl with big blue eyes. It was Janie, the girl who had spoken that morning. He said, "Why, hello, Janie," with a pleasant smile. "How are you this morning?"

The girl was frightened, and Quentin saw her mother standing some distance away with her lips drawn in a straight line. Obviously, Janie's mother had commanded the girl to apologize.

Quentin knelt so that he would be on her level. "I enjoyed church this morning. My, that's a pretty dress you have on!"

Encouraged by his smile and by what she saw in his face, Janie said, "I–I'm sorry I called you a damn Yankee."

"Well, that's all right. I've been called worse."

"It was the 'damn' Mama said was wrong. You are a Yankee, aren't you?"

"I guess so, but I'm trying to become a Southerner just like you."

Janie smiled and said, "I won't call you a damn Yankee anymore."

She turned and ran away, and as Quentin stood he found Thomas York standing beside him. "That was a good thing for that girl to do even if her mama made her do it," Thomas said.

"Beautiful child." A look of quiet understanding passed between the two men, and Quentin realized that Thomas knew what he was feeling.

"I reckon there's some that are not ready to be as forgiving," the older man said quietly. "But it will come. Don't you worry."

★ ★ ★

Johnny had started out the door with the shotgun held in the crook of his arm. He halted when his grandfather said, "Goin' huntin', Johnny?"

"I thought I'd go after some rabbits. Maybe even get a big fat coon."

"Why don't you ask Quentin to go with you?"

Johnny stared at his grandfather. "He can't hunt."

"Maybe you could teach him."

Johnny hesitated. He couldn't see how Quentin would be anything but a hindrance on a hunting trip, but he had great respect for his grandfather. Then he shrugged. "Okay. I'll ask him."

Moving outside, Johnny found Quentin putting up another run. The quail had multiplied so quickly that it was obvious they were going to need more space. "I'm going huntin'. You can go along if you want to."

Quentin lowered the hammer and looked at Johnny with surprise. "I'm not much of a hunter," he said.

"Well, we've only got one gun, but we can take turns."

Quentin put the hammer down and picked up his coat. He slipped into it and said, "I'll tell you what. Why don't you do the shootin' and let me carry the game."

"Okay," Johnny said, pleased at Quentin's words.

The two left the yard and Johnny said little. He responded to Quentin's rambling talk about the rabbits and quail and the brace of pheasants they had just received from Jim Peters. "Those birds are too pretty to eat," Quentin said.

"What do they taste like?" Johnny asked. "They're sure funny-looking things."

"Like chicken, I guess, or quail. You know, sometimes I think everything tastes more or less like chicken."

Johnny studied Quentin, aware that he sometimes said things that he did not mean. "Well, that ain't so! Pork chops don't taste like chicken!"

"I guess that's right. I was just being silly."

The hunting was good that day. The bag soon contained five rabbits, and as Johnny picked up the last one, he said, "You know, since we got those rabbits to raise, these wild ones seem mighty scrawny. Not much meat on 'em."

"Well, I don't think Romeo would last long out here in these woods. A big hawk or a fox would get him. He's too fat to run."

"When are we goin' to eat one of those things, Quentin?"

It was one of the first times the boy had called him by his given name, and Quentin felt warmed by it. "I'll tell you what. The first one that gets big enough to eat, let's skin him and have him for supper."

Johnny suddenly laughed. "You may have to fight Pru to do that. She made pets of all of 'em."

"I guess that's right. Maybe we can do it without telling her."

"Not Pru. She knows every one of 'em by name. I think she'd know all the quail, too, except there are too many of 'em."

The two hunted until the sun was low in the sky, and Quentin said, "I guess we better head for the house, Johnny."

"Okay. But let's go over by Wilson's Creek. I seen the biggest deer tracks you ever seen in your life."

"Well, I guess they would be, since I don't remember seeing any before."

"You ain't never seen deer tracks?"

"I guess maybe when I was a boy. It's been a long time."

"Come on. We might get a shot at a buck."

Quentin followed as the boy led him through the woods. He seemed to know every square inch of it, and Quentin was totally lost. "I don't even know which way the house is, Johnny," he said.

"Why, it's over that way. Are you really that lost?"

"Guess so, but come to New York some time, and we'll see how you do in all those streets."

Johnny was interested in that, and as they walked along he pumped Quentin for more information on what it was like to live in the big city.

They passed through a huge grove of first-growth timber and finally came to a creek. Johnny put his head down and said, "Right along here is where I seen them tracks. They're all washed out though."

Johnny kept his head down, looking for tracks, and the two followed the meanderings of the small creek. It was quiet in the woods—until suddenly the silence was broken by a voice that caused Quentin to nearly jump out of his shoes.

"What are you people doin' on my land?"

Quentin whirled, as did Johnny, and they saw a man step out from behind a massive hickory tree. He had a rifle in his hand, and he was one of the strangest-looking men Quentin had ever seen. He was tall, a couple of inches over six feet, gaunt but strong-looking. He had gray hair that had been hacked off with a knife, and a beard that was gray and wild. At first Quentin thought he was a very old man until he saw the clear hazel eyes and the smoothness of his skin. His eyes were deep set and peered out from under bushy, russet-colored eyebrows that clashed with the gray hair. He had a prominent nose and a wide slash of a mouth practically hidden behind the beard. He was wearing a pair of dirty, patched overalls and a black slouch hat pulled down almost over his eyes. Quentin took in all of this in an instant—and then his eyes fixed on the rope around the man's neck. It was tied in a hangman's noose and cut off so that it reached halfway to his belt. Wondering about the noose, Quentin looked at the man's rifle. It was pointed in their general direction, his finger on the trigger.

Johnny said nothing. Quentin glanced at him and saw that his face was deathly pale. Quickly Quentin said, "We were just hunting. Didn't know we had gotten onto private property."

The man did not answer. He stood there, a silent, sinister figure as immovable as stone. It was unnatural—and there was a glitter in the strange, hazel eyes that Quentin did not like. He said quickly, "Come on, Johnny. Let's get off this gentleman's land." He took Johnny's arm and at once the boy turned, and the two of them walked quickly away. Quentin felt a tension in the middle of his back, almost as if he expected to take a bullet. He did not turn around, nor did Johnny, until they had retraced their steps and moved out of sight of the strange figure.

"Who was that, I wonder?" Quentin said. He looked back but could see nothing. "Kind of a scary sort of fella."

"That's Calendar."

"You know him?"

"I've seen him before. He comes to town once in a while, but he lives in a haunted house."

"What do you mean he lives in a haunted house? I don't believe in things like that."

Johnny seemed to be breathing more rapidly than usual, and he hurried along. "Believe what you want to," he said briefly.

"Did you see that rope around his neck?" Johnny didn't answer, and Quentin saw that the boy's face was drawn tight. *He's afraid of Calendar,* Quentin thought, and resolved to question Thomas about the man.

The two arrived home just as it was getting dark, and as they cleaned the rabbits Johnny had shot, the boy didn't say a word. Johnny hung them in the smokehouse, and then the two went inside. Thomas said, "You're just in time for supper. We got company."

The company was Riley Greer, who was already seated at the table. He nodded briefly, saying in a spare tone, "Hello, Larribee."

"Good evening. Sorry to be late," he said to Eden.

"It's all right. Sit down. It's on the table."

Thomas York asked the blessing and Quentin applied himself to the meal which included spoon bread, chicken and dumplings, and slices of mountain-cured ham. One of the things that Quentin had learned to love was Eden's pickled beets. He could never seem to get enough of them. She had also fixed two sweet potato pies, which was everybody's favorite.

Finally it was Thomas who said, "You fellows had good luck huntin'."

"Johnny did all the huntin'. I just carried the game," Quentin said.

Johnny looked up at his grandfather. "We seen old man Calendar out there. He told us to get off of his place."

"I've told you not to go over to that place!" Eden said sharply.

"Aw, Ma. There's some big deer over there," Johnny protested.

"Never mind that. You mind what I tell you."

"Who is this fellow Calendar?" Quentin asked curiously.

There was a strange silence, then Thomas said, "I guess you seen the rope around his neck."

"Yes. Gave me quite a shock." Quentin shrugged. "A hangman's noose. Why would a man wear that?"

"Well, Calendar's got a strange history."

"I don't like to hear about it," Eden said quickly. She seemed flustered and shook her head. "He's a sad, tragic man."

"Quentin needs to know about him." Thomas leaned back in his chair and picked up his mug of coffee. He sipped it, then began to speak in an even tone. "His name's Benjamin Calendar, but folks around here never call him anything but Calendar. His folks died when he was just a young man, and he had a bad temper. Hit a fellow once in a fight over a game of cards. But his temper wasn't what put that noose on his neck."

Quentin noticed that Johnny was leaning forward and that Pru also was listening intently. His eyes suddenly met Eden's, and he saw something there he could not explain.

"Well, anyhow, he hired a girl to work for him. She was a bound girl, of sorts, I reckon. Well, the girl run off. He caught up with her. He tied her by the wrist to his horse's tail and started home. Afterward he swore the girl stumbled against the horse and scared the critter. He claimed it threw him and drug her off and beat her to death on some rocks."

"Nobody would ever believe that story," Greer said. "He killed the girl and made it up."

"Maybe so," Thomas said. "Anyhow, he come up on trial and old Judge Carpenter was a strange judge. He didn't know much law and made up a lot as he went along. Since there wasn't any eyewitnesses he couldn't be sure, I guess, that the man had killed the girl. So what he done was he released Calendar sort of on probation, but told him he had to wear a hangman's noose around his neck and show himself in the court in Helena once every year."

"Was he a real judge?" Quentin said with shock. "I can't imagine that ruling wouldn't be overthrown."

"We don't do much lawin' around here. Calendar went on home and he knowed Judge Carpenter meant what he said. He started wearing that noose and he's worn it ever since. I was at the court last year when he come in to show himself. Old Judge Carpenter's dead, but he left strict orders to Judge Williams that if Calendar didn't come in, to send him to the pen."

Johnny said, "That house he lives in is haunted."

"Oh, don't be foolish, Johnny!" Eden said.

"It ain't foolish, Ma! Jimmy Hawkins has to pass Calendar's house after dark sometimes. He says you can hear a woman screamin' every night. And sometimes he says you can see her tied to the tail of a giant horse that's got fiery eyes and blowin' smoke out of his nostrils."

"Oh, Jimmy Hawkins has got too much imagination," Eden said. "Let's hear no more about this."

Riley said, "I don't believe in no haints, but all the same Calendar's a dangerous fellow. More than one hunter has had a shot put close to his head to warn him off of his place." He glowered and his lips made a thin line. "If he ever throws a shot at me, I'll put him where he won't trouble nobody else."

The story of Benjamin Calendar seemed to make everyone uneasy for the rest of the meal, and Quentin left as soon as supper was over and went to his room. He had fixed it up with a lantern and a chair, and was reading one of Thomas's books, *Gulliver's Travels,* a story he had always loved and now found more entertaining than when he was a boy. He glanced out the window from time to time; the lights were still on in the parlor, and he knew that the children had gone to bed. Riley's wagon was still tied outside. The thought of Eden and Riley sitting in the parlor together disturbed him, so he tried to lose himself in the story of the huge Gulliver and his adventures in Lilliput.

★　★　★

"What about that fellow?" Greer asked Eden as they sat on the parlor couch. "Are you going to get rid of him?"

"No. He's helping us a lot. It's the only hope I've got of keeping this farm clear."

Greer was dissatisfied with her answer. "What's this about people bringing their ailments to him? I heard Miss Simms came and asked him about her stomach trouble."

"He told her about the same thing Granny did. Said she ought to make some tea out of foxglove."

Greer shook his head. "I don't like it, Eden. He ain't no doctor."

"Neither is Granny."

"We know her, though. Anyways, I got to tell you again, Eden. People are talkin' about you keepin' a man here."

"I'm not keeping a man!" Eden protested.

Suddenly Greer rose and pulled Eden to her feet. His strength was so great she felt like a child. His arms went around her, and she put her hands on his chest. "Don't do that, Riley."

"It's time for us to marry. You got three kids and so have I." He pulled her forward, and she could not avoid his kiss. He was brutal and strong and bruised her lips and held her so tightly she could not move. Finally she pulled herself away and said, "Riley, I wish you wouldn't do that." He started toward her again, but she said, "No. It's time for you to go home."

Eden knew that Riley Greer did not like being challenged. He had raised his own children in such a way that they were afraid to open their mouths against him, and his wife had been cowed into utter silence by his fits of anger. Now he said suddenly, "You're not cold, Eden."

Eden stared at him. "What do you mean by that?"

"I mean you need a man. You think I don't see it in your eyes? I know when a woman wants a man."

Anger washed through Eden Breckenridge. "It's time for you to go. Good night!" She turned and marched toward the door. He followed her, and when he'd opened it, he stopped to stare at her. "There's something in you that likes men, Eden. Well, I like that well enough. My first wife was like a scared rabbit, but you'd give a man a challenge." He reached for her again, but she stepped back.

"Good night, Riley!" she said sharply.

He grinned at her suddenly. "You'll come around," he said. "I'll show you what a good man is like. That husband of yours, Will, he wasn't all that much of a man, I always thought."

Anger burned within Eden. She shoved Riley out the door and slammed it. Trembling, she went at once to her bedroom. By the time she had undressed, put on her gown, and brushed out her hair, she had calmed down. She turned down the lamp, slipped into bed, and pulled the quilts up over her. She lay still for a long time, wide awake. Riley Greer's accusation had come as a shock. *You're not cold. You need a man,* he had said.

The room was quiet except for the ticking of the clock in the hall. Eden's mind went back to her marriage to Will. It had not been the kind of marriage she had envisioned as a young girl. Will had been demanding and thoughtless, and he had not been faithful to her. She had known that there were other women but had never challenged him.

Pushing her head back into her goose-down pillow, Eden suddenly whispered aloud, "He's right. I do need a man." Somehow the thought that she had physical desires shamed her. She felt it was wrong. Women were not supposed to have desires. Only men. But from the time of her marriage to Will, she had known that the physical act of love was something she needed, and she had been ashamed of it.

Riley Greer, of course, wanted to marry her. He wouldn't be a bad-looking man if it weren't for his expression of hardness and brutality. But the thought of being his wife was repugnant to her, and she shoved it out of her mind. *I can't marry him! I can't.*

She lay still, asking God to calm her spirits. Then she slipped out of bed and knelt, burying her face in the feather mattress. "Oh, God, help me to keep this place!" It was her prayer day and night, along with the second part, "And help me to make a home for the children."

She knelt for a long time and, as was her habit, began thanking God for all of the blessings he had brought. As she did so, she thought of Quentin Larribee, and she whispered, "Thank you for sending this man to help us."

Finally Eden got back into bed and pulled the covers up, and this time, sleep seemed to come quickly. She had always found that prayer was the best thing for sleep, at least for her, and soon she drifted off into a warm darkness.

CHAPTER Eleven

A silvery, tinkling sound caught Hannah Larribee's ear, and she looked up from where she sat to the clock that sat on the mantel. She had grown so accustomed to the tune played by the clock that it had become part of her life. Now she rose and, picking up her crutch, limped over to the wall and studied the clock thoughtfully. It had been in the family as long as she could remember. The story was that her great-grandfather had brought it over from London. She smiled slightly at the tune still playing: "London Bridge Is Falling Down." When the chiming ceased, she picked up the bronze key that she always kept on the mantel, wound the clock, and turned to go back to her knitting. She had not yet reached her chair, however, when a knock at the door turned her around. "Who could that be?" she muttered. "Must be the coal delivery."

When she went to the door and opened it, however, she was surprised to see Irene Chambers. Hannah had not seen Irene since Quentin had left New York, although she had received two rather brief notes inviting her to come—invitations Hannah had found excuses to decline.

Irene spoke rather quickly, apparently flustered. "I'm sorry to interrupt you, Hannah, but I wanted to talk to you. Have I come at a bad time?"

"No," Hannah said quietly. "Come in."

As Irene entered, Hannah noted her thick fur coat and imagined the cost but said only, "Come in by the fire. It's cold out."

"Yes. It's going to snow again, I think." Irene stood irresolutely until Hannah said, "Take that chair over there. I think you'll find it comfortable."

"It is a nice chair," Irene said. "George II, isn't it?"

"I'm not sure. It's been in the family a long time. All of this furniture has. We saved all we could when we left the home place."

"You have very nice things, indeed! I'm glad you were able to save them." Irene stepped toward a round table with an English marquetry center, triple column support, and triple down-swept legs. "That's a beautiful table. I've never seen one like it."

"Quentin and I used to play all of our games on that table when we were growing up. He's very fond of it. May I offer you some tea?"

"Yes. That would be nice."

As Hannah heated the water and then brewed the tea, she was curious. She knew that Irene Chambers had not come by simply to exchange pleasantries. But Hannah also knew that Irene would make her point without Hannah's coaxing.

"Oh, that's a lovely tea set!" Irene said.

"Yes. It was my grandmother's. I think it came from Holland, although I'm not sure."

The business of pouring the tea and then sipping it took some time, during which Irene seemed to collect herself. "Have you heard from Quentin?" she asked.

"Why, yes. I hear regularly."

"I wish he'd write me more often. I haven't heard in a week. And when he does write he doesn't tell me anything."

Quentin had told Hannah all of the details of his life at the Breckenridge place. She wondered why he had not chosen to share this with the woman he was going to marry. "He seems to be well," she said, "and as I understand it he's able to help the Breckenridge family."

"That's what I wanted to talk to you about. He's certainly done more than anyone would expect." Irene twisted her handkerchief nervously. She leaned forward and said urgently, "He's missing out on his medical career, Hannah. And I'm unhappy with what's happening. I want to see him get ahead. I just can't understand him."

"He felt very strongly about helping Mrs. Breckenridge and her children."

"But he *has* helped them! Hannah, I think what you ought to do is write to him and ask him to come home."

Ah. So this was the purpose of Irene's visit. Hannah suspected that Irene had insisted to Quentin that he return and that Quentin had not agreed. Irene spoke urgently about Quentin's sense of duty, seeming to grow more emphatic as Hannah remained unmoved.

"He has a very strong sense of duty, Miss Chambers," Hannah said quietly when Irene finally fell silent. "He'll do what he thinks is right."

Irene flushed and said rather petulantly, "Well, I think he needs to show his duty to others."

"To others?"

"Why, yes!" Irene said quickly. "To you, certainly. In your condition you must need help."

Hannah felt a quick flare of anger, sure that Irene Chambers had never given a thought to Hannah's "condition" until she could use it to help her get what she wanted. She said quietly, "I have help, Miss Chambers."

"Help? What help? You have only Quentin."

"You're mistaken. I have the Lord Jesus Christ, and he is sufficient."

Irene blinked and her face reddened. "Well, that's all very well, but Quentin has a life and I think he's wasting it." She arose abruptly. "Thank you for the tea."

Irene left without another word, and Hannah picked up her tea and sipped it.

"She didn't get what she wanted," she said to herself. "I'm afraid Quentin's in for a bad time."

★   ★   ★

By the time Irene arrived at home, her annoyance had grown into a rage. She could not bear to be crossed, and it infuriated her that Hannah would not surrender to her demand. She went at once to her room and sat down at her dressing table. As she removed her earrings, she replayed the scene with Hannah in her mind, her anger growing with each retelling. *She's hateful! I can't see why Quentin pays her any mind.*

Finally she rose and went to find her mother. She found her in the small drawing room, knitting. "Mother, I'm going to write Quentin and demand that he come home."

Mrs. Chambers nodded firmly. "I think it's only fair," she said at once. "Your father and I have talked about it, and if you would like, we will write him also."

"No. I think if I put it strongly enough, Quentin will see things more clearly."

"Why don't you talk it over with Hannah?"

Irene stared at her mother and her lip curled. "She's a frustrated old maid, Mother. She's selfish to the bone."

Mrs. Chambers looked up, surprised at the anger in her daughter's voice. "You don't like her, do you?"

"She's bad for Quentin."

"That might be a problem—after you're married."

"No, it won't. We won't be seeing much of her." Irene smiled then, adding, "I've been thinking it might be better if we get a house just outside of town. Hannah won't make that trip too often."

November had come, bringing cold blasts to the Delta, and Quentin shivered slightly, trying to ignore the cold, as he opened the cage of the rabbit hutch. He grasped a thumping young buck by the loose skin of his neck and pulled him out. Shutting the cage, he locked it carefully, then held the glossy black rabbit high and said, "There, Granny. How will this do you for Thanksgiving?"

Granny Spears had heard that Pru had an ailment and had stopped by to see if she could be of help. Quentin had intercepted her and said, "Come along. I've got a present for you."

Granny reached out and pulled the silken ears of the rabbit. "He don't look like no wild rabbit, does he, Quentin?"

"Nope. Never saw a wild rabbit this fat."

"And you're sellin' these to the riverboats?"

"All we can grow. Need to get some more breeding stock," Quentin said. "Well, I'll dress this one out for you while you go take a look at Prudence."

"That's right thoughtful of you," Granny said. Instead of going inside, she followed Quentin to the back of the house and watched as he cleaned the rabbit. His hands, though red with cold, moved with confidence; he'd had plenty of experience skinning rabbits by this time, and only a few moments later he stood with the carcass in his hand. "I'll just wrap this up for you," he said, then grinned and added, "You need to put some meat on your bones."

"So do you! Skinny as a rail!" Suddenly she reached out and took Quentin's free hand. He was so surprised that he did not resist, and she held his hand in both of hers, running her fingers over the back of his hand, her eyes half shut. Finally she looked up and said, "Some people got somethin' in their hands, Larribee. I reckon you're one of them."

Granny released his hand and went into the house without another word. Quentin stared after her and shook his head. "Strange woman. But got more sense than most doctors I've known." He knew that some of her remedies were strictly folklore, but her use of herbs came from long years of study. Some of the herb remedies Granny Spears used were more effective than some of the expensive drugs doled out to patients.

Inside the house, he wrapped the rabbit in a piece of brown paper, and as he finished Thomas came into the room. He was dragging his right leg and seemed to be in some pain. "Better have Granny take a look," Quentin said.

"Well, Granny can do lots of things, but she can't do anything about a stroke. Quentin, we're running out of honey, and Granny wants some of it."

"She likes honey that much?"

Thomas scratched his short beard thoughtfully. "It's not that she likes it, though I suppose she does—most people are partial to sourwood honey. But she uses it a lot in her healin'."

"Is that right?"

"Yes. We all use it a lot around here. Make cough medicine out of it. You can combine it with wild cherry or white pine. Or you can put yellow root and moonshine whiskey in it and it makes a good stomach medicine. That's what she's givin' Pru now."

"I don't think what Pru has is too serious, but I'm glad Granny came by."

York was still thinking about Granny's doctoring. "She mixes it with flaxseed for whoopin' cough. Or you can put sage and vinegar in it for coughs or sore throats."

"She told me she even uses it for burns."

"Yep. Not as good as some of her other remedies. But Granny's partial to sourwood, and we're plumb out." York looked down at his weakened arm and said, "I need to rob one of the begums, but I ain't up to it. Would you give me a hand?"

"Sure, Thomas. I'd do it myself, but I'm not quite sure how to handle it yet."

"I'll do the tellin', and you do the honey gatherin'."

The two men stepped outside in heavy coats. The bees were kept fifty yards from the house. Thomas used the old method of begum—a twenty-four-inch section of a hollow black gum tree. The hollow sections of the tree were pierced with two sticks run horizontally through the gum at right angles. These sticks acted as supports from which the bees would suspend their brood combs, instinctively saving the top half of the hive for their honeycombs, which they would hang from the plank lid over the top of the gum.

Thomas had brought a long, thin knife out and handed it now to Quentin, who took it rather gingerly. Actually he was afraid of bees, but he didn't want Thomas to know it. "What do I do?" he asked nervously.

"I'll pick up the top, and you just slide that knife into the crack. The comb will come right off, and you put it in this bucket."

Quentin held the knife ready, and when Thomas lifted the lid he did as instructed. The bees began swarming around him, making a zinging noise that made Quentin flinch. But all went well until he had the bucket filled—and then he felt a sharp pain close to his right eye like a hot needle being pushed into it. He managed to hold onto the bucket but slapped at the bee wildly.

"Reckon we can get away now," Thomas grinned. He replaced the lid to the begum and turned to go. Quentin followed him willingly. The sting had got him right in the corner of the eye, and it was very painful.

As they moved toward the house, they saw Johnny standing, watching. "Did they get you bad, Quentin?" he asked anxiously.

"Just one, but it's in a bad place."

"I won't never get near them bees!" Johnny declared. "I got stung all over one time." Quentin heard something in Johnny's voice he hadn't heard before—respect. "You better go in and get Granny to put somethin' on it."

By the time the three got inside, Quentin's eye was swollen almost shut.

"Quentin took a sting, Granny. You better see to him," Johnny said.

Granny came over and looked up at Quentin's eye. "Here, you set right down. I'll put somethin' on it for you."

Quentin sat down shakily. He knew that some people were deathly allergic to bees; they could go into shock, and some had even died. He had been stung as a boy, and it had affected him strongly. The room seemed to be going around, and he closed his eyes and leaned back. He felt a cool pressure on his forehead and heard Eden's voice say, "Oh, I'm so sorry, Quentin! Does it hurt?"

"Not bad."

Quentin looked up at her out of his good eye and tried to grin. "Kind of silly. A grown man gettin' put down by one bee sting."

"It affects some that way. Will couldn't stand to get stung either. He'd never have anything to do with Pa's bees."

Quentin sat quietly as she held the cool cloth to his forehead. She was leaning over, and as always he could smell a faint scent of jasmine. Through his half-shut good eye he saw that her skin was as clear as a young girl's.

Finally he reached up and took the cloth as the dizziness passed. "Guess I'm okay," he said.

"Granny's fixin' you up some kind of ointment. Just sit there."

Granny came in shortly with a small saucer. "Here, let me smear some of this on that sting."

"Ow!" Quentin protested. "What's in that anyway?"

"Never you mind. It'll take the swellin' out," Granny said. She looked down at him and nodded. "I've got to be goin'. Thanks for the rabbit."

"What about Pru?" Quentin asked.

"Nothin' serious. Probably ate somethin' that didn't agree with her. I'll come back and see her tomorrow."

"Thank you, Granny," Eden said.

"Don't forget your rabbit," Quentin called out.

Granny waited until Eden had produced the rabbit, then said, "Thankee, Quentin. You keep an eye on that youngun now. You got an eye for such things."

When she was gone, Quentin touched the tender, swollen area near his eye and said, "I think a lot of Granny."

"She takes to you, too," Eden said. She lifted her eyebrows and shook her head slightly. "She doesn't take to most folks."

"Well, she takes pity on a poor Yankee, I guess."

"I don't think so," Eden murmured. "Well, you just sit there until you're over bein' dizzy. We'll have fresh sourwood honey and biscuits for supper."

★　★　★

The bee sting did not trouble Quentin. Whatever Granny had put into the potion took the pain away, and he made a mental note to ask her what she had used.

The supper was even better than usual. They had quail, and all of them had learned to relish the tender, crisp, small birds.

"Well, no matter what, we'll always have quail," Thomas said as he crunched on a small portion of the golden-fried bird. "Shore is easier than goin' out and shootin' the varmints."

"Not as much fun though," Johnny put in. "I'd rather hunt 'em."

"These we're raising are a lot plumper than the wild birds," Eden said, tasting a bite carefully. "And they have a different taste to them."

After dinner, Quentin went to sit in the parlor. It had become a habit with him. At these times, he felt almost a member of the family. Tonight, he was reading a book he had bought in Helena on his last visit, a novel by James Fenimore Cooper. He heard a noise and looked up to see Pru standing in the doorway, wearing her nightgown and clutching the ratty old blanket she could not sleep without. Her thumb was popped into her mouth.

"Why, Pru! What are you doing out of bed?"

"My tummy hurts."

"Well, come over here and sit beside me."

At once Prudence came and sat down, leaning against Quentin. She curled up and put her head against his chest.

"Why don't you let me get you a new blanket, Pru? That one's about worn out."

"No. I like this one."

"All right. Old things are usually best, I think."

He touched her forehead and smoothed her hair back. She still had a fever. It was a puzzling sort of sickness, and it troubled him. He knew it troubled Granny, too, although she had not really said so.

He sat quietly stroking Prudence's blonde hair, marveling at how fine and silky it was. He had had little to do with children since he and Hannah had raised their brother and sisters. And even then, Hannah had done most of it. Prudence seemed light, her bones like a bird's almost. Ordinarily she was a cheerful child, chipper and always laughing, and the quietness that was in her troubled him. He well knew the diseases that could come to blot out a child's life, and he found himself experiencing a fear almost as if he were a father.

"My tummy hurts."

Quentin shifted the child around and then put his hand on her stomach. "Right there?"

"Yes. It hurts real bad."

Quentin prayed quietly, his hand on her stomach.

"That feels good, Quentin," Pru said. "It don't hurt much anymore."

"Is that right? I'm glad."

"Your hand is so warm," she said drowsily.

Quentin sat quietly and the child dropped off to sleep. Just as she did, she said, "It's all gone now. It don't hurt anymore."

Quentin did not move. He kept his hand on the child's stomach and held her in the crook of his arm. "Thank you, Lord," he murmured. "You are a great God, and you heal all of our diseases." His favorite Scripture had been, for years, the 103rd Psalm. Especially the first five verses. Hannah had loved these verses before him; he had learned their appreciation from her, and he recited them each morning as he arose, either silently or aloud. Now looking down into the face of the sleeping girl, he whispered the old familiar words:

> "Bless the LORD, O my soul: and all that is within me, bless
>   his holy name.
> Bless the LORD, O my soul, and forget not all his benefits:
> who forgiveth all thine iniquities; who healeth all thy diseases;
> who redeemeth thy life from destruction; who crowneth thee with
>   lovingkindness and tender mercies,
> who satisfieth thy mouth with good things; so that thy youth is
>   renewed like the eagle's."

In the doorway, Eden stood listening, watching, studying the face of Quentin Larribee. She had known that he was a man close to God, for she had watched Quentin's face in church. A sort of exultation lit his features during the worship service. Now she studied the tall man holding her child. She was puzzled by what she had seen. From the time Quentin had reset the dislocated shoulder of Trumbo Jones, it had been clear to her that he had some knowledge of medicine. But what she had just seen had little to do with medicine. Granny had prescribed for Pru a potion that had usually been effective with stomachaches and colic, but it had not been effective this time, and Eden had been more worried than she had shown about Prudence. She, too, had been praying with all her power for the child's recovery. But just now, she had heard Prudence's sleepy whisper, and Eden had known that, somehow, Quentin Larribee had been instrumental in taking away Pru's pain. She could not understand it. She had heard of men and women who had gone about proclaiming themselves healers sent from God, but Quentin did not seem to be this sort. There was a simplicity in the man that she admired—indeed, she reluctantly admitted to herself, her feelings had gone beyond admiration. As she stood there silently, she wondered, *What sort of man is this that has come into our lives?*

The next morning Prudence was completely well. Her grand-father said, "Well, I guess it was just a stomachache."

Prudence said, "It was Quentin. He made me all well, Grandpa."

"Is that right? Well, it's good to have a man with talent on the place." He looked up at Eden, who was standing beside Pru, and some communication passed between the two of them. Eden said nothing of what she had seen the night before, but as she went about her housework that morning, she could not get the scene out of her mind. She did not see Quentin that day except briefly at mealtimes. After supper, she sat on the front porch while her father read stories to Stuart and Prudence. Johnny was out setting up trotlines on the river with some of his friends.

A quietness hung over the land. The bite of winter was sharp in the air, and she stood on the front porch looking across to the lantern light in Quentin's window. Long thoughts came to her then, and she murmured, "He's made no advances at all—which is strange."

Eden Breckenridge knew that she was an attractive woman. Since her husband's death, almost every man she had met had, by word or by some sign, indicated a romantic interest in her. She had grown so accustomed to it that her defenses stayed up around any man. She recalled that, when Quentin first came to their home, she had, without thinking about it, put up those same defenses, expecting that sooner or later he would try to touch her, or say something with a veiled meaning.

Now she shifted uncomfortably, wondering, *Why hasn't he made any attempts, like other men? Maybe he doesn't find me attractive.*

This thought piqued her. She sat for a moment, then drawing her coat around her, crossed the yard toward the barn. She knocked on Quentin's door; there was a sound of someone moving, and then the door opened. "Why, Eden!"

"Hello, Quentin. Are you busy?"

"No. Just reading. Come in." He shut the door and said, "Take a seat by the stove there." He had rigged up a small wood-burning stove, and now it glowed a cherry red. "Feels good in this weather. I think we're going to have a bad winter. According to Granny, anyway."

"If Granny says so," Eden said as she took a seat, "it must be so."

Quentin sat down rather nervously. It was the first time Eden had been in his room since he had come there as a sick man. Now he was puzzled and asked, "Is Pru all right?"

"Oh, she's fine. That's one of the things I wanted to talk to you about."

"About Pru?"

"What did you do to her, Quentin?" she asked quietly. Her large eyes were fixed on him, and she leaned forward slightly. "She says you just put your hands on her stomach and it got well."

"Oh, I don't know, Eden!" Quentin seemed embarrassed, and he put her off with a half laugh. "I just prayed for her, and the Lord did the healing."

"I was standing in the doorway while you were praying for her. She said your hand felt warm. And then you quoted a Scripture."

"Well, I've always liked that Scripture. Don't know of any promises any better than that. Do you know it?"

"I know it's in the Psalms."

"The 103rd psalm. My sister, Hannah, taught me to lean on it a long time ago."

"Lean on it? How's that?"

"Well, it says, 'Bless the LORD, O my soul, and forget not all his benefits.' And then it gives a whole list of benefits. The first one is, 'Who forgiveth all thine iniquities.' That's salvation, I reckon. Lord knows I needed it. And the second one is, 'Who healeth all thy diseases.' I've always hung onto that. Hannah and I had quite a time with a sick brother and sisters. Not much money for doctors—so we had to send for Doctor Jesus, as Hannah always said." He smiled, and although he was not a handsome man, his lips made a pleasant shape. His teeth were good. And though he had been rather pale when he first came, he had tanned considerably since then and now looked much stronger.

"I like that," Eden said. "And it's marvelous, the way you're able to help people like this. You ought to become a doctor."

As she spoke these words, Eden saw something cross Quentin's face and knew that she had touched on something inside the man. "Have I said something wrong?"

"Oh, no. Of course not. I'm glad Prudence is better. She's a sweet child. You have fine children, Eden. I know you're very proud of them."

"Yes, I am."

Eden grew more and more puzzled as they sat. She knew that she should not have such feelings about this man she hardly knew, and a Yankee to boot. She felt embarrassment, too, knowing that she had come to his room to see whether he had similar feelings for her, but he said nothing that he could not have said in front of her father, nor had he made any attempt to come closer to her. Finally she stood, and he rose with her. "I guess I'd better go."

Quentin moved to the door and stood holding it. Eden took a step forward and then did something she had never done in her entire life. She stepped close enough to brush against Quentin, knowing that such a gesture would have aroused any other man. She looked up into his eyes and said, "I want you to know, Quentin, how much I appreciate all you've done. You've helped me more than any man ever has."

It was a strange moment for Quentin. He was intensely aware of Eden as she stood so close she was almost touching him. She *had* touched him, and his skin seemed to burn where the soft pressure of her body had swept across him. Her presence stirred hungers in him that suddenly erupted with an urgency and power he had never known. He was intensely aware that this woman was different, at least for him, from all other women. And now by the yellow light of his lantern, Quentin saw the ripe turn of her lips, the self-possessed curve of her mouth. He could not help but notice her smooth shape within her clothing, and it stirred him. He had long been aware of the loveliness of her body—the smooth roundness of her shoulders, the way she was so slender and yet so round and strong at the same time. She was shapely in a way that would strike through the defenses of any man, and now his throat was so full he could not speak. As she looked up at him, he saw that she had drawn away the curtain of reserve and that there was something almost like a challenge in her eyes. She was a complex and striking woman with a great degree of vitality and imagination—qualities that, until this moment, she had held under careful restraint around Quentin. On impulse, without conscious thought, he reached out and took her shoulders. She swayed toward him, and he said huskily, "You're so beautiful, Eden."

These were the words Eden had wanted to hear, the reason she had come to this room tonight. She knew this, and it shocked her—for she had never deliberately tried to elicit such words from any man. Will had never spoken of her beauty after they were married, although he had often praised it before. She was aware of Quentin's hands on her arms—and aware, too, that although she had been in control when she came into his room, she was not in control of what might happen now, and perhaps not even in control of herself. She had been lonelier than she had realized; the heavy responsibilities of raising her children alone and tending the farm had created in her a need for some sort of love, some sort of assurance. She raised her head and did not speak.

One moment Quentin was struggling to understand what he was feeling, and how he should respond. The next moment he leaned forward and kissed her. Her lips were soft and vulnerable and unlike anything he had ever felt before. He felt the lightly clinging touch of her hands behind his shoulders. She steadied herself and did not pull away.

For a moment they stood with something whirling rashly between them that swayed both of them with violent compulsions. For Quentin it was like a tempest howling through him.

And then Eden suddenly stepped back and color stained her cheeks. The moment was broken. She held him with a strange glance, then whispered, "I shouldn't have come here."

Quentin could not speak for a moment. He watched her face change rapidly. "I'm sorry," he said at last. "I shouldn't have done that. I didn't mean to take advantage."

Knowing that she had provoked him, Eden felt ashamed. "It's all right, Quentin. It's not your fault. Everyone's entitled to an accident. I guess I've been so tired." Then, knowing that she could say nothing else that would have meaning, she turned and left, saying, "Good night."

"Good night, Eden."

As she moved through the cold night air, Eden found that she was trembling. She had deliberately provoked Quentin Larribee; the kiss was her doing and not his. *What's the matter with me?* she cried out in her spirit.

Slowly and quietly closing his door and leaning against it, Quentin knew that he would not forget that kiss—not soon, and perhaps not ever. He had little experience with women, but he knew that that brief encounter with Eden Breckenridge had changed him. He had always regarded the prospect of life with Irene with a mixture of resignation to the inevitable and concern that he would not measure up to her expectations. Now he wondered what it would be like to spend a lifetime with a woman who stirred him as this one had. Outside, the wind began to rise with a keening whine, causing the branches of the hickory tree outside to claw at his window. It scratched almost like a wild beast trying to enter. Quentin stepped unconsciously to the center of the room and stood, unable to put the thought of Eden out of his mind.

CHAPTER *Twelve*

*O*tis Sanderson signed his name to the check with a flourish, then blew on it before looking up. Finally he lifted his eyes and said with approval, "This is the biggest check you've gotten so far, Eden. Things are going well. I'm glad to see it."

He was also glad to see the thrill in Eden's eyes when she saw the amount. "It'll be enough to make a payment on the place," she said quietly.

"Quentin didn't come in today with you," he said.

"He's building a new quail run. The other one was getting too small."

Leaning back in his chair, Sanderson ran his hand over his remaining hair and said thoughtfully, "People are beginning to open up to Quentin. It's a bit hard for some to accept a Yankee, but he's found some good friends here." A frown came to his face briefly. "Of course, some are never going to quit fighting that war. Till they go to their grave, they'll hate everybody that wore a blue uniform."

"I hope that will change, Otis."

Sanderson's eyes narrowed as he studied the woman in front of him. She was wearing a blue dress that he had never seen before; he expected that it was new—perhaps the first new one she had had since before the war. Her eyes seemed troubled, and he said gently, "Didn't mean anything, Eden. It's just the way things are."

"He's been such a help to us, Otis. We would have gone under like so many others if Quentin hadn't come."

"I think he's a good man and you're right. I don't know your business, but I suspect you had gone about as far as you could go."

Eden looked thoughtful for a moment or two, then seemed to push those thoughts aside briskly and rose. "I've got to be going. I've got to go to the bank." She smiled and said, "It always gives me pleasure to make the payment. The bankers always seem so surprised when anyone is able to make a payment these days."

"I'll see you in church then, Eden. We've got a guest speaker coming. I understand he's a humdinger."

Rising, Sanderson escorted Eden down the narrow corridors of goods piled almost to the ceiling. When they reached the front door, he saw Doctor Vance coming toward them. Vance was a large man, tall and heavy, who walked with a shambling gait. His gray hair and beard were untrimmed, and remnants of his breakfast or, perhaps, even yesterday's breakfast had found a home not only on his beard but on his vest. He had served in the Army of the Tennessee as a staff surgeon, and the bitterness that had seeped into him during those terrible years was still a shadow in his eyes. He stepped aside and touched his hat mumbling, "Mornin', Miss Breckenridge."

"Good morning, Doctor," Eden smiled and moved on out into the street.

Vance stood watching her for a moment, then swung around to face Sanderson. "What do you know about that fellow Larribee that's living out at the Breckenridge place, Otis?"

Sanderson had already heard of Doctor Vance's unhappiness over Quentin Larribee. He shrugged his thin shoulders, saying, "A good man from all I know, Doctor. He's been a godsend to Eden and her family. They'd have lost their place if it hadn't been for him coming along with this scheme to raise game for the riverboats."

"That's going well for them, is it?"

"Very well indeed!"

"Well, I'm glad to hear that. I always felt for Eden. She had a tough life married to that husband of hers. He was a rough fellow."

Sanderson did not answer, for he knew Edward Vance well enough to know that more was coming. He stood waiting. Finally Vance scowled. "What bothers me is this doctoring this fellow is doing."

"Why, it's just minor things. I don't think there's any problem."

"That's what you think! That's the way people get killed. When amateurs jump in and start treating folks."

"I never heard you say anything about Granny Spears."

Vance clawed at his beard with an irritated motion. "She just gives mostly herb potions. Can't do much damage there. But this fellow Larribee sewed up the Robertson boy when he cut his leg open."

"I didn't hear about that. They didn't bring him in to a doctor?"

"Well, they were way out in the woods and couldn't get to town. The way I heard it, he was bleedin' pretty bad. They took him to the Breckenridge place, and Larribee sewed him up."

"Did you see the job he did?"

Unwillingly Vance nodded. His mouth was a thin, white line. "It was all right," he admitted finally. "But who knows what he'll be doing next. Taking out an appendix maybe."

"Oh, I don't think he'd go that far."

Edward Vance was a good doctor, rough from his years of service with the Confederate Army. He was also an inveterate gossip, and now his eyes narrowed, and he said in a lower tone, "Otis, what about this fellow living out there? You think Eden's interested in him? She hasn't been a widow long, you know."

"I wouldn't know about that, Doctor."

"Course Riley Greer's planning to marry her. He has for a long time."

Otis said quietly, "She'll never marry him, Doctor. You can bet on that."

After the doctor made his purchase and left, Sanderson went home for lunch. He lived down the street in a white frame house, and his wife, Edna, listened as he told her about his day. He mentioned Doctor Vance's interest in Larribee and ended by saying, "I worry about Eden. She might up and marry Riley Greer."

"No, I don't think so." Edna Sanderson was a short, heavyset woman with snapping black eyes and a no-nonsense tone of voice. She thought for a moment, then shook her head. "Eden's a smart woman. She had a hard time with her first man. Greer's a lot like him."

"I never thought about that."

"Well, Will Breckenridge had a bit more grace about him, but deep down he wasn't a kind man. That's what Eden needs—kindness. And she won't get it from Riley Greer. Mark my words."

"What about this Larribee? You think she might be interested in him?"

"I can't say. She won't talk about it, but he's a Yankee and that's against him."

The two spoke quietly for a time, and then Sanderson said, "I wonder how many widows there are in the South right now looking for a man."

"Not just the South. The war took so many men. It turned this country upside down," Edna said. "Eden Breckenridge is just one more casualty."

*   *   *

Quentin pulled off his heavy wool coat. The winter sky was hard, but a pale sun threw some warmth over the earth. The worst months of winter had been bitter, but it seemed that the days were growing milder. Quentin had come out to dig postholes and build another shed for the pheasants to nest in, and now he'd grown warm enough to work in his shirtsleeves. He sawed a board, watching the golden dust drop on the earth and thought how, when he had first come to the farm, he had been awkward, unable even to saw a straight line. Now, with pride, he sawed the board accurately, then nailed it in place. He paused long enough to take a drink of water from the jug he had brought with him, then leaned back against a post set in the ground—one corner of the pheasant run he was working on. He watched the birds, admiring the sheen of their feathers and thinking, not for the first time, *They're such pretty critters. It's a shame to kill 'em and eat 'em. Of course, I guess you could say the same thing about a deer.* He began working again, but he suddenly stopped in the middle of hammering a nail and thought with some surprise, *I've had more peace since I've been in this place than I've had all my life. I guess Hannah and I had things so tough I didn't have time to know what it was like just to slow down and enjoy life.*

The thought disturbed him, making him feel disloyal. Letters had come regularly from Irene, urging him to return, and it had become more and more difficult for him to write back. He had said all he knew to say.

At this stage of their game-raising operation, it would be possible for Eden to hire a man to replace him. She had become as involved as Quentin in the sale of their animals, and Johnny knew as much about the feeding and the care of the birds and the rabbits as Quentin did. Otis Sanderson was a fair and just man, and Quentin knew that Otis would see to it that Eden was not cheated in business.

More than once he had muttered, "It's time to go." But he had not been able to bring himself to do it. He had settled into the routine here, and it fitted him. He got up in the morning and ate breakfast with the family, then worked on building more runs or hutches, then carried the game to Helena. The evenings were slow and leisurely, and he looked forward to hunting with Johnny, who seemed now to accept him—although he didn't show it as freely as the younger children did, perhaps feeling that it was unmanly. He had become so fond of Prudence and of Stuart that he knew there would be a wrenching dislocation in all of them when he left.

Johnny emerged from the house and nearly flew toward Quentin—running, as young boys will, not because there was anything to hurry for but just out of the exuberance of youth. Quentin smiled as the boy pulled up next to him and brushed his red hair out from his forehead. "Ma says we're going to town. We're going to celebrate."

"Celebrate what?"

Johnny scratched his head and shrugged his shoulders. "There's a social at the church. We're all going."

"Well, that'll be good," Quentin said.

Johnny immediately began working alongside him without being asked, talking unself-consciously about a new rifle he was saving up for and what all he would do with it when he got it.

Quentin was surprised when suddenly Johnny, after driving a nail with firm blows, stopped and turned to face him. There was something in the boy's attitude that captured Quentin's full attention, and he waited until Johnny said rather awkwardly, "Hey, Quentin. You know . . ."

Quentin waited, but Johnny seemed unable to get it out, whatever it was. "What is it, Johnny?" he asked gently.

"Well, shoot. It's just—I reckon we'd have lost this place if it wasn't for you." Johnny seemed relieved now that the words were out. "I guess I've wanted to tell you—well, I didn't like you when you came. Your bein' a Yankee and all. But I was real scared and so was Ma. We didn't know what we were going to do. But now with all this money coming in from the quail, the rabbits, and the pheasants . . . why, we're going to make it." He looked down at the ground and dug his toe in the dirt. When he looked up his eyes were glowing, and he said, "I guess I ain't never said thank you for that." He put his hand out suddenly, and Quentin took it. It was hard and firm and strong, and Quentin felt a sudden joy at the admission of the young boy.

"I'm glad I was able to help, Johnny."

It was a strange moment and one that neither knew how to handle very well. Quentin laughed shortly and made an arch with the saw. "You know," he said, "you've made this business go, Johnny. You can handle it without me now."

Johnny looked up, alert. He studied Larribee for a moment and then said anxiously, "You ain't goin' nowhere, are you?"

The moment had come. "Well, someday I will."

Johnny did not answer.

Later that day, when he was alone with his mother, Johnny said, "Quentin says he's gonna have to go sometime."

Eden felt a sudden and strange hollowness in her chest. "When did he say that?" she said.

"This afternoon when we were out building the new pheasant house."

Eden turned to Johnny. "What brought that on?"

"I don't know, Ma. We were just talkin' and I—well, I thanked him for all he had done. And he said that I could do it as well as he could. Keep things going."

"Is that all he said?"

"I said, 'You ain't goin', are you, Quentin?' And he said, 'Someday I will.'"

Eden tried not to let Johnny see the shock she felt. "Oh, he probably won't go anywhere," she said rather faintly.

Johnny stood looking carefully at Eden, probably trying to gauge her reaction, then turned and left the room.

Eden continued with her work, but her mind was elsewhere. She had never forgotten Quentin's kiss, or the touch of his hands, and although neither of them had spoken of it, there was a shared bond between them now that could be neither denied nor erased. How different it would be without him on the place! More than once as they sat in the parlor or walked through the woods at night, the thought had come to Eden that, except for physical intimacy, they had become a great deal like husband and wife. They talked over the aspects of the business, the ailments and problems of the children. She could not hide from herself that she loved the man, and that she had been waiting for him to speak. It puzzled her that he had not, and now she could not avoid the possibility that she might be losing him.

★ ★ ★

The social at church was a success. Thomas, who disliked such things, had stayed home with Stuart, but Quentin had taken the rest of the family. It had been a good time for him, and he had realized suddenly that despite the fact that some still despised him for being born in the North, he had made many friends. It came as a shock to him to realize that he probably had more friends in Helena, Arkansas, than he had in New York City. He *knew* many people in the city, but he had not grown close to many.

On the trip home, Quentin and Eden were silent. Johnny rattled on, as did Prudence, as usual, but when they arrived at the farm they found Thomas sitting on the porch. "Stuart went to sleep," he announced. "He couldn't stay up any longer. I guess I'll go myself. Was it a good social?"

"Oh, it was fine!" Eden smiled. "I wish you could have been there, Pa."

"Maybe next time."

Eden had the usual battle getting Johnny to bed, and he went protesting that it was too early a bedtime for anything except chickens. Eden said firmly, "You've got more sense than a chicken, I do declare! Now go to bed! You too, Prudence."

Quentin slapped Johnny on the shoulder and said, "Mind your ma, boy. That's the way to grow up healthy."

"I bet you didn't always mind your ma," Johnny complained.

"Well, as a matter of fact, I did mostly," Quentin said, and memory swept back over him. "She was a fine woman, and I missed her when I lost her."

His words seemed to reach Johnny. He bit his lip. "Okay. I'm going. Good night, Ma." He kissed her, which was unusual. He had grown beyond the age at which boys like to kiss mothers, and now Eden's eyes widened in surprise. She smiled and kissed him on the cheek. "Good night, son."

Prudence was very sleepy, but she insisted that Quentin put her to bed and tell her a story. It had become a ritual they both enjoyed.

Eden listened to the sound of Quentin's voice coming from Pru's bedroom. When he came out he was smiling.

"What's so funny?" she asked.

"I make up the wildest stories I can think of and she takes them all seriously. They can't get too wild for her. She's got quite an imagination."

"Come along. I made coffee and there's some cake left."

The two sat in the kitchen. Once again, Eden felt the strange sensation of familiar intimacy. There was a peacefulness about sitting quietly with him that she liked, and as they talked, she for some reason found herself talking about her marriage. She had said little about William Breckenridge to Quentin, and now she communicated more through her attitude, her tone of voice, than through her words. Quentin did not take his eyes from her as she spoke.

"He wasn't cruel or unkind or anything like that. But he was not—thoughtful. And he never showed much affection to the children."

"Or to you either, I suspect."

Eden suddenly stared at him. "Why do you say that, Quentin?"

"Because if a man has affection for one person, he'll usually have it for others."

"I don't want to be critical. He was a good provider. We just weren't well suited, I suppose, in some ways."

The silence seemed to thicken then and filled the room. Finally she got up, walked to the window, and stared out. She folded her arms across her breasts and said, "I think I had such high expectations about marriage. Ever since I was a little girl I thought about what it would be like to have a husband and a home and children. It was about all I ever thought about, Quentin."

Quentin rose and walked over to stand beside her. He saw that the moon was a thin sliver, but the stars spangled the sky. "I don't think it's a bad thing to bring high expectations to a marriage."

"Maybe it is. A person can be so disappointed when things don't work out."

Quentin understood a little bit more about this woman. She was a loving woman, he knew that. He had not forgotten their kiss either, or how it had affected him. *She craves love,* he thought, *and her husband didn't give it to her. He didn't speak it, perhaps, so there's a sadness in her.*

She stood silently for a time and then turned to face him. "After Will died I was terrified, Quentin. I was afraid we'd lose this place. I still have bad dreams about that sometimes."

"Why, it'll be all right, Eden." Quentin reached out and touched her shoulders. "You won't lose this place."

His touch was light, but he felt her body stir subtly in response. She looked up, and he saw diamonds glittering in her eyes. Tears swam there, and he was shocked. Her lips trembled, and she said, "If you hadn't come, Quentin, I'd have been lost. All of us would. How can I ever thank you for that?"

This is what Quentin had come for, to help this woman and her family. But he was not thinking of that now. He was thinking of how beautiful she was. He felt strangely light-headed, and at the same time the blood was pounding through his veins, for she stirred him as no woman had. He already knew she had the power to do that. The effect of that first kiss was still working in him, pushing him on. It had been weeks ago now, but he had not been able to put it out of his mind, and he suspected that she had not either. He felt as if they were on the edge of a great mystery. He looked into her eyes, helpless. She called his name, whispering it, and her nearness sharpened all his long-felt hungers. He said hoarsely, "You know how to stir a man, Eden." He put his arms around her and kissed her, but it was a gentle, easy kiss. He held himself back, wanting to comfort her, knowing that she was sad. Despite his restraint, there was a warning bell ringing, and he knew that he should not be touching this woman. He had not come here for this, and now he was confused.

Eden saw his confusion. She put her arms around him and leaned her head against his chest. "You're a gentle man, Quentin." She was silent for a moment, then he barely heard her say, "I didn't know what that was like." She lifted her head then and put her hand on his cheek. The silence rested on both of them. She leaned against him, the fullness of her body touching him and stirring him, and then she said, "I never thought I could love a man again—but I have a heart for you."

Her words rocked Quentin to the bone. He was aware of the faint odor of lilac, of the pressure of the curves of her body, womanly and firm against his chest. He was aware of his own desires stirring within him, but then a jarring thought interrupted: of Irene, and his commitment to her. And then another: *Even if I were to love Eden, the specter of her husband, the man I killed, will always stand between us.*

Not knowing how to extricate himself, he said quietly, "I expect that's just gratitude, but you don't need to feel that grateful. I know you can't help it. That's the kind of woman you are." He was aware that what he said made little sense; he was babbling.

Eden looked up at him with a shock. She had just confessed that she loved him, and she had expected some response from him—but not this. Something was wrong, and she did not know what it was. Before she could even speak, he straightened up and said, "Good night, Eden." His voice was tight, it seemed, and he could not meet her eyes. Whirling, he rushed from the room, leaving her standing, watching him.

A heaviness washed over Eden. She thought, *He doesn't love me.* It was a painful thought. She had always known that Will

Breckenridge had not loved her—at least not as she wanted to be loved. Now, after all this time, she had thought she saw love in Quentin's eyes, the kind of love she had always dreamed of. She had reached out for it—and found that it was not there. A sob caught in her throat, and she felt more alone and lost than she had ever felt before. She stood fighting the tears that rose in her eyes, and a grief filled her, black and dark and heavy, that she did not think she could bear.

★

★

★

CHAPTER
Thirteen

think I'll go over to Lexa. I hear that the feed mill over there is a lot cheaper than Thomasons."

Eden had been ironing, and now she lifted the black iron and spat on it, watching the spittle sizzle. Without looking up, she began to smooth the wrinkles out of one of her father's shirts. "All right," she said briefly. The iron moved smoothly over the material, and the wrinkles disappeared into a smooth, shiny surface.

Quentin stood awkwardly in the doorway watching her. It had been three days since the social, and Quentin had never before known such awkwardness. He could not get her words out of his mind, *I never thought I could love a man—but I have a heart for you.* Now, as he stood ill at ease before her, he seemed to hear them spoken again. Her face was half turned away, but he could see that her expression was tense. He had been unable to think of anything to say that could make things any different. Every night he had racked his brain trying to think of a way out of the situation, but he could not. He turned away. "I'll be back late this afternoon."

Eden did not answer, but as he left she lifted the iron and stared out the window. She watched as he climbed into the wagon, spoke to the team, and then drove off. A strange heaviness had come over her, and the pleasure she had found by overcoming her financial burden seemed overshadowed by it. Her father had asked her that very morning, "What's wrong, Eden? You seem depressed." She had denied it and forced a smile, but now as she stood watching the wagon and team disappear down the road, she knew that something had come into her life that would not change.

She replaced the iron over the grate on the hot coals, picked up the spare, and began ironing again. As she worked, she tried to drive thoughts of the scene between Quentin and herself out of her mind, but they would not leave. She could not forget the tenderness she had felt toward him, nor the gentleness he had showed toward her. She had always been a sensitive woman, and she was aware that she needed love and assurance more than most women. It troubled her that, among the couples she knew, marriage slowly deteriorated into an almost businesslike affair. It was strange to her that a love that was so warm and vibrant and glowing and consumed a woman's whole heart before marriage and during the first years could die down until, apparently for some, nothing was left but ashes. She had determined that this would never happen to her, and she had worked hard at her marriage with Will. He had always responded to her physically, but the little things she craved—the tender word, the secret little jokes, the day-by-day small intimacies that she had always dreamed of in a marriage— had never been there.

Slowly she picked up one of Quentin's shirts and began to iron it. Just touching his garment was hard for her, and she finished it hurriedly.

She was still ironing when her father came in holding Stuart by the hand. "This young man has tired me out," he grinned.

Stuart's sturdy, one-year-old frame reminded Eden a great deal of her father before he had been crippled by the stroke. Stuart held his head at the same angle, and his facial features were a great deal like those of her father.

Will had never seen Stuart, who had been conceived during one short leave from the war. Now the boy was growing up without a father. Eden cast a sudden look at her father, grateful that there was a man around.

Stuart tottered across the room and plopped himself down before the fire. He pulled out a set of blocks that Thomas had made for him and began playing with them.

Sitting down on one of the cane-bottomed chairs and soaking up the heat of the kitchen, Thomas watched Eden as she ironed in silence. "Things look pretty good, moneywise," he said.

"Yes. They do. The business is going well."

She said nothing else, and he watched her, thinking. "You're lonely, daughter," he said finally.

Eden glanced up, a strange expression in her eyes. "What do you mean, *lonely?*"

Thomas York knew this daughter of his well. They had struggled through the lean years of the war together, and during those long, lonely weeks and months and years, they'd had only each other to speak with. Even before that, as she was growing up, the two had been closer than most fathers and daughters. Eden was all that he had left of his wife, Eileen. She had died giving birth to Eden, and he had never remarried. Since that day he had loved the child greatly for Eileen's sake, and they knew each other as well as two people can.

"Had you ever thought of Quentin as a man you might marry?" he asked.

"What!" The question seemed to shock Eden. Straightening up, she glanced over at her father and nervously brushed a lock of hair back from her forehead. "What are you talking about?"

"Do you think I'm blind, daughter?"

Because of their closeness, Thomas was surprised that Eden could not meet his eyes—and that she seemed unable to form a reply. But he knew that she was an honest woman and would not evade the issue. When at last she looked up at him, there was hurt in her eyes. As she paused, trying to frame a reply, Thomas studied her—the strong, rounded shoulders, the fine womanly lines of her figure. Her face was a mirror that changed as her feelings changed. And now he saw that the pride that had always been in her had been broken, and her eyes mirrored something close to shame and despair. Now her lips made a small change at the corners, and he watched a shadow and shape of odd things come into her expression. She straightened up and gave him a level look. Her voice had a tone that seemed almost dead compared to her usual vibrant voice. "He didn't care for me, Pa."

Her words shocked Thomas. He had seen in Quentin Larribee a man who had the gentleness and insight that Will Breckenridge had lacked. Those were qualities he wanted his daughter's man to have; lack of them in her first marriage had been a source of grief to her, which she never spoke of, but he had known about it. Now he watched her, knowing that there was nothing he could do or say. He got up and shuffled out of the room, disappointment heavy on him.

★ ★ ★

"Mama, there's a buggy stopping outside." Pru was staring out the window holding Stuart up.

It was late afternoon and the golden rays of the sun threw bars across the floor of the kitchen.

"Who is it, Pru?"

"I don't know. I never seen 'em before. Fine-dressed lady, and man's not getting out."

"Probably somebody that's lost, I expect." She wiped her hands on her apron and moved out of the kitchen and down the hallway that led to the front door. The knock came when she was halfway there, and she opened it and nodded to the woman who stood there.

"Are you Mrs. Breckenridge?"

"Yes. I'm Mrs. Breckenridge."

"My name is Irene Chambers, Mrs. Breckenridge. I would like to speak with Quentin Larribee."

Shock ran through Eden. She took in the woman in one swift glance, noting the fine clothes. She was wearing a dark green wool dress with delicate white lace around the high collar, long sleeves, and a hem that showed beneath her ankle-length cloak. The cloak matched the dress in material and color but was trimmed with fur around the collar, the front, and the hem. She was also carrying a fur muff and had on a black bonnet decorated with feathers, lined with fur, and tied under her chin with dark green ribbon.

Eden tried to see the woman's left hand, but it was hidden in the muff. Her first thought came involuntarily and swiftly. *She couldn't be Quentin's wife, for her name is Chambers.*

"Quentin's not here now. He should be back soon. Would you care to come in and wait?"

"That would be nice. It's cold outside." Irene turned and called to the driver. "I'll be here for a time."

"Yes, ma'am."

"If you'd like for your friend to come in and wait in the kitchen, it'll be warmer."

"Oh, I don't expect to be here that long."

Irene stepped into the hall, and Eden said, "There's a fire in the parlor. It'll be warmer there."

Irene followed Eden down the hall and into the parlor, a small room with only a sofa, three chairs, and a table. The walls were covered with lithographs and prints. A small fire crackled in the fireplace, and Eden said, "Could I get you something warm to drink? Coffee or tea?"

"If it's not too much trouble."

"Not at all." Eden left, glad to have a moment to get her thoughts together.

In the kitchen, Pru said, "Who is she, Mama?"

"She's looking for Quentin."

Quickly she set the kettle over the fire, and soon it was boiling. She brewed the tea and poured two cups, then put sugar and fresh cream in a blue-and-white set of china that had been her grandmother's. She carried it carefully back and set it on the table before her visitor.

Irene fixed her tea and sipped it. "This is very good," she said. "It's cold outside."

"Yes, it is."

"Does it often get this cold in the South?"

"It's been colder than usual. I take it you're from the North?"

"From New York City." She hesitated and said, "Has Quentin ever spoken of me?"

"I don't think so, Miss Chambers."

Eden's answer caused Irene's eyes to narrow slightly. "I'm surprised at that," she said with some asperity. She seemed to hesitate for a moment, then said, "Do you know Quentin well?"

"We are in business together."

The words were cool and cautious, for Eden could see a watchfulness in the woman's eyes. There was, she understood at once, a sense of possession about Miss Chambers, and resentment. She said no more, allowing the burden of the conversation to fall upon Irene Chambers.

"Do you expect Quentin back soon?"

"He's gone to the mill at Lexa with my son. That's a little town a few miles from here. They should have been back earlier."

Irene bit her lip nervously, then said, "I've been worried about Quentin."

"Worried? Why would you be worried?"

"Well," Irene said, her eyes fixed on Eden's face, "we've delayed our wedding for so long that naturally I've been concerned."

Eden sat very still. "Have you been engaged long?" she asked quietly.

"Oh, yes. He's such a dear man, isn't he? He has such a promising career. None of his friends could understand why he left to come South, but I suppose he's told you about all this."

"No. He's never spoken of it."

"Why, he's one of the most promising young surgeons in New York, Mrs. Breckenridge! He'll take over my father's practice one day." As Irene continued speaking about Quentin's prospects, Eden could barely hear what the woman was saying, and could not speak. Finally Irene fell silent too, and then said, "I think perhaps I'd better go back into town. Would you kindly tell Quentin that I'm at the Palace Hotel?"

"Yes, I'll tell him."

Irene moved out of the room and quickly down the hall. She opened the door herself, then turned and said, "It's been a pleasure meeting you, Mrs. Breckenridge."

Eden could think of no proper answer, so she simply said, "I'll tell Quentin you're waiting for him."

"Thank you very much."

Eden shut the door, turned, and leaned her back against it. Prudence came out and said, "Who was that woman, Mama?"

Eden did not answer for a long moment. Then she said, "That's the lady Quentin's engaged to marry."

★　★　★

As Irene rode back to town, she replayed the scene with Eden Breckenridge in her mind. She was rather shocked at how attractive Eden was. She had expected a plain woman, and instead she found one with the true beauty that Irene had often been annoyed to see in the Southern women who visited New York. She called up a vision of Eden Breckenridge's clear skin, fine blonde hair, and especially the deep blue eyes—as well as her narrow waist and the well-developed figure—and felt displeased. But she felt better when she recalled the expression of shock and hurt Eden had tried unsuccessfully to mask.

She had finally given up on letters and had decided to come see Quentin personally. Now as the buggy bounced over the rough road, she thought, *I waited too long. I should have come a long time ago.* She remembered the expression on Eden's face. *Yes, if I'd waited any longer, it might have been too late. But as soon as I get Quentin away from her, I can put everything back in order again.*

★   ★   ★

Only thirty minutes after Irene Chambers left, Quentin entered the house. Eden had been waiting for him. She saw him pull the wagon into the shed where the feed was kept, and he and Johnny unloaded it. She stood waiting until he entered the house. Johnny headed for the kitchen, saying, "Hello, Mama. Can I have some hot chocolate?"

"Yes."

Pulling off his hat, Quentin said, "Well, I got a good price on the feed."

"Your fiancée, Miss Chambers, is at the Palace Hotel. She's waiting for you."

Quentin felt as if he had been punched in the pit of his stomach. He could not think of a word to say. He saw that Eden's face was pale and knew that he had hurt this woman dreadfully. He wished fervently that he had managed things differently, but there was no turning back the clock. "Eden," he said, "I have to explain—"

"Can you explain what sort of game you've been playing?" Eden was holding herself very tightly. Her voice was controlled, but he saw the anger that lurked in her eyes—and the shame.

"If you'll just let me try to tell you what happened—"

"I don't want to hear it," Eden said, and then her voice broke. "Just leave, Quentin, and don't ever come back."

Seeing that Eden was on the verge of breaking down, Quentin knew that there were no words he could offer to bring healing to this woman. He felt a sudden desire to go to her, but knew that she was in no mood to listen. "I'll write to you," he said quietly. "I'll get my things. You won't have any trouble with the business. Otis will help you with it."

"I'll send you your share of the money."

"No. I don't want any money."

"What *did* you want? Oh, why did you come here, Quentin?" For one moment Eden's control slipped and there was a plaintive sadness in her voice, but then she caught herself. Her lips tightened, and she turned and left the room.

"I'll write! I'll explain why I came."

"Just go, Quentin!" Eden went to her room almost blindly, for the tears were filling her eyes, burning, great scalding tears that ran down her cheeks. She was unable to stop them, and when she stepped inside and shut the door behind her, she leaned back against it, her body shaking with great sobs she was unable to control. She could not think. But even though her mind was reeling, she knew one thing: she was closing the door on hope.

Quentin went quickly to his room and packed what little he had. He moved outside, got into the wagon, and drove off. He looked back as he came to the turn in the road, and a great sadness came to him. "I may have made things worse," he said. He tried to comfort himself with the fact that he had at least brought some financial stability to the Breckenridges, but he knew that the pain that he had given Eden Breckenridge would not be assuaged by that.

He drove to the livery stable and said, "Abe, would you have somebody drive this wagon back to Mrs. Breckenridge?"

"Why sure, Quentin," Abe Simmons, the blacksmith, said. He saw the suitcase and said, "You going on a trip?"

"Yes. Making a little trip, Abe."

He left the livery stable and made his way to the Palace Hotel. He did not know what to expect of Irene. He knew that he had treated her shabbily, and he felt as if he were about to face a firing squad. Going to the desk, he said, "You have a Miss Chambers here."

"Room 207."

As soon as she heard his knock at the door, Irene composed her face into a joyous smile, threw open the door, and leaped into

Quentin's arms, exclaiming, "It's so good to see you!" She pressed herself against him, pulled his head down, and kissed him. Then she took his arm. "Come inside." She pulled him inside and said, "My, you're so brown! I can't believe it! And you've gained weight."

"I guess so." He hesitated, then said, "I'm surprised to see you."

"I couldn't wait any longer, Quentin," she said. She was smart enough to know that gentleness was what was called for here, and she was prepared to be more gentle with Quentin than she had ever been since he had known her. "I have to know what's in your heart."

Quentin blinked. He seemed surprised by her attitude—which was exactly her intention. "I know you're unhappy with me," he said at last, cautiously, "but this was something I had to do."

"I know you did," she said reassuringly.

Quentin hesitated again, then continued, "I thought and thought about it, but I just couldn't leave that family destitute when I was responsible for it. You know, Irene, a verse in Scripture came to me before I came here. I couldn't get away from it."

"What verse was that?"

"It's in the book of Job. It simply says, 'I will not lay mine honor in the dust.'"

"That's very poetic. Very beautiful."

"I just couldn't do it, Irene. I know you and your family are displeased with me, but that verse kept coming to me. A man has to have honor. It's like a cup of water. Once you spill it in the dust, it's gone forever. So I had to do this one thing. I could not lay mine honor in the dust," he said quietly.

"I understand." She was wise enough to remain quiet for a time, and then she said, "I met Mrs. Breckenridge."

"Did you tell her anything about me?"

"Just that we were engaged, and that I was lonely, and that I thought you needed to be back in your profession."

Quentin nodded and said, "I'm ready to go now."

"Can you tell me what happened, Quentin?"

Quentin began telling her the details of the business. She watched his face carefully, trying to read his feelings for Eden Breckenridge, but he seemed dull and tired. Finally she said, "Well, you've done what you came for."

"Yes, I suppose so."

"That's good." Irene put her arms around him. Putting her head against his chest, she said, "I'm proud of you. Are you ready to come home?"

She felt his arms come around her hesitantly, awkwardly. At first he was silent, and then there was a forced, unconvincing heartiness in his voice when he said, "Yes. I'm ready to go. We can leave anytime."

Yes, it's good that I didn't wait any longer, she thought. *I was almost too late.*

PART
Three

CHAPTER
Fourteen

Mrs. Lillian Van Oaks reclined in her bed, diamond rings flashing from most of her fingers as she waved them in the air. She had been relating her interminable symptoms for half an hour—enough to keep an entire hospital busy, Quentin thought irreverently. *If this woman wasn't married to a multimillionaire, what a dull creature she would be.* Her husband, Simon, was a railroad builder, and although not as famous or as wealthy as Cornelius Vanderbilt, nevertheless made a heavy impact on trade and finances through the nation. Quentin had met him only once and had been rather shocked to discover what an unimpressive man he was—small, gray, and nondescript. His wife, however, made up for this by her flamboyant dress and ostentatious jewelry, which glittered like a kaleidoscope. The lavaliere that encircled her neck must have cost enough to feed a small European nation for a year!

Irene had been ecstatic when Mrs. Van Oaks had sent for Quentin. "It's a beginning, Quentin!" she had exclaimed, her eyes flashing. "She knows *everybody,* and you must make a good impression on her. Make sure you wear a new suit."

Obediently Quentin had bought a new suit just for the occasion of calling on Mrs. Van Oaks at her brownstone mansion on Thirty-first Street, the exclusive home of millionaires in New York City. He had paid more for it than for any suit he had ever owned, and even now, amid the opulence of Mrs. Van Oaks's bedroom, he felt strangely out of place in it—as if a stranger had donned a costume and taken his name. He fingered the fine material of his coat sleeve and thought, *This sleeve alone must have cost thirty dollars.*

His chain of thought was broken when Mrs. Van Oaks said, "And I have biliousness. Oh, Doctor Larribee, you won't believe how I suffer!" Rolling her eyes up, Mrs. Van Oaks sighed deeply and heavily, reminding Quentin of actresses he had seen on the stage. He forced himself to listen to tales of Mrs. Van Oaks's biliousness, as well as the irregularities of her bowel habits. When she had finished, he said, "On the whole, you seem to be in fairly good condition, Mrs. Van Oaks."

"Good condition!" The eyes of his patient flashed. "How can you say that! Can't you see that I'm not doing at all well? Why, I've had at least half a dozen doctors, including Doctor Morgan from London. They all agree that my condition is precarious."

Quentin tried desperately to think of some reply. The truth was that Lillian Van Oaks, at the age of fifty, was as healthy as a horse. She was overweight, and from all reports she ate like a starved wolf every time she sat to dine. Finally he suggested, "I think I would like to see you lose some weight and perhaps get a little more exercise."

A silence fell over the room. Mrs. Van Oaks stared at him, disgust in her eyes. "Exercise! How can a woman in my condition exercise? And I have to keep my strength up. I'm a sick woman, I tell you!"

Thoroughly disgusted, Quentin managed to mask his true feelings while he prescribed a harmless tonic, then rose to go, hoping fervently that he would not be called back. He had not labored to become a doctor just to pacify wealthy hypochondriacs. He closed his bag, rose, and forced himself to smile. "We'll hope that this will help."

"Oh, I'm sure it will, Doctor," Mrs. Van Oaks said smugly. She put out her hand, then squeezed his with a frightfully strong grip for such a sick woman. He had to pry his hand loose, saying hastily, "Call me if you need me."

As he made his escape, he muttered under his breath, "She doesn't need a doctor. She needs to get out of bed and work off some of that fat."

Leaving the mansion, he got into his buggy and spoke to his horse, whom he had named Socrates. "Get up, Soc!" he said. "Let's get away from here!"

The gelding uttered a slobbering sigh as if he were being badly mistreated. "I've had enough of hypochondriacs," Quentin growled. "There's nothing wrong with you. Now get up!" He actually slapped the horse with the buggy whip, which startled Socrates into a brisk trot. Quentin grinned briefly. He had become fond of this horse, the first he had ever owned in New York. He threaded his way expertly through the busy streets and headed toward home. It had been a long day and a tiring one for him. He had worked at the hospital all morning, then had spent the afternoon making house calls. All of the patients had been wealthy, and few of them had actually been sick. This was the practice he would take over from his future father-in-law, and as he headed north down Broadway, he thought wearily, *How can I be so tired? I can put in all day at the hospital, walk from room to room as I make my rounds, then stand for hours in the operating room, and not be this exhausted!* In truth, small talk did not come easily to Quentin. He found it especially difficult to deal with bored people who sent for a doctor simply to fill the empty hours. Not all were like that, of course, but the day had tired him, and he spoke to the horse again. "Get up, Soc. Stop dragging your feet—or hooves, I guess."

A flock of pigeons burst from the top of one of the buildings he passed, scoring the dusky sky as they circled, uttering their peculiar dulcet sound. The sight of the birds evoked a sudden vivid memory, and he murmured, "I wonder how Johnny's doing with the pigeons? He ought to have all the boxes filled by this time." The memory was painful, for each time his thoughts went back to Helena, he could almost hear Eden's voice telling him to leave and never come back. He forced his mind away, but the image of Pru's face came to him unbidden. He had become very fond of the children in a short time, and now he shook his head angrily. *Got to forget about that—I've done all I can.* He tapped Socrates again with the whip, causing the animal to swivel his head, giving Quentin a reproachful look.

★ ★ ★

"Have some of this almond cake, Brother Pettigrew."

"I don't mind if I do, Hannah." Horace Pettigrew took a large slice of cake from the plate Hannah extended toward him, leaned back, and took a large bite. "Excellent as always! You're a fine cook, Hannah."

"I've had a lot of practice."

"I'm sure you have." Horace Pettigrew knew the background of the Larribees very well; he knew how Hannah and Quentin had struggled to raise a family after the death of their parents. He had dropped by, as he did often, to visit with Hannah. Many of his pastoral calls were made out of duty, but it was refreshing to sit with Hannah Larribee. He was always impressed at her grasp of Scripture, and once referred to her as "my walking concordance." She was able to speak of theology in a clear, levelheaded fashion that most of Pettigrew's teachers at seminary would have envied. The two had been talking for half an hour about the question of sanctification, then as Pettigrew washed the last morsel of cake down with the steaming tea from the blue china cup, he casually asked the question that he had come to ask. "And how's Quentin doing, Hannah?"

For a moment Hannah did not answer—and that hesitation told the minister a great deal. She said finally, "He's . . . different since he came back from Arkansas."

"Different how? I haven't really had a chance to talk with him. He's been so busy."

Hannah set her cup down carefully, then laced her hands together. She was wearing a light green dress, and Pettigrew marked again what a very attractive woman she was. *What a waste that she has never married or had children.* He waited until finally she said reluctantly, "He's restless and somehow seems tense."

"Well, he's getting married. That's a big step."

Hannah shot a quick glance at Pettigrew. She almost said what had been on her mind for days: *An engagement shouldn't make people tense and cross!* She would not, however, say a word against Quentin. "I suppose you might be right," she said finally.

Pettigrew was a perceptive man. He sat there quietly for a moment, then shook his head. "The few chance words I have had with him since his return, I believe I'd have to agree, Hannah. He seems somehow . . . well, to be *out* of things. He was always so interested at church. Now he just sits and stares at me, and I know his mind's a blank." He grinned ruefully. "I've seen that often enough from the pulpit."

"We hardly ever talk anymore, Brother Pettigrew. Of course he's very busy with his fiancée. It's a new world he's entering, and he has to adapt to it." The words were sharp and acerbic, and she quickly caught herself, saying, "I won't complain, although it's going to be very lonesome without him."

"You don't think of moving in with them?"

"No! Indeed not!"

Catching the sharpness of Hannah's tone, Pettigrew said quickly, "Well, that might be best. After all, you have your own ways." He felt like a man walking in dangerous territory. He himself was not happy with Quentin's choice of a bride. He had told his wife, "Quentin needs a simple woman—after all, he's a simple man. That woman will drive him crazy, Martha, sooner or later."

"Does it bother you, Brother Pettigrew, that Miss Chambers has chosen another church for the wedding?"

"Why, not at all. That's a bride's choice. And of course, I have been asked to be there to conduct part of the ceremony."

Hannah started to reply, but at that moment heard the door open. "There's Quentin," she said. Getting to her feet, she crossed the room with her hobbling gait and greeted him. "Hello, Quentin. Brother Pettigrew's here."

Quentin crossed the room to shake his hand. "How are you, Brother Pettigrew?"

"Doing very well. I just stopped by to get some of Hannah's tea and cakes. Better than any restaurant in New York."

"Here. Sit down, Quentin. You look tired."

Heeding Hannah's advice, Quentin sat down. Pettigrew sensed the strain in him, and after a ten-minute chat, rose. "I must be going. I have several calls to make. No, I'll show myself out, Hannah."

As he walked to his buggy, Pettigrew shook his head. "Something's wrong with Quentin," he muttered. "He's just not himself."

Inside, Hannah was aware that Quentin seemed unusually depressed. "What's wrong? Did you have a bad day?"

"No. Not that. But I've got to go to another party tonight."

"Another party!"

"Well, not a party, exactly. Sort of a dinner engagement. Cornelius Vanderbilt will be there."

Hannah was not impressed, as most people would have been. Vanderbilt was probably the wealthiest man in America; he could have anyone he wanted in for dinner. "How'd that come about?" she asked.

"Irene managed it somehow."

"Well, those parties always start late. Do you want something to eat now?"

"No. I'm not hungry."

Hannah hesitated, then said, "I wish you didn't have to go. We have so little time together."

"I know, but Irene says this is good for the practice." A sour look came to Quentin's face. "I suppose it is, but I didn't study medicine to go to dinner parties."

Hannah fingered the material of her skirt for a moment. When she looked up, she felt an overwhelming sense of compassion. She loved this brother of hers with all of her heart. He was her only treasure on earth. They were closer than any brother and sister she had ever encountered. Now the knowledge that she was losing him was a dagger in her heart. She knew that Irene Chambers did not like her, and once Irene was safely married to Quentin, that would be the end of that. There was nothing to be done about it, however. *I can't just tell him not to marry her,* she thought painfully. She rose and left the room, saying, "I'll wait up for you, Quentin."

Quentin stared after her, knowing that somehow he had lost something. He had always been able to talk to Hannah, but lately a wall had come between them. Heavily he rose and moved down the hall to his bedroom. Pausing in the middle of the floor, he eyed the evening clothes that he had to wear for the party. Irene had picked them out, and he hated the outfit already. *Dress up like a monkey and perform! That's what I do,* he thought angrily. An impulse came to him to throw the clothes out the window. It gave him a savage pleasure to think of it, but he knew he would do no such thing. Stretching out on the bed, he closed his eyes and tried to sleep.

★   ★   ★

The dining room of the Collingwoods' home was immense. Quentin, seated with Irene on his right and a strangely mute gentlemen on his left, felt oppressed by it all. He stared around the room, wondering, *Why would anybody want a room this big to eat a meal in?* It had to be at least twenty by twenty-five feet, with a fourteen-foot ceiling intricately painted with fine designs on a white background. The walls were painted a bright blue above the dado rail; there was blue-and-green striped paper on the bottom half of the walls. Pictures of landscapes covered the walls in gilt frames, and the four floor-length windows were covered with light blue silk draperies and edged with gold fringe which hung delicately, framing the windows. Gold fringe also hung above the mirror over the white marble fireplace. The floor was made of rich, dark oak and covered by a large area rug in different hues of green, blue, and gold. The furniture was all heavy and made of mahogany, the table long enough, it seemed, to seat at least fifty people. The chairs were covered in gold and blue jacquard material, and the table was exquisitely set with fine china, crystal, and silver.

It was ostentatious—something designed by a man who had to search for new ways to throw money away. Quentin glanced over at Frank Collingwood, his host, a cheerful-looking man in his middle fifties with hair so black that Quentin suspected it was dyed. Collingwood seemed a human enough fellow for a man with millions, all made on the stock market in a way Quentin could not understand. His sharp, dark eyes had taken Quentin's measure, and he had said, "So you're the new heir to Oscar. Getting the daughter and the practice in one fell swoop."

Quentin had managed to hide the distaste he felt. He had heard it said often. Indeed, it had been said before to his face, and he knew that that was how he was thought of throughout the city.

He could hear Irene, beside him, speaking with Martha Collingwood, their hostess, and as usual managed to find a way to encourage Mrs. Collingwood to recommend Quentin to her friends.

"We're just a poor couple starting out, Mrs. Collingwood," she was saying charmingly. Her words were belied by the diamond necklace that hung around her neck and by the gown she wore—made of deep blue silk, very low-cut, with short sleeves and a full skirt. It had a small frill around the neckline made of the finest white lace, and the skirt had layers of flounces, one of which was pinned up at the back with a large fabric bow. "You know how that is, I'm sure."

Mrs. Collingwood, Quentin was sure, had no idea what that was like. Nevertheless, she said airily, "Oh, yes. Frank and I had our struggles, just as other young couples do, but your fiancé is such a brilliant doctor. Everyone is speaking about him. He'll have no difficulty—after all, he is inheriting a wonderful practice from your father. I hope he's properly grateful."

"I'm sure he is, Mrs. Collingwood."

Across the wide table, Leslie Simmons was seated beside Doctor Franklin Sutter. Les kept his eye fixed on Irene. Actually, he loved this woman and had been hurt more than he showed when she had chosen Quentin. He knew Quentin Larribee was a better doctor, but he also knew that Quentin was not the kind of man who could step into Oscar Chambers's shoes. That required a talent for flattering people which Quentin did not possess—and never would. His skill with the knife was his only asset, for his bedside manner would never be suitable for millionaires such as Frank Collingwood.

"Now Quentin's got it all, hasn't he, Doctor Sutter?"

Franklin Sutter did not answer for a moment. His face was worn and he looked tired. "I suppose so, but he'll be doing a lot of this—mingling with high society. I hope he likes it."

"He doesn't," Simmons said abruptly. "Look at him. He'd like to get up and bolt right now."

"So would I. I don't know why I agreed to come to this thing. Quentin kept after me and I finally agreed."

Les Simmons was not surprised. He shrugged. "You never did like parties, Doctor. I was surprised that you chose to come."

"I thought I'd give Quentin a little moral support. He feels completely out of place at these things."

"He doesn't have any social graces, that's for sure. But he's got it all now."

Doctor Sutter gave Simmons a sharp glance. "You wish you had it, don't you, Les?"

"Of course I do! You think I'm stupid?" He turned to face the older man and shrugged. "I've never made a secret of it. I've loved Irene for a long time. And what man wouldn't want to have a practice like Oscar's handed to him on a silver platter?"

"Not every man wants that."

"That's true," Les agreed quickly. "And I'll tell you one thing. Quentin's unhappy. Look at him. He's trying to smile and he can't even manage that."

Doctor Sutter's rather sad eyes flickered over toward Quentin. Quentin did look miserable as he sat there. Finally Sutter said, "Well, I've been unhappy for years, but I hate to see Quentin follow in my footsteps."

"You know what's wrong with you two?" Les said. He was an astute man in many ways, and now he spoke bluntly. "You've got ideals, Doctor. Those things can be dangerous for a man."

The words angered Doctor Franklin Sutter, but when he swiveled his head to meet the level glance of the younger doctor, he choked off his angry reply and said, "You're right, Les. Ideals are dangerous, and as I look at Quentin I see myself as I was at his age. I had high ideals when I started, but they got lost somewhere along the way. I hope that doesn't happen to Quentin."

★　★　★

"Oh, darling!" Irene exclaimed as she pressed herself against Quentin. They were standing outside her door. "It went so wonderfully, didn't you think?"

"I guess so," Quentin muttered. He was intensely aware of the pressure of her body against his. He lowered his head to kiss her, and she surrendered, but only for a moment. She was always this way—allowing him to get stirred up, then withdrawing. Sometimes Quentin felt like a hungry, chained dog, thrown a bit of meat and lunging for it, only to see it drawn back. That dog would become bad-natured and ill-tempered, which is how he felt now as Irene put her hand on his chest. "None of that now. After we're married, it will be different."

Suddenly, Quentin reached out and pulled her to him. She struggled helplessly against his strength. His lips came down on hers for a moment, and he felt her resistance. Then his passion seemed to fade, and she put her hands on his chest and wrenched backwards. "Now, Quentin. Behave yourself." Irene reached up and touched her hair; she seemed to be pleased at his insistence. "It won't be long now. You'll just have to be patient." She laughed, saying, "You're quite a caveman. I declare, I'm afraid of how it might be to be married to such a man." She laughed at his expression, then turned and said, "Good night. Don't forget. We're having lunch with the Claytons tomorrow. It's important."

Quentin watched her go, then turned and got into the carriage. He drove home and unhitched Socrates, feeling a strange sense of incongruity. "Unhitching a horse in a dress suit. That doesn't make much sense."

Inside, Hannah was waiting for him, as he had known she would be. "I kept some coffee warm for you."

"Good," Quentin said. He plunked down in the chair and accepted the cup when Hannah brought it to him. He took a sip. "That's good, Hannah," he said. "Better than anything they had at that party."

"Tell me about it."

"Too much food, too many people serving it, and too much silly talk."

Hannah could not help but smile at his summary. "I take it you had a bad evening. Did Irene enjoy it?"

"Of course she did. Everybody did. Why wouldn't everybody enjoy being with one of the richest men in America and eating too much and drinking too much and listening to all the talk that doesn't amount to anything? I didn't get a chance to talk to Doctor Sutter at all. We'd just started to talk about that new surgical procedure we're working on when Irene broke it up."

I would imagine she did, Hannah thought sharply, but she said nothing. She watched as Quentin, staring morosely at the wall, swallowed his coffee. Finally she asked quietly, "Quentin, are you happy?" It was a question she had never put to him directly, and now he gave her one of the strangest looks she had ever received from him.

"Why wouldn't I be happy, Hannah? I've got everything!" His voice was tight, and he rose suddenly and left the room abruptly, saying only, "Good night."

Hannah sat in the silence of the room. The marble clock ticked silently, and she stared at it for a time blindly, then arose and picked up her crutch. She looked around the room. This world that had been so safe and secure for so long was not so any longer.

CHAPTER *Fifteen*

*T*homas York paused abruptly, his eyes falling on the calendar glued to the wall over the washstand. The picture irritated him, as it always did. The calendar illustration depicted a man on a horse jumping over a fence. Staring at it, he said under his breath, as he always did, "That feller sure can't draw horses!"

His eyes narrowed as he noted the date: April 10, 1866. *Just two months since Quentin left—seems a lot longer than that.* He straightened up, gave the calendar a rueful look, then turned and left the house, pausing only to pick up a basket woven of white oak strips.

He was not the only one keeping track of the passage of time since Quentin's departure. Eden seldom spoke of him, but both Johnny and Pru mentioned him often. Thomas let his mind dwell on Eden. *Something happened between the two of them—and it's scarred Eden pretty bad.* And that was not his only worry regarding Eden.

He saw Pru in the swing Quentin had made for her, and called out, "Come on, Pru. Let's take a walk."

"All right, Grandpa." She came to him at once, and the two left the yard, making their way down the worn path that led to the deep woods that flanked the ridge behind the house. The sun was low in the sky, creating an orange haze over the land. "Look." Thomas pointed. "There's a bunch of papaws over there."

Following her grandfather's gesture, Prudence said rather soberly, "All right, Grandpa. I'll go get them." Thomas moved painfully after her as she crossed a rise and began to pick the wild fruit. They looked like stubby cucumbers, and York reached out and took one. "Maybe I'd better try it to see if it's ripe." He peeled the thin skin off with a razor-sharp pocketknife. The fruit looked somewhat like a banana with huge, black seeds. He tasted it, then held it out and said, "Here. Try it, Prudence. See if it's good."

Prudence took a bite and chewed on it thoughtfully. "It's good, Grandpa," she said. "Tastes kind of like pears and sweet potato custard mixed together."

"Smells good, too."

"Mama always likes to put some in bread and puddings."

"You remember the song I taught you about 'em?"

At once Prudence broke into a song:

"Where oh where is little Sally?
Where oh where is little Sally?
Where oh where is little Sally?
Way down yonder in the papaw patch."

Her grandfather joined in as they sang,

"She's pickin' up papaws put 'em in her pocket.
Pickin' up papaws put 'em in her pocket.
Pickin' up papaws put 'em in her pocket.
Way down yonder in the papaw patch."

"You can sing better than I can, Prudence. That's for sure."

Prudence filled the basket with papaws, then looked up with a worried expression in her eyes. "I'm worried about Mama."

"She'll be all right, honey."

"But she's been sick for a month now. What's wrong with her?"

"Oh, she's just got some kind of ailment," York said evasively. "It'll pass away."

But Thomas, too, was concerned about Eden's health. She had been ailing for longer than the children knew. She had not complained, but she had begun losing her bright, sharp ways some time ago. Now some days she could barely drag herself around the house. He had urged her to have Doctor Vance in, but she had put him off, saying, "We can't afford it right now."

"Come on, Prudence. Maybe your ma can eat some of these papaws."

Back at the house, they found Eden sitting on the porch with her head back. She straightened up at once and said quickly, "My! I guess I dozed off a little. I don't know what's the matter with me."

"Look, Mama. We found you some papaws."

"You always favored papaws, daughter." Thomas urged. "Why don't you try one?"

"Well, I think I will."

Eden took the fruit, borrowed her father's knife, and peeled it. She took a bite and then said, "Oh, that's good!" But she didn't look to Thomas as if she were enjoying the fruit, or much of anything else. "Just leave this here and you go in and start supper," she said to Pru. "I'll be in and help you later."

"I can do it myself, Mama. You just rest." Prudence left at once, pausing only to glance at Stuart, who was digging a hole in the dirt at the edge of the porch.

York waited for Eden to eat more of the papaw, but she merely held onto it. There was a dull look in her eyes, and he said tentatively, "You're feelin' poorly today."

"Oh, I'm all right."

"You always say that. We ought to have Doctor Vance in."

"When Granny came by yesterday, she made me some chamomile tea. It made me feel a lot better."

York said nothing, for Eden did not look better. Her color had faded to a pallor, and she had none of the liveliness that he had come to expect in her.

The two sat for a time, and finally Eden said, "I hope Johnny sells that game. We need the money."

"He came back about an hour ago, but he couldn't get rid of much of it. The *Lady Belle* had stocked up at Memphis before they left. Didn't need any more fresh game."

It had become a familiar story. Word had gotten around, and the business of supplying riverboats with fresh pen-grown animals had been easy to get into. Over the space of only a couple of months, the market had become flooded. No longer did the captains eagerly snap up all their fresh game; now the pens and hutches and runs were full, and there was little market for them. The loss of income had been a blow for the Breckenridges, and now, once again, Eden and her father were concerned about making the payment on their farm. "We'll make out," York said firmly. "I'm thinkin' maybe I'll take some of the rabbits around house-to-house down in Helena. Lots of town folks there will appreciate good fat rabbits."

"You're not able to do that, Dad."

"What do you mean not able! Me and Johnny can load the wagon up. We're goin' tomorrow." He spoke with more cheerfulness than he felt, for he had heard from Trumbo that another man was already traveling the streets of Helena.

Eden said nothing. She felt wretched, sick to the bone, and knew that something out of the ordinary was wrong with her. She had been sick every morning for days, and her stomach was sore and swollen. She might have thought it was gas or something she had eaten, but she had eaten very little. Now she could not eat— her appetite seemed to be gone, too. She forced herself to get up. "I'll help Prudence if you'll take care of Stuart."

"Let me help. You lie down."

"Oh, I'm fine. Can't let this thing get me down."

★   ★   ★

Johnny was sitting listlessly beside the pheasant run, staring at the beautifully colored birds. He loved the pheasants, and at first he had hated it when they had to sell them. Now that the market had dropped out, he wished that he could. Looking up, he watched Trumbo, who was patching the wire fence that held the quail in. The big black man came by often, and now he turned, after he finished his job, to sit beside Johnny heavily. "Well, that's a fine bird in there. They shore is good eatin' too."

"Yeah, they are, Trumbo. Better than chicken, I think."

Trumbo glanced at his young friend and saw his downcast expression. "Somethin' botherin' you, Johnny?"

"It's Mama. She's sick, and she just can't seem to get over it."

"Your grandpa, he told me she was doing poorly. She be all right though. Folks get sick and then they get better. Granny just needs to come by and give her a potion."

"She's already done that, but it didn't help."

"Well, don't you fret none about it. You jes' put your trust in the good Lord. He's gonna take care of you and your mama. Wait and see."

Johnny stared down at his feet. He did not answer for a long time, then he looked up with misery in his eyes. "I'm afraid we're gonna lose this place, Trumbo. We can't sell no game anymore. Other people going into the business."

"Well, yo' grandpa, he say he's going into Helena and sell it door-to-door. You two can do that together. Why, I 'spect you make a heap of money!"

Johnny Breckenridge was ordinarily a cheerful young man, but he had been shaken by too many blows in his young life. Now he could not bring himself to believe Trumbo's words. "No," he muttered. "We're gonna lose it—and you know what?"

"What's that?"

"I don't reckon as how God's good like the preacher says."

Trumbo shook his head. "Hey now, boy! Don't you get to sayin' things like dat! Just 'cause a little trouble comes don't mean the good Lord don't care 'bout you."

"He *don't* care about me! He don't care about anything!" Johnny felt the tears rise in his eyes. Ashamed, he rose and fled blindly away.

Trumbo started to follow him, and then shook his head. "Can't help dat boy none. Dis heah family shore is in bad trouble!"

★ ★ ★

Eden had forced herself to dress more carefully than usual. Riley Greer was coming by for supper, and she had put on her second-best dress. It was made out of moss-green cotton with flecks of light beige woven into the fabric. The high neckline was edged with a fabric ruffle as were the cuffs on the long, loose sleeves, and the bodice had dark green buttons down the front for decoration. She had washed her hair and was feeling somewhat better. When she slipped into the dress, however, she noticed that her stomach was still distended. After some thought, she changed into a simple dark blue dress that fit her rather loosely. Her stomach ached, as it had all day, but she ignored it and went in at once to help start supper.

She had known little bad health in her life, and she was determined to simply outlast this illness, whatever it was. She made flour dumplings, a glazed pork roast, a pot of parsnips, and scalloped potatoes.

More than once while fixing the meal, she was caught by sudden pains, and she felt the nausea that had come so often. But she prayed, "Lord, let me get through this meal. And please help whatever problem this is—this sickness, heal me of it, Lord!"

At supper that night Riley Greer ate heartily. He was not an observant man and did not seem to notice that Eden ate almost nothing, although the family did. It had been Eden who had asked him to dinner, and now she wondered why she had given the invitation.

"Well, now this is what I call a fine meal," Riley said. He was freshly shaven and had gotten a haircut, so he looked very presentable. Actually he was a handsome man, in a way, although his features were blunt. Good health made his cheeks red, and he dominated the talk around the table, speaking mostly of farming. Then he said, "I seen Calendar today. That fellow's crazy. He ought to be put away."

Thomas had been toying with his glazed parsnips. He said quietly, "I knew Ben Calendar when he was a young man. He had a hot temper, but so do a lot of other men."

"He had more than a hot temper," Greer said. "He killed that girl, and he'd kill somebody else if he had a chance."

"I never believed he killed that girl."

"A jury believed it, and a judge."

"I never thought the trial was fair. Young Ben never even had a decent lawyer. He hired old Carl McClintock, who was drunk every waking moment. Put up no defense at all. Just hollered and raved. *He* was the one that should have been committed."

"Well, the jury said he killed her, and the judge sentenced him. Should have hung him. That's what."

Eden took little part in the conversation and finally after supper was over, Greer said, "Step outside to the wagon. I got something for you, Eden."

Apprehensively, Eden followed him outside. She had eaten a little, and already her stomach was beginning to complain. Riley stopped beside the wagon, reached into it, and handed her a package.

"What's this? It's not my birthday."

"No. It's for your wedding." Greer grinned. "I ordered some white material. Had one of the women folks in the store choose it for a wedding dress. See if you like it."

Almost numbly, Eden opened the package and saw that it was a beautiful white silk with an overlay of fine, delicate lace. She ran her hand over it but said, "Riley, I wish you hadn't done this."

"Look, Eden," Greer said quietly. "I'm just a rough sort of fellow, but I care for you. And what's going to happen to you? Everybody knows that crazy business of selling quail and rabbits has failed. It was bound to. The only thing that's solid is land and farming. And you're going to lose this place, Eden. You know you are."

Sick with fear and nausea, Eden could only shake her head. "I don't know what to say."

"Just say you'll marry me. Think about your pa. What's gonna happen to him if you lose this place? He'll have to go to the poorhouse. You know what it's like there. You're gonna lose it all."

Eden said desperately, "Just give me a little time, Riley."

Riley seemed to be struggling within himself, holding back. Finally he patted her shoulder clumsily and said, "I just want what's best for all of us. We'll put these two farms together. Why, we'll have one of the best places in the county. I can farm both of them, hire a man, and we'll prosper. Besides, I need a woman, and you need a man. It's not natural for a man and woman not to have somebody."

Eden somehow managed to endure the rest of the evening, but before she went to bed she vomited violently. Then she washed her face and lay wearily down on the bed, feeling a terrible desperation. The future loomed before her, black and ominous and unknown. Helpless, she cried out, "Oh, God, what can I do? Help me!"

CHAPTER
Sixteen

A light rain out of a dark sky had begun to fall earlier in the day—only a shower that settled the summer dust, but it had given Doctor Vance a light soaking that irritated him. He was a man easily irritated—good at heart, giving of himself to the community, yet still at times a hard man to get along with.

Now as he rode along with his chin on his chest, weary from a hard day's traveling throughout the Delta country surrounding Helena, he longed for home and dry clothes. On either side, the flat country made him long for the high hills of North Carolina where he had grown up. The flatness of the Delta had never suited him, and Vance wondered as his mare picked her way along the muddy, crooked road why he had spent his life here. When he had first come to Arkansas, Helena had been much smaller even than now. He spoke aloud to break the loneliness of the surroundings. "I said that day I'd hate to spend the rest of my life here!" Something suddenly descended on his neck and bit him viciously. He slapped at it, stared at the mangled carcass of the yellow fly, and then wiped his hands on his trousers. He finished by saying grimly, "And by gab that's just what I've gone and done."

He looked ahead where the road bent around into a copse of thick oaks and shook his head. He was coming from the home of a family he did not know, and they had given him poor directions when he left. The roads around Helena were poor to begin with, and the spring rains the previous week had brought the creeks and branches up out of their banks. Vance glanced up at the sky, which promised even more rain, hunched himself, and slapped the lines on the mare's back. "Get up, Suzie! We've got a far piece to go."

The mare's hooves made squelching noises as she pulled them free from the black mud of the road, and the wheels sank in places almost to the hub. Not at all happy about his situation, Vance considered turning back when he reached a creek that rushed along with an ominous sound. But he was heading for the Breckenridge farm and thought he was not far from the main road that led to it. He stayed in Helena as much as he could, but being one of the few doctors in the county, from time to time he found it necessary to venture out into the rural areas. Now, staring at the roiling creek carrying its load of black Delta dirt toward the Mississippi, he sighed heavily. "Come on, Suzie. It's just a little creek." The horse shied but finally plunged ahead.

The bottom of the creek was rough and uneven, and just as Vance thought he was safe from the suck and pull of the stream, he felt the wagon lurch to one side. It threw him off balance, and he almost fell over the side of the wagon. As soon as the buggy emerged, he called, "Whoa, Suzie!" Looking back, he saw with disgust that the left rear wheel had dropped off. Staring glumly at it, he got out and considered unhitching the mare and riding bareback—but Suzie was not a horse given to that sort of thing. Wearily he hitched her to a sapling and, picking up his black bag, went sloshing down the road. It was heavy going and soon he was huffing and puffing, for he was a heavy man unaccustomed to exercise.

To Vance's utter disgust, it began to rain again. The water collected on the brim of his hat and spilled over onto his chest, and his clothes were as soaked as if he had been thrown into the creek. Finally he reached what appeared to be, more or less, a fork in the road. Uncertainly, he leaned against a tree, trying to catch his breath. He was debating which fork to take when suddenly he realized that he was not alone. With a sudden wrench he threw himself around, half lifting his bag and throwing up his hand, for a man stood in the shadows of one of the massive pin oak trees. For a moment Vance thought it was a robber or bandit, but then he recognized Ben Calendar.

Vance sighed with relief even though, like everyone else in the town of Helena, he knew of Calendar, and some of what he had heard was not good. There had been stories that the strange hermitlike figure was capable of violence, and certainly his appearance did not belie that rumor. Calendar stood immobile, dressed in, as usual, a pair of ragged overalls and a black slouch hat. He was soaked to the skin and the water poured off the hat's crown, but the steady hazel eyes glared out with malevolence, unwavering.

"Well, hello, Calendar," Dr. Vance said quickly. "You startled me there." He waited for Calendar to reply, to at least make some sign, but there was no response. Vance thought, *Some day somebody will make that man give a civil reply!* However, he said quickly, "My wagon shucked a wheel back at the branch. I need some help to get it on. Be glad to pay you for your trouble."

The hazel eyes that had, in Vance's opinion, a feral threatening quality did not flicker. It was as if Vance had not spoken at all. A rifle was held loosely in the strong-looking right hand of the bedraggled figure, and he stood as if carved out of stone.

Doctor Vance waited. When he got no reply he said wearily, "All right. Who lives down the way? I'm looking for the Breckenridge place."

"Down the main road three miles."

The voice was rusty, a deep baritone, but seemed to be out of use. Without another word Calendar came out of the shadows and turned back down the road Vance had been following. Uncertainly, Vance watched him, then decided that, for all his silence, the man was going to help. He followed Calendar, but neither man said a word until they reached the creek. Laying the rifle aside, Calendar waded out into the creek, picked up the wheel, and brought it back. Leaning it against the wagon, he stared at it, then began fishing around in his pockets. He came up with a nail and nodded. "When I pick the wagon up, you slip the wheel on."

Quickly Vance took the wheel and positioned himself. He watched as Calendar moved toward the back and got a grip on the back of the wagon, then suddenly the wagon rose as easily as if it weighed nothing at all. Vance slipped the wheel onto the hub, then said, "All right. You can let it down." The wagon settled then and Calendar approached. He fitted the nail to the slot. Taking out a large bowie knife, he used the knife's butt to bend the nail so that it could not slip out.

Relieved, Vance said, "That's a good job. How much do I owe you?"

Another chilling look from Ben Calendar, but not even a nod or a word. Calendar picked up his rifle and, without a backward look, disappeared into the thick woods.

The encounter disturbed Vance. He untied the mare, climbed back into the wagon, then quickly drove away. *Strange sort of fellow,* he thought. *I don't think he's ever spoken a word to me in his life until today.*

He drove quickly and found, as Calendar had indicated, the main road only a short way down the muddy track. He turned off onto it with relief; thirty minutes later he pulled into the Breckenridge place. Tying up the wagon, he stomped the mud off his feet as well as he could, and then mounted the steps and knocked on the door. It opened almost at once, and he was greeted by Thomas York.

"I'm glad to see you, Doctor. Come in," York said at once, a worried expression in his eyes. He looked down at Vance's sodden clothing and muddy boots and said, "It's a bad day. Come in the kitchen and dry out by the fire. Could you drink some coffee?"

"I could drink anything you've got, Thomas," the doctor grumbled. Soon he was in the kitchen with his coat hung before the stove. Thomas had taken his boots and scraped the mud off, and the doctor, who had downed half a pot of boiling coffee and was feeling somewhat redeemed, now wore a pair of Thomas's socks. He sat lolling back in the chair holding the cup, sipping it from time to time, and watched as the two older children returned his gaze. "What's that baby's name? I forgot," he said.

"This is Stuart, Doctor," Prudence said.

"I remember the night he came into the world. He was a stubborn fellow."

"That he was," Thomas agreed. The doctor engaged in small talk, for the rural people depended on him to chronicle what was going on in town. Finally he said, "I lost a wheel in the creek. That fellow Calendar appeared from nowhere." He took a big sip of the black coffee and shook his head. "Like an Indian. He wasn't there—and then he was. I'll have to admit, though, I was glad to see him. He said hardly a word, but at least he helped me put my wagon back together."

"I've always thought that was the biggest waste of a life—Ben Calendar," Thomas said. "I knew his father. A good man. His mother, too. The Calendars were always good people. One bad break, and it ruined Ben's life."

"He's a strange fellow. Gave me the shivers," Doctor Vance said. He pulled himself together and finished the coffee, then set the cup down. "Well, I can't wait for these things to dry. I'd better see the patient."

Vance followed Thomas out of the kitchen down the hall. "Right in there, Doctor. She may be asleep."

Stepping inside the door, Vance advanced to the bed and set his bag down on the floor. He was stiff and somewhat chilled from his wetting, but he forgot that as he looked down on the patient. He usually saw Eden at church, and had always thought she was one of the most beautiful women he had ever seen. But now she was pale, her lips especially, and the lines of pain on her face were as plain as a printed page. "Eden," he said and sat down beside her. He waited until her eyes fluttered, and then when she looked at him and started to rise, he said, "It's all right. Just lie there a minute."

"Doctor Vance, I'm glad you came."

"Should have sent for me earlier," Vance grumbled. He reached out and put his hand on her wrist and with the practice of many years, he listened and felt and began to pull together the information that would help him to make a diagnosis. His was a rough sort of medical practice. He had come as a young man into the Delta, fresh out of medical school, and had had to learn much of his trade by trial and error. It was a hard school, but a good one, and now as he studied the patient he tried to identify her condition.

She never had a happy marriage with Will, he thought. *She kept it covered up, but I saw through it. She was too sensitive for him. Lord knows nobody ever accused Will Breckenridge of being sensitive. Good man in some ways, but not what this woman needed. Now she'll be looking for another man, for she's the kind of woman who needs a husband.*

Vance questioned her and listened as she mentioned nausea, vomiting, fatigue, and abdominal pain. "And my stomach. It's all swollen."

Drawing the covers back, Vance placed his hand on her stomach. She had always been a slim woman, very trim, showing no sign at all of having borne three children. But now he saw at once that there was a definite swelling.

All the information filed in his mind, and Vance was shocked at his conclusion. He sat there for a while questioning her further but not really listening to the answers, for he had already arrived at a rough conclusion. Finally he said, "Do you have any idea what's wrong with you, Eden?"

"No. Not an idea in the world. I know I'm as sick as I've ever been."

For a moment Vance hesitated, then said, "You must have considered the possibility that you're pregnant."

Eden lay perfectly still for a moment, and then her eyes turned to him and he saw utter astonishment in them. "That's not possible, Doctor."

Vance had expected some sort of answer like this, and he could not deny the honesty that he saw in this woman's eyes. He had become a psychologist of sorts, at least able to read through the outward appearance of most people. He had known this woman for a long time, and now he wanted to believe her. Nevertheless, it was not uncommon for widows, especially since the war, to come to him with a secret. He had long felt that Eden Breckenridge was a passionate woman, and as good as she was, she was still human. He finally said, "What about your periods, Eden?"

"Doctor Vance, you know how irregular they've always been."

Vance stroked his chin thoughtfully. "Yes, that's true enough." But then he added slowly, "You have all the symptoms. Nausea, morning sickness, and certainly that swelling would suggest that you're going to have a baby."

Eden sat up in the bed. She looked directly into his eyes. "That's impossible, Doctor. I've known only one man in my life and that was my husband. You know he's been dead for over a year."

Vance could not protest. "Well," he said slowly, "then we'll have to find what the problem is." He talked to her for some time about taking care of herself, but both of them were aware that he was not utterly convinced of the truth of her word. Finally he rose, snapped his bag shut, and said, "I'll make up a prescription for you." He headed toward the door, then turned and gave Eden one look, on the verge of asking her whether she was telling him the truth. But, seeing something in her eyes, his lips tightened and he shook his head. "Be sure you take your medicine and get plenty of rest."

"I will, Doctor."

Vance did not tarry at the Breckenridge place. He actually had no other possible diagnosis in mind besides pregnancy, but he left a tonic containing laudanum and gave Thomas instructions that she was to take it regularly.

"What do you think it is, Doctor?" Thomas asked anxiously.

"Hard to say." Vance's answer was evasive. "These things go away often without any help from us doctors. Let me know if she gets worse."

All the way back to town Vance pondered what he had just experienced. Like most doctors, he was a man who had seen the hard side of life. He had not allowed it to harden his spirit, however, and he shook his head saying, "I can't believe that of Eden Breckenridge, but the facts are there."

Later that evening, sitting down to a good, hot dinner, he related what had happened at the Breckenridge place. He knew that his wife would never reveal anything that he told her about his patients. When he had finished, he shrugged his shoulders. "I don't know what to say, Martha. I've always thought Eden Breckenridge was one of the finest women I've known."

"She is a good woman." Martha Vance, being a good woman herself, could recognize that quality. She was not intimately acquainted with Eden Breckenridge, but she had seen her enough at church and from time to time at gatherings in town to form an opinion. "What did she say?"

"She just said it was impossible."

"But she seemed to be pregnant?"

"Had all the symptoms."

"Well, it'll have to be something else then," Martha Vance said firmly. "I can't believe that she's a loose woman."

Martha Vance may have been able to keep a secret, but Lucy Gere was not. She cooked for the Vances and had ears sharper than any fox in the woods. She had heard enough of the conversation to come to believe one thing—that Eden Breckenridge was pregnant. She was not by intent a vicious gossiper, but nevertheless she did tell two people, and those two told others, and so it went. Within a few days, all over Helena, particularly in the Baptist church where Eden was a member, the tongues were wagging, and rumors cannot be stopped. They are like blowing thistles into the wind; no man can hope to recapture them again.

Reverend Nelson Jordan first heard the rumor when he was called aside by Otis Sanderson. He'd gone into Otis's store to buy a new razor, and was standing examining several. He had almost settled on a mother-of-pearl, which he could not afford, when Sanderson said suddenly, "Come into the office, Pastor."

Looking up with surprise, Nelson Jordan put the razor down and followed Sanderson back past rows of merchandise into the small, cluttered office. Sanderson did not sit down, nor did he offer the preacher a seat. He said bluntly, "The word's around that Eden Breckenridge is pregnant."

"Why, I don't believe it!" Jordan said.

Sanderson chewed on his lower lip. "I don't believe it either. But that's the gossip that's going around."

"Who told you?"

"I heard it from half a dozen people. You know how it is with gossip. Mrs. Beddington told me."

"Why, that woman's got a tongue long enough to sit in the living room and lick the skillet in the kitchen."

"Yes, she has, but Meyers Offenbach, he's a square man, not one loose with his tongue. He came to me and asked me about it. He had heard the same rumor."

Nelson Jordan settled back on his heels. He locked his hands behind his back and for a moment stood there. "I don't believe it. I'm going out and talk to Mrs. Breckenridge myself."

"You do that, preacher. That's why I asked you back here. Scotch this snake, if we can, before it gets any worse."

Nelson Jordan stepped inside the house. Taking his hat off, he smiled down at Prudence, who said, "I'm cooking Mama's supper."

"Well, let me see what you're doing, Prudence. Maybe I can help."

Prudence stared at him. "Men can't cook!" she announced firmly.

"That's what my wife says, but let me see anyway."

The preacher followed Prudence into the kitchen, and when she stopped beside the table, he said, "What are you cooking?"

"Mama's so sick all she can eat is boiled eggs, so I'm boiling some for her."

"Well, that's good for a bad stomach."

Prudence waved suddenly at the eggs laid out on a towel. "Some of these are old eggs and some were just laid. They got all mixed up."

"How are you going to tell which ones are the good ones?"

"Like this," Prudence said, flashing him a smile. Picking up an egg, she held it over a quart glass jar full of water. She let the egg slide inside and it went right to the bottom. "That's a good egg," she said.

"How do you know?"

"I just know." Prudence fished the egg out with a spoon and picked up another one. This one did not sink to the bottom but remained suspended halfway. "That's probably about two days old," she said judiciously. Picking another out, she found one finally that simply bobbed along the top. "That's an old egg."

Jordan was fascinated. "What's in that water?" he asked.

"Just a pinch of salt," Prudence said.

Nelson Jordan had always been fond of the Breckenridge children. But Johnny had avoided him when he'd arrived at the house; Jordan had seen the boy take one look and go around back. Now he said, "I guess I'd better go see your mother, Prudence."

Prudence looked up and tears welled up in her eyes. "She's real sick, Brother Jordan. I hope God will heal her."

"I'm sure he will." Jordan put his hand on the girl's head and then followed as she led him to the bedroom. Stepping inside, he was shocked by Eden's appearance but fought to keep it from showing on his face. "Hello, Sister Breckenridge," he said. She was sitting in a rocker. When she put out her hand and smiled faintly, he took it. He could tell she had a fever of some kind. Her face was pale and her eyes seemed sunken back in her head. "I've heard you've been ailing," he said.

Eden Breckenridge was a direct woman. She knew this man well and trusted him. But she suspected that this was more than just a pastoral call on an ailing parishioner—she suspected that he had heard rumors about her. Even though no one had come to her with an accusation, some of her neighbors were behaving in a most uncomfortable fashion. Eden knew the power of gossip, and she suspected that somehow word had gotten out. Doctor Vance was a good man, but he was not *that* good.

For a while she let Jordan talk uneasily about what was happening in the church, then she said without preamble, "What would happen if I died, Brother Nelson? Oh, I don't mean my soul or my spirit. I trusted Jesus when I was twelve years old. But what would happen to my children? And who would take care of my father?"

Jordan leaned forward and said earnestly, "Don't talk like that, Eden. You're not likely to die."

"Something's wrong with me. I don't know what it is, but I'm getting worse every day."

Nelson sat looking at her thoughtfully for a moment, then he said quietly, "When I was at Antietam, a bullet took me right in the chest. Should have killed me right off, but instead I lay there all day long, bodies on top of me. I thought I was going to die, and I prayed that God would go ahead and take me, I was in such pain. But God was with me. I lived when I shouldn't have." He reached out and took Eden's hand. "Nothing is too difficult for God."

"Did you hear what some people are saying? That I'm pregnant?"

Eden could see that her directness shook Jordan. He paused, then answered, "Yes. I've heard the rumor."

"Do you believe it?"

"I won't believe it if you say it's not true."

"It's not true," Eden said firmly. "I've never been with a man except for my husband, Will."

"Then I believe you, sister. Now, we're going to pray this thing through."

Jordan knelt beside the bed and prayed fervently for her healing, not only of the body but of the spirit. He prayed for the protection of her children, for the preservation of her home. Eden was touched by his tenderness and his fervency, and by the time he finished there were tears in her eyes.

"There, sister. Trust in God. I'll be coming back often, and so will my wife. Is there anything you need?"

"No. Thank you for coming, Pastor."

After the pastor left, Prudence came in carrying a tray. "Mama, I want you to eat some of these." On the tray was a bowl that contained three peeled hard-boiled eggs.

"Why, they look delicious," Eden said. She sprinkled on some salt with the saltshaker on the tray and took a bite. Suddenly the nausea rose up and she shoved it away. "I can't! I can't eat anymore right now. Just leave them, honey."

Prudence suddenly threw herself at her mother, knocking the eggs to the floor. "God won't let you die, Mama! I know he won't." Prudence clung to her mother, and Eden felt a fear wash over her, a black and awful fear that came from deep inside. She did not fear death—but she could not stand the thought that her children would be left orphans.

★ ★ ★

Awakening from a nap, Eden looked out her bedroom window and saw Johnny coming across the yard. It had been two days since the pastor's visit, and he had said little to her. Now she caught one glimpse of his face and called out, "Johnny, come here!"

When he came into her room, she saw that he had made attempts to clean up his face, but there was blood on his shirt. "What happened, son?"

"Nothin', Mama."

"Tell me."

Johnny's face twisted and he looked down at the floor. "I whipped Billy McCoy."

"Why, he's two years older than you are!"

"I know it, but I whipped him anyhow."

"What did you fight about?" Eden said, but she already knew.

"Aw, it was nothin', Mama."

"Did he say something bad about me?"

Johnny Breckenridge swallowed. He lifted his eyes and Eden saw that they were filled with torment. "He said . . . he said you were going to have a baby."

"It's not true, Johnny."

"Why do people say it, Mama?"

"Some of them are just mean. Others don't know any better. Whatever's wrong with me, it makes me look like I'm expecting a child, but I'm not. It's impossible." She reached out, and Johnny came into her arms. "I'm proud you fought for me, Johnny."

He stayed in her arms for a moment. Then, to hide the sobs that were threatening to overcome him, he said, "I've got to go, Mama."

Leaving the room, he ran outside, almost stumbling over Stuart who was crawling around the floor. "Look out!" Pru yelled. "You're going to hurt Stuart." Coming closer, she said, "Why, you're crying!"

"Am not!"

"You are too!" Prudence looked frightened. It had been a long time since she had seen her brother cry. "What's going to happen, Johnny?"

"I don't know," Johnny said. "I don't know."

All the rest of the afternoon, Prudence was filled with apprehension. She was an imaginative child, and the very imagination that could cause her to create songs and draw things could also create a sense of foreboding. She knew something dreadful was wrong and yet, feeling protective of her mother, she was reluctant to go to her for comfort.

Finally she went out to the barn and sat down on the bed that Quentin had used. She was still for a long time, thinking. Then she saw a book on the table beside the bed and picked it up and opened it. She had learned to read a little, but Quentin's handwritten text was beyond her comprehension, and she quickly gave up on it. Opening the book idly at the cover, she saw in print the name *Quentin Larribee*. She sounded out the words. Beneath it she sounded out the rest, mostly numbers—*2130 West 113th Ave.* Below that—*New York City*.

She ran her fingers over the name, as if by touching the dried ink she could touch the man. She cried out then, "Oh, Quentin, come back! Come back and help us!"

CHAPTER
Seventeen

Darling, you look like a man on his way to be hanged." Irene laughed up into Quentin's face. Her eyes were sparkling with excitement. She squeezed his arm and said, "You ought to be thrilled to go on a shopping trip in the most famous shopping district in America."

Quentin forced a smile. "Well, anything we can do together is exciting." He looked over at Fuller's Department Store at Broadway and Fifth Avenue. It covered a square block and rose up six stories high. It was the beginning of New York's famous "Ladies' Mile." A sinking feeling came to Quentin as he realized that Irene was probably going to visit all six stories, with him in tow.

"Come on, dear. They've just installed a vertical railroad."

"A vertical railroad! What in the name of common sense is that? Railroads are horizontal, not vertical."

"Not this one." She pulled him inside excitedly and pointed. "There it is. Some people call it an elevator."

Despite himself, Quentin's curiosity quickened. He walked closer and looked into what seemed to be a room divided by an iron grill. "What does it do?"

"It goes up, silly. Come along."

Gingerly, Quentin stepped onto the vertical railroad, and a young man with slick black hair asked, "What floor?"

Irene said, "Six, please."

"Six it is."

The young man pulled a lever, and the whole small room gave a jerk that made Quentin feel as if he were falling. He grabbed at Irene and held her with one hand and groped for the wall with the other. The young man turned and winked, saying with an air of self-importance, "Don't worry, sir. It's perfectly safe."

At first, Quentin didn't find the shopping trip as unpleasant as he had expected, for the shops were varied and interesting. Their first stop was an elegant milliner, where Irene tried on hats of all shapes and colors with ribbons flying. Next they went to a glovers, where it took almost an hour for her to decide on a pair of white satin gloves, and Quentin's interest began to flag. "They're a little long for evening wear," she said. She counted the buttons made of pearls that looked real. When Quentin heard the price he flinched, but Irene did not appear to notice.

The longest stop was at a French dressmaker's shop where Quentin shifted from foot to foot wearily until finally his legs began to ache. *I wonder why I get more tired just standing around than I do working?* he wondered.

Finally Irene took pity on him. "I've worn you out, you poor dear. I'm going to be one of those women whose husband never goes anyplace with them." She reached up and patted his cheek. "After we're married, we're going to shop together and have all sorts of activities. Now, you go on back to your hospital. But don't forget we're having dinner with the Van Pelts tonight."

"I'll remember."

Quentin made his escape gladly. On Fifth Avenue, he caught a hansom cab that delivered him to the hospital. With a sigh of relief, he climbed outside and paid the fare, adding a healthy tip. He felt as if he had just been released from prison. "Got to stop feeling like that," he murmured. "That's part of being married to Irene."

The rest of the day went well. He was at his best seeing patients, and he stayed so busy moving from bed to bed and from patient to patient that he thought of nothing else. In fact, at the end of the day, he was shocked when he pulled out his watch and saw the time. "Oh, my!" he muttered. "I'll never make it."

"Make what?"

Quentin turned to see Les Simmons standing in the door. He moved over and said, "I've got to be at the Van Pelts. We're having dinner with them tonight."

Simmons turned and accompanied him down the hall. Strangely enough, the two had become rather good friends. Neither of them deceived himself or the other. Les entertained an enormous envy for Quentin and made no secret of his affection for Irene. Now as the two strolled along, he said, "Congratulations."

"On what? My engagement or getting my certificate to practice medicine?"

Les grinned crookedly. "I'll never congratulate you on getting Irene."

Quentin suddenly laughed. "You are a rascal, Les Simmons! But an entertaining one."

"An honest one, too." Les suddenly stopped. Seizing Quentin's arm, he drew him around. "It's all wrong, you know."

"What's all wrong?"

"You and Irene getting married."

"Now, Les—"

"Don't interrupt me. I'm resigned to losing her, but I'm telling you right now, you won't be happy with Irene. You're far too noble."

"Noble! What are you talking about?"

"You want to give your life to patients and to medicine. That's fine if you're a bachelor, but Irene's not made that way. She wants to have supper every night with the Van Pelts or the president. She likes to go shopping." He saw Quentin's wince and laughed. "I'll bet you've been doing that today."

"Doesn't hurt a man to go shopping with his fiancée."

"It wouldn't hurt me, but it hurts you. You'd rather be here treating an open sore on a beggar than going shopping. Tell the truth."

Quentin struggled between honesty and an outright lie, and finally he shrugged. "We'll have to make some adjustments, but every couple has to do that."

Les Simmons suddenly became intensely serious. He was a short, muscular man with sharp black eyes set in a blocky face and thick, stubby hands. He was, indeed, a scoundrel in some ways, but there was a basic honesty in him and he knew his limitations. "I'll never be as good a doctor as you will be, Quent. Everybody knows you're the best. But I'd be a better husband for Irene. In the first place, you don't really care about her like I do."

"Don't be a fool, Les!"

"You're the fool, Quent. You came from a poor family. You had it rough growing up. That does something to a person. Irene never had any of that, and she'll never know how to live with having less. She doesn't understand poverty, and she doesn't understand hard work. It's not her fault she was born rich. Her parents made life easy."

"I think I could learn to take prosperity."

"No, you can't," Les said thoughtfully. "You're just not cut out that way. You're sort of a male Joan of Arc or something. You're the stuff heroes are made of."

"Les, you're talking blasted nonsense!"

But Simmons for once was totally serious. "I'm going to tell you a secret. I'm selfish enough to enjoy the good life, but you're not. And I'll tell you something else. You're going to make Irene miserable—and you're going to be miserable, too, Quentin."

The words seemed to toll like a funeral bell in Quentin's ears. He tried to meet Simmons's gaze but could not. He had struggled with some of these same thoughts himself. But spoken aloud by Simmons, they hit him with more force. He shook his head and said, "I've got to go. See you later, Les."

Simmons watched him go and bit his lower lip. "I'm not one for liking another fellow, but I like that one as much as any. He's making a bad mistake, and it won't be long before he finds that out!"

Hannah turned from the stove as she heard Quentin's footsteps. She missed the sound of his whistling when he arrived home; she had not heard him whistle for weeks. It had always been a source of comfort to her, his cheerful whistling—he did it so beautifully. She turned from the stove when he came inside. As they hugged, she said, "Did you have a good day?"

"Yes. Irene and I went shopping."

"What did you buy?"

"Nothing." Quentin grinned wryly. "She bought enough for both of us. Say, they've got a room at the shops that goes up through a building. They call it a vertical railroad."

"It does what?"

"I'm telling you it goes straight up. You get in it and it goes up in the air six stories. You just stand there and the whole room goes up."

"Have they got horses at the top pulling it up?"

"No. It's run by steam. Pretty scary. I want to take you there sometime. You ought to try it."

"No, thanks. I'd just as soon not."

Quentin nodded absently. "All right. I've got to go to the Van Pelts for dinner tonight."

Hannah ignored his comment. "There's a letter that came for you. A rather strange one."

"What do you mean strange?"

She moved swiftly across the room. Picking up an envelope from the table, she said, "Here. Looks like a child's handwriting."

"It is. It's from Prudence." He made out the printed letters on the envelope and gave her a wondering look. "I wonder where she got this address." He opened it and his eyes flew over it swiftly. Hannah saw his brow furrow, and when he'd scanned it, he handed it to her wordlessly. It was very brief, printed in large letters, some of them awkwardly made.

Dear Quentin,

Mama is sick and I'm afraid for her. I found where you live in the front of a book you left. Please come and help us. I'm scared Mama's going to die. I gave this letter to Trumbo to mail. I hope you get it because we need you.

Love,
PRUDENCE

Taking the letter back, Quentin read it again, then looked up into Hannah's eyes. He could not think clearly, but the stark simplicity and urgency of the child's plea hit him hard. He moistened his lips, then shook his head. "Hannah," he said quietly, "what am I to do?"

Hannah's mind was working quickly. She knew her brother better than he knew himself. "You'll have to go help, of course."

"You mean—*now?*"

"If the woman is that sick, she needs you now."

"But Pru's only eight."

"This letter's from a frightened child, but you must make your own decision."

Quentin stood holding the paper. He stared at the words as if he could extract more meaning from them, and finally he said thickly, "I don't know what to do. Eden told me never to come back. I don't know if she'd see me if I did." He waited for Hannah to answer, but she stood silently, studying his face. He turned from her, folded the paper, and stuck it in his pocket. Moving slowly, he left the room, and she heard his footsteps going down the hall. The door closed, and Hannah stood for a moment, then shut off the stove and went into the parlor. She sat down, bowed her head, and began to pray. "Lord, give Quentin a bit of good sense . . ."

Hannah didn't know how long she sat there, for often when she prayed she became lost in time. Now she heard Quentin's footsteps; looking up, she saw that he had put on his coat, and his mouth was set in a grim line. "I've got to go, Hannah. You're right." He hesitated then studied her. "What will Irene say?"

"I think you know."

Quentin dropped his head. When he looked up, pure misery was sketched on his countenance. "I guess I do," he said briefly. He turned and left without another word. Hannah began to pray fervently, for she knew that this brother of hers was at a crossroads.

*   *   *

"Have you lost your mind, Quentin?" Irene said shrilly. She had listened while he had told her of the letter. Now she scanned it, then looked up angrily. "A child writes you a letter like this—and you're going to throw away everything and go running back?"

"Prudence is pretty levelheaded for a child, Irene. I don't think she'd write unless it was serious."

"If the woman needed help, why didn't she write?"

"I don't think she'd do that. She's not one to ask for help."

"If she doesn't ask for help, then you're not obligated to go," Irene said. She calmed herself then, knowing that beneath what seemed to be a flexible, compliant nature, a streak of rock-hard stubbornness lurked in Quentin Larribee. She had seen it before when he had informed her he had to go to Arkansas the first time, and now she knew she must be very tactful.

"Quentin, you must think this out," she said, and then she drew him to sit beside her on the couch. Taking his hand in hers, she leaned against him. "I know you feel a deep sense of obligation to this woman, but you have to use common sense."

"It's not just Eden," Quentin said quickly. "It's the whole family."

Irene had to bite her tongue to keep from attacking Eden, but she managed to conceal her true feelings. "I understand that, and I think it's sweet of you to be so thoughtful."

"They're all so helpless, Irene!"

"But just think what you've already done for them. You left your work and put off all our plans once. Surely they wouldn't expect you to do it all again."

"Eden's a proud woman. She'd never beg for help."

She'd do anything to get you! The thought sprang into Irene's mind, but she said carefully, "This is a letter from a child, Quentin. Her mother is sick and she's frightened. That's very understandable. But children are often overemotional. You can't leave and go rushing off like a knight in shining armor!"

"I never thought of myself as that," Quentin said at once. "I just feel obligated to do what I can."

But Irene was suddenly taken with the figure of speech she had used. "It's exactly what you are—or what you want to be," she said.

"Want to be what?"

"A knight. You've always had that romantic streak in you, Quentin. I saw it long ago. You think of medicine that way. It's not just a profession with you, it's a—a *calling.*"

Quentin stared at Irene and shook his head. "I just want to help people, Irene. Isn't that what all doctors are supposed to do?"

Irene Chambers had seen too many doctors who cared only for money and position to argue this with Quentin. She realized that Quentin had no idea how rare his sort of idealism was in the real world of medicine. Giving up on this line, she pressed closer to him and said, "But darling, our wedding is getting close. There are so many things to be done."

"I wouldn't be gone long, Irene."

"That's what you said last time—and you were gone for months!"

"This is different. I'll just go down there, do what I can for Eden, then come right back."

Irene pulled away from Quentin. He had not responded to her touch and this angered her. She had always been able to stir him in this way, but now she saw that his face was set stubbornly.

"Quentin, you've got to think of *me* for a change. I'm the woman you're going to marry—not Eden Breckenridge!" Her voice was becoming shrill and her back was stiff with indignation.

Quentin stood with his head down. When he spoke, it was only to repeat miserably, "I won't be gone long, Irene."

And then Irene lost her temper. "It's that woman!" she snapped bitterly. "You're going back because of her!"

"Well, of course, it's because of her. She's ill."

But Irene had long suspected that there was more to Quentin's earlier trip to Arkansas than he had admitted. She had seen Eden's beauty, and the very fact that Quentin never mentioned her was a signal that aroused Irene's jealousy. She stood stiffly, fists clenched by her side, and took a deep breath. "If you leave, Quentin, this time it's over between us."

"Why, you don't mean that, Irene!"

"I do mean it! You're acting like a child! Our wedding isn't far off, and there are things to do. You're working into the practice. Are you going to drop that?" Even as her voice grew more strident, she began to feel more confident. This tactic couldn't fail—she could not imagine that he would give up all that lay before him. "Quentin," she said more quietly. "I mean it. If you care for me at all, you won't go."

"Don't put it like that, Irene," Quentin said quickly. "It's a call for help. I have to go."

Irene stood still as a statue, her mind working furiously. It was clear that she would not be able to keep Quentin from going back to Arkansas. She had chosen Quentin not only because she knew that he had a brilliant future as a surgeon, but also because she was certain that she could mold him into the man she wanted beside her. She had created a picture of her life, and it featured a husband who fit into society. Now she saw for the first time a side of

Quentin Larribee that shocked her. Even though she had been aware of his idealism, she had been convinced that she would be able to teach him the truths that controlled life. She had, in fact, been determined to make another man of Quentin—one that suited her dreams of rising in the social world of New York. She had seen his rough edges but was confident that, given time, she could smooth them over.

But now she saw that beneath Quentin's mild manner lay a vein of iron. The truth was, she would never be able to change him in the ways that mattered. She could change what he wore and his table manners—but in some areas she would never be able to move him.

Still she stood, suddenly aware that she was standing at a crossroad. This was a test. Being a strong woman, she knew that the time had come to risk all.

"Quentin, I'm hurt that you've taken this stand."

"I can't do anything else, Irene."

"Nothing I can say will change your mind?"

"Ask me anything else—"

"No." Irene drew herself up straight and said firmly, "If you go away and leave me like this, it's over between us, Quentin."

Shock hit Quentin, for her statement was carved in stone. "You can't mean that, Irene!"

"I do mean it. Oh, Quentin, don't force me to make this choice!" Irene reached out to touch his cheek—somewhat startled to realize that she truly did want him to come to her.

"Irene—I just *can't!*"

Irene felt something inside—something like a door closing. She knew what she must do. "I can see that you've got your mind made up. Here, take your ring, and I never want to see you again as long as I live!" She stripped off the simple ring with the small stone, all Quentin had been able to afford, and held it out. Automatically he opened his hand and took it. He started to speak, but in her anger she gave him no chance. "You never appreciated anything my father did for you! You never cared for me! No, don't try to say that you did. You left once for months and now, practically on the eve of our marriage, you're running off again! Well, go on back to that woman and make sure you never come into this house again!"

Irene saw Quentin's fingers closing around the ring as she turned away from him. Back stiff, she stalked to her room and did not come out for two hours. When she did, her face was still tight with anger. She went at once to the larger parlor where her mother was writing a letter. "Mother, something has happened . . ."

At first, Louise Chambers listened wide-eyed to Irene's explanation, but gradually her expression grew more calm, and when Irene finished speaking, Louise stood and put her arm around her daughter. "I know this is hard for you, dear, but I must say, I'm not completely surprised. I have never fully approved of the idea of Quentin as your husband. He's a fine doctor, but he's . . . unrefined. In the long run it will be best."

"How can it be best? I'll be humiliated! Jilted by a country bumpkin!"

"You're the one who is breaking the engagement. Everyone will understand that. Dear, he's not the man for you."

Louise spoke for some time, and gradually, despite her emotional upheaval, Irene began to hear what her mother was saying.

"You agree with me, don't you?" Louise continued. "I know you were attracted to him, but mostly that was because he could take over your father's practice. And there are others who can do that."

Instantly Irene thought of Les Simmons. She said nothing, but her eyes sought her mother's. Her mother had always favored Les, who came from an aristocratic background. Irene knew that they were both thinking the same thing. Taking a deep breath, she said, "I believe I made a serious error, Mother. It'll be embarrassing."

"Not at all. We'll take a trip out of town for a while after we let the word get out." She smiled, then said cautiously, watching Irene carefully, "At least this will make one young man very happy. Les will be camping on your doorstep again."

"He will, won't he?" Irene said, and then her mind began to work. "It would be foolish to let Quentin ruin my life. Come along, Mother. Let's go make our plans . . ."

★　★　★

"She told me never to come back. She said she never wanted to see me again."

Hannah listened as Quentin repeated the results of his conference with Irene. She said nothing, but she saw the distress in his face. He looked at her suddenly and said wryly, "Well, I can tell you one thing. I won't be taking over Oscar's practice."

"I wouldn't think so."

"No. Irene would never permit that."

The two were sitting in the parlor. Hannah had simply let Quentin talk until the tension had run out of him. Now he managed an ironic grin. "Well, I don't know what to do now."

"You're going to practice medicine."

"I just told you. I can never take over Oscar Chambers's practice."

"You didn't want it anyway, did you?"

"Why . . ." Surprise washed across Quentin's face as the thought struck him. "I guess I really didn't. It's not the kind of medicine I want to practice. Anyway, I've got to go to Arkansas." He hesitated, then said, "I don't know how long I'll be gone, Hannah. I hate to leave you here."

"Don't hate it, because you're not going to."

Quentin stared at Hannah with surprise. "What does that mean?"

"It means I'm going with you, Quentin. You're not leaving me this time."

"To Arkansas! You can't do that, Hannah. What about this place?"

"What about it? It's just a rented apartment."

"But all your things are here."

"Do you like it here in New York, Quentin?"

"Actually, I hate it."

"Have you felt that way long?"

"A long time. What about you?"

"I hate it, too. I always have," Hannah said simply. "I know I want to leave here."

"And go to Arkansas?"

"You're going to be a doctor, aren't you? You can be a doctor there as well as anyplace else."

And then Quentin felt as if a load had been lifted from his shoulders. He felt light and free, and something close to happiness came to him for the first time in months. He realized suddenly that he had been greatly worried about leaving Hannah alone. "All right," he said. "But you don't know how rough it is in Arkansas. It's pretty primitive."

"We grew up primitive, didn't we? Well, we can do it again."

Quentin rose to his feet. His eyes had a new light of excitement. He seemed already, Hannah noticed, to have forgotten Irene Chambers. How wrong that marriage would have been! Hannah had always thought so. She rose and picked up her crutch. "If we're going to leave right away, it's going to take a lot of work."

Quentin reached over and put his hand on her arm. He said, "You're a wonder, Hannah." The two looked at each other, smiles on their faces. Even though neither knew what their new life would be like, for some reason neither felt a moment's anxiety. Together, they would find their way, as they always had.

CHAPTER
Eighteen

As the *Robert E. Lee* swung in from the main channel and came to a shuddering halt at the dock, Hannah felt apprehensive. She watched as the gangplank was lowered from the bow until it touched the dock, thinking how strange it all was, more like illusion than reality. She recalled how frantically she had worked over the past week to get their furniture stored, sorting out only necessary personal things. Quentin had resigned at the hospital, and in a flurry of activity the two had tied up the loose ends of their lives in New York and left for Arkansas. She had seen that Quentin was terribly worried about Eden, although he had said little about her.

The shrill piercing cry of a steamboat leaving the wharf startled Hannah, and she gripped her crutch more tightly and shrugged off her doubts. *We've prayed and we're trusting God and that's all there is to it.* The thought gave her strength, and she looked around to see Quentin approaching in the line of passengers headed for the gangplank. He was carrying two bags and when he reached her, he smiled. "Well, are you ready to become an Arkansan?"

"Yes," Hannah replied. She studied his face, looking for signs of anxiety, but saw none. "Well, let's get ashore," she said firmly. "We have a lot to do." Turning, she made her way along the deck, keeping her place in the line that filed down the gangplank. At the foot a man reached out to give her a hand, and she took it saying, "Thank you very much."

When Quentin had joined her on the docks, she said, "What about our trunks?"

"I'll go rent a buggy. We'll have to stay at a hotel until we find a regular place." He glanced across the dock milling with departing and arriving passengers. "Come along. I'll introduce you to Ed Gibbons. He owns the stable. He'll rent us a rig."

The two walked up over the levee and there at the foot, right at the north end of town, stood Ed Gibbons's livery stable. As they approached, Quentin said, "There's Ed."

Ed Gibbons was standing in front of his stable. Quentin saw Ed's eyes fasten on him as he approached, but to Quentin's surprise, Ed's back straightened and his eyes grew narrow and hard.

"Hello, Ed," Quentin smiled. "How are you?"

Gibbons nodded. "Very well." His voice was clipped and short; he studied Quentin coldly for a moment, then looked at Hannah.

"Hannah, I'd like you to meet Ed Gibbons. Ed, this is my sister, Hannah."

"I'm glad to know you, miss."

Quentin had been on good terms with Gibbons and had expected a warmer welcome. He waited for Gibbons to remark on his return, but when he studied the man's square, blocky face, he was puzzled to see only hardness. "We've just gotten in from New York, Ed, on the *Robert E. Lee*."

"So I see."

Just the bare words; nothing more. Quentin knew that something was wrong. *I wonder if he's angry because I left?* he asked himself. But there was nothing to be done about it now, so he said, "I'd like to rent a rig, Ed. I'll be buying one soon, but I need one now to get our things to the hotel."

"That bay over there. You can have her." Gibbons indicated a tall, rangy bay gelding hitched to a two-seated buggy. Quentin would have expected him to walk with them over to the rig and offer to help Hannah into the seat, but Gibbons stayed planted where he was. "That'll be three dollars a day."

Quentin was startled both at Gibbons's manner and at his demand for payment in advance, but he pulled out his wallet and counted out the three bills. "Maybe you can help me find a good buy in a horse and a light buggy," he said, studying the man.

"Maybe."

The stark reply confirmed that something was wrong, but Quentin said simply, "Come along, Hannah." He led her to the buggy, helped her in, then climbed in and spoke to the bay.

As they drove back to the levee, Hannah said in a puzzled tone, "He's not very friendly."

"No," Quentin admitted. "He was fine when I was here before. Something's eating at him."

He thought about Gibbons while he loaded their trunks and the bags. When he climbed back in, he said, "When we get a house we'll have our furniture shipped. It may be a little rough until then."

"It doesn't matter."

"Well, let's go to the hotel and get settled."

There was little choice of hotels in Helena. Other than rooming houses, the Palace Hotel was the only place. Quentin handed Hannah down and the two entered the lobby. Quentin nodded. "Hello, Mr. Thompson."

Joseph Thompson, who owned the Palace, was behind the desk. He was a tall, rangy man in his late forties with a sweeping mustache. He nodded briefly, saying, "Well, hello, Mr. Larribee." There was a moment's hesitation, and he asked, "What can I do for you?"

"I'd like a room for myself and another for my sister. This is my sister, Miss Hannah Larribee."

"I'm glad to know you, Miss Larribee."

"You have a couple of rooms, I hope."

"Certainly. If you'll just register here, I'll have someone take your luggage up." He lifted his head and called out, "Frank! Frank! Take these folks up to 203 and 205."

"I'll be looking for a house, so we won't be here long, Mr. Thompson."

"Should be able to find something."

Thompson's tone and expression were cool. He was not as unfriendly as Gibbons had been, but Quentin again had the sense of stepping into something he did not understand. He nodded and said, "If you hear of anything, let me know."

"I'll do that."

It took less than an hour to get settled, and then Quentin said, "You're probably tired, Hannah. Why don't you lie down and take a nap?"

"I'm not tired. I slept well last night. What are you going to do?"

"I'm going out to see Eden and the children."

"I'd like to go with you," Hannah said quickly. "If you think it would be all right."

"Of course it would. Come along. There's still plenty of time to drive out."

They left the hotel and he helped her into the buggy. "I want to make one stop before we go. I'd like to check with Otis Sanderson."

"Who is he?"

"He owns the biggest store in town. He helped us get started in the business. Good man."

He pulled the buggy up in front of the store and helped Hannah down. As they entered, he noticed the eternal checker game going on and remembered the first time he'd come to Helena. He recognized some of the men and nodded but received little greeting in reply.

Inside, he saw Sanderson standing behind the counter weighing out coffee beans and putting them into small paper bags. When he approached, he said, "Hello, Otis."

Sanderson looked up and surprise washed across his face. "Why, Quentin," he said. "You're back."

"And I brought my sister with me. Hannah, this is Otis Sanderson. Otis, my sister, Miss Hannah Larribee."

"Glad to know you, Miss Larribee."

An awkward silence fell over the group, and Quentin felt a deepening of the discomfort that had been with him ever since he had spoken to Ed Gibbons. Sanderson had always been a friend to him, but now there was clearly a constraint in his manner. "Is something wrong, Otis?" Quentin asked.

Sanderson shot a quick glance at Hannah.

"You can speak in front of Hannah," Quentin said. "We have no secrets."

"I'm not sure that would apply in this case. Got something rather serious to tell you." He looked around and said, "Come into the office." He led the two to his small office. "Have a seat, Miss Hannah."

"I'll stand." Hannah was studying the man. She liked his appearance. He was not prepossessing but there was something solid about the man, and she had heard enough from Quentin to know that he was dependable.

Sanderson fidgeted, running his hands through his sandy hair. "Blast it, Quentin! I wish you hadn't come back."

The sharpness of Sanderson's words caught Quentin off guard. "Something's wrong," he said. "What is it? Is something wrong with Eden? Something wrong out at the farm?"

"You don't know?"

"We just got in. I got a letter from Prudence saying that her mother was sick. She asked me to come." He hesitated then said, "Look, Otis, I might as well tell you. When I was here before, I was in training to become a doctor. I went back to New York, completed my training, and now I'm coming to Helena to set up a practice."

"You don't tell me!" Otis exclaimed. His eyes narrowed and he studied Quentin carefully. "You never said anything about all that when you were here before."

"I know. I should have. But I'm telling you now. In any case, what's wrong with Eden?"

Sanderson took a deep breath and expelled it slowly. He fumbled at the watch chain that dangled from his vest, glancing a couple of times at Hannah. "It might be better if I told you alone."

"No. I want Hannah to hear it, whatever it is. Quick, man, tell me! What is it? What's wrong with her?"

"Doctor Vance thinks she's pregnant."

Sanderson could see that his bald statement had great impact on both Quentin and Hannah; that was one of the things he had wanted to find out. Quentin blinked, and his lips drew into a pale line. "Who's the man?" he finally asked.

"Most people around here think it's you." Sanderson saw that this statement came as an even greater shock than the previous one. Hannah was watching her brother with a calmness that Sanderson couldn't help but admire. "Eden hasn't been doing well, and Doc Vance went out to see to her. She claims she's not having a baby, but Doc says she's got all the symptoms."

"And people are talking about us. Is that it?"

"That's it, Quentin."

"That explains why Ed Gibbons and Mr. Thompson were cold."

"People don't know what to make of it. It looks bad, Quentin," Otis said quietly. "You show up, stay awhile, and then you leave. Then after you're gone, Mrs. Breckenridge appears to be pregnant."

"Well, go on and ask me," Quentin demanded, staring hard at Sanderson.

"All right, I will," Otis said. "Is there any truth in it?"

"Not a word!" Quentin stood, his back straight and his arms down at his sides. "Eden Breckenridge is the finest woman I've ever known."

Otis had learned to judge men, and now as he studied Quentin he reached a decision quickly. "If you say it, I believe it, Quentin." He hesitated, then shook his head. "But a lot of people won't."

"I've got to get out there, Otis. And here's what I want you to do. I need to find a place. I'm going to hang my shingle out here, and Hannah and I need a house we can live in and make part of it into an office. Do you know of anything like that?"

"Why, as a matter of fact, the Edwards place is for rent. Even got some furniture in it."

"Who owns it?"

"I do." Sanderson suddenly smiled. "Bought it to speculate. You can move right in. There's two big parlors you could make into offices, I suppose. Kitchen in the back, bedrooms upstairs."

"I'll be a little short of money," Quentin said with some hesitation.

"We'll thrash that out. Maybe you can help my rheumatism."

"Maybe I can," Quentin said. He shook his head. "I've got to go to the Breckenridge place. Come along, Hannah. See if you can hire somebody to clean the place up, Otis. I'll be back soon, and we'll need to move in right away."

"I'll take care of it, Quentin."

When the two of them were in the buggy and headed out of town, Quentin turned to face Hannah. "Something's wrong in all this, Hannah."

"Quentin, people won't go to a doctor they don't trust, and with these rumors flying around about you and Mrs. Breckenridge, it'll be hard for you."

"So it will." He set his jaw and said, "But we're here and we're going to stay."

★   ★   ★

"There's the place, Hannah," Quentin said.

Hannah looked up and saw the house and asked quietly, "What are you expecting, Quentin?"

"I don't know. I haven't the faintest idea."

They drew up in the yard, and Quentin stepped down. He heard the sound of his name and turned to see Prudence flying out of the house. Her face was beaming, and she threw herself at him with abandon, calling his name. He caught her up and hugged her with a sudden joy. *At least there's something right,* he thought. He held her for a moment, kissed her on the cheek, and then said, "Hannah, I want you to meet Miss Prudence Breckenridge. Prudence, this is my sister, Miss Hannah."

"How do you do, Prudence?" Hannah smiled as she got down from the buggy.

"Hello," Prudence said shyly. Then she looked back to Quentin, her face wreathed in smiles. "I knew you'd come," she whispered.

Johnny came around the side of the house and stopped still. Quentin moved toward him at once and put his hand out, saying, "I'm glad to see you, Johnny."

For a moment Quentin thought Johnny wouldn't take his hand, but then something came into the boy's face and he reached out. His hand was hard and firm. Johnny struggled for a moment, then said, "Pru told me she wrote you a letter, but I didn't think nothin' would come of it."

"I've come back to help if I can, Johnny. How's your mother?"

"She ain't so good."

"Is your grandfather here?"

"He's inside taking care of Stuart."

Quentin turned and said, "Come along, Hannah, and meet the rest of the family."

Both Johnny and Prudence followed Hannah up the steps, staring curiously at her crutch. "I have to have a little help," she said, noticing their stares. "I had an accident when I was younger."

Prudence said, "You do real good, Miss Hannah."

"Thank you, Prudence."

They found Thomas waiting for them inside next to the window, so Quentin assumed that he had been watching their arrival.

The two men shook hands. After introducing Hannah, Quentin said, "We're moving here, Thomas. I was in training to be a doctor, and I've finished my study. I'm opening an office in Helena."

Thomas York studied the younger man and said, "I always thought there was something different about you. And you're a real doctor?"

"Well, I have a piece of paper that says so." He reached out suddenly and took Stuart, who squealed. "This young man is growing like a weed!"

Thomas glanced in the direction of the bedroom and said, "You'll be wanting to see Eden."

"Yes." Putting Stuart down, Quentin said, "Hannah, maybe you could help entertain Stuart while I go see the patient."

Hannah came at once and said, "Hello, Stuart. Would you like to show me your toys?"

Stuart nodded and without a word began showing her his wooden blocks.

Thomas accompanied Quentin down the hall but stopped him halfway to the bedroom. "She's not good, Quentin. I'm worried about her. She gets worse every day, it seems." He hesitated, then said, "Do you know what they're saying in town?"

"Yes, I know. Do you believe any of it, Thomas?"

"Of course not. But something's wrong with her."

Quentin felt a sudden surge of affection for this man who had endured such hardship without complaint. Almost fiercely, Quentin said, "God will do something." He gripped Thomas's shoulder, and then turned and entered Eden's bedroom.

Eden was standing in the middle of the room. She was wearing a gray dress, and even before he looked into her eyes he could see the thickening of her body. Then he looked up at her face. She was pale, and the planes of her face were more clearly outlined, for though the body was heavier her face seemed drawn. He said quietly, "Eden, I've come back."

"I saw you through the window." She seemed tentative, almost in shock at his return.

"Sit down, Eden. I have some things to tell you."

Eden sat down in the rocking chair beside the window. Quentin drew up a straight cane-bottomed chair and sat directly in front of her. He hesitated only for a moment then said, "Let me begin by saying that I'm no longer an engaged man. I was engaged to Irene, but she broke it off." He watched her face and saw something change in her eyes, but she did not speak. "The second thing I have to tell you is that I'm a doctor. When I first came here, I was determined to help you as much as I could, and leave as quickly as possible. I was in the final stages of my medical training, but I wanted to keep my background out of it. Well, I've finished my training now. I'm a fully certified doctor." He went on to tell her, speaking quietly, how he had finished his medical training, and then he said, "I got a letter from Prudence saying that you were very ill. She was worried so we prayed about it, my sister and I, and we decided to leave New York and to set up a practice in Helena."

A silence fell over the room. Quentin could not read her expression, but he knew that this was not the strong and vibrant Eden Breckenridge he had known before. He said finally, "I know you told me not to come back, and I know I treated you miserably, yet somehow I felt that God wanted me to come. I'm hoping I can find out what's wrong with you, Eden—and praying that I can do something about it."

Eden studied his face, noting that his brown hair was somewhat longer. She had thought often, since his departure, of his homely features—and had often berated herself for throwing herself at a man who did not care for her. But now that he had stepped back into her life, she was confused. Miserably, she said, "Do you know what they're saying about me—about us?"

"Yes. Blasted foolishness!"

At his sharp words she looked up and said, "They say I'm having a baby, but I'm not, Quentin. I'm not!"

"Of course not. And they say I'm the father, and we know that's impossible."

She put her hand on her stomach. "I don't understand it," she said desperately. "It's exactly as if I *were* having a child. I'm sick all the time, especially in the morning; I have pains and aches, and my stomach is growing larger. What's happening, Quentin? What's happening to me?"

Quentin hesitated, then suddenly stood and, reaching down, pulled her to her feet. She was startled, frightened, uncertain—but then he put his arms around her and pulled her head down onto his chest. He stroked her hair; her body shook as she asked herself, *Should I allow this?* And then she began to weep—silently at first, trying to restrain the tears, but they would not be held back. She wept freely then, and clung to him as a child would cling to a parent.

Quentin murmured soft words, meaningless words, and finally Eden felt her sobbing begin to subside. Still he held her and whispered, "Eden, God is able to do all things. I believe he's brought me to this place to help you. We know the truth—which is that you are a good woman, no matter what the rumors are. I'm here and I'm not leaving."

With her face pressed against Quentin's chest and his arms around her, holding her close, Eden felt that her misery and doubts and fears had been lifted. Her problems were still there—but this man who held her had come back out of nowhere, with his calm words and his prayers and his confidence. She felt like a drowning person, sinking into the dark, into the depths, and then a rescuer had plucked her out and held her up and assured her that she'd be safe.

Lifting her tearstained face, Eden whispered, "Quentin, I'm glad you came back."

Quentin held her tightly and said, "I'm glad, too, Eden."

PART
Four

CHAPTER
Nineteen

For ten minutes, Quentin sat staring up at a fly crawling across the ceiling—something he ordinarily would not even have noticed. But boredom had captured him. Drowsily, he tilted his chair back. The sun was at its zenith, and June had brought hot weather to Arkansas. He reached up and loosened his tie, wondering why he had worn it. He watched the fly trace his way in a semicircular direction, finally reversing himself and covering the same territory for what seemed like the fifth time.

"I guess I don't have any more purpose than you do, fly," Quentin said, his voice breaking the silence in the room. He brought his chair down, rubbed his stiff neck, then got up and nervously stalked back and forth from one wall to the other. The office was no more than twelve feet square, and the furniture consisted of a pine desk, a brown leather chair, and a line of cabinets along one wall that were mostly bare except for a few bottles, boxes, and glass vials.

Out the window, Quentin saw two dogs circling each other warily, their bristles raised. He waited for them to lunge at each other, but finally the smaller of the two, a brown and white nondescript animal, backed off and sulked away. The other, a brindle terrier of some sort, seemed to consider prolonging the war, but then plumped himself down and began to scratch his left ear.

Pine Street was deserted except for two men lackadaisically putting up a building of some sort. They moved slowly, and their muffled voices filtered through the window. He watched them for a time, then stepped into the waiting room, hoping to see a patient. There were none, of course—only four rickety chairs and a collection of old newspapers—just as there had been none, with a rare exception or two, in the two weeks since he had opened his office. He had known it would be difficult to start a practice, but now he was almost ready to believe that it was impossible. As Hannah had predicted, the rumors floating around about Eden Breckenridge and himself served to keep people away. That and the fact that he had been born north of the Mason-Dixon Line.

The three rooms upstairs that he and Hannah had converted into an abode were no more attractive than the waiting room. The floor was a leprous brown, and the walls had been covered with an assortment of old newspapers and periodical covers. Since Quentin wasn't sure how long they would stay in that building, he did not think it worthwhile to redecorate. Hannah had agreed.

Now as he left the office, not bothering to lock the door, Quentin thought of Hannah. She had practically taken up residence at the Breckenridge place, taking over the household chores, cooking and cleaning as well as taking care of Stuart. Her main job was caring for Eden, who had grown weaker.

Eden's condition was never out of Quentin's mind. He had examined her carefully, had read every book he could find, trying to arrive at a diagnosis, but had come up with nothing. He had written to Dr. Sutter in New York and to three other physicans, but none of their answers had been of any help. Sutter had expressed his sympathy, but had little to offer otherwise. He had closed by saying:

> *There is such a thing as a false pregnancy. You may remember that Queen Mary, daughter of Henry VIII and Catherine of Aragon, wanted a child desperately. She'd married Philip of Spain and the two of them longed for a male heir so that the future king of England would be a staunch Catholic. She was along in years by that time, but then she apparently got pregnant. She had every symptom, according to history. Everyone was convinced that she was carrying a child—no one more so than Mary herself. But in the end it was discovered that it was a "false pregnancy." There had never been a conception, but every doctor in the royal court was convinced by what seemed to be absolute evidence.*

Quentin had thought much of this, and even now it was in his mind as he strolled Pine Street. The sound of a steamboat whistle caught Quentin's attention, and dissatisfaction stirred within him. He had been shocked to learn that the business he had started at the farm had fallen off to practically nothing. He had written to Jim Peters to ask if his own business had fallen off as well. The pens and hutches out at the farm were stuffed with animals, and orders were very slow in coming in. He knew that the finances of the place burdened Thomas and Eden, and now with her sickness matters were even worse.

Turning down Cherry Street he passed several people. All of them knew who he was. Most of them neither spoke nor returned his greeting. His pride was stung. He had come to be a help to these people, and now they had shut the door in his face! He passed the barbershop and turned into Otis Sanderson's store, where he found the shopkeeper waiting on the banker's wife, Mrs. Emma Finch. The Finches were members of the Baptist church Quentin had attended during his first stay. She had been pleasant enough then, but now there was a chill in her dark brown eyes, and she turned away from him as he walked by.

Otis Sanderson noticed her movement and his mouth tightened. "Hello, Doctor," he said. "What can I help you with?"

Quentin watched as Mrs. Finch moved away, carrying her purchases. When he turned back toward Sanderson, he managed a grin. "I think Mrs. Finch is unhappy with me."

Sanderson looked away sadly. "Well, she'll come around. How's business?"

"Nonexistent."

The shop owner shook his head. "Too bad. Doc Vance needs help. He's getting on and can't handle all the sick folks."

Quentin said, "I need some shaving soap, some potatoes, and some black shoe polish." He wandered around the store while Sanderson gathered the items he needed, then paid for them and turned to leave. But he found his way blocked by two men who had entered. One of them was Riley Greer, who regarded Quentin with a malevolent light in his smallish eyes. The other man was tall and lithe, as so many Southern men were. He had sandy hair and pale blue eyes that were fastened now on Quentin. He was wearing a checked shirt, faded blue trousers, and a slouch hat shoved back on his head. Something about the man sounded an alarm in Quentin, and as he looked for a way to pass by, Greer said, "This is him, Faye—the big important Yankee doctor."

The lanky man stared at Quentin, clearly hostile. "My name's Satterfield. I served under General Stonewall Jackson. Who'd you fight for, Yankee?"

Sanderson stepped forward to say, "Satterfield, behave yourself. We don't want any trouble."

Faye Satterfield laughed softly, and Quentin tensed at the quiet menace in his laughter. Then Satterfield said, "How many of our good Southern boys did you kill when you was a blue belly, Larribee?"

"I was a noncombatant in the medical arm."

"A noncombatant. You mean you won't fight?" He winked at Greer, then his hand shot out and he gripped Quentin's arm with a steely grasp.

With a hard wrench, Quentin jerked his arm loose. "This is no place for this kind of thing, Satterfield," he said. "You want to talk to me, come to my office."

Quentin was not prepared for what happened next. He caught only a glimpse of a quick movement, then a smashing blow landed over his right eye, driving him backwards. The room went around, and he fell into a display of frying pans and pots and crockery with a thunderous crash. The force of the blow dazed him. He was struggling to get to his feet when strong hands seized him by the lapels and jerked him to his feet. He knew he was about to be struck again—and then Otis Sanderson was there, forcing his hands between the two men.

"Now that's enough of that, Satterfield! Be on your way! Get out of my store!"

Pain shot through Quentin, and his right eye was blinded by a sudden flow of blood. He put his hand up to cover it and caught a glimpse of Satterfield still standing nearby, grinning at him. "Well, Yankee, I'd say you better think about moving on. Helena ain't gonna be too healthy for you. You might try back up north. Come on, Riley. Let's get out of here. The place stinks of Yankees."

Sanderson watched the pair go, then said, "That's a bad cut you got there. Come on to the back. We'll wash it off."

Quentin followed the shopkeeper to the back and discovered, when he had washed the wound and looked at it, that there was a split that would need a couple of stitches.

"You want me to get Doc Vance to sew you up?"

"No. I'll do it myself."

Sanderson stared at him, but he did not argue. He got Quentin's bag and watched as Quentin, studying his reflection in the mirror, gave himself two stitches, not flinching at all as he drew the wound together and tied the knot. He finished with a small piece of plaster and then said, "I guess that was my official welcome to Helena."

"Satterfield's not a bad man in some ways. He's good to his family and he's good to his neighbors. He's always ready to help. Still bitter about the war, though. He lost two brothers, you know."

"I can see that. Well, I'm going out to the farm."

"Tell Eden that we'll get her to Memphis to a hospital if she'll agree to go."

"I'll tell her, but you know her better than I do. I don't think she'd ever take charity."

Frustrated, Sanderson watched Quentin walk away. It disturbed him that the town had refused to accept Quentin since his return. He had done his best, but the leaders of the society in the small river town had unified against Quentin. Except for the pastor and a few others, Quentin's name was anathema.

★　★　★

Hannah had the attention of everyone in the kitchen, for she had announced, "I'm going to make some molasses popcorn balls." She discovered, to her surprise, that none of them had ever heard of them; even for Thomas it was a novelty. She spoke briskly as she prepared the syrup. "You just put in a cup of sugar, about a third of a cup of water, and add a pinch of salt." She picked up a jug of sorghum and tilted it up. It glugged three times, and she nodded. "That ought to be about right." She added a fourth of a cup of butter and some vanilla and then stirred it thoroughly. "Now, we'll pop the corn."

She had bought popcorn and a saucepan from Sanderson's store, and now the children watched with fascination as she put the large pan on the stove with a wire covering. Stuart pulled at her dress, and she lifted him up so that he could watch the kernels popping. "Bang!" he said loudly. "Popcorn is bang!"

"That's right, Stuart. Now you wait and see what we do with this."

Hannah had settled into life at the Breckenridge household more easily than anyone might have expected. With Thomas unable to do the housework, and Eden needing somebody to care for her, Hannah hadn't even asked permission—she had simply told Eden on her first visit, "You need help for a little while. I'm moving in and taking care of you."

She had moved into a spare bedroom and gone to work. Although it had been a little awkward at first, within three days everyone in the family was depending on her. They discovered that she was expert at taking care of Stuart, who dearly loved her for her stories, and the others enjoyed her cooking.

As the syrup cooked, she said, "Prudence, get a cup of cold water." She waited until Prudence brought it and said, "Now, pick up the spoon and put a drop of this syrup in there. If it makes a ball, it's ready."

Prudence nodded, reached out with the wooden spoon, and managed to drop a dollop of the syrup into the water. "It made a ball," she said.

"Then we're ready. Now, Johnny, you and Prudence wash your hands. Johnny, you get a pan of water." When Johnny brought the water, she said, "Now, we'll pour this popcorn out here, and you start ladling syrup over it, and you make it up into little balls—or as big as you think you can handle."

It was like a game for the children, and soon even Thomas had wet his hands and was busily engaged in making the balls. He grinned and said, "Where did you learn to do this, Hannah?"

"Oh, I learned that when I was no older than Prudence here. We always had molasses popcorn balls for a treat at our house. Now, you make up the balls, and I'm going to take something in for Eden."

Moving efficiently despite her lame leg, she fixed a tray and headed down the hallway. The crutch made a soft thumping on the hard pine. She found Eden sitting up in bed. "I brought you something good to eat, Eden."

"I'm not really very hungry, Hannah."

"Nonsense. Of course you're hungry. You haven't had anything this good before."

"What is it?"

"Just a little broth of my own secret recipe. And have you ever had honey custard?"

"Honey custard? I don't think so."

"Real good for getting sick folks well." She set the tray down on the table and sat down beside Eden. "There. You try some of this. This broth might be a mite hot."

Eden ate some of the broth and then tasted the honey custard. Her eyes opened. "Why, this is very good!"

Hannah nodded. "Nothing like baked honey custard." She studied Eden's face, looking for some improvement but seeing none. In fact, during the days she had been there, she had seen a steady deterioration in the woman's condition. Hannah was worried about her.

Eden ate half of the custard, then handed it back, turning her gaze on Hannah. "I can't tell you how grateful I am for all your help," she said. "I don't know what we would have done without you."

"Oh, posh! It's nothing."

"Don't say that. It *is* something. And you're very good with children, Hannah." She hesitated and then said, "It's a shame you didn't have children of your own."

"Well, I raised my brother and sisters, Quentin and I did."

Eden asked, "Did you never think of marriage?"

Hannah paused. "No," she said quietly. "That was not to be."

"You're still a young woman."

"A crippled woman." There was no bitterness in Hannah's tone, but she knew she looked resigned.

"Why, you get around better than anybody on the place, Hannah."

Hannah changed the subject—not to protect herself, but because she saw that Eden needed encouragement. "You know, Quentin tells me that, for many people, their emotions hurt them worse than what's ailing in their bodies."

"It's hard not to feel useless. I'm lying here, I can't take care of my children, I don't know what's going to happen to me." Eden turned her face toward Hannah, fear showing in her eyes. "I don't know why the Lord is letting all this happen."

"I suppose all of us ask that question when hard times come. I asked it myself after my accident—why I was crippled. But there's no answer."

"It's so unfair."

"'Whom the Lord loveth he chasteneth.' You know that Scripture."

"I know, and I try to be patient," Eden murmured. "But it's hard."

Hannah picked up the worn black Bible that lay on the table beside Eden's bed. She turned the pages until she found the passage she sought and then said, "My favorite psalm when things look bad is the third. Do you remember that one? It starts out, 'LORD, how are they increased that trouble me! Many are they that rise up against me.'"

"I remember. Why do you like that psalm?"

"Because this is a prayer that David made when his son Absalom was trying to kill him. And you remember that Absalom was his favorite child, but Absalom turned against his father and led a revolt. David had to flee Jerusalem, afraid for his life. Absalom had raised a powerful army, and David had only a few of his mighty men. So that night it looked like David had pretty much reached the end of his rope."

"I remember now how much David loved that boy."

"Yes, he did. And that made it worse. It always does when someone we love hurts us, doesn't it?"

"Yes."

"Anyway, David was out there in the darkness about to die, or so he thought, and verse two says, 'Many there be which say of my soul, There is no help for him in God.' But in the next verse David said, 'But thou, O LORD, art a shield for me; my glory, and the lifter up of mine head. I cried unto the LORD with my voice, and he heard me out of his holy hill.'" Hannah lifted her eyes and smiled. "David cried unto God, and he knew that God heard him. And I always loved that next verse. I bet you don't remember it."

"No, I don't. What is it?"

Hannah put her finger on the verse. "It says, 'I laid me down and slept.'" She shook her head. "Isn't that a beautiful thought? There in the darkness, facing an awful death, with the dearest thing he had in the world turned against him, David went to sleep. I've always loved that verse. It shows what confidence David had in the Lord."

"Read the rest of it, Hannah."

"'I laid me down and slept; I awaked; for the LORD sustained me. I will not be afraid of ten thousands of people, that have set themselves against me round about.' Isn't that beautiful?"

The two women sat together until Hannah heard the sound of a horse approaching. She took her crutch and hobbled to the window. "It's Quentin," she said. Turning back to Eden, she added, "He's very partial to you, Eden."

After a pause, Eden said, "What about the woman he was going to marry?"

"Irene Chambers? She would have made him miserable." Hannah sat again. "Poor Quentin—I don't think he ever figured out how he got engaged to her. That woman wanted him because she wanted a husband and somebody to step into her father's practice. But he never loved her. I always knew that."

Hannah's words moved Eden, and she thought back to the time Quentin took her in his arms and kissed her, when she confessed her love for him. She had been ashamed of that—but now, somehow, Hannah's words poured balm over that hurt. She looked up at Hannah and tears came to her eyes. "I'm glad you told me, Hannah."

★　★　★

Out in the yard, Quentin dismounted and went to speak to Johnny, who was feeding the rabbits. "They're looking good, Johnny," he said. "Fat and plump."

"What are we going to do with them all, Quentin?" Johnny said with a worried look. "We can't sell 'em."

"I've written to Jim Peters in Memphis. He's a pretty sharp fellow, Jim is, and he's in the same business. I bet he's hit the same problem and already found a way out of it." He laid his hand on the boy's shoulder and found a smile. "It'll be all right. Don't worry."

"Do you really think so?"

"I do. Now, I'm going in to see your mother."

Leaving Johnny outside, Quentin stepped into the living room, but he was hailed by Prudence. "Come into the kitchen! See what we've got!"

Stepping into the kitchen, Quentin smelled something sweet. Thomas was sitting at the table with his hands, stained dark, in some concoction in a bowl. "What in the world are you doing, Thomas?"

"Making molasses popcorn balls."

"I know who taught you that." Quentin grinned. "Hannah and I have stuffed ourselves on those all of our lives."

"They're mighty good, too. Have one."

Quentin took the popcorn ball Prudence was holding out to him. "They're good!" she said.

"You're telling me! I was eating these things before you were born, Prudence." He bit into the delicacy and said, "They're as tasty as ever."

"What's the matter with your head? Did you bump it?" Prudence asked.

"Just a little accident," Quentin said. "I bet you learned how to make these balls. You can make them all by yourself next time."

"Sure I can." Prudence nodded.

"Guess I'll step inside and see how my patient is doing."

He reached the hall and turned to see that Thomas, smiling, had followed him, his hands still sticky with the syrup. "I want to tell you something, Quentin. That sister of yours has about saved our lives."

"She's a wonder, isn't she? I don't know anybody like her."

"She's good with Eden. Sits by her for hours. I was no company to her, really, nor the children for long. But those two women talk, talk, talk. It's been good for Eden." His eyes went to the patch on Quentin's forehead, but he said nothing except, "How's the practice going?"

"Not too well, Thomas."

Seeing the discouragement in Quentin's face, Thomas said quickly, "It'll pick up. People need time."

"Sure. I'd better go see Eden."

"You're stayin' for supper, aren't you?"

"Wouldn't miss it."

In the bedroom, Quentin greeted Hannah, who rose at once. "Well, I'd better start supper. We've got ham, and Prudence is going to teach me to make redeye gravy."

"What's got red eyes?"

"I don't know. It's a secret, but she said she'd show me."

As soon as Hannah left, Quentin sat in the chair across from Eden, who watched him carefully. "Did you have a busy day?" she asked quietly.

"Oh, not too busy."

He took her pulse and asked her several questions, studying her face as she answered. The answers were always the same, but Quentin was not deceived, and knew that Eden wasn't either.

"I'm getting worse, aren't I, Quentin?" Eden said.

Quentin had always believed in being honest with patients. He did not answer for a time, then he murmured, "I don't understand it."

Still holding her wrist, Quentin looked at her and found that, as usual, her gaze was direct, honest. He was strongly aware of the beauty of her eyes, their blue so dark that they seemed to have no bottom. Those eyes stood out even more now that her face was drawn and thin. She looked ill indeed. She made a little gesture with her shoulders; Hannah must have just bathed her, for there was a fragrance of freshness that slid through the armor of his reserve. He longed to see her in health again with that fire that had drawn him at first and made her lovely; he longed to hear her laugh. Studying her now, he was aware of her not just as a patient but as a woman—her hair long and heavy, the turn of her lips. Even as ill as she was, he could still sense in her a woman's soft depth and quiet strength.

She whispered, "Why did you come back, Quentin?"

Unable to answer for a moment, he thought of all that had brought him here, of her husband dead and buried on a battlefield far away but in some ways more alive than he had ever been, standing between them. Quentin had known for a long time that he had a feeling for this woman that he would never lose. He shifted his weight, removed his hand from her wrist, and clasped his hands together. "Prudence asked me to."

She waited, looking deep into him. "Was that your only reason?"

A stubborn honesty lay at the heart of Quentin's character. He was unbendable in his belief that to always speak the truth was best. He looked down at his hands for a moment, then looked up. "I thought about you and I had to come."

Eden said nothing for a few moments, but as he watched that lovely face, Quentin saw a change come over it, a softening. "I'm glad you came, Quentin," she said quietly.

"You'll get better. I know you will."

"What's wrong with me? Do you know?"

"No," he said. "But I will." He took her hand and held it in both of his. For all its frailty, there was a strength to it, and he felt an impulse to kiss it, but he refrained. "I don't know, but I will," he repeated. He bowed his head and began to pray, desperately hoping that, as before, he would feel that strong urging from God telling him to pray for Eden as he had prayed for others God had subsequently healed. And Quentin did pray for her healing; he needed no command for that. But always, when God had responded to Quentin's prayers and the laying on of his hands by healing the patient quickly, beyond the effectiveness of medicine, it had been when God had given him a special urging to pray. And that did not come. He waited for a long time, praying silently. Then he looked up and saw Eden watching him. It broke his heart to see the grief in her eyes, and the longing for health. "It'll be all right," he said. "I'll go wash up."

★ ★ ★

Just before supper, Trumbo came rumbling up in his wagon. Quentin stepped out onto the porch. "What's wrong?"

"Mistuh Quentin, there's a child done got hurt."

"I'll get my bag." As he grabbed it, Quentin called out to the others, "Don't wait for me. I don't know how long I'll be."

"I'll keep something warm," Hannah said.

Running to the wagon, he tossed his bag in and pulled himself up. Trumbo spoke to the mules, and they lunged forward. Quentin asked, "Who is it? One of your children?"

"No, but it's a black child." Trumbo gave Quentin Larribee a sideways look. "She ain't got no money. I better tell you that now."

"What difference does that make?"

Trumbo laughed. "I knowed you'd say that," he said. "Get up there, mules!"

The six-year-old girl had broken her leg in a fall from a tree. Her mother, an attractive black woman with two other children, seemed to have no man, and Quentin did not ask. Trumbo helped by applying the ether, and while the child was asleep he expertly set the leg and made a quick plaster cast for it.

"Is she gonna be all right, Docta?" the mother asked.

"Sure, Ellie. She'll be fine."

"I ain't got no money."

"That's all right."

When he was going back out to the wagon with Trumbo, the woman came with a sack. "I got these here sweet potatoes."

Surrounded by evidence of the woman's poverty, Quentin was tempted to refuse the gift; he knew that she needed the sweet potatoes worse than he did. But he had learned a lesson somewhere along the way: it would be ungrateful to refuse a gift. He took the sack. "May the Lord restore you these potatoes a hundredfold, Ellie."

On the way home, Trumbo did not speak till they were nearly back at the farm. "How about Miss Breckenridge? Is she gettin' better?"

"No. She's not."

The wagon wheels rumbled over the rutted road as the men sat in worried silence. Trumbo said, "I prays for her every day, Mistuh Quentin."

"So do I, Trumbo—so do I!"

CHAPTER
Twenty

*E*den sat in a cane rocker on the front porch, watching as Stuart dug industriously in the soft ground with a cast-off spoon. He had excavated a hole nearly deep enough to crawl into and was smeared with the black soil from head to foot. She smiled briefly, thinking, *That boy is going to grow up to be a mole. He likes to dig better than any child I ever saw.* The sight of her youngest gave her a particular pang, however, for with her illness she had not been able to care for him as she should.

Inside, she heard Hannah and Prudence singing loudly.

"Oh, I'm a good old rebel,
Now that's what I am
For this fair land of freedom,
I do not care at all
I'm glad I fit against it,
I only wish we'd won!"

Eden smiled at the sound of Hannah singing a rebel song. She was filled with gratitude for Hannah Larribee; the woman seemed to her almost as an angel sent from heaven. Having been an independent woman all her life, Eden would not have dreamed that she could accept another woman's help so easily; but Hannah's gentle, unassuming spirit had helped Eden to make that adjustment. She marveled at how quickly Hannah had won the confidence of all three of the children. As she listened to the singing, she thought of what her father had said of Hannah: "Some man's missing a blessing by letting that woman get away!"

The sun, risen halfway to its zenith, poured an effulgent summer heat that already was baking the earth. Out beside the barn Johnny and Thomas were hunting for night crawlers, and Eden thought with a slight pang of how quickly Johnny was growing up. She studied his sunburned face and thatch of reddish hair and tried to see some of Will, but could not. It was as if she had forgotten Will's face.

At the sound of an approaching horse, she sat up straighter. Riley Greer came galloping in on his iron gray stallion. He rode into the yard, stepped to the ground, and looped the reins over the hitching post. Seeing her on the porch, he came up the stairs, saying, "Good morning, Eden." His face was red with heat, his light gray shirt darkened under the armpits. Taking off his hat, he mopped his face with a limp blue bandanna. "Gonna be hotter than the hinges on Hades' door," he muttered. For a moment he hesitated, then took a seat beside her, asking, "How are you feeling today?"

"Maybe a little better."

Greer obviously had come with something on his mind. There was little subtlety in the man, and now he turned to face her as if tackling a task that he'd made up his mind to finish. "Eden, you've heard all this talk going around about you and Larribee."

"Yes. I know it."

Greer seemed to wait for her to say more, to deny the charge, but she simply sat there. Hannah had washed her hair with rainwater earlier, and the heavy weight of it hung down her back. Small tendrils on her forehead stirred with the slight breeze. She brushed back a lock, lifting her eyes to study Greer.

He seemed to grow uncomfortable under her direct gaze, but he forged ahead. "Listen, Eden, I think it's time we got married. You got no protection against that kind of talk, but if we was married, I could take care of it." He nodded and lifted one huge fist. "I'd stop the mouth of any man who made a remark about you."

Eden knew this was his way, to answer any problem with force. "What about the women who talk about me? Will you whip them too, Riley?"

Greer blinked with surprise and shifted uncomfortably. He found no answer, and grated, "The talk will stop if we get married."

For a long moment Eden sat there watching the big man. She had no illusions about the kind of future she would have with him; it was clear from his history that he was not a man who was gentle with women. An image of Ruth Greer, his dead wife, rose from her memory: a woman whose face was scored with lines laid down by the stress of years of callous treatment. Eden remembered the defeat and misery that had lurked in Ruth Greer's eyes, and suddenly she knew what she had to do. It was not a new thought, but the memory of Greer's first wife brought a determination to end it all. Firmly she said, "Riley, you don't care for me."

"What? I wouldn't have asked you to marry me if I didn't."

"No. You want a bigger farm, and this one adjoins yours."

"You're tellin' me I want to marry you just for this farm?"

Eden was tired, and the pressure of his gaze disturbed her. Still she knew she had to have it out. "I'll give you an answer now. It would be a mistake to agree to marry you, Riley. You could never make me happy, and I'm the last woman in the world you need for a wife."

Eden's words, though calmly spoken, struck Greer like a blow. Anger reddened his face, and Eden knew that he wanted to strike her. Seeing that impulse so clearly on his face convinced her that she had done the right thing. "Please go, Riley. We're going to be neighbors for a long time, but don't come back with any more talk about marrying."

Standing up so quickly the chair fell over backwards, Greer glared down at her. "It's all true, I reckon. You're all swelled up there with Larribee's kid. Well, I gave you a chance. Now you'll lose this place—and I'll buy it at auction." He turned and stalked away. Getting into the saddle, he gave her one baleful glance, then kicked his horse's side. The animal gave a startled leap and soon carried Greer out of sight, leaving a cloud of fine dust hanging over the road.

As Greer disappeared, Hannah stepped outside and lifted the chair upright. Her expression was uncertain and concerned, and Eden looked up and expelled a deep breath. "Well, that's over. I told him I'd never marry him."

"You did a good day's work, then," Hannah said firmly. "Now, don't you fret about it. The Lord's going to undertake, and when God undertakes, the thing is as good as done." She reached out and brushed a lock of fine hair from Eden's brow. "Don't worry about losing this place. It's not going to happen."

Eden blinked with surprise, for she had said nothing to Hannah about her fears. She smiled then, and reached up for Hannah's hand. "You're good for me, Hannah—indeed you are!"

"Most of the things we worry about never happen." Hannah looked down at Stuart, saying, "It'll take a river to get that boy cleaned up." She limped down the steps, grabbed Stuart by the arm, and dragged him over to the pump. She washed the worst of the mud off, then dragged him protesting into the house, saying to Eden, "I'm going into town to clean up the house and Quentin's office. Thomas will be here if you need anything, and Prudence is going to cook a lunch."

"All right, Hannah."

Hannah looked down at Stuart, who was struggling to get away from her firm grip. "I think I'll take Stuart along with me. He and I haven't had much time together. You want to go to town? Maybe I'll buy you some candy."

"Yes, ma'am!"

"Well, come on. I'll wash you down." Twenty minutes later she came back outside, where Thomas stood beside the team he'd hitched for her. "Can you drive a team, Hannah?" he asked.

"Don't be foolish! Of course I can drive." She got up into the wagon with an agility that belied her handicap, put her crutch in the back, and said, "Now, put Stuart up here and we're off."

Lifting the boy, Thomas cautioned. "Now you mind Hannah. You hear me, Stuart?"

"Yes, sir. Candy!" He grinned.

Hannah spoke to the horses and they left at a fast trot.

Thomas watched them go, then went up to sit beside Eden. "That woman's a marvel. I never knew she could drive a team."

"I expect," Eden said quietly with a slight smile, "Hannah Larribee can do whatever she decides." With scarcely a break she said, "Dad, I told Riley I'd never marry him."

Thomas's eyes opened wide for a moment, then he smiled. "Fine," he said. "That's good to hear. He's not a man I'd like to see you married to."

★　★　★

The wheels of the buggy rattled over the cobblestones as Hannah drove down Cherry Street, listening as Stuart babbled on. He was interested in everything, it seemed. Now, seeing the general store, he said, "Candy, Hannah. Candy!"

"Not now. We've got to go clean the doctor's office. We'll have some lunch, and then we'll get candy."

This was too difficult a concept for Stuart, whose only concept of time was *now*, but he quieted down when she admonished him sharply.

Pulling up in front of the house, Hannah got down, balancing on her left leg while she got her crutch out. "Come on, Stuart." She took him from the wagon and said, "Let's go see the doctor."

Inside, Hannah was startled to see at least half a dozen patients waiting in the outer office. They all turned to look at her. "Good day," she said, then made her way upstairs, helping Stuart as he navigated the steep stairway.

For the next hour, she cleaned the house. When it satisfied her, she packed a few of her clothes in a brown paper bag. "Come on, Stuart. We can go get some candy now."

Downstairs, all the patients but one, a tall rawboned woman in a baggy brown dress, had gone. Hannah nodded pleasantly and said, "The doctor still busy?"

"I reckon so." The woman eyed Hannah and said, "It hadn't ort to be long if you want to wait. You got leg trouble?"

Hannah shook her head. "No. I'm Doctor Larribee's sister."

The woman looked at her with fresh interest. "Don't know whether I ort to see the doctor or not. I ain't got but only a quarter."

"You wait on the doctor. Don't worry about money."

The woman shook her head. "They told me he was helpin' folks that didn't have nothin'. I didn't believe it, but I come in anyhow. Lord knows I need some help!"

"You wait right there. I'm sure Doctor Larribee can help you."

Hannah knocked on the door. When Quentin's voice said, "Come in!" she opened it and stepped inside. He smiled and nodded. "Hello, Hannah." Turning to a short, rotund man who was putting on his shirt, he said cheerfully, "You'll be all right, Harold. Just take that medicine regularly. Come back to see me if you have any troubles."

Harold, obviously a farmer, poorly dressed and bowed with toil, said, "How much, Doc?"

"Wait until the crops come in. We'll settle up then."

Relief swept across the sunburned face. "Thanks, Doctor Larribee. I'll make it right with you."

As soon as he left the office, Hannah said, "Things are picking up."

"Quite a bit. Word got around that a free doctor is in town." He smiled at her and shook his head. "It feels good to work again, though. What are you doing in town?"

"I came to clean up the house."

"Well, I could do that, Hannah."

"No, you can't. You've got doctoring to do. Come to supper tonight."

She felt a twitch at her skirt and turned to see Stuart whispering, "Can we go, Aunt Hannah?"

Quentin grinned at the boy. "Where you going, Stuart?"

"Candy!"

"A man of few words. I like that." Quentin reached into his pocket, pulled out a coin, and handed it to him. "Here. Buy yourself something good to eat."

"You come to supper tonight," Hannah reminded him.

"All right. I'll be there."

Leaving the office, Hannah led Stuart to Sanderson's store. Their first stop was the jars of candy, and she allowed him to pick his favorites. Out of the bag containing his purchases, she gave him one licorice stick and said firmly, "Now, you chew on that and make it last."

While the boy was sucking noisily on the licorice stick and smearing his face with it, she moved about, picking up some pins and needles and a few groceries. She paid the clerk, then said, "Come on, Stuart."

As they stepped outside, she almost bumped into a large man who seemed to fill the doorway for a moment. She looked up, startled, to see a bewhiskered face.

She waited for the man to step back and remove his hat, but he did neither; he simply remained in the doorway looking down at her. He had odd-colored eyes, a dark hazel. She had always said that eyes were a mirror of the soul, but as she looked into the man's eyes, she could discern little about him. It was as if some sort of curtain were drawn over the pupils, concealing their depths. And then, for just an instant, something came into those eyes, and Hannah had the impression of loneliness—not the minor loneliness everyone experiences, but rather the infinite depths of isolation that can destroy the soul. And then the eyes changed, as if the curtain had once again fallen, and he turned and moved past her to enter the store.

When she stepped outside in the bright sunlight, she saw that Reverend Nelson Jordan had observed the encounter. He glanced inside, shrugging briefly. "That's only Ben Calendar. Don't mind him. He has no manners for anyone."

The two watched as, minutes later, Calendar came out with a heavy sack of feed on his shoulder. He walked to the wagon, tossed it in, then reentered the store.

"Doesn't he have any friends at all?"

"Not that I know of."

A thought came to Hannah then. "Brother Nelson," she asked abruptly, "have you ever talked to him about his soul?"

"Why, I don't think I ever have." Surprise washed across the preacher's face, and he studied Hannah carefully. "He's not the kind of man you can talk to."

"Why not? He's a man, isn't he?"

Uncomfortably, Jordan shifted his feet. He glanced at Stuart, who had gone to the edge of the porch and stepped off. He watched as the boy began to kick the dust of the street while sucking on the blackened length of licorice. "I guess I've been remiss. I know what reception I'd get."

"That shouldn't bother you. A man who's been through a war shouldn't mind getting a little harsh language from a man who needs God."

"You're right, Sister Laribee. I think sometimes we're pretty selective about who we share the gospel with—and that's not what Jesus did."

Hannah was watching the pastor's face while he spoke, vaguely aware that Calendar had passed behind her with another sack of feed on his shoulder. She was startled when he let out a hoarse yell.

She whirled quickly and saw Calendar rushing into the street—and then she saw Stuart!

The boy had wandered to the middle of the dusty street with his head down. He was kicking the dust, watching it rise in clouds, while the black length of licorice dangled from his mouth. But behind him, a team was rushing down the street at a fast gallop, pulling a buggy. In one glance, Hannah took it all in. The driver had seen the boy; he had risen to his feet and was sawing at the reins, trying to pull the plunging team to a halt. But there was no chance of that—Stuart was right in the path of the team, oblivious to his danger. Hannah let out a cry and heard Nelson Jordan yell, "Look out!" as he broke into a run.

Hannah seemed unable to move. She could see that Nelson Jordan had no chance of getting to the boy. The horses were bearing down, their eyes wild as the driver hauled back on the reins with all his might.

Calendar, though, was closer to Stuart than Jordan was. Legs pumping, he reached Stuart—but too late to avoid the team of horses. Hannah saw Calendar's arms shoot out, catching Stuart in the back, sending him flying headlong to roll in the dust. The flying hooves of the horses grazed Stuart, but it was Calendar who took the full force of the impact. With a thud, Calendar was knocked to the ground, and then the horses trampled his body. The wheels of the buggy lurched as they bounced over Calendar, the driver screaming wildly.

Nelson Jordan was the first to reach the fallen man. He fell to his knees and put his hands on Calendar's shoulders, while Hannah ran to Stuart. The boy's eyes were wide with fright, and he began sobbing and holding on to Hannah with both arms, burying his face against her breast. "It's all right, Stuart. You're not hurt." She picked him up with her free arm; using her crutch, she went quickly to Calendar, who lay motionless on his back. As others ran toward them, Jordan looked up at her. "He's hurt pretty bad, I'm afraid, Hannah."

The driver of the buggy had gotten the team stopped. He jumped down and ran back to them, his face pasty white. He tried a couple of times to speak, and finally choked out in a tremulous voice, "The boy ran right out in front of me. It wasn't my fault!"

"You shouldn't have been running that team down the main street!" Jordan snapped angrily. He turned back toward the bloody face of Calendar.

Hannah dropped her crutch, knelt in the dirt, and put her hand on his head. "Get my brother!" she cried. With a trembling hand, she pulled a handkerchief out of her pocket and began wiping the blood that was pouring from a cut over Calendar's right eye. She thought he might be dead until she saw his chest rising, heaving— then his eyes opened. There was confusion in those eyes, and he stared at her without speaking for a moment.

"Just be still," Hannah whispered. "The doctor will be here in a minute."

The words seemed to galvanize Ben Calendar. He pushed Hannah's hands away and rolled until he was on his hands and knees. He straightened up slowly, first to his knees, then unsteadily to his feet.

Nelson reached forward, saying, "Take it easy. You may have something broken."

Calendar gasped, "Get away from me—all of you!" He staggered toward his wagon.

Hannah followed him, begging, "Please wait. You're bleeding. Wait and see my brother."

But Calendar ignored her. He hung onto the seat of the wagon for a moment, then climbed in, his face pale, blood dripping on the collar of his shirt. He reached forward, picked up the lines, and said hoarsely, "Get up!"

Hannah watched helplessly as the team moved out. She was aware that a crowd had gathered, and then she heard Quentin's voice. "Hannah, what happened?"

As she explained, Quentin stooped to check Stuart. He stood up then and said, "Stuart's all right. What about Calendar? They said he was hurt."

"He *was* hurt. He's got a terrible cut, and he could hardly get in the wagon."

"That team ran right over him, Doctor," Jordan added. "And I think the wheels of the wagon hit him, too. He's got to be busted up inside."

Hannah was terribly shaken. She only half-heard Nelson explaining what he had seen of Calendar's injuries. Finally, he said, "He saved that boy's life, Doctor. As sure as you're born."

Quentin studied Hannah's face, then said, "Come on, Hannah. You need to sit down for a while."

He hustled the three of them back to his office, got her a cup of water, then cleaned the dust off Stuart while she composed herself. Stuart put his hands on her knee and looked up into her face, saying, "What's the matter, Hannah?"

"Nothing, Stuart. I'm just upset." Hannah had had time to think. She looked up and said, "That man was hurt, Quentin, badly hurt. He could barely get into the wagon, and he nearly fell over as he drove away."

"He's probably in shock," Quentin said. "Come along. I'll take you and Stuart home, then I'll go see about him."

As soon as they had delivered Stuart and given a report of what had happened to Eden and Thomas, Quentin said, "I'm going to see about Calendar."

"I'm going with you," Hannah said flatly.

Quentin started to disagree, but seeing her face, he nodded. "Come along then." He helped her up into the buggy and then climbed in. "I think we'd better hurry. I'm concerned about him."

He drove quickly, Hannah having to hang on over some of the rough spots. At Calendar's house, they saw the team still hitched but wandering free, pulling the wagon after it. Leaping off the wagon, Quentin helped Hannah down, then grabbed his bag. "I hope he doesn't shoot at us. I've heard he's prone to do that."

But Hannah had no fear of that. She had seen the agony in the man's face. Quentin knocked on the door; there was no answer. "Mr. Calendar!" he shouted. "Are you all right?"

There was no answer—then Hannah said, "Did you hear that?"

"No. What was it?"

"We've got to go in," she said firmly. The door was only half closed, and she pushed it back. Stepping inside, she halted momentarily so that Quentin ran into her back. Calendar was stretched out on the floor, facedown. Quentin, moving quickly, knelt beside the man. "Calendar," he said, and put his hand on the man's shoulder.

"Don't—touch me."

"Where do you hurt?"

"Back," Calendar gasped. "Can't stand to move. Down my legs, too."

"I'm going to roll you over on your back, Calendar. I'll be as careful as I can, but it'll hurt." He looked at Hannah and said, "Find a bed and get it ready."

As Hannah moved out of the room, Quentin, moving carefully and supporting Calendar as well as he could, rolled the injured man over. He heard Calendar's quick intake of breath as a shudder of pain ran through him. "Can you move your arms?" Quentin asked.

Calendar moved his arms experimentally.

"Good! Nothing wrong there. Now, your right leg."

Calendar tried to move his leg, but gasped out a short cry of agony. "I can move it, but it's about to kill me," he panted.

"What about the other one?"

As Hannah came back in, Quentin said, "Your back's not broken. I think you've got a disc problem."

"What's that?"

"Part of your backbone."

"Am I going to die?"

"No, but you're going to be out of action for a while." He looked up at Hannah and said, "We got to find something firm for him to lie on."

"Well, that bed won't do. It sags."

"You stay with him, Hannah. I'll rig something up."

It took some time for Quentin to find boards to put over the bed's sagging springs. He put the cotton ticking over the boards, then looked in vain for any sheets. Finding none, he covered the ticking with a blanket and then went back to find Hannah sitting on the floor beside Calendar.

"We've got to move him, Hannah. Ben," he said, using the man's name for the first time, "this is going to hurt like blazes. I'll tell you what. I'm going to feed you some laudanum to kill the pain." Opening his bag, he found the bottle and said, "Get a cup, Hannah." He poured a liberal dose into the cup she brought him from the kitchen and then said, "Lift your head." He watched as Calendar swallowed the bitter concoction and then said, "Just lie there."

As the two of them watched, Calendar's eyes quickly grew droopy.

"That's a massive dose I gave him, but he's in terrible pain. We've got to get him into bed."

It was a struggle, and the laudanum did not take away all of Calendar's pain. Fifteen minutes later, the two of them stared down at the big man lying flat on his back, his face twisted. Quentin said, "I've got to sew that cut, and I've got to fix up some kind of traction to take the pressure off that disc. Hannah, start a fire and heat up some blankets. He's gone into shock; heat will be good for the soreness." They had stripped off the man's shirt, and Hannah was appalled at the enormous bruises and contusions on Calendar's back.

The two worked steadily. It took a while for Quentin to rig up a crude traction apparatus by tying strips of cloth around

Calendar's feet and attaching some metal bits he found in the barn. "I'll have to do better than that, but that'll do for now."

"Are you sure his back's not broken?"

"Yes." Quentin shook his head. "He's in bad shape, though. He'll need a lot of care. I don't know who would take him in."

Hannah looked up at her brother. "You and I'll take care of him, Quentin."

"Be a big job," Quentin said. "He'll be pretty helpless for a while." He looked at Hannah's set face and nodded. "All right. If you say so."

"I say so," Hannah said. "You'd better sew that cut up now. I'll heat some water."

CHAPTER
Twenty-One

Nothing pleased Doctor Edward Vance more than a breakfast of buckwheat cakes larded with creamy, yellow butter and drowned with blackstrap molasses. He ordinarily polished off several large portions, but this morning he seemed preoccupied—so much so that his wife said, "What's the matter with you, Ed? You usually bolt my buckwheat cakes like a grizzly bear."

For a moment, Vance toyed with a morsel on the end of his fork, then put it down and shook his head. "I can't stop thinking about Quentin Larribee and Eden Breckenridge." His eyes were troubled and he turned to gaze out the window. For a time he watched as a yellow cat was driven across the yard by swoops of a mockingbird. It was a scene he often marveled at, that a large cat could be intimidated by such a frail creature. But this morning his mind was not on the cat and the bird, and he picked up his coffee, sipped it, then set it down abruptly. "I may have been wrong about that young man, Martha."

"About Quentin Larribee?"

"Yes. I'll say this for him. He's not greedy."

"From what I hear he's doing good work on the farms outside of town. There's no money in that, of course."

"No, there's not. I've kept up with him pretty carefully, and from all reports he's a fine doctor. He works hard at least."

Martha Vance considered her husband, then asked, "What about Eden?"

"I just don't know—I just don't know, Martha. She looks pregnant, but she vows she's not. I don't know what to think."

"Be careful, Ed. I've always considered Eden Breckenridge a good woman, and I still do."

Irritably, Vance clawed at his beard, then shook his head. "Well, blast it, Martha, I always thought so too." Picking up his fork he swirled a morsel of the cake in the blackstrap, put it in his mouth, and chewed it. "I suppose the gossip mill is working overtime on Hannah Larribee."

"Well, it is strange. A single woman alone with a man—it just gives people one more thing to talk about."

"Why, the man's not able to move! And I didn't see any of our good people lining up to care for Calendar. It was a pretty good thing what Calendar did. He saved that boy's life as sure as I'm sitting here."

"He's such a strange man. And nobody really understands him. Going around with that hangman's noose around his neck, it's enough to frighten little children."

"Not only little children. He gives anybody a fright when they see him."

"Was he badly hurt, Ed?"

"Bad enough. Larribee asked me to go to see what I thought. And the fellow did do me a service fixing my buggy. He's in poor condition, Martha. I never saw such bruises!"

"Will he be all right?"

"Oh, yes. He's got some damage to the spine. Probably a disc problem. The woman's safe enough."

Martha Vance sipped her coffee, then shrugged. "Well, people will talk. Miss Larribee's not doing her reputation any good staying all alone with a man."

"I don't suppose she is. Well, in any case I suppose people have to have something to gossip about."

"It's not right, though. You know it isn't, Ed," Martha said quickly. She sipped her coffee and said thoughtfully, "Some people move into a town and people hardly know they're there. They're quiet and don't make any noise about the way they live, but the Larribees have certainly made an impact on this place!"

★   ★   ★

Carefully, Ben Calendar raised his head and, bracing his hands against the hard mattress, struggled to an upright position. The pain was less than he'd expected, and as he moved carefully, he listened to the voice that drifted to him from somewhere else in the house. He had become accustomed to Hannah Larribee's singing. Now her words came to him clearly.

"My Jesus, I love thee, I know thou art mine
For thee all the follies of sin I resign;
My gracious redeemer, my Savior art thou:
If ever I loved thee, my Jesus, tis now."

Something about the woman's voice tugged at him. He had been alone for so long, in such bitterness of spirit, that when Hannah Larribee had first invaded his home and taken over his life, he had resented everything about her. She had ignored his protests, his curses, his insults, and gone about renovating his house and taking care of him with a brisk efficiency that had finally silenced him. As she sang, something in him responded in a way he could not explain.

"I love thee because thou has first loved me
And purchased my pardon on Calvary's tree;
I love thee for wearing the thorns on thy brow:
If ever I loved thee, my Jesus, tis now."

The voice had been drawing closer, and his door opened. Hannah entered, bearing a tray of food carefully balanced in one hand. With the other she used her crutch. "Well, you're looking better, Mr. Calendar," she said cheerfully. Putting the tray down, she said, "I made you some fresh biscuits, and the ham you had in your smokehouse is delicious. I've already tried it."

"I'm not hungry." Calendar was indeed hungry, but he hated to be dependent. He gazed at this woman, curious. He had wanted to question her, but long custom had sewed shut his lips.

"You eat every bite of that," Hannah nodded. "You've got to keep your strength up." She sat beside him, and Calendar ate quietly.

When he had finished, she took the tray and left the room, but she was soon back bearing a basin of water and a towel. As she put it down, he said, "What are you going to do now?"

"I'm going to change the bandage on your forehead, and then give you a bath."

Startled, Calendar glared at her. "You can change the bandage, but you ain't givin' me no bath!"

Hannah did not answer. Efficiently, she removed the plaster, gazed at the cut on his head, and said, "It's healing up nicely. You're going to have a scar though. Now, let's take those weights off."

She removed the weights that Quentin had arranged for traction, and a sigh of relief escaped Calendar's lips. "I hate those things!"

"They're doing you good, though. Now, I'm going to clean you up."

Calendar protested again, but Hannah ignored him and began washing his face, stopping once to say, "If you'd just shave these whiskers off, it'd be a lot easier." She washed his upper body then said, "Now, doesn't that feel better?"

Calendar said rather ungraciously, "It's all right. Leave those weights off."

"I suppose I can for a while." She took the water out, and he could hear her singing—which, to his surprise, pleased him, and he hoped she would keep it up. His house was always silent except for, perhaps, one of his dogs thumping on the floor as he scratched. He had grown accustomed to the silence, but now Hannah Larribee had brought song and activity to his house, and Calendar was not anxious to return to the silence. She came in again and began to clean the room. "I'm worried about my stock," he said.

"You don't have to worry about that. Trumbo's taking care of them."

Unable to think of anything else to complain about, Calendar lay back and endured the dull gnawing of pain.

Looking at his face, Hannah said, "You're having quite a bit of pain today."

"Not too bad."

"You need some more laudanum."

"No. I don't want any more of that stuff."

"Don't be foolish. There's no reason to hurt when you don't have to." She gave him a healthy dose of laudanum. He was very susceptible to it, and she sat beside him, making small talk, while he gradually became drowsy. When she stopped talking, he found himself asking a question he would never have asked while wide awake. "How'd you get crippled?"

"Why, it was an accident." She said no more.

Barely awake, he muttered, "Have you ever been married?"

"No, I never have."

Calendar considered this. He was almost unconscious, but he roused himself and studied her face. She was wearing a simple green dress, and he noted, as he had before, how well-formed she was. Her auburn hair was swept back and tied and there was an attractiveness about her that he could not ignore. "Don't you hate God for letting it happen to you?"

"No, I haven't."

"If God loved you, why would he let it happen to you?"

"I don't know, Mr. Calendar. There are many things I don't know, but I do know one thing, and that is that God is love."

"How can you think that? You're all crippled up. Look all around you. People suffering everywhere. Would God let people suffer if he was love?"

Hannah leaned forward and her voice was gentle. "There is evil in the world and suffering, but it didn't come from God. It came from the heart of man. That's why Jesus came, Mr. Calendar, to put things right. He's begun a work of redemption, and he's going to finish it. One day there won't be any pain, any suffering. All will be happiness and joy because Jesus will sit on the throne. But even now, I can love God with a handicap, knowing that he loves me. I believe that he could give me a perfect body right now, but he hasn't chosen to do so. That doesn't make me love him any less. I simply think of the day when he went to the cross and died. That was for me and for you."

She continued to speak for some time about the love of God, and her face glowed; Calendar watched her, taking it all in. He had been a pariah for so long that he had forgotten what it was like to be talked to as a human being. He had let bitterness fill his soul. And now he said, "I'm glad you feel like that—I wish I could."

"You can, Ben." Unconsciously, Hannah used his first name. He had been such a strange, alien being when she had first come to care for him that she had been half afraid, but he was so like a child, so helpless and pitiful, that her heart had gone out to him. Now she leaned forward and said, "You've had a hard life, but you have a lot of years ahead of you, Ben."

Calendar did not speak for a long time. His eyelids sagged, and finally he mumbled, "I guess . . . you know about me."

"No. Why don't you tell me? I've heard things, but I'd like to hear what you have to say."

Calendar was so still that Hannah thought he was asleep, but then his lips moved. She leaned forward to catch his words. "I loved her—I would never have hurt her in a million years!"

And then he said no more. Hannah looked down on him, thinking of what he had just said. She knew the story—that he had been a hard man, that he had murdered a young servant girl. But somehow, she knew that what she had just heard Ben say was the truth. "Whatever happened," she said under her breath, "it's not like they say."

★   ★   ★

Fatigue dragged at Quentin's shoulders as he got out of his buggy and approached the house. He spoke to Thomas, who was sitting on the porch playing some sort of a game with Stuart. He could hear the voices of Johnny and Prudence off in the house somewhere, and when he had climbed the steps, he said, "How is she, Thomas?"

"About the same. You look like you've had a hard day."

"Lots of sick people. There's some cholera over by Burden Springs—at least I think it is. But I hope not." He shifted his weight and added, "I stopped on the way in to see Calendar."

"How's he doing?"

"Much better. He's able to sit up and walk around some now." Quentin looked at Stuart, sitting playing with his blocks, and murmured, "If it hadn't been for Calendar, I don't know if we'd have Stuart with us."

"I thank God every day for that, Quentin."

Quentin rose and said, "I'll go in and see Eden."

Inside, he smelled meat frying and realized he was ravenously hungry. He had eaten nothing since breakfast, and now hunger came at him like an armed man. He entered the bedroom and found Eden sitting in a rocking chair, reading. She looked up. "Hello, Quentin." She studied his face and said, "You're worn out."

"A long day. I just came from Calendar's. He's going to be all right."

He sat down across from her and told her of some of the patients he had seen that day, but he was worried about Eden, and his mind was not on what he was saying. For days he'd tried to keep silent, but now he could hold his tongue no longer. "You're not going to marry Greer."

It was the first time Quentin had spoken of this, and Eden shook her head. "No. I'm not. He doesn't care for me, and I don't care for him."

"I'm glad of that. I didn't think he was the man to make you happy."

"He wouldn't be getting much if he got me. I couldn't be a wife to him."

Quentin straightened up and said, "Eden, I think you ought to let me take you to Memphis or even to St. Louis."

"What for?"

"To a hospital. I haven't been able to diagnose your case. There are doctors in those places who have much more experience."

"I couldn't do that."

Quentin was discouraged. Her sickness had mystified him, and now he said, "Let me take you away from here, then. Sell out. We'll go somewhere and make a fresh start."

Eden looked surprised. She looked at him steadily for a few moments, as if waiting for him to say something else, and then said, "I can't run away from my problems, Quentin. None of us can."

Quentin was still. If only he had not killed this woman's husband! If not for that, he would have insisted on her marrying him. But the ghost of Will Breckenridge was there before him. He said heavily, "I guess I'll wash up before supper."

After he left, Eden began reading again. She had prayed and sought God in every way she knew, but nothing had seemed to work. She had never doubted God's power to heal. He was the Almighty One. But he had not healed in her case. Now she began to pray again, and as she prayed, God began to speak to her heart. She sat very still, knowing that this was one of the few times in her life when God was giving her something directly. Like many believers, she was afraid of visions and distrusted, to some degree, people who said, "God told me to do this." Nevertheless, in the quietness of her room, sitting with her Bible on her lap, she felt the presence of the Lord come upon her—and in that silence, Eden Breckenridge knew what God wanted her to do.

The congregation of Grace Baptist Church ordinarily was not easily shaken, but when Eden Breckenridge came in Sunday morning along with all of her family, a muted whisper ran through the worshipers. Every eye was turned toward her, most of them filled with avid curiosity.

As the song service began, Otis Sanderson was very much aware that the congregation was more interested in the appearance of Eden than in the hymns he was urging them to sing. Finally, with a disgusted shrug, he gave up and said, "The service is yours, Pastor."

Standing in the pulpit, Reverend Jordan deliberately kept his eyes away from Eden and her family. Without comment, he read his text and plunged into the sermon, which happened that morning to be on faith. Jordan knew his congregation, and he was an excellent preacher. But this morning, his words were flying out the window unheeded, for this was the first appearance of Eden since word had gotten out that she was expecting a child. Valiantly he forged ahead, until finally he came to the end of the message, feeling defeated. He said, "We will sing one concluding hymn—"

He broke off abruptly, for Eden had risen to her feet. Her face was pale, but there was a calmness in her countenance and a steadiness in her voice as she said, "Pastor, might I say a few words?"

"Why, of course you can, Mrs. Breckenridge."

Every eye was on Eden as she stepped out of the pew and made her way to the front. Slowly she turned, and her eyes scanned the congregation. Many were unable to meet her gaze, but all paid attention as she began to speak. "I know almost all of you," Eden said in a quiet tone, "and this church has always been dear to my heart. I've always felt that this was a place where the members of the body of Christ could find love—and forgiveness."

Her last word caught the attention of every listener, and most of them wondered: *Is she going to confess her sin and ask us to forgive her?*

Eden suddenly met Quentin's eyes. He was watching her steadfastly, his lips drawn into a tight line. She had not told him what she was going to say. He had been surprised when she had asked him and her father to bring her to church. Quentin had felt that might not be wise, but she had insisted. Now she looked out over the congregation and began to speak again. "I would like to ask this church to pray for me."

Again a murmur passed through the congregation, and several dug their elbows into the side of their spouse, feeling that a confession was coming.

"I know that it has been told in our community that I am expecting a child." Eden held her head up and said in a loud, clear voice, "That is not so. My husband is dead, and I have never known a man since he died. Before God, I am not guilty of the things that have been said of me in this town."

Astonishment showed in the face of almost everyone. Nelson Jordan studied his congregation, and saw a variety of reactions in their expressions—and most of them, he realized, were feeling shame. Almost all of them, he would guess, had spoken about Eden's condition; if they had not passed the rumor along, they had at least listened. Many of them dropped their heads, apparently unable to meet her gaze.

"I do not ask you to forgive me for a sin I have not committed, but I do ask you to pray for my physical healing. I know that God is able to do all things, and I'm asking you to join with me in a prayer of faith that God will give me physical strength, and that he will heal me."

For a moment no one moved. Then, abruptly, Doctor Edward Vance, who was sitting halfway back in the church, rose to his feet. He came forward, and when he reached Eden he put his hands out and took hers. He looked into her eyes and said loudly enough to be heard all over the church, "Sister Breckenridge, I ask you to forgive me. I have offended God, and I have wronged you by my lack of faith in you, and I ask you to forgive me."

Eden blinked back tears and whispered so quietly that only the physician heard, "Of course I do, Doctor."

Quentin saw others were moving out into the aisles, and to his astonishment, soon there was a double line waiting to speak to Eden. He knew that her simple words had touched a chord in these people, and was astonished to see men he would not have suspected capable of such a thing wiping their eyes. Someone began a hymn, and he found himself singing and weeping along with the rest.

Seeing Eden surrounded by so many, he began to feel something happening in his own heart—something he had felt before. He gripped the back of the seat, remembering the times God had commanded him to pray for people and he had seen them healed. Now he knew in his heart that, at last, God wanted him to pray for Eden. He moved out of his seat and stood in line. He could not have explained his feelings, for he did not understand them himself, but in his heart there was a steady note of joy because he knew that God was in this.

When he finally reached Eden, tears were running down her cheeks. He took her hands and leaned forward. "God is going to restore you, Eden. He just told me so!"

CHAPTER
Twenty-Two

"Eden's had quite a bit of company, Granny." A look of approval was spread across Thomas York's face. He smiled, adding, "I think her little talk at church cleared the air quite a bit."

"I heered about it," Granny said. She shifted the sweet-gum twig from one side of her mouth to the other, adding, "If I'd have been there in her place, I'd have said worse."

"Well, it worked anyway." Even as he spoke a woman emerged from the bedroom and Granny nodded. "Hello, Emma."

"Oh, Granny." Emma Carstairs came at once and nodded. "I'm glad to see you. Been meaning to ask you to stop by my place. I've got a few ailin's."

"Be glad to, Emma." Granny left the visitor talking with Thomas about her ailments thinking, *She's strong as a horse, but she enjoys a little attention.* When she entered the room she went at once to Eden who was sitting in her rocking chair beside the window. Granny sat down on the bed and studied her with a cynical appraisal. In all truth Eden did not look any better physically—if anything somewhat worse.

"You look tard. I reckon you've had too much visitin'."

Eden smiled faintly. "I have had quite a few, but it's been good. How are you, Granny?"

"Me? Why, just like always. I'm able to sit up and take nourishment."

The two women sat talking until Hannah came in saying, "Hello, Granny." She received the older woman's greeting, then said, "I'm going over to take some food to Ben."

"How is he doin', Hannah?" Granny inquired.

"He's able to get around some, but still in a lot of pain. I'll be back in time to fix supper."

As soon as the door closed, Eden said, "Granny, that woman has been a godsend! She's just been such a wonderful help to me. As a matter of fact, I think she's one of the best people I've ever met."

Granny grinned suddenly. "Like her brother?"

The question flustered Eden, and her cheeks showed a tinge of color. Granny saw Eden's confusion and filed it away in her mind.

★ ★ ★

Hearing a buggy coming, Calendar grasped the arms of the chair and rose, holding himself stiffly. The pain was constant, but it was not the blinding, searing type that had prostrated him. Moving carefully, he went to the door and opened it just as Hannah came in, carrying a basket in one hand. She looked at him in surprise. "Why, you shouldn't be doing this, Ben!"

"Got to do somethin'," he said. "I'll go crazy pretty soon if I can't get outside."

Hannah entered the house. "I brought you some fixin's. Come in and talk to me. I'm hungry myself. I brought enough for the two of us."

She made her way to the kitchen, and as he followed her he marveled again at how well she was able to maneuver. She was wearing a pale green dress, and her hair was loosely tied in back. He had always admired auburn hair.

Hannah put the meal of ham, fresh green beans, and newly baked cornbread onto the table. She seated herself and said, "Now we'll thank the Lord for it." Without waiting she bowed her head, and Calendar did the same. "Lord, we thank you for this food which you have provided. Thank you for the healing that you're doing in Ben, and we pray that you would give him perfect health and strength. And I pray for Eden, that you would do a healing in her. In Jesus' name."

Calendar ate hungrily, saying once, "You're a fine cook, Miss Larribee."

"Oh, for heaven's sakes, Ben, call me Hannah. After all this time I think it will be all right."

Calendar paused and said awkwardly, "All right then, Hannah."

"That sounds better."

The two ate, and Hannah gave him the news, such as she had. After he had eaten a piece of the fresh apple pie she had baked, she cleaned up quickly and then came to sit down again. "Ben, I want to ask a favor of you."

"A favor? Why sure. You just name it."

Hannah shook her head, saying, "You shouldn't promise to do something before you know what it is."

"I reckon anything you'd ask me would be right. And after all you've done for me I couldn't rightly refuse you anything. What is it?" He was curious and saw that there was some sort of humor in her gray-green eyes. During his period of recuperation he had grown to look forward to listening to her. They liked the same writers, including Mark Twain and James Fenimore Cooper, and she was introducing him to Longfellow. He did not know poetry, but he was beginning to like it. Now as he studied her face he was impressed again by what an attractive woman she was.

Hannah took a deep breath and said, "I want you to shave."

Calendar had been expecting something else. Certainly not this! "Sh—shave!" he stammered. "Why do you want me to do that?"

"Because you look awful," Hannah said frankly. "You're all woolly and you're enough to scare the children."

"I reckon I do. From what I hear, the women say to the kids when they're mean, 'Look out or Ben Calendar will get you.'"

"Well, part of it's that awful woolly beard. Some men have nice smooth beards, but yours is woolly as it can be. So I want you to shave."

Calendar stroked his beard thoughtfully, then saw that she was waiting. "All right," he said. "I'll do it. The scissors are in the table over there."

"Well, I can do that part of it." Hannah got the scissors and wrapped a sheet around his neck. "This is going to be messy," she said. "Now you just sit still. I wouldn't want to cut a piece of your ear off."

Calendar sat very still while Hannah snipped at the beard. It began to fall onto the floor in swatches, and it gave him an odd feeling as if he were losing part of himself. He was very conscious of her touch as from time to time she moved his head around. Something stirred within him that he had thought long dead.

Finally Hannah said, "That's as close as I can get. You'd better shave yourself. I'd probably cut your throat. You sit here and I'll bring the hot water. Where's your razor?"

She busied herself and five minutes later Calendar was scraping the razor down over his skin. "Haven't used this thing in years," he said. "It's dull." Still he managed the job, and finally she took a towel soaked in water and let him wash his face. He said, "I wish I had a mirror, but I don't."

"My goodness, you look so—different!" Hannah exclaimed, her eyes large with surprise.

Calendar indeed was a different man, so transformed that Hannah Larribee was shocked. His skin was white except for the forehead and around the eyes, where he had been burned to a bronze color. It gave him an odd look, as if he wore a mask. Hannah was taken aback by his masculine good looks. "You look twenty years younger," she said.

Calendar rubbed his cheeks, saying with a touch of wonder, "Burns like fire. I feel downright naked!" He grinned suddenly, his teeth very white and strong. "Now I'll have to shave every day. Nothing looks worse than a man with stubble."

Hannah felt uncomfortable for some reason she couldn't understand. "I guess I'd better go," she said quickly and rose, but his voice stopped her.

"Stay and talk a while. Gets lonesome around here." He surprised himself with this and said quickly, "I reckon you've spoiled me, Hannah. I was used to being alone. Never thought about it. But now I get lonely."

Hannah Larribee dropped her head. "I know what that's like," she murmured.

Studying her carefully, Calendar said, "You ought to get married."

Hannah looked up and met his gaze. "With my handicap?"

"Why, Hannah, you're the most complete woman I ever met! You're woman enough for any man."

The words seemed to strike Hannah, and she could not answer. Calendar's hazel eyes were fixed on her. She could not think of an answer and finally shook her head silently.

After a pause, Calendar said quietly, "You know, I'd like to show you this place when I'm able to get around."

"I'd like to see it."

"I've let it go down, but I'm thinkin' I might try to put it in better shape when I'm able."

"I hope you do, Ben." Hannah lifted her eyes. She could not forget his words, and she asked abruptly, "Did you mean what you said? That I'm woman enough for any man?"

"Wouldn't have said it if I hadn't meant it, Hannah."

The silence that fell embarrassed them both, then Hannah smiled and rose. "Come along, Ben. We can sit on the porch and talk about Mark Twain."

★ ★ ★

For the first time since starting his practice, Quentin had seen a steady procession of patients. They had started filing in by ten o'clock, and now it was almost three. It did not take much discernment to understand that Eden's talk at church had something to do with it. But Quentin had also discovered that Doctor Vance was channeling part of his patient load to him.

He held a baby in the crook of one arm and poked his fat stomach, smiling as he did so. "He's fine, Mrs. Kennedy. Just cutting a new tooth." He handed the baby back, and the anxious mother breathed a sigh of relief.

"I guess I shouldn't have bothered you bringing him in—but he's my first, and I guess I'm a worry wart."

"Better safe than sorry. You come anytime."

"How much do I owe you, Doctor?"

"Oh, I suppose a dollar would be about right."

Mrs. Kennedy looked up with surprise and said, "That's not much."

"It's enough for what I did."

After Mrs. Kennedy had left, Quentin moved to his desk and stared down at the cash that had accumulated there. He did not count it, but a feeling of warm satisfaction came to him. He was at last doing the thing that he had longed to do for many years.

He picked up his bag and left the office, locking it carefully behind him. He glanced at the sign stating his office hours, then hitched his mare and climbed into the buggy. As he drove down the side street, he passed the Baptist church and saw Reverend Jordan watering his flowers out in the front yard. The preacher loved flowers; when they were in season, he decorated the church with them.

"Hello, Doctor." Nelson Jordan came over to stand beside the buggy. "I hear you been pretty busy today."

"It's made a difference, these past few days, Brother Jordan." Quentin grinned. "I feel like a doctor at last—seeing patients."

"Well, I haven't got over what happened in church last Sunday. It's funny, Quentin, but one thing can turn a church around. The Spirit of God moved, and I've sensed a new spirit."

Quentin nodded, then said slowly, "Pastor, I want you to join me right now in a prayer."

"Of course." Jordan quickly stepped closer. "What is it, Quentin?"

"I've seen people healed by the power of God. No medicine, no drugs, no surgery. Just a sovereign act of God in answer to prayer."

"So have I."

"I've been praying for Eden now ever since I got back, but nothing's happened. I just haven't been able to pray the prayer of faith. Something seems to be blocking it."

"How have you been praying?"

"Why, I asked that God would heal her."

Quentin hesitated briefly, then related how several times God had moved on him and told him to pray for certain individuals, and they had been healed. Then he shook his head. "I'm praying for Eden, but I haven't had that same feeling."

"Well, I think sometimes we want to make God fit into our plans," the pastor said. He thought for a moment and then added, "You know your Bible. Sometimes God answers in strange ways— in a manner that we don't expect. It may be that way with Eden. You know," Jordan said slowly, "the Bible says the Spirit of God is like a river. Not like a channel or a canal. When we dig a canal, the idea is to get from point A to point B in as straight a line as possible. But a river doesn't do that. It doesn't flow straight. It meanders, it takes cuts, and it bends back on itself. You just can't command a river to go in a straight line. I've often thought that we try to get God channeled into a straight line to suit our convenience." The pastor grinned briefly and said, "It's almost like he was our servant and we were telling him what to do." Then he sobered and said, "Let's pray that whichever way God wants to work in Eden's life— no matter what it is—that he will do it as a sovereign God."

The two men prayed, and when they had finished Quentin felt somehow lighter. "It's been a help talking with you, Brother Jordan. I'm going to see Eden now. I'll tell her about our agreeing in prayer."

He left Helena and drove rapidly for a while. Finally he turned off the main road and stopped beside a stream, for God seemed to be speaking to him again. He got out of the buggy and let the horse drink from the stream. The sun was hot and the wind was blowing gently. Overhead red-winged blackbirds wheeled and turned in the sky. He paid little heed to this but threw his whole heart into trusting God. "Lord," he said aloud, "I've been expecting you to send a miracle—and I still expect it. But you do it in any way you choose. Please show me what I should do . . ."

For a long time Quentin stayed there. Finally, slowly, something began to build in him. He stood beside the bubbling stream and let God speak to him. It did not come all at once, but after an hour of meditation and prayer he straightened, looked up, and smiled. "Lord, I take this as a word from you, and I'm going to obey. I ask you to guide me in everything that I do."

★   ★   ★

Quentin burst into the sitting room where Eden sat reading. "Eden, how much do you trust me?" His voice was urgent, authoritative.

Eden looked up with surprise. Quentin crossed the room quickly and took her hand, pressing it as he looked directly at her, awaiting her answer.

"I trust you completely, Quentin. Why are you asking me that?"

Quentin spoke quickly, confidently. "I've been praying for a mir-acle—for God to do something in you miraculously. Something that's directly from God. But I prayed with the pastor this afternoon, and ever since then the Lord has been dealing with me." He told her how he had stopped beside the river and prayed. "Eden, I am convinced that you have a condition that surgery will correct. I believe you have a tumor. I want you to have an operation."

"An operation?"

Quentin was well aware that the very mention of surgery frightened most people—and hastened to add, "I know this frightens you, but I think it's what God wants us to do. I've been hoping that you'd be healed as I've seen others healed, but that hasn't happened."

"Are you sure this is what God wants, Quentin?"

"Yes, I'm very sure." He took in the calmness in her dark eyes and added quickly, "What we'll do is take you to New York. I know all the finest surgeons there, and I know they'll be glad to do the surgery."

Eden frowned and then asked, "Can't you do it, Quentin?"

"Why . . . there are men who've had much more experience—"

"I don't care about that," Eden said, and a hint of the strong will that lay in her surfaced, changing her expression. She held his gaze steadily. "No, I want you to do the operation, Quentin."

Eden's voice was firm, and she suddenly put the back of his hand to her cheek in a gesture that caught at his heart. The small action revealed the depth of her surrender to him. For a moment it troubled him. Then, looking into her face, he felt a growing certainty. "If that's what you want, Eden, I'll do my best." He leaned over and kissed her cheek lightly. "I can't lose you now," he whispered. "I've been looking for you all my life."

Eden looked into his face and said quietly, "I told you once, Quentin, that I cared for you." She hesitated, dropping her eyes for a moment. Then she lifted them and smiled. "I still do," she whispered.

Quentin put his arms around her, and she came to him gently and trusting. He held her as she laid her head against his chest. He stroked her hair and they said nothing. Finally he moved back, and when she lifted her face, he kissed her and said, "I love you, Eden. I didn't know a man could love a woman so much."

Eden put her head back on his chest. "I trust you for everything," she said quietly.

CHAPTER
Twenty-Three

Thomas sat in Doctor Vance's waiting room, trying to appear relaxed. He had been shocked when, the day before, Quentin had broken the news that he was going to operate on Eden. And they had wasted no time. Today they had come into town, where Doctor Vance had been waiting. The two men had used Doctor Vance's office and equipment, for Quentin was not set up for serious surgery.

They had been sitting for a long time, and now Thomas saw that both Prudence and Johnny were tense, their backs straight, fear and apprehension on their faces. Stuart had given up and now lay down on a pallet made on the floor. "Don't worry. It'll be all right," Thomas said. He made himself smile and said, "Your mama's going to be just like she always was."

Johnny's lips were tight and he could not speak. But Prudence whispered, "I'm afraid, Grandpa."

"The Bible says, 'God has not given us the spirit of fear.' We're going to see a miracle! Just believe God."

★ ★ ★

Fifteen minutes later the door opened. Thomas rose at once as Quentin entered; the children scrambled to their feet. "Is Mama all right?" Prudence asked, going to Quentin at once.

He swept her up, laughing, and kissed her. "She's going to be fine. Just fine!"

Thomas expelled his breath. Johnny seemed to almost collapse, and Thomas reached over and put his arm around his grandson. "What was it, Quentin?"

"It was a tumor. A big one."

"A tumor." Thomas pondered. "And you took it out?"

"All gone." Quentin spoke quietly. "God just seemed to be with me. I've never been so sure about a surgery in my life."

He kissed Prudence again and she begged, "Can I see her, Quentin?"

"She's asleep right now, but as soon as she's awake she'll want to see you. We'll have to wait for a while."

Doctor Vance came out a few minutes later, and when Quentin took the children out to get them something to eat, he said, "Thomas, I never saw anything like it."

"Like what, Doctor Vance?"

"That surgery was a work of art! I tell you, God has put something special in Quentin Larribee's hands. He's so quick and sure! Never a wasted moment." Vance shook his head in disbelief. "I've seen some of the big-time surgeons, but none like Quentin."

"You think she'll be all right, Doctor?"

"No doubt about it. She's asleep now, and she'll have some pain when she wakes up. But God has answered."

★   ★   ★

Eden came out of a deep sleep. She was vaguely aware of the pain, but she was also aware of a face hovering over her. She blinked her eyes, and Quentin's eyes swam into focus. "Quentin?" she asked.

"Don't try to talk."

She lay there holding one of his hands in both of hers. She felt his other hand on her head stroking her hair. She did not speak for a long time, but then she said, "Quentin, don't leave me."

And she heard his voice, warm and firm and filled with the love she had always longed for, say, "I won't leave you, Eden—not ever!"

CHAPTER
Twenty-Four

For a moment Calendar paused, lifted the brush from the shiny back of the gelding, and admired the animal. He had a deep love for horses. When the gelding snorted, turned his head, and nipped at his shoulder, he tapped the velvet nose smartly. "No. You can't have a bite of me. Now mind your manners." He continued brushing, pleased that he could bend over with only a slight pain in his back. Just being able to move around, to work and to care for his animals, had been a blessing.

A sound caught his ears, and he turned to look outside the barn. Quentin Larribee was driving up in his buggy. He quickly led the gelding into the stall and poured out a plentiful mound of oats. "Have a good lunch," he muttered, then turned and went outside.

"How are you, Doctor?" Calendar greeted his visitor. "Get out and have some sweet tea. It's hotter than blazes today."

"Sure is," Quentin agreed. It was near the end of June, and the fierce sun overhead beat down upon him. His clothes were damp and wilted, and a fine layer of dust clung to his face. Taking out his handkerchief, he wiped his face and grinned. "You Southerners know how to take hot weather. I'd like to take you up to New York sometime and see how you do in twenty below."

"Not for me." Calendar grinned. "Come on inside."

The two made their way toward the house, and Quentin studied Calendar's walk with a careful eye. "God's done a work in you, Ben. I've seen people not nearly as badly hurt as you who were never able to walk again."

Calendar did not answer until they had mounted the steps. He moved somewhat stiffly and carefully, but he turned and a sober light touched his eyes. "I've been thinking about that a lot. My brother Cass was thrown from a horse when he was sixteen. He broke his neck, and he died right there. Why wasn't it me, Doc?"

"Nobody can say about things like that, Ben. It wasn't your time. God's got his hand on all of us."

"You really believe that with all the misery around us?"

"I have to, Ben. What's the alternative?" Quentin studied the tall man before him. He was still somewhat unaccustomed to the smoothly shaven face, and he noted from a small cut that Calendar had already shaved that day.

"Come on in and rest yourself."

Quentin sat down with relief on a chair in the kitchen. Calendar fetched the jug of tea from the springhouse and filled two large tumblers. As the two men sat sipping the tea, Quentin spoke idly about some of the calls he had made, but he noted that Calendar seemed troubled.

Finally he came out with it.

"I guess I'm not much of a hand to speak my thanks, Doctor Larribee, but I wouldn't have made it without you."

"Oh, I think you might have. Hannah had more to do with it than I did."

Calendar looked down for a moment. He moved the glass of tea around in his large hands and studied it as if it had some meaning. Finally he looked up and said, "I don't know what to make of your sister. I've never met a woman like Hannah."

"She's the best woman I've ever known," Quentin remarked. "She's had a hard life, though." He told Calendar how the two of them had raised the other children. "She was in love with a man once, but he died in the war. That always grieved me. He was a good man, Ben. Hannah would have made a wonderful wife for him."

"She never took another man?"

"No. She's sensitive about her handicap."

Calendar snorted. "That's not right! She's as good a woman as any I ever saw—handicap or not."

"I'm glad you think so, Ben. I wish you'd tell her. You might not know it, she's so independent, but she's like any woman. She likes to be told that she's pretty and nice things like that."

Calendar suddenly grinned. "I'd be no hand at that. No practice."

"Practice up and give her a try."

Calendar sat silently, apparently mulling thoughts that he found difficult to express. Finally he cleared his throat and said, "If I wasn't such a lost cause, I'd—"

Calendar broke off, and Quentin suddenly had a quick insight. This man had a feeling for Hannah. He studied Calendar thinking, *His life's been so strange. I don't know if he could ever be married. He's been a hermit for so long.* "Have you thought much about God, Ben? You know he never gives up on us. No matter how far we get away from him or how far we run, he's still there waiting to give us a chance."

Calendar stared at Quentin. "You really believe that?"

"Of course I do. The Bible says he came to seek and save that which was lost." He began to speak of the Lord Jesus Christ, and Calendar listened, his hands clasped before him. Quentin noted that they were not entirely steady. He ended by saying, "You know, it would be hard to get in to see the president of the United States. It's a lot easier to get in to see God."

Calendar looked up. "What do you mean by that?"

"I mean he's ready to save those that call upon him. I want you to think about it, Ben."

"I will. I'll think on it right hard, Doc." He hesitated, then added, "To tell the truth, I've been thinking on it quite a bit."

Quentin felt that this was as far as God would have him to go. He got up and a thought came to him. "You know, next week there's that Fourth of July celebration. I think you ought to come."

"Me? Why, I can't do that."

"Sure you can. It'll be Eden's first outing since the operation— and Hannah would be glad to see you."

The words caught at Ben Calendar, but he did not answer. After Quentin had left, he stood in the yard watching the dust from the buggy rise in the air. He looked down at the dog that came to whine and nudge at him. "What do you think, Caesar? What would happen if I went to that celebration?" The hound sat down and stared up at his master, and Calendar returned his gaze. "I wonder," he mused, then turned and walked back toward the house.

★ ★ ★

When Quentin arrived at the Breckenridge house, he went in at once to find Eden. He found her animatedly teaching Prudence how to put up jam. The kitchen was filled with the fragrant odor of fruit and sugar boiling on the stove, and Quentin asked, "When do I get some of this jam? I'm hungry."

"Not for a while." Eden smiled. She looked fit, and color had come back into her cheeks. "Now, you watch these and don't let them boil over, Prudence," she said. "I'm going to take Quentin out to show him the finest tomatoes in the country. You can take some home to Hannah."

"Nothing I like better than fresh tomatoes."

They moved out of the house and Quentin remarked, "You're doing so well. I'm glad to see it."

"I feel wonderful. Oh, Quentin," she said and turned to him, her eyes aglow, "it's so wonderful just to wake up in the morning and not dread the day! I thank God every moment for what he's done for me." She reached out suddenly and took his hand. "And I can never thank you enough."

He held her hand and his feelings were stirred powerfully. He started to speak and longed to tell her of his love, but he could not. "I was glad I was able to help," he said. "Well, let's go see those tomatoes."

Eden's countenance fell slightly, as if she had been expecting him to say something different. She watched him for a moment, waiting, then said quickly, "All right."

For the next fifteen minutes they moved among the tomato plants selecting the ripest and best, which Eden put in a bucket. She was just handing the bucket to Quentin when he heard approaching hoofbeats. "Somebody's coming in an awful hurry."

The two watched as a cloud of dust rose on the road, and Eden said, "That's Clay Satterfield."

"Faye's boy?"

"Yes. It's his oldest boy."

The two walked to the edge of the garden patch and the young boy, no more than twelve or thirteen, pulled up his horse. His face seemed pale despite his sunburn, and fear was evident in his eyes. "They sent me to git you," he said, holding the mare, which was panting and coated with straw.

"What is it, son?" Quentin said quickly.

"Doc Vance says for you to come quick. My brother's been hurt turrible bad."

"I'll come as quick as I can. That horse is pretty well used up. You want to ride in the buggy and leave him here?"

"No. He'll make it back. You go on, Doc. Hurry!"

Quentin ran back to the house for his doctor's bag, calling over his shoulder, "I'll see you later, Eden." The boy followed him to the house with the buggy. Quickly they exchanged places, and Quentin struck the surprised mare a blow with the buggy whip. "Get up!" he said brusquely, and the horse shot forward, throwing Quentin backwards.

Clay Satterfield's horse may have been tired, but Clay kicked it into a dead run. Quentin followed, bumping and jolting over the old ruts. The dust rose like a plume behind him, and finally they turned onto a side road and the jolting became worse. He was afraid he would break an axle, but still he urged the horse forward.

Finally they pulled up in front of a house set in a clearing and surrounded by fields. Quickly Quentin leaped out of the buggy, grabbed his bag, and started toward the house. But Quentin halted halfway up the steps when Faye Satterfield stepped outside, his face hard, and shouted, "Get off my place, you damn Yankee!"

Faye looked angry enough to kill. But Doctor Vance came outside and grabbed Satterfield's arm. "Shut your mouth, Faye! You've got a dying boy in there, and this man's the only hope we've got! Now shut up and get out of here!"

Quentin had already experienced Satterfield's violent temper, and he expected him to flare up. But a woman came out, her face lined with fear, and took the man's arm. "Faye, let him look at Donnie."

Satterfield hesitated. His lips became a straight line, but he muttered with a nod, "All right. You kin go in."

Quentin followed Doctor Vance inside, where he found the injured boy lying on a clean cloth on the kitchen table.

"Bad head injury. He got kicked by a horse," Vance muttered.

Stepping at once to the head of the table, Quentin needed no more than a quick glance to make his diagnosis. "Bone shattered. We'll have to do a trephination."

Doctor Vance looked worried. "I've never done an operation like that. Have you ever seen one?"

"Yes. I've done two myself."

"Thank God!" Vance expelled his breath. He gripped Quentin's arm. "We've got to hurry though. His color is worse and his breathing is more shallow."

"It'll be better when we remove the pressure." He took a closer look at the injury, then muttered, "I wish we had a plate."

"We got plates." Faye Satterfield suddenly appeared. "What do you want a plate for?"

"Not a plate you eat off of, Satterfield. We're going to have to remove some of this bone in your son's skull. You see where it's shattered here? Those fragments of bone have got to come out. When we take it out it'll leave a soft spot. What we need is a piece of silver plate as thin as possible. I could put that back in and it would shore up the skull."

Satterfield stared at Larribee, then nodded. "I'll get the plate. Don't you worry about that. How big does it have to be?"

"About this big around—about an inch and a half." Quentin held up his hands over the boy's skull. "It'll have to cover this area. But it's got to be smooth and very thin."

Satterfield stared at Quentin, his pale blue eyes unreadable, then he said, "I'll take keer of that—you take keer of my boy." Then he wheeled and dashed out the door.

"Where's he going to get a plate, Ed?"

"Faye's a good metalworker, a blacksmith," Vance said. "He'll do it, I think."

"All right. We'd better get started." He turned to the woman. "Ida, we're going to need lots of hot water."

"It's on the fire. I can make all you want." The woman twisted her hands nervously and looked down at her son. "He's so still, and he . . . he looks so bad!"

"He'll be better when we get the pressure relieved," Doctor Vance said. "Now, Ida, you keep the other children out and give us hot water."

The two men began to prepare for the operation by making an operating room, of sorts, out of the kitchen. Both men had brought their bags, and they laid out such instruments as they had. Between them they had enough to do the surgery.

Vance suddenly asked, "What are the boy's chances?"

Quentin thought for a moment. "I think he's got a good chance if we can relieve this pressure, unless there's some damage we can't see."

They had finished their preparation when Faye Satterfield entered. "How's this?" he asked. He held up a small polished disk that gleamed in the sunlight that came in through the window.

Quentin took it and marveled at the smoothness of it. "Just right," he said. "What did you make it out of?"

"Silver dollar. I beat it out fine and polished it up good and smooth. Will it do?"

"This will do fine." Quentin hesitated. "Faye, I need Doctor Vance to help me with the surgery. I'll need you to administer the anesthetic."

"What's that?"

"This." Quentin took out a small can of ether. "Put this on a small cloth, just a few drops, and let Donnie breathe it. It'll put him to sleep. But from time to time, if he starts waking up, you'll have to put another drop or two on there." He studied the man carefully, wondering if he was up to it. "Some people can't stand to see a thing like this. But it's very important that Donnie remain perfectly still. If he moves while I'm taking the bone out, it would be bad."

Faye said instantly, "I went through the whole war, Doc. Seen lots of bad things. Course this is my own son, but I kin do it." He hesitated, then asked, "Has he got a chance, Doc?"

"A very good chance, Faye. This operation has been done for hundreds of years. Why, the Egyptians did this sort of thing back when the pyramids were going up. I know it sounds strange, but all it means is that we're going to replace part of your boy's skull with this little plate . . ."

Quentin finished explaining the operation to Faye, then looked at Doctor Vance and nodded. "All right then. We're ready to start." He opened the can of ether and put a few drops on the cloth, holding it at arm's length. "Here, Faye. Keep the top on the can, because the fumes will get all of us."

Satterfield took the cloth and held it gently over his son's face. Quentin waited and saw that the breathing became more regular. "All right. We can start now."

Faye Satterfield waited until Quentin stood over his son's head, a shiny instrument in his hand, then he pulled out a pistol and laid it on the table beside the instruments.

Quentin studied the pistol, then lifted his eyes to meet Satterfield's. "What's that for, Faye?"

"It's for you in case my boy dies."

Quentin Larribee had not one doubt in the world that Faye Satterfield meant exactly what he said. He studied the hard light in Satterfield's eyes, then moved over to where his bag was. Reaching inside, he removed the thirty-eight he always carried, came back, and laid it down on the makeshift operating table.

"What's that for?" Satterfield demanded, eyeing the weapon.

"If this boy's going to die, Faye," Quentin said calmly. "I'll know it at least sixty seconds before you do. In that case the gun's for you."

Suddenly Faye Satterfield grinned. "It looks like you got the best of the argument, Doc." He picked up the heavy pistol and turned the cylinder until the shells fell out. He put them in his pocket, then laid the empty weapon back down on the table.

Quentin studied the man before him, then nodded. "Before we start this I want all three of us to pray over Donnie."

Satterfield blinked. "I ain't a prayin' man, Doc."

"Then it's time you started." He waited for a moment, holding Satterfield's gaze, and finally the man's eyes dropped. Quentin bowed his head, as did Doctor Vance, and there was a moment's silence. Quentin prayed aloud, "Oh, God, give us skill to help this boy. He belongs to you, and we know he's beloved of this father and this mother. All is in your hands, Lord. We're your servants, and we ask in the name of Jesus that you give success to this surgery."

Faye did not raise his head at first, but when he did there was a strange light in them. Quentin moved to the head of the table. He began making an incision, and Vance at once stemmed the flow of blood. Quentin glanced up quickly to see how Satterfield was taking it and saw that the man's face was set, his hands steady.

Picking up the scalpel, Quentin explained what he was doing. It was a habit he'd picked up in the hospital in New York, and he was aware that Satterfield needed all the encouragement he could get. Faye Satterfield was an uneducated man, hard in many ways. But Quentin could see that he loved his son deeply.

"You can see the indentation here, Faye," he said quietly. "Now what I'm going to do is make an incision right across it. There won't be a great deal of blood, for the arteries and veins are small in our scalps. Doctor Vance will keep the blood cleaned up as I make the cut."

With one firm movement Quentin made an incision across the shaven skull, then said, "Now I'll make two other incisions at the ends of this one—like this." Quentin's voice was conversational, as if he were talking about the weather. He wanted to eliminate as much as possible the strangeness of the act of surgery for Satterfield. He waited as Vance cleaned away the blood with small pads of cloth, then said, "Now we can get to it. Faye, put three more drops of ether on the cloth."

With sweat beading his forehead, carefully Satterfield applied the drops. "That right, Doc?"

"Fine. Just right. You're doing it just as well as I ever saw." Quentin's scalpel moved quickly, and the fractured area of the skull was laid bare. "You see how the skull is broken, Faye? See those splinters? Well, they've got to come out. The trephine, Dr. Vance."

Vance handed a circular object with sharp teeth to Quentin. "This is for removing all that broken bone," Quentin said. "It won't hurt Donnie a bit, and it will get all this damaged bone out of the way."

Vance and Satterfield watched as Larribee used the trephine. Quentin moved so skillfully that the circle of bone was freed in what seemed an impossibly short time.

"Small forceps," Quentin said, and taking the instrument, with one smooth motion lifted the broken disk of bone. The gray matter of the brain was exposed, and Quentin said quickly to take Satterfield's mind off this, "Now see those small splinters? I'll just take them out, and we'll be ready to close."

Quentin moved more slowly now, for he wanted to be absolutely certain that all of the bits of shattered skull were removed. Twice during this time he instructed Faye to add a few drops of ether, but Donnie never stirred. Dr. Vance took his pulse several times, and commented once, "His color is good, Doctor. He's doing fine."

Quentin didn't speak for a time, and his hands moved surely. Finally he looked up with a smile. "That's it. Now the plate, Doctor." He waited as Vance cleaned the disk, then took it and held it up to the light. "This is fine work, Faye. I've never seen better."

Quentin set the small disk in place, then folded the flaps of skin over until it was covered.

"Would you like to do the sutures, Dr. Vance?"

"No, you finish up."

Quentin took the curved needle threaded with gut and began to sew up the flaps. He moved slowly, taking smaller stitches than most surgeons, and when he tied the last knot, he turned to Faye. "All done, Faye."

"Will he be all right?"

Quentin removed the cloth from Donnie's face and studied the still features. "I believe he will. It wasn't a bad skull fracture—not as bad as a great many I've seen. We got all the splinters and the pressure is relieved. He'll need good care, but I'd say he's going to be fine. What do you think, Doctor Vance?"

Vance shook his head wonderingly. "I agree—and let me tell you, Quentin, that's the finest job of surgery I've ever seen in my life."

Quentin smiled, then turned to Satterfield. "Go tell your wife, Faye. Your boy's going to be fine."

Faye held the doctor's eyes for a moment but did not say a word. Then he made a choking noise and dropped his head. When he looked up his lips were trembling and tears glistened in his eyes. "I went through the whole war, Doc, and never shed a tear—but I just can't help it now!"

"It's all right to cry over a son," Doctor Vance said quietly. "Go tell your wife the good news."

As soon as Faye had left the kitchen, Vance exclaimed, "I never saw anything like it, Quentin. God's given you a marvelous touch."

Quentin started to answer, but then a loud unearthly scream erupted. "What was that!" he exclaimed.

Vance grinned. "Oh, that's just Ida. She's a shoutin' Methodist."

"Well, she'll have to take her shoutin' outside." Quentin grinned. "I don't want this boy disturbed for a while."

"Oh, she don't shout long. That may be all of it. Let's go out and talk to 'em. I could do a little shoutin' myself."

Quentin moved into the parlor, where he was almost knocked down by Ida Satterfield. She threw her arms around him, her face wet with tears. She was saying, "Thank God! Thank God!" over and over again.

Quentin patted the woman's shoulders. "Now, Mrs. Satterfield, the boy's going to take lots of care, but the Lord was with us. He's going to be fine."

"Doc," Faye Satterfield spoke up. His cheeks were moving with some emotion he was trying to suppress. He shifted his weight around and looked down, and then looked up with a faint smile. "I never thought I'd ask a Yankee to set down in my house—but it would pleasure me if you would set and take something."

Quentin suddenly felt a great happiness and contentment. He nodded. "Be glad to, Faye." But he was thinking, *If I can make peace with an unreconstructed rebel like Faye Satterfield, I can do it with anybody!*

CHAPTER
Twenty-Five

Hannah slipped the dress over her head, fastened it, then turned to examine herself in the mirror. The dress was made out of peach-colored fabric, with a tight-fitting bodice that buttoned down the front to the waist. It had a small white lawn collar, and the elbow-length sleeves ended with a ruffle of lace. The skirt was double, with the overskirt turned back to reveal a lining of a light pumpkin color.

She heard firecrackers popping outside as they had been all day long celebrating the Fourth of July. She studied the dress carefully, remembering the argument she had had with Quentin. He had insisted that both of them buy new clothes for the celebration, and when she had protested he had said, "Think of it as something in honor of Eden. It'll be her first outing since the operation."

Slowly Hannah turned and moved to the window. The new shoes she had bought, shiny black leather buttoned up and snug, gave an unaccustomed tightness and squeaked, it seemed to her, as she walked. Pulling the curtains back, she looked out the window and saw a group of small boys setting off firecrackers and yelling and screaming like wild Indians. All up and down the streets of Helena, people were milling around dressed in their finery.

Somehow Hannah had been unable to join in the spirit of celebration. During the time she had been caring for Ben Calendar her life had been full. It had been something to do, and she was a woman who needed to keep busy. Of late, however, she had become more and more aware that sooner or later Quentin must marry. But what would happen to her then? One of two things. Either she would move away and live alone, or else she would make an uncomfortable third in a household. Both situations brought a sense of gloom to Hannah.

"Hannah, are you ready?" A banging on her door turned her around, and she moved quickly to open it.

"Well, look at you!" Quentin beamed and stepped inside. His eyes were bright, and he was wearing a light gray suit jacket, a white shirt with a black tie, and a pair of gray-and-black striped slacks. "You look beautiful, Hannah, just beautiful!"

His words pleased Hannah and she moved closer. Bracing the crutch easily under her arm, she straightened his tie. "You look beautiful, too," she said.

"Come along. We're missing the celebration." They started out of the house, but Quentin said, "Let's not forget the box lunch."

"I'm not going to get involved in such a silly thing." Quentin had explained to her that it was customary for unmarried ladies to bring a box lunch. Then the men would bid for the pleasure of sharing the lunch with them. "It's too much like buying a woman."

"Oh, don't be silly! It's just in good fun. Come along now. No arguments." He ignored her protests and moved into the kitchen. The box lunch was tied up neatly with a string. He carried it as they left the house and walked down the streets.

Helena, it seemed, had drawn to itself more people than it could hold. Farmers from the outlying areas and many citizens of smaller towns were all there. There would be a band concert, square dancing, political speeches of course, and food of all kinds. More importantly to the young people, a small carnival had set up on the end of Cherry Street, and now there was the sound of a calliope, and a merry-go-round spun with squealing children aboard the gaily painted horses.

They passed through the crowd, stopping here and there to look at the shooting galleries where customers shot for a chance at dolls and other prizes. The air was filled with the smell of barbecue, roast beef, and candied apples. Quentin bought an apple and bit into it, then handed it to Hannah. She tasted it and made a face. "Sweet and sour. I'll take mine separate."

Quentin, however, devoured the apple and then led Hannah further. They were greeted by many people, and Hannah was proud at how many people went out of their way to speak to Doctor Larribee. He had become, in a very short time, quite well known. Many, however, did not know her, and she felt an uneasiness and embarrassment about the gazes that came her way.

Their walk was interrupted by a tall, bluff man with red cheeks and muttonchop whiskers. His hair was gray, but there was a youthful manner in his smooth face. "Ah, my dear Doctor Larribee," he said loudly in a voice that sounded as if he were accustomed to being heard.

"May I introduce my sister. Hannah, this is Judge Harlan Nettles, and this is my sister, Miss Hannah Larribee."

"Delighted to make your acquaintance, Miss Larribee." Judge Nettles bowed in an old-fashioned way and took the hand that she extended. "I was not aware that you had such a beautiful sister, Doctor. You've been keeping her in hiding." Nettles was a man of flowery speeches. He was given to dramatics, and he often shocked people in his courtroom by his dramatic presentations and by his verdicts. He was a man who loved politics, and it was common knowledge that at the next election he would be running for governor. "Well now, Doctor Larribee. Have you been thinking over my suggestion?"

"Yes, I have, but I'm afraid I can't agree, Judge."

"But you must! You must join our ranks, Miss Larribee—those of us who would enlist your brother."

"Enlist him for what, Judge Nettles?"

"Why, everyone has agreed that Doctor Larribee should serve on the town council. It's a natural thing, and we will not take no for an answer. You will join us in encouraging him, will you not?"

Hannah smiled. "Yes. I think it would be a very good thing. He's so modest that he would never seek it for himself."

"Well, now that I have you on our side, I have no fears. It's a pleasure to meet you, Miss Larribee. Doctor, I'm taking this as a yes." He moved away, greeting men and women with a handshake.

Quentin protested. "Hannah, why did you say that? I'm no hand for civic affairs."

"It's an honor, Quentin, and you have to do it."

Quentin grumbled, but he saw that Hannah was pleased. They continued to make their way down to the end of the street. When they arrived there Quentin said abruptly, "Look. There's Eden. Come along." They made their way through the crowds out to the open space where the riding horses, buggies, and wagons were tied, and Quentin arrived just in time to reach up and hand Eden down. He held her hand tightly as he swept off his hat with a free hand. "You look absolutely beautiful, Eden! Doesn't she, Hannah?"

Eden indeed was lovely, wearing a light yellow and green dress with a white collar around the rounded neckline. It had elbow-length sleeves ending in a white lace ruffle and tiny white ribbon bows in a line down the front of the bodice. But the rosy color in her cheeks pleased Quentin most of all.

Quentin reached up and took Stuart. "I'll have to hang onto you, Stuart. How about you ride on my shoulders?"

"Yes, sir!" Stuart yelled, and was seated at once on Quentin's shoulders.

"Carry my hat, will you, Eden? I don't want to lose it. I paid too much for it."

"You look so distinguished," Eden said.

"Yes, you do," Thomas agreed. "If you drop dead, Quent, we won't have to do a thing to you but stick a lily in your hand."

"What an awful thing to say!" Hannah exclaimed. But she liked Thomas York very much, and he came to her at once to walk beside her.

For the next two hours the party visited every attraction. At the horse race, they cheered Faye Satterfield, who won easily on a chestnut gelding. Faye came over after having received his prize and said, "Now I'm ready to pay my doctor bill."

"Wait'll the crops come in, Faye," Quentin urged.

"Nothing doing." He pulled off some bills and said, "Will that do it? It's only money, and I owe you more than that. I'm mighty grateful to you, Doc." His eyes were warm, and he shook his head. "It's a miracle the way Donnie's coming around. As good as new."

Quent shrugged off the praise, and finally they made their way to the carnival. They stopped to look at a Flying Jenny. Quentin said, "I built one of those for my brothers and sisters back on the farm. But this one is huge!"

The Flying Jenny was nothing but a single long pole with a car on each end large enough for two people. It was supported in the center by a large pole three feet high. The central shaft was driven in a circle by a system of gears powered by a matched set of mules on a treadmill which was set back about twenty feet.

"Can we ride it?" Johnny demanded at once.

"It looks so dangerous," Eden said. "What if it breaks—or if the car falls off?"

"We'll risk it." Quentin grinned. He paid the fare. "Johnny, you hang on to Prudence. I'll hang on to your ma."

Eden flushed, but the four settled into their seats, and the bearded owner asked, "Fast or slow?"

"As fast as she'll go!" Quentin said. "Don't spare the mules."

The mules settled in and the Jenny began to spin. Almost at once Eden found herself thrown against Quentin, who put his arm around her and held her close. "Don't worry," he said. "I'm here."

She looked up at him and laughed. "And what would you do if the car fell?"

"I'd save you some way." Quentin was feeling light-headed, for things had changed so drastically. He had found a life, and he knew that in Helena he had made a place for himself.

Finally the afternoon began to draw down, and Thomas said, "It's about time for the box supper. I'm gonna buy me a box put up by a good cookin' widow woman."

They made their way to the square where the dance platform had seen good service that day with dancing and band music. Quentin had stopped off there earlier to leave Hannah's box, and now they took their places in the crowd that was standing around. Judge Harlan Nettles was in his element. He was obviously in charge of the event, and now he was saying in his trumpetlike voice, "All right. Get ready to pay for your best girls, men! This money's going to go for a good cause. We need to buy a home for old folks who can't take care of themselves. Now, don't be stingy, boys." He picked up a box and looked at the name. "Now, what am I bid for this fine lunch and one of the finest girls in Helena to join you in eating it? Betty Simms, come right on up here."

A blushing girl made her way to the front and stood there awkwardly. The judge argued and wheedled until Betty's lunch box sold for seven dollars.

Quentin enjoyed himself. The judge had a quick sense of humor. He knew everyone, it seemed, in the county and probably in most of the state and made witty remarks about some of them. They were never offensive, and the crowd was happy.

The auction went on for some time, the most heated contest being for a young woman named Sally Bates who was evidently courted by two young men. They evidently had made this a test of some kind, for the lunch finally sold for forty-three dollars.

Thomas laughed saying, "Buck Tyler will be broke for a month. I hope he gets his money's worth out of that lunch."

Hannah had enjoyed the auction, but she suddenly saw the judge pick up a box that she recognized as the one she had packed. She tried to shrink back and would have left, but Quentin held her back. "None of that," he whispered.

Judge Nettles smiled broadly. "Now we have a real treat for you fellas. Most of you know our new doctor, Quentin Larribee. He's not much to look at, Doctor Larribee, but his sister is. This box belongs to Miss Hannah Larribee and it's filled with fried chicken, biscuits, peach pie, all kinds of goodies. You come right up here, Miss Larribee, and let the folks from Helena give you a greeting. You fellas, I want to hear bids."

Seeing that Hannah was terribly embarrassed, Eden put her arm around her. "Go on, Hannah. It'll be fun."

Hannah flashed a grateful look and made her way to the front. As always she was conscious in a crowd of the crutch that she used, but she kept her head high and turned and faced the crowd. Her face was rather pale, but she had determined to tough it out. She kept her eyes fixed on Quentin, who was smiling at her and winked broadly.

"All right, men. What's your bid?"

A tall rawboned man standing in the front and obviously a little the worse for drink cried out, "Why durn it all. I'll stake that filly out. I'll bid five dollars."

The judge gave the man a withering look. "Why, Zeke Tanner, you're a cheapskate. That's no bid for a fine lady like Miss Larribee!"

"That's right, Zeke. You've got no manners or taste at all." The speaker was a short, muscular man with a fancy suit. "Ten dollars, Judge."

"Well now, Sheriff Wright, that's more like it. I'm glad to see that the law enforcement branch of our government has good taste."

But Zeke Tanner gave the sheriff a hard look. "I'll make it fifteen."

"Twenty."

The bidding went up rather quickly, and finally when the drunk bid twenty-nine dollars the sheriff turned and faced him coldly. He was wearing a pearl-handed pistol on his hip and he placed his hand on it. He glared at his opponent and said, "I bid thirty dollars—and if you top it, Zeke, I'll put you where the dogs won't bite you!"

A laugh went up from all the crowd. Zeke Tanner glared at the sheriff but turned and pushed his way out of the crowd.

"All right," Judge Nettles said. "That's thirty dollars once. Thirty dollars twice—"

"One hundred dollars!"

A gasp went over the crowd and everyone turned to look as a tall man stepped out from the side. The man was dressed in a fine gray suit, polished boots, and a white Stetson. But the thing that everyone saw was the hangman's noose hanging around his neck.

"Calendar! Is that you?" Judge Nettles gasped.

"It's me, Judge."

Hannah Larribee was so shocked she could not speak. Calendar came up and stood beside her, and when he arrived he took his hat off. His hair was prematurely gray, but it was the kind of gray that was lively and full of life and glistened. His eyes were wrinkled at the corners from being out in the sun, and he was tanned and fit looking. He looked down at Hannah and a silence fell over the crowd. Everyone leaned forward to hear, and the words came clearly, "Is this all right with you, Miss Larribee?"

Quentin Larribee was watching his sister. He loved her more than ever for the courage she had shown, and now he saw that she was moved. He watched as her eyes met those of Ben Calendar. Finally, seeing that she was speechless, he stepped forward and called out loudly, "It's all right with me, Ben. Now, Hannah, take your man."

The spell was broken for Hannah and she shot a grateful look at Quentin and turned and said quietly, "Yes, Ben. I'd be honored."

A quick buzz of talk ran around the crowd. Everyone knew Ben Calendar—but not this man. It was hard for some of them to make the mental adjustment, for the handsome fellow that stood before them dressed in a fine suit had nothing about him of the ragged, rough-bearded man that most of them had seen only at a distance.

Judge Harlan Nettles had a quick mind. He had grown up in Helena, and had been, as a young man, a spectator at the trial of Ben Calendar. He had not been convinced of the man's guilt then, and he had been disgusted with the sentence. He had often wondered what sort of a judge would come up with a sentence like that, disgracing a man for the rest of his life by tying a noose around his neck.

And Nettles was also a politician. He had a sense of the dramatic, and he suddenly had an inspiration. He fully planned to run for governor, and he knew that the lives of politicians often are controlled by one single moment or one single phrase. Now he knew that he had a chance to imprint his name on the minds of the citizens of Arkansas. It took only a few seconds for him to reach his conclusion, but as Ben Calendar turned to get the box, he said, "Ben Calendar, come here."

Calendar stopped abruptly and looked up at the judge. He glanced down at Hannah and then moved over to stand directly in front of the big man. "Yes, Judge."

Choosing his words carefully, Judge Nettles began to speak. Everyone leaned forward to catch them. He was a practiced orator and lifted his voice just enough to reach the ears of the crowd. He was not unaware that Ed Collins, the editor of the *Arkansas Gazette*, was there, and that whatever he said would be printed in the biggest newspaper in the state.

"Some of you may not know this man, Ben Calendar, but something is in my heart today. I'm a man of the law. Without the law we're lost. But the law is not cold. It is a living thing. It strikes down the guilty but it frees the innocent . . ."

Everyone including Quentin listened intently as the judge spoke of the law. And like the rest he wondered where this was headed.

No one wondered more than Ben Calendar, who did not move but kept his eyes fixed on the judge. He was aware that the judge's eyes had a glint in them, but he could not imagine what brought it there.

Judge Nettles knew he had reached his speech's climax. There was always one moment in every speech that could drive the nail, and he already had this group in the palm of his hand. He also noticed that Ed Collins was writing furiously in a notebook.

"Ben Calendar, I want the law to be redemptive. You've lost some good years, but I see a change in you today and that pleases me. Not too many men get a second chance in life, but you're going to get one." He paused then and lifted his head, and his next words were sounded out clearly as a trumpet. "By the authority of the sovereign State of Arkansas, I revoke your previous sentence."

Ben Calendar flinched as if he had been hit by a bullet. He heard the gasp that went over the crowd and could not grasp what the judge's words meant.

Harlan Nettles knew full well that he had no legal authority to revoke a judge's sentence. But he also knew that it would be a simple matter to have the case reviewed and legally carry out what he was proposing right now. Either way, history would put him down as the man who took the noose off Ben Calendar's neck and set him on a new way.

"Your new sentence, Calendar, is to be a good man, be a good neighbor, serve your fellowmen, and keep yourself in the law of God and man. Now, take that cursed noose off your neck!"

Ben still could not move and it was Hannah who uttered a glad cry. She came up quickly and reaching up, slipped the noose over his neck. She whispered so quietly that only a few including the judge heard her words. "We'll keep it, Ben."

And then Ben Calendar stared at the noose. His hand went up and he touched his neck where the noose had hung for so many years. He moved his head, and then he looked back at the judge and said huskily, "Thank you, Judge. It's a sentence I aim to keep."

A cheer went up then, started by none other than Quentin Larribee. "God bless the judge! A man of mercy and truth!" The shout that followed pleased Nettles, although he waved it off. He looked at the man who would be his campaign manager for the governorship and saw a broad smile on his face. A look passed between the two, and the man raised a hand with his thumb and little finger touching with the other three fingers spread out. "It's in the bag," he mouthed, and the judge was happy.

Calendar turned almost blindly, but the judge called him back. "Wait just a minute, Ben Calendar." He waited until Ben turned back with some alarm. "Where's that hundred dollars?"

A laugh went up, but the judge held his hand out until Calendar reached in his pocket and produced the cash. "Now, take this young lady and this food and go somewhere and eat it."

Hannah took Ben's arm and the two made their way through the crowd. Everyone watched them but the judge said, "All right. We've got more lunches here. Come up here, Suzy Melton."

Hannah hardly knew what was happening, but she found herself heading for one of the tables at the outside of the square. She sat down abruptly for she felt a trembling in her knees. Calendar seated himself opposite her. He placed his hands flat on the table and bowed his head and did not speak. He was quiet for so long that Hannah was filled with wonder. She reached out and put her hands on top of his. "What is it, Ben?"

Calendar lifted his head. He turned his hands over and trapped hers, aware that they were the object of many eyes. But he did not care. "I've got a second chance, Hannah."

"You have, Ben. You have!"

Swallowing hard, Ben tightened his grip on her. "Hannah, I know you'd never marry a man who doesn't know God."

Hannah stared at him speechless. His hands were strong on hers, and she could not speak for a moment. But she knew suddenly that God was doing something very fine in this man, and she waited until he continued.

"I need—some help on this, Hannah. Do you think God would forgive a man like me?"

And then Hannah Larribee squeezed the hands of Ben Calendar, and her heart filled. She said, "Of course, Ben. Jesus came to seek and to save that which was lost."

Quentin and Eden had not gone far. They watched the pair as they sat at the table and saw what was happening. Eden whispered, "That's so sweet, Quentin."

"Do you think something will come of it?"

"Don't you?"

And then Quentin felt a great release. For years he had grieved over his sister, Hannah, but now . . . "Yes," he said. "I think it will." He longed at that moment to speak to Eden, to tell her what was on his own heart, but he could not. There was joy for Hannah, but a quiet deadly sense of desperation for himself. He turned away, and Eden, who had been expecting more than this, went with him, but the moment had passed.

★　　★　　★

The late afternoon sky was scored with white clouds. The heat of the day was passing away and there was a hint of rain in the air.

Eden had gone down to the creek, feeling the need to be alone. It had been four days since the Fourth of July celebration, and she had been expecting Quentin to come. But he had not. He sent word by Hannah that his office was filled with patients. Hannah had been radiant. She talked much about Ben, and it was obvious that these two were destined for each other. Eden was glad for Hannah.

But Quentin had not come.

Time passed, and a beaver came swimming downstream, leaving a V-shape in the water with his flat tail. Eden sat very still, but the beaver was alert. He suddenly disappeared, and Eden saw him no more.

Finally she arose and turned to go home, but before she had gone a dozen steps she heard someone coming and looked up. "Quentin," she said, keeping her voice even. "I didn't expect you."

Coming to stand before her, Quentin betrayed his anxiety. He was troubled, she saw that at once, and she asked quickly, "What's wrong? Is it sickness?"

"No. It's not that, Eden." Quentin bit his lips and then said as if he had memorized a speech. "Eden, I've got to tell you something." His voice faltered, and she had the odd sensation that he looked like a man facing a firing squad. She had never seen him like this, with something like fear in his eyes. "What is it?" she said. "It can't be that bad."

Quentin locked his hands behind his back and said in a dull voice, "There's no easy way to say this. Eden, I was conscripted into the Union Army at the end of the war ..."

Eden stood very still listening as Quentin spoke of his induction into the army. She could see that he was miserable and could not for the life of her think why. He spoke finally of the Confederate attack at Fort Stedman, and suddenly she sensed what was coming, but she did not move nor speak.

After relating how he had been half blinded by an exploding shell and forced into the line, he said, "I couldn't see anything much and I got separated from the other soldiers. I was pretty scared and the bullets were whistling around me. And then I—"

He broke off, and Eden urged him. "What happened, Quentin?"

Taking a deep breath, Quentin said, "I caught a glimpse of what looked like an enemy soldier, and he was right in front of me. I didn't even think, Eden. I didn't aim. I just lifted the musket and pulled the trigger. He ... he went down, and then I heard someone shouting that he was trying to surrender."

Quentin looked at her with tortured eyes and could say no more. Eden, in that moment, knew everything. She whispered, "It was Will, wasn't it?"

"Yes," Quentin said, his voice hoarse. "I ran to him and he was dying. There was nothing I could do, Eden."

He suddenly turned, unable to face her. He walked blindly to the creek and stopped, his hands locked at his side staring down. He did not move.

Eden took a deep breath. She accepted what she had heard. Going to stand beside him, she turned him around so that he faced her. "That's why you came, isn't it? To try to make up for what happened."

"Yes. I read your letter to your husband and I couldn't get away from it. I was engaged, as you know, but somehow I just couldn't put it aside, Eden. And so I came to see how I could help." He licked his lips and shook his head. "I wanted to tell you a thousand times, and I would have but—"

"But what, Quentin?"

He sighed and shook his head. "I think you know. I came to love you, Eden, and I knew when you found out about this that you could never care for me. You could never forget."

Eden Breckenridge was still, but many thoughts were going through her. She was shocked by the revelation she had heard— but somehow not terribly so. Her marriage to Will Breckenridge had never been happy, but she had grieved for him as was proper. She had also been shamed by this man who stood before her, for he had deceived her. She saw now why he had done so, and realized that he had acted with honor. She also knew that he was speaking the truth when he said that he loved her. She had seen that love in him long ago, and now she knew why he had been afraid to commit to it.

The silence ran on. Quentin looked down at Eden and said, "I don't know what to do, Eden. I love you, but I can't stay here and see you. I'll have to leave."

"You don't have to leave, Quentin." Eden lifted her arms and put her hands on Quentin's cheeks. The knowledge that he loved her was growing in her, and her own love for him had been there a long time. Now she whispered, "It will be all right." She pulled his head down and his arms went around her. His lips were firm and his arms held her so tightly that it gave her pain, but she did not care. She put her arms around his neck and drew him ever closer. There was a fullness in her that had been somehow captive, but now it was released, and she knew that she was a woman who was loved.

As for Quentin, he could not really believe what was happening. She lay soft in his arms, her warmth becoming a part of him, and he knew that she was full and warm and deep. That which lay between them was strong and somehow unsettling, but it was good, and finally he raised his head, still holding her as if she were something he was afraid he might somehow lose.

Faint color stained her cheeks, but she held her head high.

"What about the children, Eden?" he asked. "What will they think of me if I tell them the truth?"

Eden, being a woman and a mother, had already thought of this. "They'll think of you as a father. You've already become that to them, Quentin. They love you and trust you." She saw there was doubt in his face and shook her head. "I know you so well. Better than I thought I could know any man. I can tell what you're thinking."

"What am I thinking?"

"You're thinking it won't be honest to keep the truth from them."

He looked at her with wonder. "Yes. I was thinking that."

Eden tried to put into words what was in her heart. There was an honesty in her like a steel bar, but she was a woman who could balance reality against idealism. She knew that this man had given up a life of riches and ease for her. She knew also of his love for the children. She said quietly, "You came to help them and me.

And I think you can help them best by being a good father. There's a goodness in you, Quentin." She saw her words relieved him, and she added, "Some day, Quentin, we will tell them—but not for a long time. Not until we're sure it's right. Until then we'll have each other, and they'll have you."

Quentin felt like a man who had just been released from a dank, dark, gloomy prison into the bright sunlight. For many months he had struggled with this, and now somehow it had come right. He swung Eden around, crushing her to him. She protested, "Put me down!"

He did, but he kept her in the shelter of his arms. "I want to marry you, and I want us to grow old together. And I want us to have children and grandchildren."

Eden suddenly laughed and pushed at his chest. "You are the most unromantic man I ever heard of! Trying to ask me to marry you and talking about losing our teeth and getting old and gray!"

"That's for later," Quentin said. He smiled and pulled her close, pressing her head against his chest. They stood quietly for a long time, knowing that they would remember this moment all of their lives. She felt his hands stroking her hair and the warmth of his body as she held him tightly. Then he straightened up and said, "I just thought. I'll have to ask your dad's permission. Come along."

"What will you do if he says no?"

"I'll run off with you."

Eden laughed and the sound was delightful. She took his hand and they started back toward the house. "And so we'll elope with three wild children."

"Yes. It'll be fun."

Warmth swelled in Eden, and she said quietly, "I love you, Quentin—as I have never loved anyone before."

It was what he needed to hear. He tightened his hand and then said, "Come on. It's our time, Eden."

The two made their way back down the path, and as they reached the clearing where the house was, Eden began calling out, "Dad—Johnny—Prudence—Stuart! Come quick! We've got something to tell you!"